MANA HARVEST

Sword to Ploughshare LitRPG

Wolfe Locke
James Falcon

Cover design by: Ahmet Nergez
Library of Congress Control Number: 2018675309
Printed in the United States of America

This book is dedicated to the Dukes of Harem and Silver Pen for their feedback, support, and general good will.

Anything worth doing, is worth doing yourself.

SVEN, THE SHATTERFIST - THE RETIRED S RANKED
ADVENTURER

CONTENTS

Title Page

Copyright

Dedication

Epigraph

Chapter 1: The Lower Quarter   1

Chapter 2: Crowd Control   12

Chapter 3: The Land Writ   23

Chapter 4 Starting System   34

Chapter 5: Apple Bitters   44

Chapter 6: Oak Tree Farm   50

Chapter 7: And Then There Was One   57

Chapter 8: Up in the Morning   62

Chapter 9: The Well   69

Chapter 10: The Dried Creek   74

Chapter 11: Flow   78

Chapter 12: The Crystal Cavern   83

Chapter 13: Old Memories   90

Chapter 14: Invitation   95

Chapter 15: Practical Magic   101

Chapter 16: Fireside   105

Chapter 17: Pre-Game   109

Chapter 18: Festival of the Thankful Feast   113

Chapter 19: A Feast For Friends   118

Chapter 20: The Next Morning   126

Chapter 21: A Real Farmer   131

Chapter 22: Till The Soil   137

Chapter 23: One Step At A Time   143

Chapter 24: The Sleeper Has Awakened   148

Chapter 25: One of Us   153

Chapter 26: Morning Chores   160

Chapter 27: A Man and His Horse   164

Chapter 28: Glacial Freeze   171

Chapter 29: Pints and Bitters   177

Chapter 30: The Price of a Story   184

Chapter 31: Out of the Bar   192

Chapter 32: Dedicated Service To The Magic Knight Corps   201

Chapter 33: The Departed   208

Chapter 34: Raspberry Tart   215

Chapter 35: Farmers Market   221

Chapter 35: Boots on the Ground   227

Chapter 36: Three Bronze Reserved   237

Chapter 37: Turnips, or Turnips   244

Chapter 38: The Other Side of A Cliff   250

Chapter 39: Into the Thick of It   262

Chapter 40: Starting Trial   268

Chapter 41: Your Own Reasons   275

Chapter 42: Next Stop   285

Chapter 43: Tinker, Tailer   294

Chapter 44: Between Us   304

Chapter 45: Leyline   314

Chapter 46: Extra Duty   321

Epilogue Part 1: A Few Months Later   337

Epilogue Part 2: Constable   342

Want More LitRPG?   347

* Author's Notes *   349

Books By This Author   351

CHAPTER 1: THE LOWER QUARTER

"Come on, Eric. We've still got to get through the Lower Quarter before midnight," Cid shouted out toward his partner, a new guard by the name of Eric who'd been assigned to Cid as part of his left seat, right seat introduction to the profession.

"Aye, that's a rough neighborhood, too," the lad said, picking up the pace behind Cid. "Heard there was trouble there last night and the night before. A stabbing after a dice game. That's where Corporal Derin got hurt, right? Breaking it up?"

Cid shook his head. "Derin'll be alright after a few days' rest. He's probably okay already. At this point, he's just sandbagging it, but that's all the more reason to go there now. Sergeant Gavin's patrol will be stopping by at around three. It'll be good for us Guards to have more of a presence tonight. Make ourselves known and shown. Make sure things stay quiet."

Eric was one of the new recruits in a big batch of new regrets, but he was coming along quickly. He'd make full Guard before long and get his provisional status upgraded. The Commander often gave Cid the more promising of the recruits. They often joined him on his nightly patrols to get a real sense of what being a Guard was actually like and so Cid could watch out for them. If they weren't being watched over, it was easy for them to get involved with more than they could handle before they were ready. He could usually tell who'd do well in the Guards and who might prefer a different career. Cid was pretty sure Eric would be one that stayed.

They both carried lights to guide their way— oil lamps, not the mage lights that were common in some of the other areas of service. Cid made sure they stepped loudly to announce their presence. They weren't an undercover unit, and Cid wasn't in the business of trapping people or catching them by surprise. He'd always been a believer that what people did on their own time, outside of the public eye, was their own business.

There was one team of Guards that did that kind of job — led by a one-eyed brawler named Julian. While Cid treated the team with professional respect, he found their work to be a little unsavory. It left a bad taste in his mouth. Hardhearth was a hard place to live, and sometimes its citizens ended up on the wrong side of the law in their struggles to survive. But if they weren't hurting anyone, Cid believed in looking the other way, or at least giving them the option to hide what they were doing when they heard a Guard coming.

Julian didn't.

This job takes all types. And Julian had done great work for the Guards. He'd personally run a sting operation just last winter that had taken out a group of smugglers who'd managed to build a secret den beneath the docks to move alchemy components. Julian was always quick with a joke, too — especially after a few pints of ale.

They turned right onto Saint's Row, a place of beggars and alms, and descended a narrow set of steps into the Lower Quarter. Cid kept his senses on high alert. This stairway was dangerous: narrow and winding with alleyways leading into the densest parts of the city at regular intervals. An easy place for a man to be killed, especially at night. Cid knew a few Guards who had been, just as much as he knew a few who had an ax to grind with the Guards.

"Keep your wits about you," Cid cautioned. "Thieves and cutthroats hide in the alleys sometimes. Even a Guard can make an easy target if you've got a blind spot. Check the doorways too."

"Aye," Eric said.

Cid could hear the fear in the lad's tone. He wondered for a moment if it was a good idea to take the young recruit into the depths of the Lower Quarter tonight. He'd oftentimes done it before. Every young Guard had to see what they were up against. It was better to get it out of the way sooner rather than later.

But never so soon after another Guard had been stabbed. *It's a good experience that the lad needs, but the rougher elements might be feeling braver than they should.*

Cid reasoned the concerns away. There was always the Lower Post if they got into trouble. It was the worst assignment in the city, often used as a punishment for Guards who'd disgraced themselves in some way. The men there were often rude and surly, but it was good to have a place to hide if things got too hot to handle. Or at the very least, it was a good place to ditch the recruit.

The Market and Commons had been lit by Mage Fire Lanterns, but down there, the streets were lit by flickering oil lamps, if they were lit by anything at all. Magic was too expensive to waste in the Lower Quarter, and no respectable mage would come down this far to work a light spell.

No respectable mage, Cid grumbled internally.

There were plenty of mages of ill repute who plied their trade in the worst parts of the city. They kept a low profile and didn't advertise what they were doing. They certainly weren't going to waste their abilities making lamps.

It was a quiet night in the Lower Quarter, and the

streets were silent except for their echoing footsteps. Cid kept scanning his surroundings. It was dark here even with the oil lamps and easy enough for someone to hide in the shadows. Many a Guard had gotten into trouble when they let their attention lapse down there.

It only took a second.

"Hey! Get back here!"

A voice called from up ahead, slurred from drink. Cid's hand drifted toward the hilt of his blade, and he was pleased to see Eric doing the same. The lad had good instincts.

"Little lady! Where ya going?"

He could see them up ahead now. Two stumbling drunks following a red-haired woman in a bright green dress. A prostitute, by the look of her. Most women wouldn't dare be out on the streets this late wearing so few clothes, and she had a steely quality to her stride that suggested she'd dealt with this sort of man before.

"Hey! You're walking too fast!" the first drunk shouted again, stumbling even more as he tried to catch up.

"What you doing?" snapped the second drunk. "Why you following her? She's MINE! I got here first!"

"What do you do for a living?" the first man asked, drawing himself up to his full height. "Cobbler, what? Actor? I'm a mage. Mages get first dibs."

"Bullshit!"

The non-mage threw a punch, but he was so drunk that the blow went wild. He lost his balance and staggered into a building. The mage grabbed the woman by one arm as she tried to flee.

"Hey!" she shouted. "Knock it off!"

"I already paid!" the man shouted. "I want what I'm

owed. A man pays, he gets what he's owed!"

Cid quickened his pace. It was time to intervene.

"Guards!" he said, raising his voice so it carried. "Break it up, you three. It's almost midnight. Time to go back to your houses."

"Bitch tried to cheat me!" the mage bleated. "Guards trying to cheat me too now? I want what I'm owed!"

"Lady, give him his money back, and we all walk away free," Cid said. "No need for anyone to be harmed here tonight."

He'd spoken too soon. The second drunk had caught up and now barreled into the mage, arms flailing wildly as he tried— and failed— to land a punch.

"Bleak," Eric said. "These guys couldn't fight to save their lives, even stone-cold sober."

Cid waded into the fray, grabbed both men by the collar, and separated them. "I said break it up. Now!"

"Do you know who I am?" the mage huffed. "Do you know what I do?"

"No, and I don't care."

"I'm a mage. I'm a mage! And you're what, a City Guard? You have no right to tell me what to do. You have no right to even talk to me!"

Cid rolled his eyes. He was used to the arrogance of magic users by now. The Guards had to deal with them a lot, but as it turned out, a mage had to follow the same laws a common man did. Luckily, most mages didn't have enough power to break out of prison— especially down here.

"I'll cut you some slack, because I know you've been drinking," he said. "A drunk man's words are rarely wise, but I'll warn you not to say that kind of thing again. Not around me. The Guards are here to keep the peace by the order of

Lord Vanstone and the king himself. We work for the people of Hardhearth."

"I'll call a bolt of lightning down on your head!" the mage shouted. "I'll strike you right in the eye!"

Cid blinked. "Weird threat."

The mage wriggled out of his grasp like a snake and dropped to the ground. Many gagging sounds resounded through the alley as the alcohol threatened to make a reappearance. The whole thing was turned into a spectacle when the mage realized they were all waiting for him to stop. After a few moments, he wriggled back to his feet with difficulty. He stood in front of Cid, swaying a bit, clearly trying to conjure up a spell.

"Li— hic!— ghtning," he said, shaking his head when nothing happened. Raising his finger, he pointed right at Cid. "I said lightning."

Nothing happened again, and Cid fought back a laugh. The mage was wild-eyed and wild-haired, clearly in no state to be doing magic.

"Calm down," he said, crossing his arms. "Walk away. Go home, and get some good rest. Sleep off the drinks, because you don't want to pick a fight with us, trust me."

But the mage was in no mood to listen. He tried once more to cast lightning. When that failed, he gritted his teeth and howled in frustration.

"Fine," he said with a huff and a stomp. After slapping the side of his head for a minute, he grinned. "[Ice Bolt] it is."

This one worked, and a large, javelin-shaped shard of ice flew straight at Cid's head.

"Seriously?" Cid said, dropping to the ground. "This is how you want to be?"

He could hear the ice whistling as it passed over him and shattered harmlessly against a wall on the far side of the street. The mage was already preparing to cast again, and Cid looked around for something he could use to break his focus.

It won't take much. He's probably had a gallon of ale.

There was a small paving stone on the ground next to him that had worked its way loose from the road. He picked it up.

This'll work.

He hurled the stone at the mage. While it did nothing but bounce off the man's chest, it was enough to break his concentration— and the spell.

"Bloody Guards!" he snapped and rubbed his chest. He scowled towards Cid and Eric as his hands began moving in a complicated pattern. The sluggishness seemed to evaporate from his movements, though his eyes still glazed over from the drinks. "Let's see what you can do with this one."

This time the man's lightning spell worked, and he cast a clearly recognizable version of [Lightning Shield]. Cid knew the spell from his time working with the Magic Knight Corps, although Bran always did a better version of it. The Corps' version created a crackling ball of floating lightning half a mile wide— enough to cover an entire squadron of knights riding fast. This man could barely make a shield large enough to cover his head.

Still, it was dangerous. [Lightning Shield] would electrocute anyone who came too close. Cid didn't intend to get too close. The mage was cackling drunkenly and staggering around, joke-threatening both the other man and the prostitute. He was a menace, and it wasn't safe to let this go on any longer.

"Stand back," he said to Eric, and the boy obediently fell

back to the other side of the narrow street. *Good lad.*

Then, Cid reached into the pocket of his uniform and pulled out a small cloth bag. The secret weapon of the Guard. It was just a bag of sand, but it had taken down better men than this pathetic mage. He poured a little— just enough— into one hand and threw it, trying to aim for the center of the lightning ball. It had a better chance of doing its job that way.

He heard a shriek, and the lightning vanished instantly as the mage frantically rubbed his eyes, trying to clear them of sand. This mage was easily distractible, and it seemed he couldn't focus on more than one thing at a time.

"Always does the trick," Cid said to Eric. "Pocket sand. Not exactly honorable, but I never claimed to be an honorable man. The goal is not to get killed. Always is."

The young man looked suitably impressed, and Cid turned his attention back to the mage. It was time to finish the fight.

Before the other man could regroup, Cid punched him hard in the face. One blow was enough to knock him out, and Cid grabbed the mage's collar as he sagged to the ground to keep his head from hitting the hard paving stones. The man might have attacked a City Guard, but there was no need to kill him.

"You see," he said, turning back to Eric, "what's important is to end the fight quickly. The longer it goes on, the more chance there is for something to go wrong, especially down here. Now, let's get this fool out of here."

"There's a cart just down the street," Eric said. "No horse, but I bet between the two of us, we could drag it to Lower Post, at least."

Cid grinned. *Good lad. The boy keeps aware of his surroundings, even with chaos around him. It's a quality a Guard needs to have.*

"Take him to the cart, then," he said. "I'll join you in a moment once I've finished up with these two."

He handed the unconscious mage off to Eric and turned to the others. The other man looked suitably abashed, but the prostitute pulled her shawl higher on her shoulders and looked back at him boldly.

"S— sorry," the man said. He seemed to have sobered up a bit over the course of the fight. "Won't happen again, sir."

"I'm no sir, but see that it doesn't. I'm here most nights, and I'll know if it does. I've got a good look at you now, and I never forget a face."

This wasn't precisely true. This guy looked pretty generic in the way that all dodgy magic types looked alike, and Cid bet he could blend into a crowd with little trouble. But it seemed to have the desired effect. The man visibly gulped and kept his eyes fixed on the cobblestones. He'd think twice before causing trouble again.

"Off with you," Cid said, and the man sprinted off into the night. The prostitute watched him go, waiting until he was safely out of sight before she spoke.

"Thanks," she said. "Hoped you guys would intervene."

"You should head home," Cid said. "It's not safe to be out on the streets this late."

She shrugged. "This is the time I earn my keep. Need money to live. Most men won't hurt me."

"And the ones that would?"

"Then I better hope my luck holds," she said. "It has so far. I'll light a candle for the Lady tonight. She'll protect me."

"At some point, it won't hold," he insisted. "I've seen enough dead wh— women down here to know how it goes."

He'd been about to say 'whores', but he didn't want to be rude to the lady.

"No good staying safe and sound inside if I starve to death in my home," she said, and now there was an edge of bitterness to her voice. "You want to help out? Talk to that lord of yours. Get him to clean this area up, give us jobs, and a real market. I don't do this because I love the work, you know."

"But—"

"See ya," she said, sauntering off down the street and into the darkness.

Cid sighed. This job was hard sometimes, but there was nothing to be done about it. He'd talk to the commander as she'd suggested, for all the good it would do. Lord Vanstone was a good man but a lord through and through. He'd never had to skip a meal for lack of coin.

Eric had loaded the mage onto the empty cart and was waiting patiently for Cid to join him.

"He's been making a lot of noise," the lad said when he arrived. "I think he's going to wake up soon."

"All the more reason to get him out of here. We can drop him off quick and be on our way."

"Aye."

Eric grabbed one of the traces as Cid grabbed the other, and they started to drag the cart toward Lower Post.

"Tell you what," Cid said, turning toward the younger Guardsman. "If we finish patrol by two, I'll take you to a nice tavern near the Saint's Row, and we'll talk about what you want to do with your life. I think you've got a nice future with the Guards, if you want it."

The lad grinned so wide Cid could see his white teeth gleaming in the moonlight. "Captain Dawnshield, there's nowhere else I'd rather be."

CHAPTER 2: CROWD CONTROL

"She sat and spun in the tower high. And she waited, and she waited for the dragon to die!"

It was the latest tune to sweep Hardhearth, and half the market was singing or humming some scrap of it. Cid whistled along as he made his way through the crowd. He liked to check in with the local vendors when he was on morning rounds Tuesdays just to be sure all was well and no one was being cheated. A lot could go wrong in a market, and over the years, he'd seen almost all of the options.

He made a beeline for the pastry-seller first. She always gave him something to take away, and her pie crusts were perfect. It was good to have something in his belly to sustain him as he made his way around the city.

"How are things, Molly?" he asked, trying to look hungry. "Everyone treating you fairly?"

"Aye," she said. She was an older woman with tight gray curls half-hidden under a lacy bonnet. "The only trouble is that dratted song."

"What song do you mean?" Cid asked with a glint of mischief in his eye. "The one about the elderly dragon and the maiden? Goes like this—"

"Don't even start," Molly said, her eyes boring into him. "It's been stuck in my head all day. Every time I manage to clear it out, someone comes up to me singing it, and there it is again. Take your pastry and begone with you."

"What kind of pastry?"

His stomach was growling.

"Here." She pushed a folded cloth napkin across the counter toward him, and he opened it up. Inside was a flaky pie in the rough shape of a cat, clearly fresh-baked. He could see the steam rising off of it.

"It's a good one today," she said. "Put a little chicken in there for you. And potatoes, peas, and some of my special gravy to boot."

"Looks delicious, Molly," Cid said, wrapping the pie back up again and slipping it into his pocket. "Can't wait to eat it."

"See you bring the napkin back next week. I'm not made of money!"

Shaking her head, she turned to her next customer. Cid grinned. He knew well enough when he was dismissed, and he made his way through the market in high spirits. Once he was out of Molly's earshot, he started whistling the dragon song again.

The fishmongers had already packed up their stalls by mid-morning. They set up at dawn and were usually sold out within the hour, but Cid checked in with the butchers, the cheese mongers, and the vegetable sellers. Most of them had a little something for him, and he ended the morning with a pocket full of food. It was nice to think it was just because the market people liked him— and they did, well enough. But they also knew that it was wise to stay on the good side of the Guards, just in case they ever needed a little extra help.

There was a patch of green a few streets over, and Cid headed there to eat his makeshift breakfast in the open air. He'd been on night duty the past few days, and it was nice to feel the sun on his face. He started with Molly's pastry, wolfing it down while it was still warm from the oven. Then, he took a look at what else he'd been given.

He had a thin slice of cured prime meat from the butcher's stand, a sliver of a rich white cheese, and a fresh roll with salt baked into the crust. The three would go well together as an afternoon snack. The red onion he'd gotten from the vegetable seller was less useful, but the Guards' cook might appreciate it, at least. They got a good allotment of produce from the city stores, but every bit of extra food helped. Most Guards had a big appetite, especially the young recruits.

He had just re-wrapped his food and put it away when he heard it: one of the city emergency bells going off near the eastern gate. Hardhearth had six towers, each with an alarm bell on it that could be rung if the city was under attack. They were rarely used— few were foolish enough to attack Hardhearth— but when one went off, it was all hands on deck for the Guards and any Magic Knights or Mages in town.

Cid looked around, trying to figure out which tower was sounding the alarm. The noise was coming from the south and east. That meant Queensgate— and it also meant that he was probably the closest Guard to it. He took off at a run, unsheathing his sword as he went. Whatever he encountered there was likely to be ugly.

He soon found himself pushing against a crowd of panicked townspeople trying to escape the threat. They were shrieking and wild-eyed with fear— more of a mob than a group of people. And Cid knew well how dangerous a mob could be.

"Hey!" he shouted as a young boy stumbled on a loose

cobblestone and went down. When nobody halted and the boy was getting trampled, he shouted even louder, "Hey!"

The crowd didn't stop. They surged forward past and over the lad, paying no attention to the danger he was in. If Cid didn't step in, he'd be crushed to death.

"Hey!" he shouted, shoving his way through. Luckily, he was almost twice the size of the average Hardhearth citizen, and his time in the Guards had made him strong. It was still difficult pushing against the flow of the crowd, but for most men, it would have been almost impossible.

He reached the boy, grabbed him by the collar, and pulled him up. He was weeping, his face bruised and scraped from his time under the mob's feet, but he didn't seem seriously injured.

Lucky, that.

Cid had showed up just in time.

"What's going on?" he asked, trying to shelter the boy from the worst of the crush. "What are people running from?"

"U— undead," the boy stammered. "In the cemetery! Th — they came out of nowhere, and j— just started rising from the ground. I don't know why!"

Cid grimaced. *Obviously not out of nowhere.*

Undead meant a necromancer was at work. Likely, it wasn't a skilled one either if they were wasting their time with the Hardhearth cemetery. It was probably a disgraced mage from somewhere in the lower city, someone who'd learned a new trick or uncovered a scroll and wanted to see if he could pull off the spell.

Seems like this necromancer didn't know how to control the dead once summoned. Cid sighed. It wasn't an uncommon issue, but it was an issue that was well above Cid's pay grade. To tackle this at the source, he'd need to find either a Battlemage or a priest.

"Eddie!"

A blond woman was rushing toward them with a fierce look on her face. Her hair had come loose from its pins in the chaos and was hanging down around her shoulders.

"Eddie!" she shouted. "Are you all right?"

"Aye, ma," the boy responded, wiping his nose. "The Guard saved me."

She turned to Cid. "Thank you, sir. I've been looking for him all over. Been so worried. How can I ever repay you for your kindness?"

"I'm no sir, I work for a living," he said. "And you can repay me by getting away from here and staying alive. It's not safe."

She gave him a rough curtsey, grabbed the boy by the arm, and vanished into the crowd. Cid sighed and turned toward the cemetery.

Hopefully they'll be all right, but that's up to them now.

When he got there, the situation was worse than he'd feared. Whoever had done this had raised almost half the dead buried there, and the cemetery gates were hanging wide open. Luckily, the Undead were not cunning or intelligent creatures and had no idea what funneling meant.

They'd formed a massive cluster at the gate that had kept too many of them from getting through yet. Still, a few got out. He could see a few staggering around High Street in front of the temple, chasing pigeons and pressing their faces against shop windows.

No bloodlust in this lot. Looks like we got lucky.

Then again, the people buried in Hardhearth Cemetery

were mostly ordinary merchants and councilmen, not warriors. They'd been peaceful while alive, and it made sense that they'd stay that way in death. It took skill for a necromancer to turn the Undead into real monsters— and it was becoming increasingly clear that whoever was behind the risen dead was a rank amateur.

Still, it would take an effort to clean this up. At least no one had been seriously hurt— yet. But the longer the Undead stayed on the loose, the more likely it was that something would go wrong. He needed to put this to bed as quickly as possible.

Cid made a beeline toward the closest Undead— a former judge in a tattered wig and tunic. The creature was banging its head against a tailor's window, apparently trying to get in.

Hoping to replace the old rags he's wearing, maybe.

"Alright," Cid said, brandishing his sword. "Git. Go back home."

It turned toward him, baring its yellow teeth, and advanced on him.

"Well, I tried to give you an easy out."

Look at me. Talking to a zombie. I've been on night patrol too long.

He raised his broadsword and cut the creature down. It lay twitching on the ground, still trying to attack him until he severed its head from its shoulders. He wrapped his cape around his face, trying to seal the stench of rotting flesh. He hated dealing with Undead. They always made him feel sullied, as if some of their unclean qualities rubbed off on him every time he was near them. If he ever found himself face to face with the necromancer behind it, he'd have words for them, that was for sure.

He left the body for the city sanitation workers to clean up and moved toward the other Undead. Agitated somehow by their comrade's second death, they were running back and forth on the street while screeching. They tried to attack when they noticed he was coming toward them, but they were no match for a trained Guard. He took them down one by one, trying to decapitate them neatly each time. It was less work for the city workers that way— fewer body parts to gather.

Another man might have taken his time and used the fight to train a little, but Cid wasn't the type. He believed in finishing things quickly, conserving his energy, and getting out. It was one reason he'd survived so long in the job— long after many of his comrades had died or left the Guards for good. It didn't take long for the Undead on the street to be thinned out and taken care of, and he turned his attention to the cemetery gates.

A few more zombies had escaped through the narrow opening, and they wandered toward High Street, looking dazed and confused. Cid cut them down as he approached the gate, then took a moment to assess the situation. The Undead might have been pathetic, but they were still dangerous.

Most people in upper Hardhearth didn't know how to fight, and if what he'd seen already was any indication, they were too horrified by the Undead to be much use against them. He needed to get this cemetery closed and make sure it stayed that way. The latch was broken, but if he could find some kind of bar, something to bind the gates together....

Hopefully someone's been digging graves recently.

He climbed the wall to look inside. The entire cemetery was crawling with Undead, and the whole place reeked. Trying not to gag, he scanned the area for what he needed.

There.

A shovel, planted in the earth not too far from where he stood now. It was perfect. If he could grab it, he could use it to force the gates closed until he was able to find a mage to work a spell reversal. He vaulted over the wall, avoiding the Undead who shuffled toward him, and pulled the shovel out of the ground. Then, he quickly climbed back out onto the street and drew his sword again.

Holding his sword in one hand with the shovel in the other, he jogged back toward the front of the cemetery. A few more Undead had escaped into the street while he was gone, and he made quick work of them then braced one armored shoulder against the gates and pushed.

The zombies tried to fight back, scrabbling their rotting fingers against his chainmail, but he was stronger. They couldn't hurt him from behind the gate, and bit by bit, he forced them back away from the High Street. Once he had the doors firmly closed, he jammed the shovel between them as a makeshift latch. The dead pushed hard, but the shovel held.

For now.

Hopefully he could get someone to put them down soon.

"Hey!"

Right on cue, a priest was running toward him, sandals slapping on the pavement. He had a round face, big, blinking eyes, and looked way too young to be in charge of anything.

"This your cemetery?" Cid asked.

"Yes! Yes! What's going on? I was leading services at Lowgate Temple when I heard the news. Came as quick as I could. This is horrible!"

Cid kept a wary eye on the gates just in case the Undead started to break through. "Some amateur raised them. Things are alright here— lots of scared people, but nobody's hurt. But if you could—"

"Of course! Of course. Let me just—"

The priest fumbled in his jacket pocket and brought out a scroll. His hands were shaking as he unfurled it.

Poor lad. Likely his first time. This is probably the most excitement he's seen since coming to Hardhearth.

"I banish ye," the priest said in an uncertain voice. "In the name of all the gods and goddesses, all the lords and ladies, and the protector of Hardhearth."

He went on to read the same text in a variety of languages, and Cid relaxed. One by one, like dying flies, the Undead were dropping to the ground. The situation was under control.

Once the last of them was down, he clapped the priest on the shoulder. The other man winced.

"Ow," he said.

"Sorry. Look, I'm off. Seems like you can take it from here. I'll go back to the post and tell them to send sanitation for the bodies."

"Oh. That's not your job?"

"No," Cid said. "Got to spread the work around and give the other lads something to do. Right?"

"Um," the priest said, looking at the corpses with disgust. "Right."

The sun was high in the sky now, and his shift was nearing its end. Cid was in a merry mood as he headed back toward the Guard post.

"She sat and spun in the tower high," he sang. "And she waited, and she waited for the dragon to die!"

Report to Lord Vanstone, then done for the day. Not too shabby.

A sudden movement in the alleyway ahead of him caught his eye, and he tensed, ready for danger. Another Undead? No. Too small.

A little girl with ropes of dark braided hair stepped out of the shadows, holding a scroll. Looked to be a Lower City kid. He knew the type, always ready to cause mischief of some kind or other.

And carrying a scroll....

His jaw dropped, making a connection. "Did you do this?"

She didn't respond, opting to stare back at him regretfully.

"Seriously," Cid said, taking a hesitant step toward her. "This is your fault?"

The might-be necromancer shrugged her shoulders then sprinted away into the alleyway before he could catch her. She dropped the scroll, and Cid grimaced, grabbing it up.

It's been used. He looked down the alley after, staring after the darkness the little girl had disappeared into. With the scroll in hand, he shrugged. *Hope she doesn't try this kind of thing again.*

He'd have to send some Guards down to the High Street on an awareness campaign about magical artifacts and why they were dangerous for most people. That, at least, wasn't his problem to deal with.

Cid smiled and kept whistling the dragon song as he pulled his leftover snacks out of his pocket and headed toward the Guard house— one of three small barracks in the city.

Fighting the Undead always made him hungry, and his shift was practically over.

Maybe I need to think about a new job....

CHAPTER 3: THE LAND WRIT

Cid Dawnshield's leather pack was heavy on his back as he walked the last few miles north toward the town of Haven and away from the city of Hardhearth, the only home he had known for most of his life. It was not the easiest of routes, but for somebody like him who was used to forced bi-quarterly marches and training, it was just another day.

His tan leather boots were caked in mud and had reddened from the dust of the road. He hoped the town had a tavern where he could sit for a bit and have a pint before continuing on to his final destination. He had things to do and was eager to get around to them.

Would be nice if my old horse Nightshade was here for me to set my pack on and carry some of this gear. His former horse had been reassigned to his replacement, young Bill Wargwell, a fresh out of training guard who just started doing rounds when Cid had announced his retirement. *Barely green behind the ears.*

Cid shook his head fondly in consideration of the boy. He had spirit, and Cid thought Bill would be a good fit for the Guard. That aside, Cid wasn't overly comfortable leaving his horse with the lad. Cid had hoped he'd be allowed to buy Nightshade from the City Guards when he left as had been custom, but in the end, the Lord Commander Vanstone of Hardhearth hadn't allowed him to cut a deal for what he could afford.

Probably for the best, is what Cid wanted to say, but his aching back disagreed. He knew the horse was getting on in age— *just like I am—* and his muzzle was going gray, but Nightshade still had a few years of good work left in him. Cid had bonded with the horse over the years. It had been hard watching Bill lead Nightshade away, but the lad was kind and had a good way with the horse. Cid knew his old friend would be fine. *He's a Warhorse. They get the best treatment the city can afford. Unlike us Guards, horses are not so easily replaced.*

But just in case, Cid had left Bill with a good wool horse blanket and a stern warning of consequences should he not use one for Nightshade on the cold days.

Which is how Cid now found himself on foot and alone after twenty years in the Guards. He was bound for a village he hadn't seen in almost a decade, and even that was more a passing view on his way to somewhere else— a somewhere he'd never considered seriously as a place to end up in his old age.

He'd almost forgotten about Haven.

It wasn't until a few months before submitting his papers for retirement when he'd finally told his mate Bran he was turning in his spurs and calling it a day. Bran was a Knight Errant in the Magic Knight Corps. He specifically served as a Battlemage, and while they were notorious for being secretive and self-serving, Bran and Cid had still managed to strike up a friendship. He often came in to town on leave or when he had a free weekend.

Those times had come less and less often as the Knight moved up the ranks. He and Cid had struck up a friendship when they were much younger over pints of ale and games of cards in the local taverns, united by a love of women, ale, and on occasion, gambling.

Most of the time, Cid didn't call out Bran when he cheated at cards. It was one of the reasons the two men had been good friends throughout the years, the other being how often they'd been grouped up during times of crisis in the city. They were in different services, but they'd fought alongside each other more than a few times.

Teaming up with different parts of the city's forces wasn't uncommon. Threats appeared often and in many different forms. It wasn't odd to see a monster den form beneath the city and the City Guard to need a supplemental force or for a new dungeon to form near densely populated areas and need to be subjugated and put down.

The City Guard was just that, so Cid still got to see Bran from time to time. It was after one such occasion that Cid revealed his retirement to his old friend.

"And where are you thinking you'll be bound?" Bran had asked. "Off to the Gold Coast to sip greenwine for the rest of your days? Bask in the sun with one of those little umbrellas in a drink? Eat oysters off a plate and drink straight out of coconuts with a straw? I've heard there are many, many beautiful girls there too. They all swim in the bay before dawn, or so I've also heard."

"No, not the Gold Coast. That pace of life isn't what I'm looking for, and I don't just want to sit around the rest of my life either."

He'd shrugged when Bran looked at him oddly and shook his head. "Can't imagine spending my retirement doing anything but sitting on the Gold Coast and living lavishly."

Cid ran his hand through his hair. "Truth be told, I'm also not sure I can afford it. A Guard's pension isn't exactly a wealthy man's level of coin. Definitely nothing like that fortune I've heard they throw around at your kind when you're done." He'd grinned in jest before his old friend could cut back.

"I'll have to come visit, wherever you end up. I don't have many true friends left anymore. The life we live isn't exactly risk free," Bran had said, patting Cid on the shoulder before staring blankly into the distance.

A soft lull had settled over them, and Cid had to be honest with his old friend. "I'll have to send word once I reach wherever it is, and I'm sure you'll be enjoying the Gold Coast sooner than you think. Truth be told, I don't think I could sit still or relax. Not after so many years of always being so active with the potential of danger around every corner. I think sitting around would make me crazy, and I want to DO something, you know?"

"Trust me, I know the feeling," Bran said with a nod. "Still think you're crazy."

Cid sighed. "I just— I need to keep my hands full. I need to keep myself busy, just not too busy. The right level of busy. Something that makes me feel like I've accomplished something by the end of the day but doesn't leave me regretting my life's choices," Cid replied, wondering about what the next phase of his life would look like.

"What a shame, I'll say. Well, I can't force my dream on you," Bran responded with an almost sad tone. "I'm serious though, Cid, I'd come visit you."

"Why would you want to spend the little vacation time you get to come see me? Especially if I don't know where I'll be or what I'll do yet," Cid asked.

"Well, I've always wanted to see the Gold Coast. After this mission, I've been relocated indefinitely, and the Gold Coast is much better than the place I'm bound for now," Bran said with a grimace. "But here I am, spending my time off with you instead of visiting my favorite place. So indulge me a bit, would you? Pray tell, where else would you go if not literal Paradise? You've gotta have some kind of ideas, so what are you leaning towards? Have you possibly thought about adventuring?"

Cid had, in fact, spent the last few weeks trying his best *not* to think about it. As much as he tried to avoid thinking about what he would do next, it was a problem that had been turning over and over in his head.

He just didn't know if the choices he had made or would make were the right ones. He couldn't decide on the nearly unlimited options and opportunities before him, judging everything based on risk, reward, and interest. He wouldn't know if his choices were correct, if he'd made a mistake in retiring, if he found happiness in what came next. It all added up, mounting, causing him a headache and a twitch in his eye.

Breathe, Cid, breathe.

As much thought as he'd put into it, he hadn't figured out a solution yet. Once he turned in his gear, he'd have to turn in his key to his room in the Guards' barracks as well. He'd need to find new lodging with quickness.

Cid sighed. "In truth? I've no idea, but adventuring like all those guild guys do doesn't have a lot of draw for me. It's basically what I've been doing but for better pay and more danger. You've seen it, right? Groups of five go out excited and full of life, and a group of four comes back a little more grim faced, I don't want that. I'm trying to enjoy my life after this, and I definitely don't need that kind of negativity. I don't want to have to live through that kind of grind again."

Bran's metal armor rattled as he gave Nightshade a few pats. He looked up at the sky for a long moment before turning back toward Cid. "A few words of advice?"

"I'll hear you out," Cid said with a nod.

"Get started on that plan, my friend. Things move fast once you're ready to move on. The higher ups— they won't take kindly to you leaving. You know how they are, and they'll make you give up the horse too, mark my words on that."

Cid grimaced and smacked his lips, patting his trusty steed affectionately. "I can hope."

Bran shook his head. "They'll never give you terms you can afford right now, but you should be able to get Nightshade back in time. It'll just take some navigating."

"I know.," Cid said, sighing. "Wish things could be easier, but good warbeasts are harder to come by than a good soldier, and I'm just a Guardsman."

"You've done good work over the years. Don't discount yourself." They stared at Nightshade, both lost to their own thoughts until Bran continued speaking. "If you're serious about buying the horse, you'll need a place with enough land, water, and food for the both of you. Ever thought about being a farmer?"

Farmer? Cid had to fight an urge to laugh out loud. Everybody looked down on farming— even he did. *But maybe they shouldn't. Maybe I shouldn't. Is it really that bad?* Besides, the Corps did offer cheap plots of land to every former soldier and Guardsman, a tradition going back to ancient times: the sword to ploughshare. However, nobody he knew had ever taken them up on the offer. It was just too ridiculous an idea.

"I'm serious," Bran said, his eyes hard like stone. "A man like you— good with animals, likes being outside, doesn't mind hard work— might like farming. It's like a natural fit and would probably be good for you— good for your spirit too. It would get you close to the land. You know, make things grow. New life and all. It would probably do you some good to enjoy a different pace away from the city. All that stuff seems like good reasons. I would if I were you and somehow didn't want to settle down on the Gold Coast."

"What? Bran, I don't know anything about farming," Cid

said. "I definitely don't know about all that spirituality stuff."

Now it was Bran's turn to laugh. "Mate, you've fought undead, werebeasts, and dumb drunks. How hard can it be? You remember that staring death and danger right in the face, right? How many monsters have you slain? No small amount, I'm sure. If you can do all that, then you can try your hand at farming."

He wasn't sure what it was, but something about Bran's tone had made him consider it. His thoughts had turned toward a tiny village that he'd ridden through. A place he'd only been just once years before where he'd seen a farm with a "for sale" sign posted outside.

"Farming may not be that hard, but aside from fighting, I don't exactly have a lot of other talents suited for that kind of life," Cid responded.

Bran bolted upright and grinned. "You'd be surprised. Some skills get applied to other fields of work quickly." He looked around and lowered his voice. "This will have to stay between us— I'm serious— but I think I've got an idea for your situation. Hear me out, and then after, you can decide if you want to try farming or not." Brand reached into a pouch he was carrying and pulled out a crest bearing the seal of the Magic Knight Corps.

"I'm still not sold on the whole idea," Cid said.

"Listen, I'm heading out myself soon. I can't tell you the details, but it'll be awhile before I can check on you to see how you're holding up once this retirement is settled." Bran's voice grew serious. "Just rumors for now, but it's concerning enough for the higher ups to warrant an armed response from us, so you'll need to get on without me awhile, yeah?"

"I get that, but what does that have to do with me and farming?" Cid asked, looking around as the strange atmosphere grew between them.

"Just give me your arm, I want to give you something. This will only hurt a little," Bran commanded, and the tone of his voice let Cid know it wasn't really a choice. "And don't you ever tell anyone I did this. If anyone asks, you woke up in a bar with no recollection, not even a little bit, of what happened. It would... not be good for me if it got out I did this for you. We Knights guard our secrets, and magic is one of those."

"Uh... ok?" Cid wasn't sure how to feel, but he wasn't going to stop it now.

Bran grabbed his arm and brought the crest down. It glowed with arcane energy as it seeped into Cid's skin with a hiss. The Knight began to chant, and a pulse of power passed through the crest into Cid. Though it burned, he could already feel the change within him. The familiar notifications, the blue screens that helped guide their lives on a daily basis, appeared before him and made Cid aware of what had changed within him.

Notification: Blessing of the Magic Knight's Crest
Details: Cid Dawnshield, you have received the Blessing of the Magic Knight's Crest. The elemental spells of fire, earth, water, and air are now yours to use. A rare privilege given only to a few. Use it well and you become accustomed to this new power, experiment as you may.

Cid Dawnshield	
Race	Human
Class	Guard (Rank B)

Level	34
Sub-Class	Unassigned
Level	NA
Attributes	
Strength	18
Agility	9
Endurance	28
Magic	4
Abilities	
Refraction	Taunt
Subdue	Hidden Pocket

New Subclass: Mage Unlocked! Yet to be assigned!

Higher level of proficiency required
to receive class bonuses.

New abilities gained!			
Fire 1	Water 1	Wind 1	Earth 1

That's... pretty good. Bran actually helped me be able to use magic. I never would have been able to without him. Cid looked up and nodded at Bran in thanks. The gift he'd received was something only a true ally and companion would give.

Magic was something only a few had the aptitude to learn, much less unlock. It all depended on the mana within a person. With that one act, Bran had made a believer of Cid, and the next step was just finishing out his time.

"You won't regret this my friend."

****

Cid smiled. The memory was a good one. Bran was a good friend to him, a friend any man was lucky to find once in their life. Now, there he was on the road toward Haven with a pack full of the few belongings he owned on his back, his sword on his hip, and a Land Writ folded in his back pocket.

Lord Commander Vanstone had given him a hard look when he approached the Commander's office to buy the land under the old program and get a final signature on his retirement packet. It wasn't much money, but the program was generous. A single signature traded a monthly pension for payments on land, but that land was his and would be for the rest of his life.

The only catch was the land had subrights assigned by the Kingdom to the Magic Knights Corps, but the details of those subrights were not made out to him. Any concerns Cid might have had were waved away by dreams of a better life than that of a uniform, a personal chest, and a barracks bed.

"You sure about this?" the Lord Commander asked, brows furrowing under his shock of gray hair. "Never picked you out for a farmer, Dawnshield. We could still use you in the Guard. If there's something you don't like, you can always stay and try to change it from within. You still have room to get promoted."

"I'm sure," was the quick reply.

Cid had already convinced himself, and this was just the last step. One door closed and another opened. The next thing he had to look forward to was stepping off and putting one foot in front of the other until he arrived.

It was a tough call, writing off the little bit of money he'd get from the Kingdom, but it was a better choice. A Guard's pension didn't exactly leave much to live on, and even if he had to work hard to get by, it was still a far better opportunity for a chance at a better life.

But the closer he got to Haven, the less sure he became and less time he spent in his memories. The road was dry and dusty, the day was hot, and he felt the loss of Nightshade more keenly the longer the journey lasted. He was considering turning around and telling the first person of any authority in the Guards that he'd made a terrible mistake and wanted to re-enlist. Those thoughts vanished in an instant when he turned a bend in the road and saw his destination in its entirety.

Haven.

And even though Bran had been the one to put him on this path, Cid was excited to commit to it.

CHAPTER 4
STARTING SYSTEM

Cid stood on the top of the hill overlooking Haven. The village was laid out in the valley beneath him. It was a cluster of red brick, thatched rooftops, and roads full of bustling busy villagers. Haven was surrounded by lush green farmland that bordered an untamed wilderness of thick foliage and overgrown forest. A small brook ran through and curved around the center of town in a series of half loops. It was spanned by a series of brown stone walls and moss-covered bridges. It was charming, and— best of all— there was a small building by the water that looked like a tavern.

Cid grinned. *The sign with a flagon of ale really gives it away. Finally! I can slack off this thirst with a pint or two.* It was a beautiful view, and much to his surprise, Cid found himself many times happier than he thought possible. He was grinning from ear to ear with the widest smile he'd had in a long time. *A new life.*

He could be happy here.

Well, maybe. Let's see if I can just learn how to farm. This is a good beginning. It's ok to take it easy though since this is meant to be my retirement. No need to rush the rest of my life.

He held up his hand, flexed his wrist, and tried to activate [Fire 1]. It didn't come naturally to him, and the ability wasn't as easy to use as he'd assumed. Flames briefly appeared but then went out. Cid sighed and hung his head. *It's fine. This is new, and I still don't have it figured out. No need to get flustered.*

If I can unlock magic this late in life, I can figure out farming and how to use the magic.

With a deep breath, Cid shouldered his pack one last time and headed down the hill into town. He felt good and partially ran down while whistling a jaunty song he'd learned from sailors when they made port to drop off their goods at Hardhearth. The lyrics were unprintable and not fit for the innocent, but the tune was catchy and made it really easy to keep pace— and unless you knew the words, you'd never know it was inappropriate.

When he approached the open gates of Haven, Cid let the tune die down slowly. *Can't be making a bad impression from the get-go.* He spied a scrawny teenage lad with a mop of red hair standing on the railing of one of the bridges. Judging from the gangly limbs, the lad was just on the cusp of manhood.

The lad was throwing rocks in the water, watching them splash. He didn't even bother trying to give them a proper skip. He jumped down from the railing when he saw Cid approaching him.

"Who're you, sir?" the kid asked with a wary glance, throwing a suspicious side eye that lingered on the dagger Cid kept strapped to his leg and then to the pack on his back. "You lost? You don't look like you're from around here."

These small villages tend to not get many visitors. They can be skittish around newcomers and have their own ways. I need to not make a bad impression right away. Cid kept his distance. He didn't want to spook the lad anymore than he already had.

"My name is Cid Dawnshield. I'm here under the Sword to Ploughshare program. I used to be a city guard. I'm looking for Daryl Nightgreen, the Village Elder. I've got a Land Writ granted to me by my former commander for the property of Oak Tree Farm. I've been told it should be just outside of town."

The lad stood up a little straighter after Cid said he was

a guard, and seemingly reassured by the disclosure. "Daryl Nightgreen? That's my grandfather you're looking for then! I'm Lyle Nightgreen. I keep watch ov...." The lad's voice cut abruptly. "Wait, Oak Tree Farm, you said? You sure that's the name on your Land writ? Oh man. Who made that call...?"

Cid tried not to get worked up. The lad, Lyle, looked over at him and then away after he glanced over the land writ. He looked uneasy. Cid took a deep breath. *I'm sure it's nothing bad.* But Cid took another deep breath and prepared himself. He wasn't sure and needed clarity. *It's probably bad. Of course it would be bad.*

"What's wrong with Oak Tree Farm? Should I be concerned? What's the deal? Bandits? Hobgoblins? Kobolds? Spiders?" Cid pressed, pulling out the wax sealed paper to look it over and be sure.

By Decree of the Kingdom of the White Tower,

Cid Dawnshield, under the "Sword to Ploughshare" program is entitled to the property known as "Oak Tree Farm". All rights, privileges and ownership pass to him. All payments shall be arranged by the Office of Coin, White Tower Branch.

Given under my hand in the muck and mire,
Lord Commander Vanstone

Yep. It's all there. Can't fight that kind of authority. 'By Decree of the Kingdom of the White Tower, One Oak Tree Farm. Owner. Cid Dawnshield'. Sure enough, there it was: the name of the farm printed in bold black ink at the top of the writ and the authority that bestowed it upon him.

The lad raised his hands and waved away the concern. "Oh no, nothing like that. It's just nobody has been up there for a while. The land has taken back a lot of it, or so my Grandpa likes to say," Lyle said. "Old Mr. Talley got sick of his duties and sold the place back to the Crown and went off to live on a beach somewhere. We'd all given up on it ever being a farm again. Not enough hands around here to work the soil."

"Well," Cid said, trying to sound more confident than he felt. *I knew that deal was too good to be true. It's probably all gone fallow. I'll be lucky to grow a weed, much less potatoes.* "That's why I'm here. I'll fix it up. You'll see. I'll be growing nine foot tall corn stalks in no time."

The lad smiled, revealing a jagged scar under a cheek that Cid had missed earlier. *A knife scar. That looks like it's from a dirk.* "Alright then. I'll hold you to that. Nine feet tall, and not an inch shorter, or else you'll owe me." The young lad looked around, twiddling his fingers excitedly until he turned back to Cid. "Said your name was Cid, right? Damn-something or other, yeah?"

Cid grinned. "Dawnshield. It's Cid Dawnshield."

"Doesn't really matter," the lad said with a shrug. "Just follow me, and I'll take you to see my Grandfather."

He threw one last stone into the water and scampered off toward the center of town. A few times, he looked back to make sure Cid was following him. Haven wasn't large, and it only took a few moments to get to the Nightgreen house.

It was a neat brick building with a thatched roof— much like the other houses in town— and the front garden was wild with flowers, and beneath it all, Cid could smell the scent of wild garlic. A small bronze plaque on the front gate marked it as the Village Elder's office with the family name and title.

A bandy-legged man with wild white hair emerged from the backyard as they approached. He looked like an older version of Lyle, and he waved away Cid's attempt to shake his hand and call him sir.

"No need for all that formality, I work for a living," he said with a good natured smile. "I've been expecting you. It's

Cid, right? A friend of yours from the Magic Knight Corps sent me a letter yesterday explaining that you'd be coming into town. Said I was to look after you. I've been waiting to get a look at the man who'd be brave enough to take on the challenges of Oak Tree Farm. You've got a strong constitution, right? Or is it endurance?" he asked, waving away the question. "Whatever that true grit is being called these days."

Cid's stomach sank. Brave enough? Is he telling me the property is overrun by monsters? Or is this one of those country jokes. It could be spiders. Giant ones. It's going to be spiders. I'm going to get up there, and there's going to be spiders.

"I don't know what you mean by 'brave enough'," Cid replied. He looked towards the center of Haven and around at the surrounding town before turning back to Daryl. "I'm just trying to grow turnips and potatoes. I came here once on a mission with Bran, years and years ago, when I was still new to the Guard. Had a long weekend and needed a change of pace from the city scene after. Haven seemed like a breath of fresh air and was stunned the first time I saw it. I was surprised anything was still available for purchase then."

It sounded a little dumb when he said it like that, but Daryl Nightgreen laughed out loud when he heard it.

"Well, it sure is different from the city, I'll give you that." Daryl caught his breath after his loud bout of laughter, crows feet crinkling the corners of his eyes. He nodded, covering his mouth for a few minutes until he recollected himself. "Yes, there's plenty of land available, even today. I don't know what you've heard, but farming is hard work, and we've got special qualifications to live here."

Cid hadn't heard of anything of the sort before. He wanted to ask what Daryl meant but remained silent, figuring the older man would probably tell him if he just waited.

"Not just anybody is meant for Haven," he said,

scrutinizing Cid. After a few minutes, he cracked a grin and winked. "Elbow grease and dirty palms tend to scare off the city types. Those types don't like that you can't just throw money at the dirt to make things grow. I've seen people expect the land to provide for them without putting any work into it," Daryl continued with a good natured laugh.

"Doesn't seem quite right. I assure you, I don't mind putting in work." Cid was tired from his travels and ready to see what he'd have to deal with in the near future, but he didn't want to cut off the elder of the Nightgreens. Being rude to what was effectively the town leader would be a bad way to start off his journey in his new home.

"Hopefully we don't give you any cause to regret your purchase." Daryl held up a hand to stifle the questions Cid had. "You'll see what I mean when you get there. Just know that if you ever feel like you need a break, you can come on over, and we'll get you fixed up with a good meal. You're one of us now. I hope you come to think of this place as home."

"Thanks, I do appreciate the warm welcome." Cid wanted to shake the older man's hand, but Daryl still refused any attempts.

Daryl pat Cid on the shoulder and looked over at Lyle, giving the kid a hard, serious look. "After I've completed business with Mr. Cid, can you take him up to the farm when he is ready?"

"Of course, Grandpa," Lyle answered with a nod.

"Alright." Daryl waved the lad away, calling after him as he darted away, "Don't go too far, I'll send him to you when our business is done, okay?"

"Sure, Grandpa," the lad replied over his shoulder, sticking a thumbs up their direction.

Cid grinned at the boy's antics. It was obvious to tell Lyle was ready to get back to what he was doing. *Dropping rocks is a lot more fun than signing paperwork and small talk. I don't question it at all.*

The lad was already halfway down the road, kicking up dirt clods. At one point, he grabbed a stick and started swinging it around like a sword. Cid grinned, knowing the boy was ready to get in trouble.

Daryl shook his head, sighing. "Troublesome. That lad is trouble. Endless energy, and he uses it all to get up to no good." Daryl stared after the boy for a few seconds, crossing his arms. He tutted once and turned back to Cid. "Whelp, it's my fault. I've been too lenient with him. I can't help it. He gives me that silly grin, and I just forget that I'm supposed to be scolding him."

"Couldn't imagine having kids myself. Seems like you get to deal with the best and worst parts of life all at once. Was always too much for me with the Guard, and if I'm being honest, I don't think I'm too good with kids," Cid admitted.

"Takes a special kind of person to keep up with the energy of the youngins, that's for sure," Daryl grumbled as Lyle moved about, spun in circles with his stick twirling in fanciful fashion, and stabbed at some unknown foe.

Cid just watched, feeling more exhausted the longer he did so.

Daryl turned away from Lyle and back to Cid. "This looks like your first time dealing with farming and the life that comes with it, so I'm going to level with you a bit. It's going to be a dry summer here, I can tell you that much. A dry, dry summer. It's only late May, and yet, it's already this hot." He wiped sweat from his face with the side of his arm. "You'll have your work cut out for you in the weeks ahead. A lot of that work will be hard and miserable, but to make it less so, follow my advice," Daryl said, waiting for Cid to respond.

"I'm all ears. Any advice that will help me is always welcome and probably more than I know at all when it comes to farming," Cid said, focusing on the older man.

"You'll need to secure a water source up there." Daryl snapped and smacked his knee. "Right! Here's something I— as Village Elder— can do to make things easier. Let me make your ownership of the farm formal. **[Initiate Personalized Farm System]**," Daryl waved a hand.

You've been offered a Quest! Accept?	
Yes.	No.

The choice was simple, and Cid accepted.

Granted Profession Quest: What Plants Crave!	
Description:	Daryl Nightgreen has given you a Profession (Farming) Quest: Secure a water source for your farm if you want to make it through the rest of the hot months.
Reward:	None
Consequence For Failure:	Lose all crops.
This Quest is one of three conditions to unlock Class: Farmer.	

The notice disappeared, and Daryl continued, "Anyway,

you mentioned you don't know much about farming, right lad? This should help."

"I'm not a lad," Cid said with a cough. "I'm nearing forty, pension and all."

Daryl playfully rolled his eyes and smacked his lips. "And I'm almost sixty, so you're all lads to an old bear like me. I've buried pets older than you."

"Alright, that's fair," Cid said, wearily looking around in hopes he'd see Lyle. He wanted to get up to the farm, but Daryl's advice and Quest were valuable. He didn't know if he could gain more information— which he severely lacked— in regards to learning how to farm. "I don't know too much about farming. I was a town boy— grew up in a town a bit bigger than this one. My father ran a bakery, but I was never inclined that way. Baking was never for me. I saw the farmers coming in from the fields time to time, met them in the market, but—"

Daryl raised a brow and cleared his throat, causing Cid to pause mid sentence. "You know, lad, that's a long way to say you've never raised a crop in your life." Daryl laughed. "Well, that's alright, lad. There's a first time for everything, and if there's one thing Haven's good at, it's farming. We don't have much else around here. Won't be quite as exciting as your time serving the Kingdom, though some nasty things do kick up every now and then around Harvest time."

"That's alright," Cid said, rubbing a sore spot on his neck in memory of an injury from a recent takedown between him and a couple of drunks. "In twenty years, I've seen enough excitement. This is my time for a quieter life."

"You sure?" Daryl asked, eyes twinkling. "You don't want to travel the world first? I've heard some wild tales about the Gold Coast..."

Cid coughed and rolled his eyes. *Everyone is always talking about the Gold Coast.*

"Haven's more my speed and the tempo of life I want. The Golden Coast's a bit overrated," Cid grumbled. "It's long past time to get back to my roots. Haven looks a bit like where I grew up. A bit greener, though."

"Fine, fine," Daryl replied in a mock apology. "It's green for now. We'll need some more rain than we've had in quite some time if we want to keep it that way. Let's keep our eyes on the sky and our fingers crossed, lad."

Cid looked up. The sky was a brilliant blue with not a single rain cloud in sight. He'd have to get used to keeping his thoughts on the weather if he wanted to be any good at farming. *Still, that sun feels good on my face.*

"But I like your spirit!" Daryl said, clapping him on the back with surprising force. The old man was stronger than he looked. "We'll help you out if you need it and teach you everything you need to know. The system should help a lot with the farming routine. Trust me, I should know. I fed it a lot of the prompts myself. Now, I've got an idea. Let's head down to the tavern for a pint before Lyle takes you up to the farm? How's that sound? Hmm, hmm?"

"A pint does sound good, but—"

Daryl held up a hand, grinning. "You can leave your pack here if you like. No one'll take it."

Cid grinned. He was liking Haven already. "You read my mind. A drink would do wonders after ."

CHAPTER 5: APPLE BITTERS

Daryl waved off all Cid's offers to help carry the drinks and set two foaming steins of ale down on the table.

"Leave off, lad, I've got it," he said good-naturedly. "I may be old, but I can still carry two glasses of beer. Wouldn't be much of a village elder if I couldn't." Daryl paused for a second. "Wouldn't be much of a man either if I spilled it."

After Daryl set them on the table, Cid quickly grabbed one and took a big sip of ale, nodding approvingly. "Good stuff. Is that a hint of apple mixed in with the bitters? Back in Hardhearth, this kind of stuff was a bit beyond my means."

"Aye, lad. Ain't much coin to be made in service. As for what's in the brews, that's a trade secret, like most things here in Haven," Daryl replied with a wink. "What I can tell you is that it's a local brew. We don't have a lot of trade here aside from the weekly market for the nearby towns. Miss Maggie over there," Daryl started, pointing towards the bartender, "brews this one. Maybe one of these days you can get the recipe — if you prove yourself, that is."

You've been offered a Quest!
Accept?

Yes.	No.

Cid wasn't sure what the Quest would be, but he accepted regardless.

Granted Reputation Quest: Friend of Haven I	
Description:	Daryl Nightgreen has given you a Reputation (Town) Quest: Prove yourself a friend of Haven, and Miss Maggie will teach you how to brew "Apfelkorn".
Reward:	Drink Recipes, Brewing Kit
Consequence For Failure:	Permanent surcharge of the Apfelkorn drink and loss of the recipe mix.
Quest Line Finishing Condition Required:	???

New abilities gained!
Alchemy 1

The update disappeared, and Cid took another deep drag of the draught. *Alchemy will be a decent ability to learn. I'm pretty limited with what I picked up in the Guard. Not many variations of protect, cover, and subdue.*

He refocused on the taste of the Apfelkorn. It tasted like fall and the holiday season and left him wanting more. *Yeah, I'm going to need that recipe.* Cid raised his mug and looked across the bar at the tavern owner and offered a salute in gratitude.

She was leaning against the far wall talking with two burly men who must be regulars, her blonde hair tied up in a complicated braided style. *Or.... Plenty of reasons to keep going back for a drink.*

"She's a good brewer," Cid commented, almost absentminded as he enjoyed the drink.

"Aye, a good brewer. I'm sure that's exactly what you were thinking," the old man laughed. "Keep your eye on her, though. She's a keen one, she is. She'll talk you into having four or five more than you need, pocket all your money, and then rent you a room upstairs at an upcharge you wouldn't believe and quote in the morning that you were too far gone to get home safely. Usually, she's right. Shrewd businesswoman, that one."

He wasn't quite sure how to respond to that and took another sip of his drink. "Interesting."

"Anyways," Daryl started, drawing the conversation back to the matter at hand. "We're all glad to have a real hero here in Haven. Thank you for your service, lad. It's an honor. You know, I did a little time in the Magic Knight Corps myself."

Uh... Bran must have told them I was in the Corps. Urgh. I'll go along with it and ask Bran to help me sort it out when I see him next. "Former knight," Cid said quickly. "And you did? When?"

"Before your time, lad." The old man waved the question away. "Well before. And I only did two years before switching to the reserves, not that any of that mattered. Different kind of system. At any rate, I came back to town pretty quickly after my little adventure."

"Why'd you leave this place anyways? It seems nice," Cid asked, leaning forward.

"Oh, it's just the way of things around here," Daryl said. "I'll call it a little of this and that. I can't say I was much of a knight. When I joined, I could barely sit on a horse. Everyone else got a real warhorse once they got out of advanced training. As for me, I got a fat old thing from the training school. Worst horse of the lot. Called him Old Bayberry. He knew enough to stop moving whenever I fell off, and that happened often enough. He never stepped on me once, something my old bones are thankful for. Didn't kick me either, now that I think about it."

"You can always get better at riding," Cid countered. "Besides, Magic Knights do a lot more than ride horses."

"Aye. That's true enough, and true, you can get better at riding. But I'm not arguing the merits of learning to ride at my age. I'm settled in my ways and have other things to focus on than shortcomings of my youth," Daryl replied, and Cid could tell the old man didn't want him to press further.

I know enough to tell when a subject is off limits.

"But like I said, I wasn't much of a knight. You know how it is, lad, I'm sure. I saw a band of knights riding through town one day with a group of recruits coming along right behind them, and I got stars in my eyes. Pictured myself off running around the world, having adventures. I had somebody I wanted to impress. Silly stuff. I was young. The Corps— well. You know how it is."

Good thing Bran has told me enough stories. "Yep. Pretty much," Cid replied, not wanting to volunteer too much and hoping to change the subject.

"It wasn't quite what I imagined, is all." Daryl took a deep drink before talking again, "And in the end, I was better off back in Haven. I'm not a good fighter with the sword, and I still can't ride worth a sack of beans, but being Haven's village elder's the kind of job I do well. Oh, and magic! Magic is just in my blood. I came back, strutted around for a bit, and got over myself. Met Lucinda— she's my wife, you'll meet her— and things went from there. You've met Lyle. He's a good lad, a good grandson. He's growing into a good man."

"He seems like a good kid," Cid replied. "Clearly a bright lad."

"You have no idea," Daryl said. "It's funny. When I came back here for the first time, years ago, I thought a lot of things that just weren't good for me. That I'd washed out of the Corps and was coming home in shame. But in the end, it was a good thing. I've had a good life."

"Ah," Cid said, nodding his head. He'd only ever had one job: Guard, and the only life he'd been living was that of a Guard. *This good life he talks about has a draw to it.*

"But what am I doing?" the elder asked, draining his glass and smacking down on the table. "You don't want to listen to an old man's tales. I'm sure you want to get on the road and see your new place. Lyle's outside, probably still dropping those rocks in the water. Not much for a young man to do here but get in trouble. Anyways, he'll take you up there if you're ready."

Cid looked out the window. The lad was sitting by the side of the road. He looked bored half to death. *Must have run out of rocks.*

"Maggie!" Daryl said, raising an arm, and the tavern keeper strolled over, taking her time. When she got to the table, she looked Cid up and down frankly. "Come meet our newest resident."

"So, you're the one who's taking over Oak Tree Farm then?" she asked with a critical eye passing over Cid.

He nodded. "I am. Bought and paid for."

She looked over at Daryl. "Does he know what he's in for?"

The old man opened his mouth to speak, but Cid cut in before anyone could warn him about something he didn't want to handle— like spiders.

"I've heard it's in rough shape," he said. "But that's all right. I was a knight. I love a challenge."

"'Challenge' is one way of putting it," she said dryly. "Five sols pieces for the drinks."

"Don't pay her no mind," Daryl whispered as she walked away. "That's just how Maggie is. She's the same with everyone."

"I didn't take it personally," Cid said, watching her go. She said something to the table next to them, and they dissolved into laughter. *Hopefully she didn't make some quip about me. But I'm positive as soon as I leave they'll be laughing about the newcomer from the city and whatever awaits me down that road.*

Lyle Nightgreen stood up and dropped his stick as soon as they opened the door to leave, and Cid and Daryl said their goodbyes.

"Don't worry, lad," the old man said. "I'm always here if you run into trouble. We all are. That's just the way we do things here in Haven. One team, one fight— and all that."

"I'll keep it in mind," Cid replied, and he headed to his new home.

CHAPTER 6: OAK TREE FARM

It was getting late in the day, and the sun was just starting to set behind the hilltops. Cid and Lyle's shadows stretched out long ahead of them as they crossed one of the bridges that led out of town towards Cid's new property.

"Do you know what this bridge is called?" the lad asked suddenly as he leaned against the railing and looked over to the stream below.

"No idea, not a single one," Cid replied passively, not really interested. "In my experience, they always have names for people I don't know or functional names like *Crossing Area Three.*"

"Death Bridge! It's called the Death Bridge." The lad turned and looked at him with a huge grin. Cid was sure the kid was trying to spook him for laughs. He tried not to roll his eyes.

Wonderful. Alright, don't turn into a creepy kid. Please, please, please. I don't need that in my life. "Oh," Cid replied. "That's a weird thing to call a bridge."

"It's not actually called that. It's actual name is something far more boring. Support Bridge Number Three, or something like that," Lyle admitted. "So, I made the name up. I named all the bridges in town." He pointed to each, offering names as he passed over them. "That's Dragon Bridge, Pirate Bridge, and Tiger Bridge."

Cid frowned. He was at a loss for what to say. *How do you politely tell a kid you don't want to hear it?* Cid sighed and just accepted it. *No use offending anyone just because I'm grouchy. If I act uninterested long enough, maybe he'll get the hint.*

"Those are good names," he said finally, hedging his bets.

Reputation Quest: Friend of Haven I has progressed!	
You've successfully navigated your first interaction with one of the townsfolk, and it has been noticed.	
Esteem with Daryl Nightgreen has risen	Esteem with Lyle Nightgreen has greatly risen.
+1 Reputation in the Town of Haven.	
Once a reputation of +15 or higher has been reached, the residents will no longer treat you like an outsider.	

Only 15? That's not too hard to reach. This should be nice once I get a feel for the area.

"Thanks," Lyle replied, interrupting Cid's musing.

Cid could tell the lad was pleased, a small smile cresting the boy's face. "So, uh, do you like it here in Haven?" Cid asked. "You're what— fifteen, maybe sixteen at the most? What do you want to be when you get older?"

Lyle made a face and looked downward. "Fifteen, but not for much longer," the lad muttered before he kicked at the ground, continued walking along the path in silence, and ignored the rest of the question.

"I'm guessing you don't know what you want to do

then." When Lyle didn't respond, Cid started to feel slightly awkward. "Sorry about that, don't mind me. Forget I said anything," Cid said.

"It's fine. I already know what I want to do. It's just that it's here that's the problem," the lad said, kicking a stone and watching it skip away. "It's just *boring*. Almost nothing ever happens here, and I've done basically everything there is to do here. You showing up is maybe the most exciting thing that's happened in Haven since I was born. Everyone is obsessed with the Magic Knights, and I don't know. I just—" Lyle groaned in frustration, waving his hands around. "I feel like there's got to be more than just this. You're from the city, so I'm sure you know what I mean, right? I couldn't ever imagine trading the big city for a place like this, don't you know?"

Cid looked around. While they'd been talking, they had managed to move a surprising distance and were a little way outside of town now. The sun was shining, birds were chirping, and light made dappled leafy patterns on the ground. It was beautiful, peaceful, and the most exciting thing that happened was a chirping bird flying by.

It was no surprise to him that a young buck, wild with energy, would find things to be boring. He could see how a lad like Lyle Nightgreen might think it was so dull, a life or death struggle would be a better alternative— deadly dull. If Cid hadn't spent so long in the Guard, he never would've imagined enjoying a serene place like Haven. If he'd lived another life, maybe the Gold Coast would've been his choice of retirement.

He turned to the lad and looked him in the eyes. "Listen, hone in on that feeling, that want and desire. What do you want to do most?" he asked. When Lyle looked back with confusion, he tried to reword his request. "Imagine doing what it is you want to do, and tell me what comes to mind."

"I— I see a big field, and I'm riding on the back of a warhorse in armor towards... the unknown. I think I want to go on an adventure!" Lyle shouted, bouncing in place. "I want to get out of here and see the world! I want things to happen in my life I can be proud of, stories I can tell to my grandchildren like Grandpa! I don't want to be stuck in this backwater forever, dreaming of real action and the world beyond."

"Hm," Cid said. *Maybe he needs to be thinking of moving on, the Guard is always hiring.* "Have you—"

"We're here!" the lad shouted out suddenly, startling Cid.

A narrow dirt track branched off the main road and wound its way through the trees and thick overgrown brush to their right. The road was hardly more than a trail, and barely any of it could be seen through the overgrowth.

"This is the way to the farm?" Cid asked as he looked for signs of trouble, monsters, and webs. *I'll take a dark path in the woods over spiders anyday.*

"Yeah, this is it. Look." The lad pointed over at a small wooden sign. The sign was half buried by the undergrowth and was partially tilted to the side, making it even easier to miss. The words on it were caked with dust but still legible: *Oak Tree Farm.*

He'd finally made it.

"Come on Cid!" Lyle called, scampering ahead of him down the road. "I've been dying to know what you'll say when you see what the farm looks like. I already bet my grandfather you'll freak out."

Freak out. That's not at all what I want to hear. What have I gotten myself into? Cid followed him down the path toward the farm, his heart practically pounding in his chest. *Let's see what the damage is.*

As he approached, his heart sank.

Daryl Nightgreen had been right: the place was a mess. A small two-story farmhouse stood at the center of the compound. The porch was half caved in, and the little bit of porch that was still usable was covered in old and yellowed trash. There was an equally large hole in the roof. And even with that, the Farmhouse was at least in better shape than the other buildings.

Sitting catty-cornered from the farmhouse was an old brown barn. One of the wall's was completely warped. The timbers that supported it had warped and splintered, causing the barn to have a very concerning tilt to the structure. There was a tool shed with a caved-in roof not too far away from the barn, and behind that, a chicken coop.

The coop could hardly be called a coop since it was mostly just rusted wire hooked to rotting wood. Cid walked over to the tool shed to get a better look. There was a tree growing out of a hole in the ceiling, and not too far away, he spotted a dry-looking well that was missing a bucket. Everything was overgrown, and hardly anything looked like it was usable.

From what he could tell, the fields around the farm had gone fallow. They were overgrown with weeds and wild growth. Nature had retaken the land. Different parts of the property were easier to tell had once been used for pasture. He could see the stumps where fence posts had once been. In other places, he spotted water troughs, but they clearly hadn't seen livestock in years.

Oak Tree hadn't been a farm in a very long time. *But no spiders, so.. it's a win!*

Lyle coughed to get his attention. "Well?"

"Well, what?" Cid replied as he walked around the property with the lad following close behind.

"What do you think?" Lyle asked.

"It could be worse. I've slept in worse. I think it needs

some work," Cid said. "And it might be a while before this place is up and running. But it's nothing I can't fix with a little time and effort."

He hoped. Cid still didn't know the first thing about farming. His time in the countryside was almost purely limited to short term excursions with the Guard.

"Oh," the lad said, looking perplexed. "So, you're staying then? Doesn't this look like too much work?"

"Of course I'm staying," Cid responded with an eyebrow raised. *Is he trying to get me to leave?* "Make no mistake, this is mine. I bought it with my time, my service, and my toil. I own it now. It just needs some attention."

"Sorry. It's just my grandfather said you'd be *really* mad when you saw what kind of shape it was in," Lyle said. "He said you'd probably leave and try to get a plot of land somewhere else. Demand a refund like everyone else to come through. No one from out of town has wanted to put in the effort. Everybody else quit."

I've never been a quitter, and I won't be starting now. This, this may seem impossible, but impossible is nothing. Cid was already smiling. "Well, Daryl was wrong. I'm not mad at all. And I'm definitely not going to leave. It's perfect. It's mine. Finally, mine. Not much to look at— not yet— but it's home."

Granted Personal Quest: Home Sweet Home I!	
Description:	Oak Tree Farm has seen better days. The farming will need to wait until enough repairs have been done to enable basic functioning of the farm. This quest needs to be

	completed within the week due to the severity of the damage.
Reward:	+5 Reputation with residents of Haven
Consequence For Failure:	Collapse of the Tool Shed and Chicken Coop.

CHAPTER 7: AND THEN THERE WAS ONE

"Well— uh... Are you sure you're going to be alright here all alone, mister?" Lyle asked, looking around at the half-ruined farm. "I mean, this is worse than I thought. I'd heard from grandfather just how bad it had gotten here, but wow. Are you sure this is really ok? I mean, I'm not willing to stick around and help tidy up, but I'm sure grandfather would be ok with you using the guest room if you wanted to. This place doesn't look like it's fit for livestock, let alone a person."

Cid held back a laugh. The lad was clearly deadly serious and well intentioned. *I've slept in a lot worse places than this, lad. I just need to find a dry spot and make sure there aren't any animals or monsters to worry about nearby.*

"You don't need to call me 'mister'," he absentmindedly muttered. He continued looking around at the rest of the farm, but none of it got any better than it was after his initial assessment. "You can just call me Cid. And I'll be fine here tonight. I was with the Guard, remember? I reached Class B. I know how to take care of myself."

"Alright," Lyle said, looking a bit deflated. "Well, if you're ever around or need my help, you know where to find me."

"Aye, I do. Next time, lad, I'll absolutely keep that offer in mind. Looks like I've got a lot of work cut out for myself."

Lyle snickered. "You can say that again. I'm surprised you're not running away as fast as possible. I know if someone handed me this mess, I would've already begged for mercy."

"Well, if you're looking for some pocket change, I'm sure I'll have some work available for you around here in the near future. There will be plenty to do to help out. At least that's my guess from what I've seen so far. I'll need to do a more extensive look around in the morning. All I know is there's going to be lots of work, without a doubt. Regardless, I'll tell your grandpa what a great help you've been so far," Cid promised. And it was true, the lad had been a good help. "Anyways, you'd better get out of here before it gets too dark."

"Fine. Alright, Cid, I'll hold you to that." With nothing more to say, the lad turned and ran off.

Something about letting the lad run off without any protection after dark didn't sit quite right with Cid. *I wasn't a Guard for nothing.* He quickly used the [Cover] ability on the lad, and a silvery shield that only Cid could see covered the kid.

The ability should last long enough for him to get home. If anything does happen, the ability will trigger, and I'll be granted the [Haste] status to go after him with quickness. He should be fine though, he knows this land a lot better than I do.

Still, Cid kept watching the lad until he vanished into the trees. Only when he was out of sight and the [Cover] effect faded did Cid then turn toward the farmhouse. It was getting dark in earnest now, and it was time to make camp for the night.

It didn't seem likely there'd be much in the way of a comfortable place to rest, not with how the farmhouse and rest of the farm were half ruined— some areas near complete disrepair. *Luckily enough, I don't need much to get comfortable.* Cid had everything he needed right in his pack, patting it longingly as he thought of finally finding a place to rest.

Within a bedroll, he'd packed everything he needed to get comfy in his new home: a sleeping bag, a dagger, and the ability to use it if needed.

He climbed the creaking stairs toward the front door, carefully stepping around the hole in the porch. His eyes were open for tracks and signs of things to be concerned about. *Like people or giant spiders.* He didn't spot any, though he had seen a few older footprints here and there on the property. *Some of the villagers were probably doing an inspection.*

He shoved his way inside, and the door groaned painfully. Cid looked up and saw the door was halfway off its hinges, and it took him a few tries to move it. One of the hinges tore the rest of the way with the movement and hung tilted in the air, supported only by the bottom hinge. *Another thing to fix. I'll add it to the mental list of the thousand and a half things I have to do.*

But Cid wasn't unhappy about it. If he worked hard, he could make it work. The task of repairing the farm was a tall order, but it almost made him feel better to have a list of projects ahead of him. It would help with his transition away from the guard and into the next phase of his life.

He'd have to do a proper survey in the morning— take a full account of what needed to be done and what order he wanted to do it in. Already, the Quest incentivized recovering the tool shed and chicken coop, but he had a week to work on that. He had to see if anything else took precedence. He'd have to make a real checklist so he could sort and order it by priority. Hopefully the Quest was understanding of the massive project he was taking on.

With the inside of the farmhouse being in such rough shape, Cid decided it wasn't worth the risk to try and explore the second floor in the dark. *Strong or not, I don't want to risk breaking my leg if one of those steps is rotted out. Besides, no signs of monsters. Or spiders. Nobody has been here in a long time.* It was a relief. As for the stairs, they didn't exactly look fully stable.

Instead of trying to find a room upstairs, Cid did a quick check of the downstairs. The kitchen was just as rough as everything else, as was the sitting room. A door to what he assumed was a wine or root cellar was locked and heavy. *That door is also noted. I'll leave that for later when I can see better.* The spot where the bathroom was had a dusty claw tub and other unmentionables. It wouldn't be seeing use for a while.

Mostly satisfied with the quick tour of his surroundings, Cid set his pack down in the front hallway, pushed away some old leaves and sticks that had found their way in, and laid out the bedroll he'd brought with him. It was a little beat up and torn in spots, but it had served him well throughout the years. It was the sort that the Guards used when they were away on duty for short-term deployments.

Tucked into the bedroll was a thick wool blanket to wrap up in, and it was reasonably comfortable. Trying not to sneeze —the house was full of dust— he pulled a dagger out from the hidden sheath on his side and unlaced his boots.

He stretched out his toes and wrapped himself in his cloak, laying down for sleep. His hands curled around the dagger. Everything else aside, he was exhausted, and after the day's journey, he was out almost as soon as his head touched the ground.

Out, but always ready for danger. His final thought before sleep was to update his personal log.

Personal Log Entry I

End of Day One.

You've traveled to Haven and claimed Oak Tree Farm as your own. Currently, you've found no signs of monsters or brigands. The farm is in need of many repairs that will take some time to complete. The morning will reveal the extent of the damage, but sleep after a long day of travel is paramount.
You have the beginnings of a mentorship with the lad, Lyle. Keep this up, and you may have an apprentice to help with some of your tasks and to become a useful inside source of information on Haven.
You have begun to build a friendship with Daryl Nightgreen. Keep this up, and you may gain unique bonuses and access to otherwise closed inventories from vendors.

Active Quests	
What Plants Crave	Secure a water source for your farm and finish unlocking the farmer class.
Friend of Haven I	Return to Miss Maggie for partial reward. Continue to gain reputation with the residents of Haven.
Home Sweet Home I	Restore basic functioning to Oak Tree Farm. Time Remaining: 6 days 18 hours 23 minutes

CHAPTER 8: UP IN THE MORNING

Morning came and went.

Cid woke up to bright sunlight filtering through dirty windows and a few noticeable holes in the ceiling. *What time is it?* He'd hoped to get up early and get to work, but he could tell by how brightly lit the hallway was that dawn had already come and gone. He'd missed an early start to the day.

Urgh. He blinked away the fatigue from the night's rest, rubbing his eyes. *Looks like it's closer to noon than mid-morning.*

He moved a bit and tried to stretch, wanting to work out some of the morning stiffness from his body. *It's unfortunate that I lost the morning, but I can't stress it too much. Just have to work around it.* Getting up early had been a nice idea, but he'd underestimated how tired the trip had made him. *Or the drink for that matter.* He'd have to be better about that.

With a groan, he sat up and glanced around. The house looked even worse by day than it had by night— and it had already looked pretty bad by night. He had a very brief thought of giving up when he realized he'd be eating cold rations for a while. The thought of cold food wasn't one he was fond of, even though it was something he'd built up a tolerance for over the years. As he'd learned in his days as a guard, sometimes the only thing worse than the cold rations were when the cold rations were heated up.

Just going back to square one reminded him of his early days in the Guard when he'd been new, green, and had a large share of hard living. It was a life far different than the moderate comfort he'd enjoyed as his time in service and grade afforded him better accommodations. *Like the barracks instead of a field tent.*

It was almost enough to make him think about going back to the Guards and picking up right where he'd left off, but then shook his head. *No.* He wanted this farm. He'd started this new life, and he'd accepted the Quests. He wasn't a quitter, so he was going to finish it.

First thing's first. It was time to get his ducks in a row. He sat up with a groan, tucked his wool blanket back into his bedroll, and sheathed the dagger back into his side sheath. *Thankfully, I didn't need it last night, but it's better to be safe than sorry.*

Cid reached out an arm and swiped upwards into the air to bring up his stats menu.

Cid Dawnshield	
Race	Human
Class	Unassigned
Level	34
Sub-Class	Guard (Rank B)
Level	NA
Attributes	

Strength	18
Agility	9
Endurance	28
Magic	4
Abilities	
Refraction	Taunt
Subdue	Hidden Pocket
Cover	Water 1
Fire 1	Wind 1
Earth 1	Alchemy 1

Cid noticed his main class was now unassigned. *Right, that tracks.* Cid was a former Guard, and now it was official, recognized by the system itself. Though he wasn't an elite Knight Errant like Bran, his status was in a good place.

In his years in the city, Cid had picked up decent gains to strength and more to endurance while acquiring the fighting skills he needed to survive up close when a sword wasn't available— and he was good with a sword when was one was. He wasn't great with a bow— there hadn't been much ranged fighting in the narrow streets of Highbridge— but decent enough that he wasn't better off smacking them with the weapon. He could always improve if he needed it.

Hopefully in the peaceful town of Haven, he wouldn't

need it.

He was definitely faster and stronger than the other villagers, but he didn't expect there to be much out there that could give him a challenge— or be even a real threat whatsoever. It was good living, and his attributes he'd earned with the Guard would help him here on the farm.

Getting Oak Tree Farm ready would be an impossible task for someone without his augmented strength and speed. Even for him, it would be hard enough. Hopefully his other skills would be useful.

His thoughts turned to the newest abilities he added. He'd almost doubled the amount of abilities at his disposal: [Fire 1], [Water 1], [Wind 1], [Earth 1], and [Alchemy 1]. He never used magic in the Guard, and magic itself wasn't that common outside of the Mages Guild or Magic Knights.

As it was, he didn't have much of a framework or understanding of magic to really understand how to make use of magic. *I'll have to learn the best way, experience. Besides, on the farm, things might be different. I'll have to see if there is a way to learn more while I'm here in Haven.*

He smiled as an image of himself working grand magic in the field like some Archmagus came to mind. A *little magic could go a long way though, that is if I figure out the right way to apply it. Just treat it like any other tool.*

He laced up his boots. He'd wasted enough time already and took off outside to take in the lay of the land. He thought for a moment about taking his sword with him, but opted not to. Hopefully, he wouldn't need it, and he'd still have his dagger on him. He shoved the broken door open and scooted through the gap. It didn't fully open. *I'll really need to fix that soon.*

But once he was outside, his mood immediately lifted. The day was stunningly beautiful, the air crisp and clear as he stepped out onto the porch. He could already sense that it was going to be hot— the sun high in the sky with strong waves blaring down— but it wasn't bad yet.

Perfect weather for a site survey.

He inhaled deeply, enjoying the scent of new grass, and smiled. The only sounds he could hear were birdsong and rustling leaves. There was no one else around but him. Nobody was nearby, and it was strange yet blissful. After spending so many years in the city, surrounded by people, it was truly a strange feeling to be totally alone.

He liked it, feeling freedom like never before.

"Alright," he said aloud just to break the silence. He clapped his hands together with a big smile, feeling excitement bubbling up from his gut. "It's taken a while to get here, but it's time to get to work."

Cid started by doing a circuit of the land he'd bought, walking the perimeter of the plot. Oak Tree Farm's previous owner had marked it out with boundary stones, so it was easy to see where his land ended and the common land began. It wasn't a lot of land, but it was more than enough for him. He hummed as he walked, enjoying the feeling of looking over the farm.

His farm.

The fields were overgrown and full of weeds, and the fencing was even worse off than he'd seen last night. He'd have to clear the land and rebuild the fences before he could even think about bringing animals in.

Closer in, the vegetable gardens were completely overgrown with every manner of anything that wasn't a vegetable, and the ground had dried out. More than a few barbed vines crisscrossed the field.

Might be good to consult Daryl on what to do there. He needed to find a way to irrigate. Otherwise, even if he cleared out the weeds, nothing would be able to thrive, and he wanted Oak Tree to thrive. This was his new life, his new home.

And it has to be a success.

The far pastures had been partly reclaimed by the forest, and he frowned as he tested his strength against one of the young trees that had started growing there. It was too big for him to pull out of the ground at this point. He'd have to chop it down and dig up the stump.

How did the farm get into such bad shape? Why didn't anyone want it before me? Even in bad shape, it should have been bought up pretty easily.

It was mystifying to him. Oak Tree Farm was perfect and had everything a man could want, even a former City Guard. It was green, quiet, peaceful— just the right place to start a new and peaceful life. Just the right place for a fresh start. He just had to get it up and running.

After taking the boundary tour, he moved on to inspecting the buildings in the farm compound: the barn, tool shed, chicken run, and farmhouse. To his relief, they had been built well with good bones. The foundation seemed solid. While they would need a lot of work to get them back in working shape, he wouldn't have to rebuild them completely if the wood was still usable. Whoever had built them had known what he— or she— was doing.

He spent a little extra time in the barn, noting that there were stalls for both cows and horses, but the supports would need to be replaced in spots and reinforced in others. Even then, the whole thing would need to come down eventually. His mind turned briefly to Nightshade.

If only there was a way to get him back.

But it would be hard to buy him off the City Guard, especially when the guards needed every good charger they could get. And who knew if Nightshade would even want to work a plow? It would be a significant comedown for a former warhorse. *If I expanded the plot though, I might just be able to let him roam free. Would be his retirement as much as mine.*

Granted Companion Quest: No One Left Behind!	
Description:	Find a way to acquire Nightshade from the City Guard then do so. The old war horse doesn't have many more years left in him before he's put out to the field. Take care of Nightshade!
Reward:	+5 Reputation with residents of Haven
Conditional Requirement:	Stables
Consequence For Failure:	Permanent loss of the Horse Nightshade.

CHAPTER 9:
THE WELL

Permanent loss of Nightshade... The words repeated in his head, the thought not sitting well with Cid. *But if I'm going to get anything done, I need to keep moving. I can't focus on what I might lose.*

So Cid got to work and quickly finished his appraisal of the repairs needed, satisfied with the inspection of the buildings. *So far, all I've got is a big need to repair the structures and fix up a better place to sleep. Which means...*

His attention turned to the toolshed, and he glanced at the tell-tale signs of a well behind the toolshed. There was dry dirt and stacked rocks in a ring, some moss, an old shovel, rope that didn't look usable, and a dusty bucket. He walked over. *That might just about solve my water issue.* The well was dry on the outside, and Cid was already worrying as soon as he noticed a distinct lack of dampness.

The well had a narrow opening at the bottom, almost like water was being piped in from another source rather than fed by the land. As far as he could tell, that source was totally blocked with rocks and dirt, assuming the origin of the water hadn't dried up since the last owner handled the property properly.

Cid frowned as he peered down into the depths of darkness. He'd need water if he wanted to do anything with the farm, and he'd need it soon. Without the well in good condition, there wasn't much point in trying to do anything else. Cid tried to pick up the shovel to see if he could move some of the debris with it, but as soon as he went to pick it up, the head rolled off, revealing the handle had rotted clean through underneath.

Profession Quest: What Plants Crave has progressed!

You've found your first available water source.
The well is no longer functioning and seems to
have fallen into disrepair. Unlike most wells,
this one is fed by a secondary source rather than
pooling the water of the surrounding land.

Let's try this again. I need to clear it to get the well working. Cid walked back to the toolshed and, carefully as he could, started to rummage around. But when the rummaging went nowhere, he started tossing piles of rubbish out into the yard, until he found a rusted shovel with a warped wooden handle. It was ugly, but still serviceable, and for the first time since leaving the house that morning, Cid smiled. He had a big task ahead of him, but he'd start by clearing the debris from the well. After that, everything else would fall into place.

Several hours later, Cid had made a massive pile of dirt and rocks next to the well with no result for his efforts. He sat down on the ground to take a break, breathing hard. It was mid-afternoon, the day had grown hot, and he was completely parched. He'd already had to grab his pack from the house.

Cid pulled a large flask out of the pack. He shook it to see how much water was left. It was just over half full, plenty to last him through the rest of the day, but if he couldn't unplug the well soon, he'd have to go back into town and get water from the river. That would take time, time he didn't want to waste on a task he'd have to do multiple times a day if he didn't figure it out now.

He took a big drink and sighed. *Well, I'm going to have to head to town soon anyways to get more food. I'm sure Lyle will be glad to see me.* While he'd brought enough from the Guards to last him a few days, he'd already burned through about a third of his stores. Maybe he'd head back to the tavern and see if Maggie had any specialties on the menu while he was there. It would give him a reason to try and know her better.

Enough thinking about her. He had work to do. And it seemed like he wasn't getting very far either. Something he was doing wasn't working. Maybe he wasn't digging quickly enough or something. He stood up, grimacing as his knees popped, and hoisted the shovel over his shoulder. *Time to do the thing.* He tested the rope and tossed it down. *Just big enough.*

He went in.

Though, as he was climbing back into the dry well, a stand of trees in the distance caught his eye. They were waving gently in the breeze, almost like they were inviting him to come their way. He looked down at the well then back at the trees. It looked nice over there, inviting.

And they were on his land.

Maybe he could take a quick trip that way just to see whatever there was to see. *Out there. And not at the bottom of the well. I still have other stuff I need to do.* It was an easy justification, after all, he'd be surveying his property. *Right. 'Surveying the property'.*

Yeah, the well can wait. It was too hot for hard work right now anyways, and it would still be there later in the day when he got back. Cid clambered back out onto the ground, shovel still slung over one shoulder, and struck out toward the trees.

He was in good spirits now, glad he'd made his decision. This was his retirement from the Guard, after all. He deserved to not have to climb down into some dark hole in the ground. He'd done enough of that. *Yet, here I am doing it again.* He laughed, he didn't feel that bad about it.

The stand of trees was lush and green, surrounded by broad-leaved bushes. For a moment, he thought about dropping his shovel and flopping down on the grass to take a nap. But something told him to keep going. He pushed his way through the undergrowth, hacking at thorny branches with the blade of the shovel, until he found himself at a low and rocky cliff.

I own this? All of this? This is my land? Amazing.

A dry riverbed stretched out ahead of him with a narrow trickle of water at the bottom, and a thin, pathetic stream of water dripped down the cliff. It had clearly once been a real creek with a real waterfall, but something must have happened to it. *It must be blocked somewhere.*

Maybe this was why the well went dry too. If it used the same water source as the stream, maybe they'd both gone dry at the same time. He'd have to track down the site of the problem and unplug it.

Cid looked down at the shovel in his hand. It might not be enough for the task ahead. He needed better tools.

Grumbling, he shoved his way back through the bushes and into his ruined toolshed. He'd cleared out a lot of the debris inside while he was looking for the shovel, but the floor was a little more jumbled than it had been before. He took a few minutes to move the rest of the rubbish outside and swept the floor with a broom he'd found.

Then in the corner of the shed, he saw it. *That's exactly what I need. Cid grinned*

A rusty pick was leaning against the far wall. It was exactly what he needed: small enough for a small space and light enough to carry easily while at the same time being heavy-duty enough to shift boulders and densely packed dirt. Hopefully, between this and his shovel, he'd have the tools to get the job done.

CHAPTER 10: THE DRIED CREEK

Cid hoisted the pick over one shoulder, the shovel over the other, and set off back toward the dry creek, whistling as he went. He was making progress. Slowly but surely, he was moving things forward. He just had to keep at it. *I can't get too far ahead of myself, but this is the beginning, I can make things happen after this.*

In front of him, green brush and trees stood in his way while vines twisted around trunks and hung from trees. It was not enough to remember. *Better do it right. This might be a pretty frequent stop for me. A little extra effort now to save me from more hassle later.*

Cid took the time to clear away some of the overgrowth that was in the way. Each swing was clean, methodical, and not that of a farmer but that of a man-at-arms of the City Guard. He deftly made short work of the bushes that stood in his way.

After a few minutes, he'd created a narrow opening just wide enough for him to walk through. He brushed a bead of sweat off of his face with his forearm and stood back. He looked at it happily. He noticed the creek bed widened in spots and was deeper in others. *Perfect!.* If he could get the stream unblocked, he could swim in it in the heat of the day when it got too hot to work. That was just the extra motivator he needed to keep pushing forward.

Cid hopped into the dry riverbed and followed it. Eventually, it led him to the base of a cliff where only a trickle of water could be seen flowing from on high. *I'll have to make my way up.* He looked around the cliff base until he found the best spot to climb. *I'll follow the water back toward its source, and then I'll see what's the problem. Hopefully it wouldn't be too far of a walk. Or too big of a problem.*

With a grunt, Cid threw up the shovel, the pick following shortly after. He himself then followed. With one hand in front of the other, he hoisted himself up the cliff— it was a small one, more of a mound than a cliff, really— and found himself on a low and rocky hill.

With a little bit of height added to his vision, Cid saw the creek bed wound its way further upward, but he didn't see what caused the sad trickle of water at the bottom cliff. He wiped his brow again and continued on his way.

The sun was hot on his face, and he hoped he'd be able to solve the issue today. An afternoon spent relaxing in a pool of cool water was just what he needed. He didn't bother to think about the countdown timer that was running against him.

It wasn't too long before he saw it: a spring wedged in between two large boulders that must be the source of the stream— and hopefully the source of his well, too. It was immediately clear what the problem was. The spring and the rocks around it were totally overgrown with dense, gnarled tree roots. Some of the roots were warped in odd directions, and in other parts, the roots had knotted and appeared to be bigger than he was.

The atmosphere grew heavy and dense. His breath didn't come easy, and Cid had to resist the urge to leave. He almost felt like he didn't belong but shook the feeling away. *I have to figure out what happened to the water.* As for the roots, the tree they belonged to was massive. The tree towered, clearly old and ancient.

Cid dropped his tools and bent down to take a closer

look. The roots were strong and healthy, and the tree above them was tall with a dense cap of green leaves. It would be a shame to cut it down— even if he *did* need water. *I need to find another way.*

And there was something else, too. Something unusual. He cupped his hands around one of the roots, trying to block out the sun so he could see if he was just imagining things. He wasn't. The root— and the entire tree— was glowing faintly with a pale green light.

A mana tree. Cid stepped back carefully, cautiously, *reverently.* He hadn't seen it before. *How did I miss it?* It was almost like it had just appeared once he was close enough.

He'd heard of such things, but he'd never seen one himself. They were practically the stuff of legend in these lands: tall trees that grew abnormally fast and dropped magical fruit filled with mana.

They were incredibly valuable.

And this one was his.

It was exciting, but it also made his problem a lot trickier. He needed to keep the tree alive if he wanted to harvest its mana, which meant he couldn't just cut it down. He might have spent most of his life in the city, but he'd heard about what could happen if you harmed a mana tree. He had no intention of inviting that kind of bad energy into his life.

But he also needed his well to be working again, and the tree's roots were in the way of it. He'd have to work very carefully and avoid disturbing the tree or its roots. It would take finesse—

Which worried him. Cid, as a former Guard, wasn't really a finesse kind of guy.

Well, there's a first time for everything. And if I need to be a finesse guy, then so be it. Right now, here and now, I'll do what I have to.

There had to be a way. And if he wanted his new life—and his new farm— to be successful, he'd have to learn more than a few new skills. He picked up his pick and tentatively approached the rock pile.

"Sorry, tree," he said, feeling a little foolish as he did so. "I'll be careful."

Was he really talking to a tree? But who knew how smart a mana tree was? Maybe it could understand everything he was doing and saying. And if so, he definitely didn't want to offend it.

Granted Mystery Quest: I Speak For the Trees!	
Description:	???
Reward:	???
Consequence For Failure:	???

Uh... Ok? He looked up at its leafy branches. They waved gently back and forth in the breeze just like a normal tree.

But nothing was normal about a mana tree.

They were nourished solely by magic power and coveted by any and all magical practitioners across the world. He'd just have to watch what he did and said, just in case it could understand. Working carefully to avoid disturbing the tree's roots, Cid slowly started, clearing rocks away from the riverbed.

CHAPTER 11: FLOW

Little by little, Cid tried to clear away the dirt and debris from under the tree's roots, and little by little, he came to one conclusion. *This isn't working.* The dirt was just packed in too tightly and was mixed together with a red colored clay. *I may as well be trying to do something equally difficult, like trying to break a rock with an ice pick for all the good that would do me.*

It was already late afternoon. The sun was starting to sink toward the horizon, but for all of Cid's work with the pick and shovel, the stream remained stubbornly blocked, the roots holding firmly in the earth. It was uncanny, almost like they were guarding or sealing something. He'd never seen anything quite like it. *Water should be coming out, even if it's just a little. I need a new approach, to try something else, but what?*

Cid sat down on the nearest boulder to think. He tried to push back the wave of disappointment that threatened to wash over him. He'd had rosy images of his new life and had imagined farming to be less... *hard.* The thought nudged at something inside him and made him feel a bit ashamed. He'd seriously misjudged how difficult farming was.

When people in the city talked about farming and farmers, it was always with a sort of disdain, though Cid had never been one of them. It was as if farmers and anyone who lived outside the city were somehow worthy of contempt for the simpler life that they lived, and as Cid was learning very quickly, there was nothing simple about farming.

Ever since deciding to buy the land, he'd imagined

himself kicking back and relaxing a bit on a piece of rich land after a long career in the Guard— long easy strolls in the morning through orchids, cool mist cooling him as he ate fruit and veggies at leisure, amongst many other fantasies of glamour and comfort.

Not even close.

Cid was starting to realize what he'd known deep down all along, something he now had blisters to prove. Farming was hard work, and he hadn't even really started yet.

He couldn't do anything with Oak Tree Farm unless he could get the water flowing again, and he needed to get it flowing very soon. At some point, he actually needed to start planting crops. The little bit of money he'd saved up could sustain him, but it wasn't exactly amazing money to live off of — and since he'd traded his pension, it wouldn't last forever. It had always been meant to be a supplement.

But what can I do beyond what I've already done? Think, Cid, think. If this was the Guard, how would you handle it? How would Bran handle it with the Corps?

A thought dawned on Cid, an old saying. *The same water that hardens an egg destroys the mountain.* He smiled. Cid had a solution. Bran had granted him the **[Water 1]** ability a few days earlier when he left the Guard for good, saying it might come in handy sometime soon. *A parting gift that could have got the Mage Knight in a lot of trouble.*

Cid had pictured himself using it to water the fields or fill a trough so his eventual cows could drink, but maybe there were other uses for it. A basic spell wouldn't be enough to clear out and free the spring on its own, but it might give him the boost he needed so that he could do it with the tools he already had.

Now, how to make the magic happen. Cid felt a little foolish. He'd watched Bran cast major spells before, and he always had an effortless cool to him that Cid knew he didn't have. He stood up again, dropped his tools, and held his hands out in front of him.

It would be his first time attempting to use the magic, and he didn't properly know how or where to start. So, with no other ideas in mind, he simply said, "**[Water 1]**."

Unsurprisingly, nothing happened.

Cid frowned. *What would Bran do if he was here?* Cid shook his head. He already knew the answer. *Bran would just make it work.*

I need this to work, but it needs to be condensed. I'll also need to shape the flow. Cid waved his arms awkwardly, feeling like a madman. A wild-eyed dwarf had once preached on the street corner next to his house when he was a boy, claiming to be a mage, and his weird twitching gestures had lodged themselves in Cid's memory and stayed there.

Now, he felt a bit like that erratic dwarf as he tried to get his new spell to work— and without meaning to, he started to mimic the dwarf's movements as he tried to cast **[Water 1]** for the second time.

Surprising nobody, nothing happened this time either.

Don't picture the dwarf, picture Bran. He corrected himself.

Bran always slouched a bit while he worked as if he couldn't be bothered to stand up straight. Cid knew better though. The man was all about keeping his core centered, and his spellwork was fluid and smooth, his arms moving only as much as they needed to in order to get the job done. Maybe that was what he needed to do.

Cid stood back on his heels and hunched his shoulders. He raised his arms lazily and moved through the gestures Bran had taught him as if he was only half-interested in making them. He pictured streams and rivers and waterfalls emptying into cold mountain pools. He pictured ocean waves breaking on the beach and ripples of leaves falling on ponds.

A cool flow.

A drip.

Water.

A thin stream appeared out of nowhere in front of his hands and dropped down on top of the rockpile. It started to trickle down through the dirt. Cid smiled but tried not to get too excited. He had to keep it cool.

Water.

The stream grew larger, pouring into the dry riverbed. Gradually, he released the hold he had on the spell and let more water flow. He could see small rocks being carried away with the current. This was good. It was working. Not only had he performed a new spell, he'd shaped it too.

Once he was satisfied that the spell wouldn't end when he stopped actively casting it, he picked up his pickaxe and shovel and got back to work. With the **[Water 1]** spell helping to work some of the soil away, his job was much easier than it had been before. He dislodged rock after rock and tossed them into the pile behind him, grinning as he saw water— real water from the spring, not from his spell— start to seep through the roots of the Mana Tree and flow down the dried Creek bed.

Finally.

Profession Quest: What Plants Crave has been completed!
You've successfully managed to free a water source and, in doing so, have avoided damaging the roots of the Mana Tree that had contributed to the blockage.

For preserving the Mana Tree, a reward has been added for completing this Quest!

Reward: Spellweaving!

CHAPTER 12: THE CRYSTAL CAVERN

It took Cid the rest of the afternoon to clear the roots from the debris. Using **[Water 1]** tired him out faster than the labor with the shovel and pickaxe did. It was a tedious process, but Cid got it done. He managed to get the stream cleared with no harm done to the tree's roots.

He took a moment to bask in the sun as he washed the mud and clay off his tools in the now rushing water. He peered over and saw the water was starting to fill in the deeper spots of the formerly dried creek bed. *It'll be deep soon. Well, deep enough.* He smiled but was too tired to swim today. *Maybe tomorrow. That would be nice.*

For now, he turned his attention to the skill window for his newly acquired skill.

Spellweaving
Known commonly as the most basic ability of those who command magic. It allows for a basic level of elemental creation and control. With enough experience, time, and skill, one can transcend the limitations of the mortal and wield the laws of the world as their own. The possibilities are endless.

I'll have to ask Bran next time I see him for some Spellweaving tips. I'm sure he has plenty of pointers he can give me. Regardless, I'm glad I've got this step behind me so I can move forward. If this does the trick to free up the water and feed it into my well, that'll be a job well done.

He'd have to double check when he got back to the farm just to make sure the well had water in it that he could pull from. But he was fairly confident he'd solved the issue. If not, he'd be back to square one.

Well, not quite back to square one. Almost, but not completely. Cid looked over at the stream and was pleased. No matter what happened with the well, he had a stream now.

And a Mana Tree.

That wasn't nothing. Finding the tree was a good omen. Something like that just appearing— it was a blessing, and one that might just predict future success.

He was about to pack up and head back to camp when something caught his eye. A brightness that Cid hadn't spotted before. Something glimmered behind the spring in the hole left behind where a large boulder had once been and where the tree roots of the mana tree had kept all the gathered debris held tight. Squinting against the setting sun, he moved closer.

There's something in there. Cid moved forward to examine it, but it was too tight to see clearly. He reached out and moved some loose mud out of the way, noticing the whole time that the area seemed to hum with a magical energy. The mud gave way to an opening behind it, and behind the opening was something else.

I bet I can fit. The hole was just large enough for him to squeeze through. It was a tighter fit around his shoulders than he wanted. Cid just had to hope there wasn't anything horrible inside. He carried on and pushed his way through.

He crawled along the narrow passage, and the passage steadily grew wider and firmer, less dirt trail and more paved path. Soon, Cid found his curiosity building as it opened up into a large cave under the hill, and—

Cid stopped in his tracks.

Beautiful. Can those really be what I think they are?

The truth was immediately clear, identifying what he'd seen sparkling earlier. The entire cave was full of glowing mana crystals of every possible color, shape, and size. Each crystal practically hummed with power, and the very air of the cave was thick with mana.

Cid reached a hand out to touch one, quickly retracted it. The air around it crackled with electricity, and the feeling got stronger as he got closer to the crystal. It seemed likely it would have some kind of magic effect if he actually made contact with it.

Instead of examining further, Cid moved farther into the cavern and followed what appeared to be a path of laid out stone. The dim glow that radiated out from the crystals provided just enough light for him to see where he was going, and his jaw almost dropped when the cavern opened up on either side farther into a brilliant blue room full of the crystals.

It was massive— more of a cave system than a single cave— and it was all on the edge of his land. *Might even still be on my land, but I'm not sure. Judging by the size of these crystals and the Mana Tree up above, I'd say there must be a leyline or something around here.*

Granted Epic Quest: Mana Harvest!	
Description:	It is not yet time. The trials have not finished spawning in. Come back

	again later, reach the ley line at the source, and find a way to directly harvest the power that lay within. Thirty-nine days until the harvest cycle ends
Reward:	All mana based abilities will receive a +1 upgrade modifier. Title - ???
Consequence For Failure:	Decreased affinity for magic. Loss of 1 magical ability. [Randomized]

Harvest cycle? What does any of that mean? Cid knew he'd have to come back soon and explore further, see how far the cave really went, but not today. He was exhausted from digging up rocks all day, and the only tools he had were his pick and shovel. He'd need a real lantern when he came back. And maybe more delicate tools— something that might help him extract a crystal without damaging it. *Maybe something bigger than a dagger too in case I run into trouble.*

He came to a halt in the center of the cave and took a deep breath when he stepped on to a raised stone platform. The effect was immediate as waves of restorative magic crashed in on him. He felt less tired than he had when he came in, almost completely refreshed. Waves of blue pressed over him, lingering wisps of mana passing through him in waves.

It's got to be the crystals or the leyline. I'm hoping it's the crystals though. They might have healing abilities if they do, and I can really work with that. I'll have to come back later and collect some to make sure.

He looked around and saw a series of sealed doors, and each one drew him forward towards them— towards whatever trial and challenge waited behind each one. Cid shook his hand and slapped his face to focus. *I can't be exploring an unknown Dungeon. I'm not prepared, and I've other Quests to finish up.*

With a sigh, Cid turned around and headed back to the surface. Once he was out of the cave and crawl space, he rolled an old log in front of the opening to obscure it. *Just in case,* and then off he went. It was time to head back to the farm. He took one last look up at the mana tree, drinking in the sight of it, and then made ready to leave.

He picked up his tools, making his way down along the riverbank and through the stand of trees that had originally caught his eye.

Once he got back, he took a quick detour over to the well to make sure his efforts had worked. Sure enough, it was already a quarter of the way full of water and rising. He'd look back again in the morning to see where things stood. But it seemed like for now, at least, his hard work had paid off.

Good. Oak Tree Farm was off to a good start. He glanced over in the direction of the spring and the mana tree that grew over it but found nothing. *It's gone. Or maybe it's hidden by some kind of spell or ability.* He shrugged. He had other things to worry about.

He thought longingly of the bedroll in the front hallway of the farmhouse, but there was one more thing he had to do before he could sleep. He carried his pickaxe and shovel back to the toolshed— now freshly clear of trash, although it needed a lot of cleaning and repairs— and leaned them neatly against the far wall.

The toolshed groaned and seemed to wobble. Cid cringed and grabbed an old bag of nails and a rusted hammer. It wasn't much, but it was honest work. In a few minutes, Cid was attaching a support, and with it, the tool shed settled.

The little bit of construction hadn't gone without issue. All the tools fell over, and Cid had to pick them back up. *I'll need to build a rack for them. And get more tools.*

His time in the Guard had taught him to take care of his gear, and he wasn't about to change his ways now. On watch, a rusty sword or a badly maintained piece of armor could be the difference between life and death. On the farm, the stakes were lower, but he still needed to maintain what he had if he wanted to make a living. He thought about that for a minute. *Is it really lower? If I don't take care of the stuff I have and I'm reckless, I'll lose everything.*

He checked the well again. The water had risen to the top. It had a faint blue glow to it. He tossed a bucket of water on himself to clean away some of the grime of the day and pulled the bucket again, drinking thirstily.

Finally— *finally*— he made his way back to the house. The front door was still broken, and it took him a few tries to get it open. *I'll have to fix that soon. Tomorrow, I've got to really buckle down and make more progress on the Quest.*

It was really annoying being on a deadline, but for now, that didn't matter. He'd had a successful first day of work. He'd gotten his well working, he'd created a stream he could swim in, he'd discovered a hoard of unexpected wealth in the form of mana crystals buried beneath his lands.

And more.

A Dungeon to explore once I've got the bare minimum to check it out safely. All things considered, it was a pretty good day.

It wasn't enough yet. He'd have to keep up the hard work, but it was a good start. And he knew how important first days could be.

I might make something of this farm.

And with that, he took off his boots, ate some of the preserved food he'd kept in his pack, and wrapped himself up in his cloak and wool blanket after, quickly falling asleep.

CHAPTER 13: OLD MEMORIES

The moon shone through the gap in the ceiling of the farmhouse, but Cid didn't notice. He was tucked into his wool blanket oblivious to the world. He tossed and turned on the bed roll, his sleep troubled and his hand firmly clenched around the dagger he kept under his pillow.

But even though he slept restlessly, Cid dreamed.

****

The light from the torch he was holding illuminated the dank and musty tunnel, casting long eerie glows down the darkened hall and even longer shadows against the stained walls. Even with the flame of the torch, Cid couldn't see too far.

He wasn't surprised. The sewers under the city had never been an easy place for an assignment, and every step of his steel boots echoed loudly. But that was the way of a city Guard, to patrol and come out in force later to clear monster dens and nests.

It made sense that there was no way to know if monsters had found their way into the human quarter without actually checking for them. Such infestations could go undetected for weeks— or even months. Though, the sewers were known for always being a problem. Nests and infestations were common, and forays out to sweep the sewers were far more common. A recurring duty of the guard.

It had only been a few weeks since the last full clear, but rumors of activity in the sewers had warranted sending out a Guard to check it out earlier than scheduled. That specific patrol duty had fallen on Cid who, as the youngest person on his squad, hadn't already pulled the duty. This time, the rounds in the sewers below the city were his.

It wasn't a duty he was particularly pleased with, but he thought it was a hazing ritual since he was still new. Still, he had to be cautious. He still had a waypoint lodestone if things got too dangerous, but he didn't want to use it unless absolutely needed. The city Guard was not known for reimbursing their people for on the job expenses. The lodestone was not an expense that Cid was able to write off or replace easily even if he had the coin.

His boot caught against something and kicked it. Cid winced as he heard something hard scatter across the ground, something he hoped was just a rock.

Whatever it was dropped into the water of the sewers, and soon, other things could be heard swimming towards it. Cid turned the torch towards the water and saw ripples of movement on the surface, but whatever was behind those ripples, he couldn't see. He just knew better than to stay in one spot and find out. Water rats, drowned ones, fel crabs, deep ones. The list went on, and Cid was only comfortable handling water rats and fel crabs.

He breathed deep, trying to calm himself. Cid had no issues fighting outside, but the sewers were counted least among the list of the places he would have liked to find himself assigned to patrol. The only assignment he dreaded more was watch duty within the mausoleum. The walls felt like they were too close and closing in. He needed to ground himself.

"Slow is smooth, and smooth is fast," he muttered to himself as he surged forward, careful not to dislodge anymore debris. Soon, he left the waters behind and took a side tunnel, but it didn't take long for him to grow dismayed. "Today is not my day."

White webbing hung in strands, and Cid knew they could only mean one thing. Spiders. Though what manner and breed was anyone's guess until confronted face first with whatever manner of arachni made the tunnels their home. Cid shuddered and held his short sword out in front of him.

He'd heard stories from the other city Guards but hadn't had to face a spider yet. He walked along and used the edge of the blade to cut through the strands of spider silk and made sure to keep the torch steady. The last thing he wanted was to lose his light.

He didn't see a net of webbing, only becoming aware of them when he ran into them, immediately jumping backwards. A fist sized spider squirmed across the floor, and Cid nervously laughed about it while also trying to resist the urge to scream in terror and bolt. The way back was just as dangerous. Like most good people of the realm, Cid hated spiders.

And when there's one spider, you quickly find you have two or more, and then you find yourself swords up and neck deep in ichor.

Another approached, this one closer to the size of a tabby than a hand, and Cid defensively lunged out with his short sword to slay it when it moved closer— uncomfortably close. Another spider hissed and lunged forward, and Cid responded accordingly.

Spiders climbed down the ceiling on strands of white while others scurried and climbed and crawled. Cid kept up his defenses, but when he turned to run away, he found the way had been blocked. A mass of black tiny spiders moved across the entryway he had just just passed through. Corded white lines blocked the tunnel he had just come through. There would be no escape, at least not in that direction.

His heart started beating faster, and for the first time since he'd joined the Guards, Cid thought maybe he wasn't going to make it. But rather than dread, Cid found his resolve hardening.

"Fine, so be it then." He reached into a pouch for a red vial containing the essence of flame. He readied himself to quickly apply the item to the surface of his blade.

It lit up with red flame, and he attacked, his sword carving and cutting through the hard carapace of the spiders. Each attack coordinated with the movement of the torch. He used the flames to burn away the webs and kept himself from being immobilized in the strands.

Eventually, all the spiders lay at his feet, a mass of green ichor, but then something unexpected happened. Fur brushed against the back of his neck— hairy fur— and then he felt it. The mouth of the beast that had him. Cid screamed and swung in attack.

****

His eyes opened, and he found himself face to face with a hairy monster pressing down on his chest. A monster whose mouth was open, salivating, and hungry. Cid pushed it away with a quickness, drawing his dagger as he sprang up in one fluid, almost immediate, motion.

"What the heck, Cid? Don't hurt him! Put away the knife," yelled Lyle as the lad backed up toward the crooked opening of the front door, his hands raised, not wanting to start a scene. The monster ran over to the lad and stood at his side. "Settle down, ok? It's just my dog." Lyle raised a hand to show he meant no harm. "I brought you something my grandfather wanted to give you."

Cid looked around, lost in thought, and realized what

had almost happened. He put the dagger away sheepishly, thankful that nothing bad had happened to the lad or his dog. Cid cleared his throat, still feeling the sting of embarrassment and concern. "Listen Lyle, you're a good lad and all, but don't get too close if I'm sleeping. Sorry about all that."

Lyle nodded, trying to be understanding. "Nightmares?"

Cid shook his head. "Nightmares. Memories. Life as a Guard isn't exactly glorious or easy. I don't regret putting it behind me."

CHAPTER 14:
INVITATION

"I'm sorry you saw me like this. Can you give me a few minutes?" Cid asked Lyle sheepishly. "You kind of caught me at a bad time. I'm not my most put together in the mornings. I'll meet you outside once I get ready unless it can't wait. It can wait, right?"

Lyle nodded and motioned for the dog to follow him, and they headed outside. Cid crashed back onto his bedroll, feeling a little embarrassed and worried about how that situation almost played out. He turned the thought aside to focus on a task he'd been putting off that needed attention. Log updates. He opted into the mental note that helped him keep track of things.

Personal Log Entry II
Start of Day Three.
You've continued to make Oak Tree Farm your own. You've still seen no signs of monsters or other concerns about dangerous beasts or groups. The repairs have yet to begin, though you've managed to secure a water source for the farm and found a Mana Cave with a connected Leyline. You may continue to build a mentorship with Lyle, however recent actions have lowered your

esteem with the lad and scared him a bit.

Active Quests	
Friend of Haven I	Return to Miss Maggie for partial reward. Continue to gain reputation with the residents of Haven.
Home Sweet Home I	Restore basic functioning to Oak Tree Farm. Time Remaining: 4 days 8 hours 47 minutes
Mana Harvest I	Reach the Leyline within the mana cave. Time Remaining: 38 Days
No One Left Behind	Acquire Nightshade from the City Guard of Hardhearth.
I Speak For the Trees	???
Completed Quests	
What Plants Crave	Secure a water source for your farm and finish unlocking the farmer class.
Farming Class	PARTIAL CONDITION MET

He took a moment to lie back on his bedroll and take stock of the update. He'd done a decent job so far: cleared out the toolshed, got the well working, and found the cave. But he only had a few more days to get the farm up and running— even just a bare bones version of it— and he'd already used up a lot of time. It was already the start of day three, and he was still sleeping in the front hallway of the farmhouse. He needed to get this whole process moving faster.

Much faster.

Cid noticed something else. He needed a bath and some new laundry quite badly. He'd been wearing the same clothes for three days, and after yesterday's work with the stream, he was starting to smell more than he was comfortable with. He'd have to be sure to take a swim before he went to sleep tonight and try to get cleaned up. *Maybe rinse the clothes out in the stream and leave them to dry.*

There was one other thing too. Even though he'd been working hard and hadn't slept the best, he felt amazing. He'd woken up surprisingly early, given how tired he'd been the night before.

And he felt *great.*

He'd slept better than he had in weeks. *Maybe the mana cave beneath the land has restorative properties. They used to sell crystals to put in the water when I was stationed in the city. Maybe I should try that with these.*

He sniffed again and wrinkled his nose. *I need some more clothes, too.*

When he'd left Hardhearth, he'd had to give back his uniforms when he left the Guard, which meant that he didn't have much, and he'd had to cut back even further to fit all his belongings into one pack. He had one other shirt aside from the one he was wearing, but this was his only pair of pants. The knees were already starting to wear through, too.

Well, I'll do what I can.

He pulled the other shirt out of his sack and changed into it then took out some hard cheese, a sausage, and a bit of dry brown bread to start the day. Breakfast time— such as it was.

Cid was used to road rations, but that didn't mean he liked them. Now that he had a real place to live, he didn't have to eat like this anymore. He could get some real food and cook it over a fire. He'd have to go back into Haven soon and see what the market was selling.

But for now, he bit into the sausage, grimacing as he tried to chew the hard meat. *Why were these things always as hard to eat as possible?* It was like the Guard were actively trying to make the men's lives as difficult as they could.

He shoved the last of his cheese in his mouth, put his boots on, and stood up to take a look around. The farmhouse was still full of trash and debris, except for the small space he'd cleared out to sleep in. Piles of garbage were heaped outside in the yard, clearly visible from the front window. It was a depressing sight.

"I need to get rid of all this crap," he said aloud. *But, when I've time. That can wait until I manage all the literal other thousand things I can do. I'll just have to keep my area clean.*

Great. Decision made.

That was his next step after he was done talking to Lyle and then the farm duties. He'd clear everything out of the house and yard, clean out the surrounding buildings, and... what? He'd need to dispose of it somehow.

An image popped into his mind unbidden. An old memory.

****

He and Bran had had a few pints in one of the pubs in Hardhearth, and they'd wandered outside the city walls to look at the stars and throw rocks at a minor Goblin Den. Bran knew most of the constellations— had picked them up in his travels with the Magic Knight Corps— and he was always good for a story about them.

When they'd gotten into the fields, though, the temperature dropped fast.

"No worries!" Bran said, puffing up his chest. "Watch this!"

And, slouching as he usually did when he was working magic, he'd conjured up a massive bonfire— complete overkill with the [Inferno] ability.

"Whoa," Cid said. "You sure it's not going to cause a forest fire or anything?"

"Yep! Damn sure. I'm a Magic Knight. Even if it did get bad, I'll just use a water spell to try and work it out," Bran explained matter of factly.

"It's pretty big," Cid replied skeptically.

"Cid, mate," Bran said, clapping him on the back. "I'm a mage. Trust me. This fire doesn't do anything without my saying so."

It had been an impressive sight— and sure enough, the fire had stayed exactly where Bran put it. It had gone out with a snap of his fingers.

****

And now Cid himself had a **[Fire 1]** spell. That settled it. He'd burn all the trash. Maybe he could use the fire to soften the rest of his road rations until they were almost edible, too.

A knock on the door broke him from his thoughts. It was Lyle. "Sorry, mister, I can see you're still busy. I'll just tell you what my grandpa said. Tomorrow, Haven will be having its Festival of the Thankful Feast. It starts at five in the afternoon if you'd like to join us."

And with that, the lad took off, and Cid knew by the way the lad hung his shoulders that he was disappointed. *I'll have to make it up to him later, I just don't have time right now. I'll have to teach him some of the skills I learned in the guard. That might make up for it.*

CHAPTER 15:
PRACTICAL MAGIC

Cid propped the door open shortly after that. He needed to make quick progress and didn't plan on missing the Festival the next day. Preparations needed to be made, and one of those was a hot bath and a fresh set of clothes. He shook his head and chided himself for having a few too many things pulling at his attention. *One thing at a time.*

With the door propped open, Cid went to work with the farmhouse first. Little by little, he started clearing out everything that was broken, useless, or of questionable cleanliness, carted it outside, and dumped it into a pile in the yard. It was far enough from any of the buildings that they'd be safe from embers— just in case he lost control of the [Fire 1] spell once he got started with the controlled blaze.

A ripped couch, a broken headboard, a stained mattress. Old books and yellowed papers. An icebox that wouldn't stay closed and whose insulating sawdust had long gone to rot. Cupboards that had been torn off the wall from age. Moth-eaten curtain and loose bits of wood.

It all had to go. Eventually. The icebox would stay until he had something better. He did a few quick repairs to make it somewhat usable.

As for the rest, it was a slow and tedious process. The upstairs took the most time, even though there was only one room. Taking an old bed frame apart and moving it down questionably stable stairs was a process in and of itself.

Eventually, the only thing that remained untouched was the locked door leading to the basement, and Cid wasn't ready yet to go explore whatever awaited him below. So long as it remained locked from his side, it didn't need to be cleared just yet. *That'll take some time when I get around to it, and I just don't have that kind of time right now.*

It took a good part of the morning, but he finally got the house emptied out just before lunch. The house was still dirty, it just wasn't the same kind of dirty. It was manageable. He looked around and saw there was still a lot of loose dirt and leaves and had an idea.

"Here's to hoping," he muttered as he activated the [Wind 1] ability. Air began to pass through his hands in response. *Perfect.* It was a kind of practical magic and might not have been the intended use of the spell, but Cid had zero issues with using the [Wind 1] spell to blow away the dust and debris within his house. *Now, at least I've something to work with. A shell to build up. I can handle that.*

He blew a large pile of dust straight off the porch and then deactivated the magic ability. His body felt a little drained from the effort, but overall, Cid was left feeling quite pleased with his efforts and took a moment to appreciate the progress he'd made so far.

The pile of trash had already grown large enough for a decent fire, but Cid wasn't ready yet to start it. Next, he cleared out the chicken coop, but as he dragged away rusted mesh and rotted boards, Cid realized he might end up losing the chicken coop regardless of what he did.

Regardless, it still needs to get policed up. After, he handled the tool shed and the barn. When he was finished with the two of those, he gathered up all the yard trash he could find into another separate pile. *I'll burn that next once the farmhouse trash is all used up.*

Once it was all ready, Cid filled up a bucket with water from the well and prepared himself. He stood in front of the pile, and he hunched his shoulders, relaxed his arms, and thought of fires. Rising. Falling. Steady embers. Bonfires, forest fires, and flames licking across the grassland, candles, the merry crackle of a kitchen stove. All of these flickered across his mind as he tried to cast the spell with a much more targeted intensity than he'd experienced before.

Flames spewed forth from his hand as he used his magic to cast [Fire 1]. Smoke started to emerge from the pile, and it ignited with a whoosh. Cid poured more power into it and fought back a laugh as the flames rose higher. He wouldn't exactly call himself a mage— not yet, not like Bran—but he was making progress.

First, he'd used **[Water 1]** to clear the roots of the tree, then he'd used [Wind 1] to blow out his house, and now he was using **[Fire 1]** to burn his trash. All he had to do was use **[Earth 1]**, and then he'd have mastered basic elemental magic.

"Nice work for a grunt from the Guard," he said, stepping back and dropping his hands. The fire was large enough now that it could keep burning on its own without needing any extra magical input from him. He could always cast **[Fire 1]** again if he needed to.

Farming Class update!
PARTIAL CONDITION MET
Effectively removing the trash and debris from the facilities using abilities you've access to is a practical type of magic that those who wish to farm must possess. The ability to find a way to overcome

individual obstacles with the tools on hand.

2/3 conditions unlocked to gain Farmer Class.

He spent the rest of the day watching the fire and feeding it garbage and debris with a brief stop for a swim in the newly unblocked creek-bed during the hottest part of the day. If he kept it up, he'd be able to lean into the Spellweaving ability and use it to "freeze" the flames whenever he wanted to so he could step away and come back without having to start the fire again.

"Nice touch, Bran," Cid muttered, appreciating what his friend had done for him. Cid looked to the north and wondered how Bran and the others from the Guard were doing. *Nothing good, I suppose. But I hope they're staying safe. I doubt it though.* With a grunt, Cid took a deep swig of water and then got right back into it.

CHAPTER 16:
FIRESIDE

By sunset, the trash was almost all gone. Cid had been working hard throughout the day and had kept casually feeding the fire from piles of wood debris he'd stacked up for burning. He'd been looking forward to the blaze. Cid squatted down in front of the fire and enjoyed the warmth of the flame on his skin and looked up at the stars.

It didn't take long for him to get uncomfortable, and he stood up, ignoring the popping sound in his knees as he did. *Might be a little sore tomorrow.* He looked at the fire to make sure it was ok and stepped away for a moment to grab a better seat to rest on. He'd salvaged an old wooden rocking chair he'd found around back and used it to sit in relative comfort.

The chair wasn't in perfect condition— one of its legs was wonky, the back had warped a little bit from time, and the wood itself was starting to splinter in places— but it was comfortable enough and didn't take much to get it fixed up, so he could at least use it. He picked up the chair and carried it over to the burning fire and sat it down before heading back into the house. His pack was just where he'd left it next to the bedroll in the hallway. He reached in, grabbed the food inside, and headed back to the fire.

With a contented sigh, he threw his head back and laughed, enjoying the night sky and the fresh air. His belly rumbled bringing him back to reality. *Alright, alright.* He warmed up the last hunk of sausage and cheese from his rations and mashed them together on a bit of bread that he'd toasted over the flames. It was almost good. *Almost.* He'd have to head into town for more provisions in the morning.

Once his stomach was full, he leaned back in the chair to take in the moment before wondering, *what's next?* He stretched out his neck and took a look around, feeling proud of what he'd accomplished so far. Cid felt a load had come off his shoulders now that he'd gotten all of the trash taken care of.

He hadn't realized it, but the yard and the buildings being so full of garbage and debris had pressed in on him. A claustrophobic and unpleasant feeling. Now, he could really start to enjoy the space and focus on the last of his tasks before the Quest completed. *I'm making good progress, but it just feels like I'm not because of how big the workload was when I started.* After one quick glance around, Cid felt the need to change that thought. *The workload is still pretty big.*

He looked up at the stars and tried to remember some of the constellations Bran had taught him. In the city, he'd never had much use or the ability to learn them. The couple of times star navigation had come up had been when he was out on maneuvers as part of a cross service training or missions. It wasn't something the Guard focused on.

The big thing the Guard focused on was the cycle of the moon and the harvest holidays when things could get a little rowdy and out of hand easily. He lifted a finger and traced against the night sky trying to remember. *That one, the big one right above my head, was... what? The Dragon? The Lizard?*

He and Bran had always been pretty busy the handful of times they went outside the city, and when they both were off duty or on leave and wanted to get out of town, it had been to find some backwater tavern to try the ales. They tended to get pretty deep into the drinks and talk about the politics of the kingdom.

One memory stood out though, Cid dimly remembered an ancient myth about whatever constellation that was: a vicious monster, a beautiful princess, a dramatic ocean rescue.

But he couldn't really recall any of the details.

Well, it's alright if I never became a star expert. You don't need to be a star expert to appreciate the night sky. Cid slapped the top of his legs, got up, and moved over to the pile of trash and grabbed out some more wood. He idly fed the pieces of a broken table into the fire as he looked at the sky.

Wish I had a nice pint of ale right now, he mused as he spread his hands out in front of the flames and enjoyed the feeling of relaxation that rolled over him. *This is a good mood for a drink. Maybe even something a little stronger to nurse by the fire.*

Cid wished he had something, anything— literally anything at all. Part of starting over meant exactly that, working back up from the bottom. If it wasn't for his pension and the clothes on his back, Cid would have had very little to show for his time in the Guard. His thoughts turned back to the farmhouse. *I still need to do repairs, and I need to start finding some furniture to put in it. I can start off small and work my way up.*

He slumped back down in the rocking chair, thankful that it didn't break under his weight, and realized he should have taken it a bit easier getting back in it. Cid smiled, enjoying the fire, and thought of fond memories. Drinking beers around a roaring fire had been one of his favorite things to do on his nights off from the Guard. A good pint of his favorite brew at a tavern was always the go-to after a hard shift— was always a good way to relax and leave work at work.

Oh well. It was a good life, but I can't live the dream forever. It was a good thought to have. Cid had been serious when he talked about a new life after his time in the Guard, and while some of his experiences had been hard— others bordering on terrible— he'd had good times too.

He'd made good memories and met lifelong friends.

Brothers, people like Bran.

He laughed. *Brothers aren't everything, though.* His thoughts turned to Maggie, the surly barkeep from Haven. She brewed her own ale, didn't she? Maybe she'd be able to give him some kegs to go if he made a visit to her tavern. *Not give, sell. If not, maybe something smaller like some stout spirits or that apple deliciousness she sells at the tavern.*

Cid just wanted something he could take back with him to the farm when he went back into town. He could even get a little variety pack if she'd give it to him and sample what kinds of beer she had to offer.

It was a nice thought, and he imagined himself coming back to the fire in a few nights with a cold bit of ale in his hands. *That's something to look forward to.* It didn't hurt that Maggie wasn't bad looking, either. It didn't hurt at all. He got up and put more wood on the fire. It wasn't a bad way to spend the rest of his night.

CHAPTER 17:
PRE-GAME

Personal Log Entry III	
Start of Day Four. You've continued to make Oak Tree Farm your own. No monsters have been seen. You've secured a water source and have begun to build relationships with the people of Haven. You currently have an engagement to attend the Festival of the Thankful Feast.	
Active Quests	
Friend of Haven I	Return to Miss Maggie for your reward.
Home Sweet Home I	Restore basic functioning to Oak Tree Farm. Time Remaining: 3 days 11 hours 19 minutes
Mana Harvest I	Reach the Leyline within the mana cave. Time Remaining: 37 Days

No One Left Behind	Acquire Nightshade from the City Guard of Hardhearth.
I Speak For the Trees	???
Completed Quests	
What Plants Crave	Secure a water source for your farm and finish unlocking the farmer class.
Farming Class	PARTIAL CONDITION MET

Later the next day after burning most of the trash and rubbish on the property, Cid worked as tirelessly as he could. Around noon, he stood up straight, stretching his back, and wiped the sweat from his brow. He'd been working all that day and most of the day before in the vegetable garden behind the farmhouse, trying to get the land ready for planting.

The soil had completely dried out while the farm had been abandoned, and he'd spent hours pouring buckets of well water onto the ground and turning the dirt over with his shovel once the water had soaked into it and softened it up a bit. It had been a lot of hard work, but he was finally almost done. There was still a lot to do in the larger fields that surrounded the compound, but at least he could start with the garden first. Grow some initial crops, sell them in the market, and get a little experience at being a farmer before tackling the harder stuff.

Because I really have no idea how to farm, and until I get a better hang of things, I don't want to overcommit.

The land was almost ready, and he'd done enough repairs on the house safety that he could get upstairs. Once the hole was patched, Cid planned on putting his sleeping roll into the bedroom on the second floor. It wasn't much, just an empty room really, but it was home. For now, it was good enough. He had a well full of water, the sun was shining, and the farm was clear of trash. He was good to go, but he had no idea what to do next.

If I'm going to throw seeds in there, I'll need to head into town and find some. I'll need to grab the right ones.

He needed advice, that much was clear. So once he'd finally gotten the soil turned over in the garden, he headed down to the wading pool he'd created in the recently unblocked creek and dived in, making sure to scrub himself with a piece of pumice he kept in his gear. When he was done, he put on his last clean shirt and headed into town for supplies and a talk with Daryl Nightgreen. The Village Elder had offered his help any time it was needed, after all. It was time to take him up on his offer. *Besides, this gives me an excuse to go to the festival. They asked. It's only polite.*

At least I'd figured out how to wash my clothes in the stream. His pants still had a little bit of dirt on them from working in the garden all morning, but overall, he looked presentable— maybe even presentable enough to get a drink in Maggie's tavern before heading home.

Maybe.

Well. He'd cross that bridge when he came to it. It was a beautiful day, and he whistled an old soldiers' tune as he walked the short distance into Haven. A song about a tavern halfway between this world and the next— a cantina visited by honorable shades.

As he got closer, he heard the sound of loud drums and wild flute music. As he turned the final corner toward the town, he saw a large crowd of people wearing brightly colored clothing dancing in circles on the village green.

Cid stopped dead, uncertain of whether he should get any closer, but a familiar figure perched on the closest bridge caught his eye. It was Lyle. The lad was hanging back rather than joining the festivities, but he was smiling and seemed to be enjoying himself. When he saw Cid, his face lit up.

"You came!" Lyle said. "I knew you'd show up!"

"Right. Today's the Festival of Thankful Feast. Of course I'd show up," Cid responded with a smile. It has been years since he'd enjoyed a thankful feast. Usually, he just served others food as part of the extra duties of a city Guard. "I wouldn't miss this for the world. Just had to get a little work done on the farm first."

"How's it going over there? Anything I can help with?" Lyle asked.

Cid laughed. "Soon. Still getting things ready. But I've been thinking about it, and I'll have something for you to do very soon."

The lad grinned from ear to ear, and Cid felt a little guilty for fibbing to him. With everything that had been on his mind in the past few days, he hadn't been thinking of Lyle at all. He'd have to find something he could help with.

"Speaking of the farm," he said. "Is your grandpa around? I'm looking to get his advice on something."

CHAPTER 18: FESTIVAL OF THE THANKFUL FEAST

Lyle pointed toward the village green, and Cid looked in that direction. Sure enough, there was Daryl, wearing a ridiculous green outfit with a pointed hat that was equally festive. The old man was hopping on one foot in the strange leaping dance that all the villagers were doing.

"Oh," he said. "He seems busy. Maybe I should wait for him to be done."

"He'll be dancing all day if you don't stop him," Lyle said. "I'd just go talk to him now if I were you. Otherwise, you'll just be waiting till he gets tired or it's food time."

Cid took the boy's advice and picked his way through the crowd, trying not to be drawn into the dance. He was just there to talk to the Elder, after all, not to celebrate. Cid was trying to be responsible. Once he was done with this conversation, he promised himself he'd go back to Oak Tree Farm and get back to work once he had things figured out.

"Cid Dawnshield!" Daryl bellowed as he approached, his words noticeably slurred. "Happy Thanks to you!"

"Uh, Happy Thankful Feast Day? Do you have a moment? I need some advice," Cid said as he scanned the area around him, doing his best to avoid the other dancers.

"Anything for our newest Havenite!" the old man said as he pulled away from the dance and sat down at a nearby table, motioning to Cid. "Come over here and have a seat." As soon as the old man got settled, Cid noticed how hard he was breathing.

"Heh. Don't do that, it's fine. I'm fine, really. I'm not as young as I once was. I used to be able to do the Thankful Dance all day without breaking a sweat. Now look at me, Dawnshield!" The Elder motioned up and down in good humor, making himself the brunt of a joke. "Time makes fools of us all."

"Uh," Cid said. Daryl's words were grim, but he was smiling broadly as he watched the villagers twirl around the green.

"Well, anyways," the Elder said. "What brings you down here? I'm assuming you're not just here to celebrate."

"No," he admitted. "I need your help. I have no idea how to be a farmer. I've had a busy last few days, and now I'm kind of having a tough time with what comes next."

Daryl laughed. "I thought that might be the case. Well, let's start at the beginning, lad. How far have you gotten?"

Cid told him what he'd done so far at Oak Tree Farm, although he left out the part about the Mana Cavern and tree he'd discovered. He wasn't keeping it a secret, not exactly. But he wanted to learn more about what the cave was before talking about it with anyone else.

Daryl Nightgreen nodded sagely as he listened to what Cid was telling him, and he broke into a crooked smile when he heard Cid randomly start talking about a vegetable garden.

"I think you're selling yourself short, Dawnshield," he said when Cid was done. "I think you'll be a very good farmer, indeed. You've got all the right instincts, and I've got the knowledge. Between the two of us, I think we can get Oak Tree Farm back to life. I also have a book. The lad will run it over tomorrow."

"Okay. So, what do I do next? I'm guessing I need seeds, right?"

The old man's eyes twinkled. "Good, good. Aye. To grow plants, you need seeds, lad. You've got that one right."

"Right. But what should I grow?" The question had stumped Cid, and he wasn't wanting to commit to buying seeds he couldn't grow.

"Hm," Daryl said, stroking his thick beard. "Well, to give you a real answer, I'd need to see your garden— where it's situated, how much light it gets, how much water." He started counting on his fingers as he continued. "How good or bad the soil is, the PH levels, and half a dozen other factors you wouldn't understand. But I can give you a guess right now. Zucchini and pumpkins are easy to grow. I'd start with those. Maybe get some tomato seeds while you're at it. They'll all come in at different times, so you'll always have a fresh crop while you're sorting the rest of the farm out. Zucchini will be first, then tomatoes, and pumpkins last of all. If you're really terrible at farming, turnips are the way to go."

"Alright," Cid said. He liked the thought of a garden full of zucchini and tomatoes. He could do something with that.

"I'll take you to the seed store in a bit," Daryl said. "Get you set up with an account. I'm guessing you'll need supplies too?"

"Some real food would be great. I've been eating road rations for the last few days. It was all I had, and I didn't want to take the time to come into town."

The old man made a face. "I remember from my time

in the Magic Knight Corps. Vile stuff. Well, we can get you something better than that, I'm sure of it."

Cid smiled even as he felt bad about not correcting the man. *It's not my fault he assumed I'm a Magic Knight and not a Guard.* Cid changed the subject. "I can cook a real meal over the fire tonight."

"You'll do nothing of the sort, lad!" Daryl said. "Tonight, you'll stay and feast with us. It's the Festival of Thankful Feast! A day of celebration! Feast is in the name. What are you thinking, trying to work tonight?"

"Oh," Cid said. "I mean, I really do need to get back to work. If the farm's going to be viable by the end of the summer, I can't take any time off—"

"Do I need to repeat myself?" Daryl was already shaking his head. "Not today, lad. Today, you're going to see the best hospitality Haven has to offer. You're a villager now, and we want to welcome you to your new home. This is our biggest party of the year. There'll be a bonfire after the meal— and music. Maggie'll be handing out free ale, a new kind that she brewed just for the Festival."

"Hm," Cid muttered and crossed his arms. The bonfire was tempting— as was the feast after a week of eating terrible food.

"There'll be warm pumpkin," Daryl edged him on. "Warm pumpkin mixed with butter and cinnamon. Apfelkorn and sweetmeats, too."

His stomach growled. He hadn't had warm pumpkin in years, and he'd never had it with butter and cinnamon.

"Alright, you win," he said finally. "I'll stay for a bit just to see what it's like."

"Aye, lad," Daryl said firmly, standing up to rejoin the party. "And we'll have you doing at least one dance before the night is out, you can count on that."

Reputation Quest: Friend of Haven I has been completed! Granted Friend of Haven II!	
Description:	Speak with Maggie to receive your reward for completing Friend of Haven I. Prove yourself a friend of Haven. Enjoy the festival, break bread with the villagers, and embrace the custom of thankfulness.
Reward:	Three Headache Medicine. Increased Reputation with Townsfolk. Reach "Friend" status with Daryl and Lyle.
Consequence For Failure:	Loss of reputation with the townsfolk of Haven.
Quest Line Finishing Condition Required:	???

CHAPTER 19: A FEAST FOR FRIENDS

Cid didn't end up dancing around the town square or anywhere— much to Lyle's disappointment— but he *did* end up at the Nightgreen house to eat their annual Thankful Feast and break bread with them. When he showed up at the door, the first thing that Daryl did was make sure he settled in.

"Sit down, sit down," Daryl said, pulling out a chair at the foot of the table. "You'll love the food that we've made. It's not as good as when my missus was still around, but you'll still like it. Especially if my guess about you losing a little weight the last couple of days is true. Those rations don't exactly fill you up, I'm sure of it."

Cid nodded. "I hope so, but you think it's fine for just the three of us? I don't want to be a bother."

The Village Elder waved away the concerns with a hand and ushered Cid and Lyle to the formal dining area at the back of the house. The walls were covered with old drawings and sketches, and a long wooden table took up most of the space in the room. Cid sat at one end, Daryl sat at the other, and Lyle was somewhere in between. They were so far away from each other at the massive table that it felt like they had to shout in order to be heard.

"This is where we take the Feast," Daryl said. "It's a little fancy, I know. The room felt a little cozier when Lucinda was still here with us. But you know how it is. We do what we can, and traditions are important." The words hung in the air as he vanished back into the kitchen.

Lucinda? Cid wondered, an expression of confusion coming across his face. The name rang a bell, but his life had been so hectic lately that he couldn't remember where he'd heard it before.

"My grandma," Lyle mouthed trying to keep Cid from making a mistake. "She died five winters ago. Her heart just gave up. Sometimes, grandpa forgets that she passed."

"Oh. I'm sorry for your loss." Cid looked away embarrassed. *Yeah, Stupid, stupid, stupid. I should have known that. He just mentioned her too.*

Cid looked down at his empty plate, feeling a little guilty for bringing it up.

"It's okay," the lad said. "Grandpa is mostly over it, I think. It was a long time ago. I was a little kid then."

"Right." He'd forgotten how long five years could seem when you were as young as Lyle was. To Cid, it felt like the time had passed in the blink of an eye.

"Here we go!" Daryl said, returning from the kitchen with a large lidded ceramic bowl in his hands. "Mashed pumpkin. And there's more, you'll see. I know I made some promises, just uh.... don't be upset if I over promised a little bit. Just thought it was important for you to join us."

He vanished again, and Cid took the lid off the bowl. His mouth started watering when he smelled what was inside: warm pumpkin mixed with butter and cinnamon, just as Daryl had described earlier. Cid went to take a bite.

"Don't eat it yet! Don't you dare," Lyle cautioned with a look that let Cid know the lad knew the consequences first hand. "He's bringing out more."

Sure enough, he was. Daryl Nightgreen carried dish after dish out of the kitchen: roast chicken dripping with juice, slices of pork with herb seasoning, mashed potatoes with slices of butter melting on top of them, meat pies with perfectly browned crusts, and more. By the time he finally sat down, the table was practically groaning under the weight of all the food.

"Impressed?" he asked with a wide smile and eyes twinkling. "Welcome to our biggest feast day of the year."

"We're not going to be able to eat all this food," Cid said, eyeing a large chicken leg. After his week of eating road rations, he was starving.

"Correct," Daryl agreed. "That's why you'll be taking a lot of it home. A lad and his grandfather don't need all of it."

"I want the ham, though," Lyle interjected. "I don't mind a slab of it in the morning."

Daryl laughed. "We can give Cid a little. There'll be plenty left."

The lad sighed. "Fine."

"Thank you," Cid said, genuinely moved by the Village Elder's generosity. "For everything. You've been a big help."

Daryl waved his thanks away. "It's nothing, lad. You live here in Haven now. You're one of us. It's only right that you feel at home."

Cid wasn't sure how to respond to that, so he took a bite of meat. Then, he turned to Lyle.

"Is this everyone that's joining us? Just feels like you made a lot, even for leftovers," Cid asked.

He could tell by the boy's sinking face that he'd said something wrong. Lyle looked down at his plate glumly.

"It's just us. I wish my parents could be here, but I won't be seeing them now— or ever," he said finally. "They were lost in a storm when I was a little kid. Went out to look for some of our cows that had wandered off and never came back. That's why I live with my grandpa now."

"Ah," Cid said. *Put my foot in my mouth again. Twice in five minutes. That has to be a record.*

He cast about for a more cheerful topic to lighten up the mood— something that no one could possibly object to, that wouldn't stir up any bad memories.

"Want to hear a story?" he asked.

Daryl raised his eyebrows but said nothing. Lyle looked up from his plate.

"What kind of story?" the lad asked warily.

"A story from my time in the Guard back when I was just a rookie. Only a few years older than you are now. Young. Reckless. Full of adventure. Let me tell you, I made some dumb mistakes, but I also got my way out of some pretty weird situations using my wits alone."

"Okay," Lyle said slowly. "Sure. I'll hear a story."

"Excellent," Cid said, sitting back in his chair. This was a tale he'd told many times before, and he felt himself settling into the familiar rhythm of it. A tale that had bought him many a sympathetic drink in taverns throughout the years. "So like I said, I was a rookie. It was my first year in the Guard, and I was green as grass is long. There were storms on the Southern Seas that spring. Horrible storms that raged day and night. My socks were always soaked. It was terrible, and all sorts of strange creatures fled into our lands to wait out the windy season, including Rocs."

"Rocs?" the lad asked, brows furrowed. "What's a Roc?"

"A giant bird, lad," Daryl said gently, getting into the story. "A bird as big as an elephant. Even bigger if it's a female."

"Wow." The lad looked at Cid in amazement.

"There was a big one nesting outside of Hardhearth — not violent or anything— but it was harassing farmers in the area, chasing their sheep around, just generally being a nuisance. It ate a sheep or two, but that was nothing unexpected. My Commander sent me out to see if I could chase it off. We didn't want to kill it, just drive it into a more rural area where it wouldn't bother anyone. They're endangered, you know? And so I set out— alone. I was confident I could deal with the problem myself."

"Let me guess," Daryl chuckled. "There were some unexpected developments."

"That's one way of putting it. About a day into my journey, I was walking around, blowing my Roc whistle and trying to attract it to me, and then I saw the thing flying toward me. Absolutely enormous. It was far away still, but it was clearly much bigger than we'd expected it to be. I'd never seen anything that big, and it had spotted me. It was coming my way."

"Did you run?" Lyle asked, eyes wide.

"No, though I should have. I was a fool at twenty, I can tell you that much. I stood my ground as the great bird got closer and closer. It had its talons outstretched for me and a mean look in its eyes. It meant trouble, that much was for sure. I thought I could fight it off, but as soon as it got to me, it grabbed me in its claws and carried me aloft into the mountains!" Cid sighed. "I overestimated what I could do."

Lyle was fully hooked now. He was leaning forward in his seat, and Cid's misstep in bringing up his parents had clearly been forgotten. "So what happened next? How did you defeat it?"

"Getting to that part," Cid responded gravely, "The thing took me to its nest and dropped me in. I had no idea what was going on or if it was going to eat me or what. Three hatchlings were already in there, pushing me around and trying to get me to leave. They thought I was another baby bird trying to take their food. Their mother was perched nearby, watching us."

"Did she try to eat you?" Lyle blurted out.

Cid nodded his head. "She would have— if I hadn't pretended to be one of her own hatchlings!"

The lad almost fell out of his chair. "What?!"

"Yep. I grabbed all the loose feathers in the nest and put my arms up like this—" Cid made his arms look like wings. "—and I squawked just like a baby bird." He did an impression, and Lyle roared with laughter. "And the Roc was so confused that she just let me go. I had to hop all the way down the mountain in case she saw me. Terrible way to spend a holiday. Really put the hurt on my knees too."

Lyle was still laughing when Cid went back to eating, and his grandfather put a hand on his shoulder. "Help an old man out, lad?" he asked. "Take some of these empty plates to the kitchen?"

He obeyed, and Daryl waited until he was safely around the corner before turning to Cid.

"That was a kind thing you did," he said. "It's noted and appreciated."

"I don't know what you mean," Cid responded, feeling uncomfortable with the praise. "I was just telling a story."

"A Roc? Come on, lad. I can smell a tall tale from a mile away," Daryl explained, "You distracted the lad from thinking about his parents. It was a good thing to do."

"Oh, I don't—" Cid tried to say but knew it was no use.

"I'd like to give you something," Daryl said, getting up with some difficulty. "Come with me. Thankfulness is more than just a word around here."

Cid followed him out the backdoor and into a narrow tool shed at the bottom of the garden. The old man pulled a large satchel off a high shelf and handed it to him.

"These are some tools that might be useful," he said. "A new hoe, rake, and shovel. Oh, and a spade. I bought them for myself, but I'm getting on in years. They'll see more use in your hands."

"I can't just take these," Cid protested.

"Please take them. I want to see them used," Daryl responded. "And take these, too."

He pulled some packets of seeds out of a drawer.

"Remember the zucchini, pumpkin, and tomatoes I told you about? This is my special seed blend. I developed it myself. These will grow twice as fast as what you'd buy from the feed store. It's a mix, hard to tell which ones will end up growing."

Cid took the seed packets and tucked them into his pocket.

3/3 conditions unlocked to gain Farmer Class.

Unlocked Class: Farmer!

With the acquisition of working equipment and seeds, you have finally completed the last remaining condition. Upon your next waking, you may reset your assigned class data and abilities.

The status faded, and Cid nodded appreciatively for the gift holding his hand out to shake. "Thank you, Daryl."

Having the Village Elder for a friend was proving useful in surprising ways.

CHAPTER 20: THE NEXT MORNING

Cid woke with a start and was briefly surprised to find himself on Daryl Nightgreen's couch with an old blanket and the warm sun of morning streaming through an open window. *What am I doing here?* Then it came to him. After the old man had given him the seeds, he invited to knock back a few pints of ale on the back porch.

The two of them had sat in those chairs for hours after Lyle had gone to bed, swapping tales of the old days when the Kingdom was younger and when they'd still been young enough to have heroes. Eventually, when they'd run out of harrowing adventurers, they just listened to the cicadas buzzing in the darkness and enjoyed the relative quiet. Cid was surprised at the rich life that Daryl had lived. *Guess someone doesn't get to be a Village Elder without some experiences.*

When Cid had tried to walk home, Daryl had directed him to the couch and threw a blanket on him. Before he left, the old man made sure Cid took one of his newly earned Headache pills. "Sleep it off and go home in the morning."

Morning.

The status hit him, and Cid knew he needed to make a few adjustments. He quickly applied the new class of farmer and applied his old Guard class to the subslot.

Class: Farmer assigned!

New abilities granted!		
Green Thumb	Prune	Use Farming Item

Class: Mage is unassigned. Not yet proficient enough in this class to receive bonuses.

Cid Dawnshield	
Race	Human
Class	Farmer (Rank E)
Level	1
Sub-Class	Guard (Rank B)
Level	35
Attributes	
Strength	19
Agility	10

Endurance	29
Magic	5
Abilities	
Refraction	Taunt
Subdue	Hidden Pocket
Cover	Water 1
Fire 1	Wind 1
Earth 1	Alchemy 1
Green Thumb	Prune
Use Farming Item	NA

After Cid assigned his Farmer class, he was pulled out of his status and back into the present. *Haven isn't the end of my journey. It's just the beginning of another one.* Gaining the new abilities would add to his skillset and make his job on Oak Tree Farm a bit simpler.

"Hey?! You awake yet? Time to get up!" Daryl shouted from the kitchen. "I'm making breakfast and boxing up some food for you to take back to the farm."

"You don't have to do that," Cid said. But his mouth was already watering at the thought of Thankful Feast leftovers. They'd keep him fed for the rest of the week.

Breakfast turned out to be thick, flaky biscuits topped with slabs of white gravy, pork sausage, and spices like thyme with just a small slice of butter to top it off. A real country breakfast. Cid and Lyle ate greedily.

"You don't seem to like it much," Daryl said, eyes twinkling as Cid piled another three biscuits onto his plate and pulled a ladle of gravy.

"You know, Grandpa, you really should make this stuff more often," Lyle said, mouth full. "Not just when people come over." Lyle turned to Cid and shielded his hand with his mouth and whispered, "Normally, he makes really healthy food. It's terrible."

Daryl just laughed. He'd heard everything. "You're still growing, Lyle. Healthy food is good. You can't just eat a dozen eggs and whatever else you want to get large. Moderation matters. Tell him, Dawnshield."

"Healthy food is good," Cid said obediently, a sinking feeling coming over him that he might have doomed himself to healthy eating as well if he was to visit again.

"Speaking of good," Daryl said. "I was thinking, Lyle, that it might be good for you to go to school soon."

The boy's face turned red. "No. I want to adventure!"

The old man crossed his arms. Lyle did the same. Cid looked from one to the other then ate the last of his breakfast in big bites and stood up to go. This felt like the kind of thing he shouldn't get into the middle of.

"Well," he struggled to say with his mouth full. "Time for me to be off. Big day on the farm. Thanks for the seeds, Daryl."

"Aye. It's no problem. Just glad to see they're being put to good use. I was worried they'd go bad sitting in that shed for so long."

Patting his back pocket to make sure the seeds were still there, Cid hoisted his bag of new tools over his shoulder and set out for Oak Tree Farm. Haven was quiet after the previous night's festivities, and he didn't pass anyone in the streets on his way out of town.

Except—

A clanking noise coming from behind the tavern caught his attention. Maggie was cleaning up: picking up empty bottles from the village green one by one and dropping them into a bag. He almost went over to talk to her, but something in her face warned him off.

She looks like she wants to be left alone. Better to leave her to it. Something told him he didn't want to end up on Maggie's bad side.

He whistled a tune Daryl had taught him the night before as he made his way home. The lyrics were a little fuzzy in his memory, but he thought the song was about a wolf-man and a beautiful princess who fell in love but could never marry. A sad song with a merry tune— Cid's favorite. He liked the contrast. It reminded him of some of the plays he'd seen on the streets of the city when he'd pulled roving Guard duty.

By the time he rounded the corner and started up the path to Oak Tree Farm, he was in high spirits. His new seeds were practically burning a hole in his pocket, and he couldn't wait to plant them. He had everything he needed now. He was finally a farmer. A real farmer.

CHAPTER 21: A REAL FARMER

A real farmer. Cid laughed to himself at the thought. *I guess so. Or at least I will be once I actually start growing these seeds.* For now, Cid finally had all the pieces together to start, and that was more than he'd had yesterday.

As he rounded the bend and came up on Oak Tree Farm, Cid took a good look and felt a moment of pride. It was the first time he'd left his land and come back since arriving in Haven, and he felt good seeing the progress he had made, even if it wasn't as much as he'd wished for. Sure. It still needed some work— okay, a lot of work— but he was making progress. And the farm was his— all his.

Cid smiled again, thinking of how his pension was basically just paying the monthly on the farm, but it wasn't a bad arrangement. He was pleased. He'd discovered something he'd only hoped was true when he retired. *There's life after the Guard after all.*

When the thought of retiring had first started to settle in, Cid hadn't been fully sure that he'd be able to move on, find something new, be somebody different. He'd seen and heard more than his fair share of the old grey beards who sat around the taverns all day, drinking ale and smoking pipes, after leaving the Guard. None of them were ever fully able to move on or start a new life. But that wasn't him. And now, he knew that it never would be.

Shielding his eyes against the sun, he looked over his fields and winced when he saw the burn spot from all the trash he'd burned the other night. *I'll have to clean that up sometime, maybe spread the ashes around.* He looked back toward the fields, trying to decide which one to plant first. He didn't have enough seeds for all of them. Not yet. But he could do one, at least.

Eventually, he set his sights closer to him and settled on the field closest to the farmhouse— and to his now-full well. Since he'd never done this before, it made sense to start with something easy, and he didn't want to waste a lot of time carrying water back and forth. *Better to focus on getting the seeds in the ground and ready to go.*

He didn't even stop by the farmhouse to drop his things off before striding boldly into the field he'd chosen, though he did put the food in the shade. *I don't actually have a way to keep this right now.* Cid shrugged and walked over to the field. This was what he'd been waiting for all week: the moment where he finally planted something and became a farmer for real. He didn't want to waste another second.

Heart pounding, Cid put the pack with the rest of the gear down and pulled out his new shovel and the seed packets Daryl had given him.

He read the label. *Looks like Zucchini* first.

Cid always had a fondness for zucchini. His stomach rumbled thinking of some of the sweet breads he used to buy in the city that used zucchini. *Ah... chocolate.* He pushed the thought away and put the pack of seeds on the ground before he got started on the field. The old man had given him some instructions, and Cid planned to take it to heart. After all, the elder knew what he was talking about.

And I haven't lived this long by ignoring good advice.

The shovel cut into the crust of dried dirt but didn't go

much further. As soon as Cid had started to dig, he hit a rock immediately. One rock, and then another, equally large rock. He tried to move spots and dig again, but the same thing happened. The ground was too rocky and patted down to plant in.

Right. This whole farm's been out of commission for a while. Ground down top soil might be a problem.

Cid didn't know much about farming except a few bits about red clay and bad soil, something he'd be the first to admit. But Cid thought he knew what the problem was. The soil wasn't ready. Rocks had risen to the surface over years of hard winters and hardened further from disuse. No one had been there to work the land and keep the dirt healthy. He'd have to till the soil if he wanted his seeds to do well here.

Okay. Just a minor setback.

Maybe he could still plant tomorrow or the next day if he started tilling now. But without a plow or plow horse, it was going to be rough going. Daryl had given him a hoe as part of his new toolset, but working the land by hand would take hours, especially under the hot sun. Hours that he didn't have.

He sighed deeply. *I'll just have to do it then. There's no other way of getting around it.* Reluctantly, he put the seeds back in his pocket.

Soon.

But for now, the zucchinis would have to wait.

By sunset, he was breathing hard and covered in dust, his shirt a sweaty dripping mess, and for all that effort and huffing and puffing, the field was less than a quarter done. What he'd seen for all of his effort was encouraging. When he turned over the rocky soil, he uncovered rich black earth.

Good to grow in.

His crops would do well here— that was if he ever got

the field tilled. He needed to move faster. The growing season wouldn't last forever, and if he couldn't get at least one crop out of Oak Tree before fall, the farm might not succeed. He'd have to rely on the kindness of Daryl and the villagers to make it through the winter.

It wasn't the end of the world, but it would be humiliating.

No, I have to find a way to make this work.

An image popped into his mind unbidden. Bran in a winter cloak, standing in a narrow mountain pass full of rocks. They'd been on a job together— the Guard and the Magic Knight Corps working in tandem to catch a crew of bandits — and their foes had tried to block their way so they couldn't pursue them to their hidden base.

Bran had cast an earth spell easily— as if it were nothing — and the rocks had rolled out of their path on their own.

And Cid had that [Earth 1] spell now. Maybe he couldn't clear a mountain pass full of boulders, but surely he could use it till some soil faster than he could by hand. *I'm spent anyways, why not give it a try?*

He placed his hoe on the ground next to him and planted his feet in his spellcasting stance. The magic came easier than it had the previous two times he'd tried this.

I'm getting better.

Spellweaving was still thrilling to him, and he watched with wonder as the earth started to turn itself over and arrange itself in neat rows ready for planting. Meanwhile, the rocks buried in the soil unearthed themselves, practically demanding a place to go. Cid looked towards the edge of the field, and off the rocks went, arranging themselves in a long line where Cid had looked.

Those might be useful later. Could use them to build a wall or something.

A hard week's work was finished in minutes, and Cid found himself grinning like a lunatic as he took in the freshly plowed field. He'd be done here in time for an evening swim.

I could get used to this magic thing.

Before he stopped for the day, he updated his log.

Personal Log Entry IV

End of Day Five.
You've made good friends with a few of the locals of Haven. The Village Elder respects you, and the lad looks up to you. He'll make a good apprentice. The work at the farm has only just started, but you're making good progress.
Small steps are required to get up any mountain.

Active Quests	
Home Sweet Home I	Restore basic functioning to Oak Tree Farm. Time Remaining: 1 days 23 hours 7 minutes
Mana Harvest I	Reach the Leyline within the mana cave. Time Remaining: 35 Days
No One Left Behind	Acquire Nightshade from the City Guard of Hardhearth.

I Speak For the Trees	???
Completed Quests	
What Plants Crave	Secure a water source for your farm and finish unlocking the farmer class.
Friend of Haven I	Return to Miss Maggie for your reward.
Friend of Haven II	Prove yourself a friend of Haven. Enjoy the festival, break bread with the villagers, and embrace the custom of thankfulness.
Farming Class	3/3 Conditions Met! Class has been rewarded!

CHAPTER 22:
TILL THE SOIL

 Cid looked over the clean rows of dark and fertile earth and let **[Earth 1]** go. Bran had done him a great favor when he'd given him that group of basic spells. They were making his life significantly easier.

Granted Class Quest: The Path of a Magus!	
Description:	Having used all four elemental basic spells, you have started on the Path of the Magus. Further explore your Spellweaving ability to develop mastery over the basic elements of magic.
Reward:	???
Consequence For Failure:	???
This Quest will allow you to gain enough proficiency to receive bonuses.	

 I'll have to look into that. Cid paused as the blue screen vanished and saw how much work was left on his farm. *When*

I've time. But as interesting as that Path might be, I decided to become a farmer for a reason.

He wiped the sweat from his brow—and frowned. His hands were still covered in soil from tilling the field earlier, and he'd just smeared dirt all over his face.

It's time for a break anyways.

The creek water was calling his name, and there was just enough of the hot part of the day to really enjoy it. There was still plenty of time to do things that needed to get done and go for a swim. *I can still get some planting done before dark too.*

A good way to spend the day.

Before he went down the little path toward the stream, he dropped the leftover food Daryl had given him in the ruined icebox. It wasn't going to keep anything cold, but at the least it would provide a seal to keep the bugs off. *I'll need to figure that out too.* Cid sighed. *Another addition to the honey do list, minus the honey.*

He tried to look on the brightside. Hopefully the temperature down there was low enough to keep the food fresh for a day or two, at least. Cid had a big appetite after so many days of road rations, so he didn't think it would need to last much longer than that before the rest of it was eaten.

With that settled, he headed toward the water, stripped off his clothes, and jumped in. The water was cool and refreshing, and he felt his entire body relax as he floated on the surface. Between the manual tilling and the spell work, getting the first field ready had taken a lot out of him.

Farming is hard work. Cid had found a new respect for it. His hands ached like they did when he'd practice techniques with his short sword. *Much harder than it looks.*

Cid laughed as he swam about. *Ok, it may be hard work, but this is nowhere near as hard as a life in the Guard had been.*

As he looked up at the fluffy clouds above his head and enjoyed the sun on his face, Cid found it hard to believe how he'd spent so long in the cramped and narrow streets of Hardhearth. He'd had good times in the city, fun times, but it wasn't where he was meant to be. He knew that now. He just wished he'd realized it earlier.

There weren't any streams like this in Hardhearth— only the city moat— and only a fool would want to swim in those putrid waters.

Coming to Haven was the best decision I've ever made.

Something brushed his leg, and he leaped to his feet in a panic, splashing wildly. Who knew what might lurk in waters fed by a Mana Spring? Visions of sea monsters and giant poisonous jellyfish rolled through his head.

Whatever it was swam by him again, and he looked down to see a flash of silver scales under the surface of the water.

A fish. It's just a fish.

And not just any fish, either. It was a large, plump rainbow trout, just the right size for a hearty meal. There were more, too— an entire school of them swimming upstream, practically close enough for him to reach out and touch their fins. His stomach growled. It had been a long time since breakfast.

Maybe this is dinner.

Moving slowly so as not to startle the trout away, he waded to the shore and put his pants back on. They were still dirty from his work in the field, and he sighed. Now, he was covered in dust again. It really was time to get more clothes.

He stood on the riverbank for a moment, observing the current. Trout liked quiet places and cool shallow waters. Maybe he could dig a little fishing pool that might attract them. He'd need to work quickly, though, before they moved on to wherever it was they were going. He regretted leaving his spade back in the field, but there was no time to go back and get it. He'd have to start the hole with his hands and enlarge it later when he had time.

He chose a sunny part of the bank sheltered from the fastest part of the current and started digging. In almost no time at all, the small hole he'd made started filling with water. He worked until his pool was deep and wide enough for several trout to fit inside then stood back to watch and see what happened.

At first, they didn't seem interested, but gradually, the school started swimming closer and closer. Soon enough, four fat fish were splashing around inside.

I can make it bigger and use some of the rocks from the field to line the bottom.

That would keep the water from draining out of it. And making it bigger would let more trout fit inside the fishing pool comfortably. More fish meant a better chance of catching something.

Speaking of...

If he wanted a fish for dinner, he needed a pole and a line. He rummaged around in his pocket and pulled out a tangled wad of string. That settled the issue of the line.

As for the pole...

Cid moved back toward the stand of green trees that stood between him and the rest of the farm and pulled a thin branch off the closest one. It was still green and springy enough to make a good fishing rod. He pared the bark off the branch with his pocketknife and tied the string onto the end.

And a fish hook.

There was a hawthorn tree nearby, and he snapped a

sharp thorn off of one of its branches. It wasn't an ideal hook, but it would do for now. He could get a better one— either a real fish hook or a piece of bent wire— next time he went into town.

Cid deftly knotted the hook onto his line and took an experimental cast.

Good enough.

He wouldn't take his makeshift pole on a fishing trip, but it would do the job here. He poked around in the dirt under the trees until he found a few fat worms he could use for bait.

"Sorry guys," he said, skewering two of the worms onto the hook. "It's for a good cause."

That cause being dinner.

Well, the worms wouldn't know he was lying to them.

To his relief, the trout were still in the fishing hole when he got back to the riverbank. He dropped the line into the water then lay back on the grass while he waited for one of them to bite. They were wary of the hook at first, but that didn't trouble him much.

The sun was warm, and the evening was young. He could afford to wait— and imagine how good grilled trout would taste with a little bit of salt on it. He didn't yet have much in the house to season it with, but maybe he could lay it on a bed of the leftover pumpkin he'd gotten from Daryl. With a pile of roast vegetables on the side, maybe...

The rod started to bend, and he leaped to his feet, mouth watering. He'd hooked one! A large trout was flapping in the water on the end of the line, and the other fish scattered back into the creek. Grinning from ear to ear, he slowly reeled it in and pulled it out onto the bank where it flapped in the dirt.

He took his knife out of his pocket and put the fish down mercifully then held it up in front of his face. Its scales glinted in the sunlight, and Cid grinned. Hopefully, the trout were regular visitors to his part of the creek. If they were, he'd just found a way to feed himself until his crops grew without having to go back into town. Fish for dinner every day might not be the most exciting thing in the world, but it was simple and nutritious.

Still, though—

I need more spices if I'm going to be eating this much trout.

More spices, new clothes, fish hooks— it was time to make a list of purchases for the next time he went into Haven. Daryl had been generous enough to give him the seeds and tools for free, but in the future, he'd need to plan on buying whatever he needed at the local general store. Hopefully, his slim pouch of retirement money from the Guard held out long enough to cover his expenses.

Well, he'd worry about all of that later. For now, it was time to finish up a few tasks and spend the evening celebrating a productive day on Oak Tree Farm. And he needed to figure out a way to cook this fish without lighting it on fire.

One thing at a time. That's the key to getting it all done.

With that, he picked up his shirt from the rock where he'd stashed it, turned his back on the creek, and headed back toward the farmhouse. The fish and pole were under his arm, and he whistled a tune as he walked. This one didn't have words yet— it was a melody he'd made up just now, on the spot.

Maybe I can give it some lyrics. Call it 'The Old Man and the Trout'.

He liked the sound of that.

CHAPTER 23: ONE STEP AT A TIME

Cid's stomach was growling as he carried the fish back home, but he had one more thing to do before he could start making dinner. He wanted to get the seeds in the ground so they could start germinating.

There wasn't much he could do about the trout, so he dropped it on the grass next to the field, trying to keep it out of the sun, and pulled his seed packets out of his pocket. He separated out the zucchini seeds from the rest and took them with him into the field, dropping the tomato and pumpkin seeds next to the fish.

I'll have to store the others in a safe place and keep them cool and away from the light until it's time to plant them.

He wasn't quite sure if there was a best way for him to put the seeds into the soil, so he improvised a bit, digging a series of small holes with his fingers and dropping them in two at a time. He'd have to ask Daryl for advice the next time he saw him— both about planting techniques and about the best time to plant the other seeds. He knew he'd probably need to rotate them to get the best use out of the field.

The old man had given him a big bag of zucchini seeds, but the field was only half-seeded by the time Cid reached the bottom of it and dropped the last two into the ground. He stood up straight, stretched his back out, and looked over his handiwork.

There's room for me to plant more in this first batch of crops if I have some that will work.

Maybe the tomatoes would be good in the second half of the field, but that was a problem for later. He'd done just about enough work for one day.

He filled a bucket of water from the well and carried it back to the zucchini field, scattering the water over the rows with his hand so he didn't drown the fragile seeds.

I should get a watering can. It would make this a lot easier.

Another improvement to add to the ever-lengthening list. Two more loads of water later, he was done. The zucchini seeds had everything they needed to start growing: fresh water, fertile earth, and plentiful sunlight. The only thing left to do now was wait.

Wondering how long it would be before he started seeing results, Cid returned the bucket to the well and retrieved his fish and the remaining seed packets from where he'd left them at the edge of the field. The trout didn't seem much worse for wear— luckily he'd done his work quickly— and he carried it back to the house, stashed the seeds in a box he'd found and placed it in front of the door to the cellar for safekeeping. *At some point, I'll actually need to find my way down there. I can't just leave stuff by the door.* He turned away and went. He sat down on the front porch to try to figure out how he was going to make dinner.

The farmhouse didn't have a working kitchen yet. There was a wood stove that stood in one corner. It was made of good iron, but it was rusted and looked like it hadn't been lit in a long time. Everything else, minus the ice box, had been torn out and burned along with the rest of the debris. The kitchen, for all intents purposes, was still out of commission.

His shoulders sagged. *This won't work for what I need to do. Might serve someday, but not now.*

Getting the kitchen ready would have to be a high priority for the near future, but after the day he'd had, he wasn't about to solve that problem tonight. Without a functioning stove, he'd have to find some other way to cook the fish without burning it to a crisp. He knew that raw fish could be a delicacy in some parts of the world, but the idea of eating such a large trout uncooked turned his stomach a bit.

Not an option.

Luckily, he had the **[Fire 1]** spell that Bran had taught him, and he thought he might be able to control it better this time after getting more practice with his new abilities. All he needed was fuel and some way to keep the fish insulated from the flames so it cooked low and slow.

Fuel wasn't an issue. The week had been bright and sunny with nary a hint of rain. He shouldn't have a problem finding dry firewood in the nearby forest. Insulation might be tricker. He looked around the farmyard, trying to think of something he could use. It needed to cover the trout entirely, be airtight, and easy to remove when he wanted to eat...

An idea hit him. Clay.

Of course. I should have thought of it earlier. He'd heard about some of the other men in the Guard cooking in clay pots when they were out on the road. They absorbed heat well but still kept their contents from scalding. Maybe he could try a similar trick here.

Well, he didn't have any clay pots to spare, but he *did* have plenty of fresh clay on hand at the riverbank. He'd have to do an experiment to see if this worked. Sighing heavily— *does everything have to be as difficult as possible?—* he walked back to the stream and gathered a lump of clay large enough to cover his fish. He was pleased to see that several more trout had returned to his makeshift fishing hole while he was gone. That was a good sign. They liked the shallow water, and if he enlarged the hole, he could attract even more.

Once he had enough clay, he gathered a few dry branches from the bank and returned to the farmyard. He dumped them in a pile in the center of the yard, far enough from any buildings that there was no risk he'd accidentally start a larger fire than he wanted. Then, he took his dagger and gutted the fish, removing the parts he couldn't eat and slathered the trout in clay until it was thoroughly covered. Finally, he took up his Spellweaving stance and pictured a burning ember in his mind to activate the **[Fire 1]** ability.

The dry branches caught instantly, and he grinned. He was starting to get used to his magecraft, but it still carried a thrill. Hopefully that never went away.

Once the fire was well established, he gently set the fish on to cook. Then, he went to the ice box and retrieved one of Daryl's containers of pumpkin and vegetables. They'd go well with fresh trout. He put it next to the flames— not in the fire itself, but close enough to warm up— and rotated the bowl regularly until the clay covering the fish was hard and dry.

Time to see if this worked.

He extinguished the fire with a thought and cracked the clay open with his spade. Just as he'd hoped, the fish was flaky and perfectly cooked, and he spooned it into Daryl's bowl of pumpkin to let it cool. It was falling off the bone, and he had to force himself not to eat it immediately. After cooking over an open flame, it was hot enough to burn his mouth.

Incredible.

After a long day of manual labor under the hot sun, it hit the spot. He'd have to be sure to make this again— and soon. Maybe with a little more seasoning, maybe a little bit of lemon juice— or whatever he could get. He'd sort something out.

Once he was done, he sat back on the porch to enjoy what remained of the fading sunlight. The day had been a rousing success. He'd planted his first seeds, secured a food source, and enjoyed an incredible meal cooked over a roaring fire. Oak Tree Farm was well on its way to being viable.

I'll be a farmer yet.

Once the sun had vanished behind the trees for good, Cid went back inside the house to get some rest. After all, he'd have to be up with the sun tomorrow, and there'd be another busy day ahead of him. Best to sleep while he could.

With the trash cleared out of the house, he could move his bedroll out of the front hallway. He rolled it up, grabbed his cloak, and climbed the rickety stairs to the second floor bedroom. It was a large room with a wooden floor and big windows overlooking the farmyard, and he took a deep breath as he laid his bedroll out against the far wall.

Then he sneezed. The room might be clear of garbage, but it was still full of dust even after he'd blown it all away with **[Air 1]**. *Must be the hole in the roof or the door. It's too easy for dust to get in here.* He'd have to clean the house top to bottom again once he got around to those repairs.

But not now.

For now, it was time to rest. He laid back on the roll, wincing as his sore shoulders hit the wooden floor. It was better than the front hall, but it still wasn't the most comfortable sleeping situation. He'd have to get a real bed with a feather mattress when he found an opportunity. Maybe Daryl had something he could use.

Baby steps. Overall, though, he was pleased with the progress he'd made so far. He'd come a long way in a week.

And with that happy thought in mind, he drifted off to sleep.

CHAPTER 24: THE SLEEPER HAS AWAKENED

Late into the night, Cid tossed and turned on his bedroll. The moon was out and bright beams illuminated the night. All the while, Cid struggled to rest. Eventually in the wee hours of the morning, he tossed the wool blanket off of himself and sat up abruptly, sweat pouring down his face from a vague notion that he'd had another nightmare.

He looked around, grabbed his pack, and pulled out a wax candle he kept in case of emergencies and used the **[Fire 1]** ability to set the wick on fire. The room lit up from the short flame, and Cid felt his nerves begin to settle, though his heart continued to beat hard in his chest as the hairs on his arm stood on end.

Cid sighed heavily. His senses had been triggered, and when something like this happened, it was next to impossible to settle down and get back to sleep until he did something about it. It was an old habit that he'd picked up in the Guard, one that had been trained and drilled into him during long nights on watch. It was an instinct that had served him well but wasn't always accurate. More often than not, that keen and sudden awareness was a cat on the prowl or a nearby brawl that needed to be broken up.

Oak Tree Farm didn't have the same kind of issues as the city, but Cid wasn't going to just ignore that sense he had. He pulled the dagger from under his pillow, set the candle on an iron holder, and got up to do a quick patrol. *Probably nothing, but it's worth looking at.*

A quick glance told him the door was still shut. *Well... shutt-ish. I'll fix that in the morning. Or try to.* His attention turned toward the stairs, and he cast a furtive glance up them. He didn't see anything, but he knew he needed to look. Carefully and calmly, Cid walked up the stairs, the light of the candle leading the way.

He looked into one room, saw only the light of the stars through the hole in the ceiling, and thanked his luck that it hadn't rained since he'd been there. *Another task to handle.* Fresh dust marred the room, but he didn't see any signs of a disturbance. Though, he did see a few tiny prints in the dust that let him know something small had been through.

Next, he went to the other room, the master he'd cleaned up once before. Much like the first room, there was fresh dust, but no disturbances aside from a few jagged scratches on the floor from where he'd dragged furniture out when he'd cleared the debris. *So, aside from a few paw prints, nothing up here. Except...*

Cid's gaze turned to the upstairs bathroom, and he wandered over. As he approached, he heard the brief scuttering of movement and moved the candle to get a better look while holding his dagger out.

A small animal was standing there, two yellow eyes staring back at him while reflecting the flames in his hand. Cid shook it and laughed. The tiny critter hissed at him, jumped off the toilet seat, and ran out of the bathroom into the room with the hole where Cid assumed it went back to wherever its den was.

Alright, so a racoon was keeping me up.

Still, Cid wasn't ready to call it a wrap just yet. He went back down the stairs, his body just starting to settle down, and did a quick walk through the rest of the house. Just because he thought he'd cleared his home didn't mean he was ready to consider the job done. The old living room was strangely bare and off-putting. It wasn't until he got to the kitchen that he realized something.

The basement.

"Do I really need to do this?" Cid wondered aloud, groaning. *Yes, I do. And I already know there's going to be spiders. Giant, massive, horrible spiders.* He could already feel legs crawling on him and feel the webbing in his hair. He shook his head to clear his thoughts, approached the door, and looked through the glass pane on top.

It was dark and blackened as if there had been a fire. Cid felt his heart sink. *Of course it would be extra foreboding.*

He waved a hand out in front of him and gritted his teeth as he lied to himself. "I'm fine. I'm fine. This isn't hardly anything at all. I've been through worse. It's just the basement. How bad could it be? Nothing compared to the sewers, right?"

Eventually, he had to stop staring at the door and just go down. *Fine. Just gotta do it.* He undid the lock on the door and carefully, cautiously opened it up, checking to make sure nothing was on the other side. The door opened up, revealing a dark staircase that led down into dank darkness.

Cid held the candle out in front of him to get a good view, making sure that nothing was out of the ordinary. He couldn't see much in the gloom, but nothing *seemed* dangerous. With a deep breath, he took one step down the stairs— and then another. Cobwebs hung from the ceiling in wispy threads, but much to his surprise, the basement was largely absent of webbing, but something else disturbed him.

A smell. It was kind of a wet, musty, earthen smell. it set him on guard. Cid moved the candle about and, to his relief, found the basement was not anywhere near as large as he had feared. On the farthest wall, empty jars shined back at him, the fire of the candle reflecting off the glasses' surface. On an old wooden shelf, a pile of tin lids were stacked. *Canning? That's what was in the basement?*

The laugh that followed was rich with relief as anxiety fell off of him. Cid moved the candle around some more and saw a couple other shelving units, not with glass jars but with shelves full of soil. *That must have been the smell. What did they need soil in the basement for?*

Cid pondered for a moment, and then, the answer dawned on him. *Mushrooms. These are for growing mushrooms. I'll have to ask Daryl about this.* Cid smiled.

Granted Profession Quest: Mellow Mushrooms!	
Description:	Having overcome your fear, you ventured into the basement of the farmhouse at Oak Tree Farm and discovered a canning station and shelves for growing mushrooms. While both appear to be in disuse, it is possible to fix up the area, restore the canning station, and set up mushroom production.
Reward:	[Can This] [Grow Mushrooms]

Conditional Requirement:	Restore function of the basement
Consequence For Failure:	None

The blue screen faded, and Cid's mind was put at ease. The basement wasn't a place of fear. it was just another place, another tool to use as he figured out how to be a farmer. With nothing else to see, Cid went back up the stairs and settled into his bedroll. With no other disturbances, he slept peacefully.

CHAPTER 25:
ONE OF US

A fist banged loudly on the wooden door, and Cid woke up with a start. *Somebody is banging on the door. Gods. Why are they so loud?* Cid scrambled to grab his gear from his pack, and for a disorientated moment after the sleepless night he had, Cid thought he was back in his Guard Post in Hardhearth and that one of the city citizens was outside his station demanding his help and assistance.

The first time he'd heard a knock like that, he'd been a new recruit— and all new recruits had to undergo the six-month crucible, a series of swing double shifts that always included third watch. It was the Guard's way of testing the resolve and mettle of new recruits to see who had what it took to stay on the job and who would fold under the pressure of the job. During that time, Cid had often been awakened by the same sound he was hearing now: someone pounding on a door and shouting his name.

The door shuddered under the blows, and the voice called out again, "Cid! Come out, old man!"

Wait. Who's an old man? The voice outside sounded very familiar. He stood up, wincing at the kinks in his back flared up with a little bit of pain. *Is that from working around the farm, or did my back suddenly decide sleeping on a bedroll isn't good enough?*

With a quickness that defied the stiffness he felt, Cid went over to the window, opened it up, and looked outside. Lyle was standing there next to Daryl and a man he didn't recognize. The lad started pounding on the door again and hollering for Cid. Cid said nothing and watched as Lyle, red in the face, kicked the door with his shoe. Daryl gave the lad a stern rebuke, and Lyle stopped.

Time to make myself known. Cid leaned out of the window and shouted, "Hey, Lyle, what are you doing?"

The lad jumped up, startled by Cid's sudden presence, and then responded, "I'm waking you up!" Lyle stepped away from the door next to his grandpa and crossed his arms.

Cid laughed. "Wake me up by beating my door down? Don't do that. I've still got repairs to do."

Lyle looked back "Well, it worked, didn't it?"

Daryl elbowed Lyle in the ribs. "Easy, easy, lad," Daryl said placatingly before turning his attention to Cid. "For a farmer, you sure like to sleep in, Dawnshield. Bad habit you picked up in the city, I'm sure."

Cid looked up at the sky. It was light out, but the sun was still low on the horizon. "It's not that late."

"When I got out of the Magic Knights, I took to farming pretty easy in a communal. The lot of us were up before dawn," Daryl responded.

"Noted." Cid responded. All the while, he took a moment to process what the old man had said and gave him a new look of appreciation. *He was in the Mage Knights. I should have guessed that. How stupid of me to let him think I was in too. I better keep Bran's role in this to myself. I don't need anything to fall back on him just because he used the Corps Emblem to grant me magic power.* "Wait, you used to farm?"

Daryl gave Cid a big grin. "When I was, oh, not much

younger than you. Well... Maybe. I'm not sure. Time and age matter less the older you get." Daryl gave him a hard look, and Cid withered slightly under the well-intentioned judgement. "Didn't you wonder how I knew so much about planting?"

"I didn't think that much about it," Cid admitted regretfully. "I made a few assumptions that didn't pan out. I thought everyone in Haven knew that kind of thing. I just assumed you'd always been a farmer. Since... you know."

Daryl threw his head back and laughed out loud. "Well, that's one way of thinking about it, lad. But no, I come by my knowledge from experience. From dirt on my hands and sweat on my brow. A real sword to ploughshare, I was. Anyways, I'm being rude, where are my manners?" Daryl motioned to the man next to him. "You need to meet my companion."

The thin man standing next to Daryl waved. "Hi."

"I'm Cid Dawnshield," Cid said. "It's good to meet you. I don't think I caught your name."

"Oh, sorry about that. I'm Edd," the man replied. "I'm a carpenter. Daryl told me you might be in need of some help around here."

Lyle looked over at Cid, held a hand up to his mouth, and whispered, "Grandpa thought you might be in over your head."

Cid laughed. It's not like it was a lie. He felt comfortable. They meant well. *These people are good to know.*

"Anyways, I also brought some hard almond cranberry biscuits," the old man said quickly, changing the subject. "Thought you might want some fresh breakfast before we got started."

"Daryl," Cid said, crossing his arms. "Get started?" *Just who does this old man think he is?*

The elder smiled, not caring for Cid's resistance. "They're still warm! Almond cranberry biscuits with honey butter. You can't say no to that."

Cid's stomach rumbled, but his resolve remained firm. "I don't need any help. This is my farm now. I took on the project. I can see it out."

"Not a word, lad," Daryl said. "You're a Havenite now. We take care of each other, and we're happy to help. Now, come on down to the porch so you can meet Edd properly."

Cid shut the window and retreated back into his room, grumbling. He appreciated the help, but he didn't like it. He wanted to get the farm fixed up on his own.

"That's your pride talking," he said to himself as he pulled his shirt on. He knew he needed to get over it. It was more important to get the farm working on time than it was to do everything himself. But it wasn't easy. It almost felt like he was giving up in a strange, twisted sense.

Daryl, Lyle, and Edd were already sitting on the porch eating biscuits when he finished getting ready. The old man had brought them in a tin pail lined with a blue checkered napkin, and he offered it up to Cid when he saw him.

"You'll like them, I think," he said. "I'm still experimenting with the recipe, but I think this is my best batch yet. It's a variation of what my missus used to make."

"Grandpa's the best baker in town!" Lyle said around a mouthful of biscuit.

"Second best," Daryl reminded him, and Lyle looked away, not wanting to say anything.

Cid reached into the bucket and took one out. The biscuit was thick, flakey with a sheen of butter on it, and full of fresh cranberries. His mouth watered, and he took a bite. Then another and another. Finally, he stuffed the whole thing in his mouth.

"This is delicious!" he said once he'd swallowed.

Lyle grinned. "See?"

Edd walked over from the wagon they'd pulled with them and grabbed a biscuit for himself. As he ate, Daryl turned to him. "So, what do you think, Edd?" Daryl said, setting the bucket down. "Where do we start?"

Edd looked around the farm, taking in the scope of the problem. "Well, we need to get that door fixed first and plug any holes in the house. I see a lot of disrepair, but with my abilities as a carpenter, it shouldn't be a hassle."

"Agreed. I've got a lot to do still— especially that door," Cid said, taking another biscuit. "I've been meaning to get around to that."

"Not to worry, lad," Daryl said. "We'll do it for you."

"Seriously, you don't have to do that. I'm fine. I can do it —" Cid started to protest.

"Not another word about it, lad. You've proved yourself. I took a look at your field on the way in. You've tilled it well, and it's already starting to bear the fruit of your labor. I think you'll be around Haven for a while yet. You can pay us back the favor when you have time."

"Really?" Cid asked, thrilled. "Things are already growing?"

"Aye. Take a look when you've got time. We'll get your house in order. Lyle can help with the cleaning. It builds character," Daryl stated, glowering towards the lad.

"Aw, seriously? I wanted to fix the door," Lyle protested.

"Seriously," Daryl responded with seriousness. "Edd'll be fixing the door. You help me clean up. If you do a good job, you can help me fix the staircase. It looks a bit rickety."

"It is," Cid said with a nod. "I've been worried it'll cave in while I'm walking up it. I've done what I can in the meantime, but I'm not a carpenter."

Daryl gave Cid a thumbs up and replied, "Yes. Exactly. It'll be good to get that sorted."

Even though I'd hoped to do it myself. Their aid would be a great help. Having it done sooner would be better, anyway. He'd hate to break a leg on the stairs in the middle of the night. That would put a quick end to his farming career, at least for the year, and he couldn't afford that. He didn't exactly have another source of income.

"You do that," Edd said. "Clean up and work on the stairs. I'll do the door and any more advanced repairs that need to be done. If we make good time, I wonder if we can get that cow barn fixed up today too."

"Aye?" Daryl asked, peering at it from the porch. "You thinking of bringing animals in here, lad?"

"Well," Cid said. "I was hoping to. Would be nice to have some cows around, at least. Get some cheese and milk. I've a horse that's been on my mind too, and I'd like to get him back. It would be nice if I could have a place for him."

Besides, if I need to, I can also use the barn for chickens. It would be a good source of food through the winter when he couldn't grow anything.

"Alright then," Daryl said. "Cow barn it is, assuming we have time."

"I wonder if I can get some of the villagers to help out with that," Edd said. "We're fine for the house, but the barn isn't a job for just three pairs of hands."

Lyle crossed his arms. "Four!"

"Three and a half. I'll give you that much, boy," Edd responded.

Lyle scowled, and the three men laughed before Daryl

answered, "You'll be a full pair of hands when you're fifteen, but not a moment before! Now, let's get to it, lads."

Cid knew it was the right call to let things go when he saw the blue screen.

You've reached Friend status with Daryl and Lyle Nightgreen!	
Having gained enough trust and reputation with the Village Elder, you've become an unofficial Havenite. While not all townspeople will respond as kindly to an outsider, you are quickly proving yourself to be one of them.	
Reward:	Assistance from the Haven townsfolk. Daryl and Lyle will assist you as time and chance allows.

CHAPTER 26:
MORNING CHORES

Cid exited the farmhouse and worked on gathering up all the cleaning supplies he could find in the tool shed. With everyone waiting on him, he didn't bother to make an entry in his personal record. It could wait until the end of the day. It wasn't much, but thankfully Daryl and Lyle had come prepared. Edd immediately grabbed his gear and went to work on the door.

Daryl and Lyle grabbed the cleaning supplies and spent most of the morning cleaning the dirt and grime out of the farmhouse. It was hard, thankless work. At least it would have been, but Cid was extremely thankful. Scrubbing the walls, floorboards, and everything else was uncomfortable at best. He wasn't going to say no to the help, and it freed him up a bit to work more in the field now that he'd sort of stabilized Oak Tree Farm.

More than once, Daryl sent Lyle to get fresh water from the well, poured it out across the floor, and used it to mop up. Lyle threw the dirty water out when he was done and looked over at Cid, calling out, "How were you sleeping here?"

As if to emphasize the point, the lad put the empty bucket down, picked up the broom, and started coughing as he kicked up a massive cloud of dust. "It's so dirty."

Cid thought about all of his recent sleepless nights and surge of nightmares. "It wasn't relaxing at all," Cid admitted. "I didn't exactly sleep great, and it wasn't this dirty. It just gets dirty easily."

Lyle looked around skeptically before turning back to Cid again, responding, "I'm sure."

"And you're sleeping on the floor, lad? Ain't no excuse for that with warm beds and empty rooms in town," Daryl said, shaking his head. "Terrible for your back too. Cripple you early, it will. A farmer needs to get himself some good rest if he's going to work the fields all day. I'll have to see if I can find something better for you than just that old bed roll. Shame on you, really, for thinking field gear was a long term solution."

This time, Cid knew better than to protest. The old man would just overrule him anyway, and regardless, Cid knew Daryl was really just trying to look out for him. He thought he knew the reason why. *The old man's memory is starting to go, but he's the only one taking care of his grandson. I wonder if he means to burden me with the kid.*

They worked hard, and by mid-morning, the door was fixed, the house was sparkling clean, and they were getting to work on the staircase. Edd was up on the roof doing some reshingling, but he periodically popped down to see how things were going and to offer advice. Cid did his part too, though, every time he came in from the field to try and help, they waved him away.

"It was pretty bad up there. I'm glad we came," he said once he was done. "Did you know part of the roof was about to cave in. That would have been a big job to fix."

"See?" Daryl asked, not letting a good ribbing go to waste. He nudged Cid in the ribs. "Good thing we came."

Edd had ridden in on a horse just as wiry as he was, and once he was done with the roof, he cantered into town to summon some more villagers while the others ate lunch on the porch. Cid heated up the rest of the leftovers from the Thankful Feast, and Lyle's eyes went wide when he saw the

[Fire 1] spell in action. Daryl looked on distastefully, seeing that Cid didn't have a proper ice box.

As for Lyle, he was entertained. "Wow!" he said. "You're a mage too?"

Cid thought for a moment about how to spin it and ultimately decided to not. "Well, not exactly. My mate Bran's a mage. We've been doing missions together forever. I can do a few spells, that's all. It's nothing impressive, really."

"It's more than anyone else in the village can do, besides me," Daryl said thoughtfully, taking a big bite of pumpkin. "And it's a useful skill to have in these parts. You might be paying us back for our help sooner than we all thought. You'd do well to learn more about those abilities."

"Thanks! Anything I can do, just let me know," Cid said eagerly. "Seriously. You guys have helped me out so much already. I know I owe you."

"It was a neighborly favor," Daryl said firmly. "And there'll be no talk of anyone owing anything. Still, your skills might be a good thing to have around here. I'll keep them in mind, and hopefully, you share some of your good fortune as time and energy allows."

Cid nodded. "It's been good to have. Already, the practical applications for farming have really helped, and it's cut down a lot of time from some of the tasks I needed to do."

Daryl looked away then back at Cid. "Actually, there is one. I'm not quite as young and spry as I used to be, but I can probably use a little help with Lyle."

Cid looked and titled his head curiously. "What do you need help with Lyle? He's doing just fine with how he is."

The Village Elder disagreed. "He's doing ok for now, but I told you about his parents. I don't want that for him. I need to start training him up in self-defense and the way of the road."

"Alright," Cid responded. "It might not be much or as official as I'd have liked, but so long as things are like that, the lad needs to learn."

"Hey!" Edd called out. "You guys done talking yet? It's time for the next step."

CHAPTER 27: A MAN AND HIS HORSE

"Yeah, I think we're about done," Daryl replied to Edd. "If you want to go ahead and get started on the next part, it's about that time."

"This should only take a few minutes," Edd said as he walked off the property towards the curve that led from the main road back to town. Almost as soon as he disappeared from sight, the sound of hooves on a dirt path could be heard, and almost immediately, Edd reappeared, riding on a scrawny looking horse. Behind him was a procession of villagers.

"That's..." Cid's voice trailed off as he saw the large group approaching. "That's a lot of people."

"Yeah. We planned this. Everyone knew the farm was messed up pretty bad and you'd need some help. See, lad?" Daryl said. "This is part of what life is like in a small town once we start to accept you. Everyone's turned out to help. It's the Haven way."

"Alright, alright," Cid replied, feeling a little embarrassed.

Cid tried his best to catch names and thank people for coming, but too many had come for him to catch all of them. Most simply shrugged it off or grunted a thanks. It dawned on Cid the reason for why. *Daryl made this happen. But if I want to get along with the rest of the townsfolk, I'll have to get to know them all personally.*

Soon, Edd was commanding small groups to fix up the farmhouse in places he couldn't quite finish earlier while other groups set about doing small repairs around the farm. At some point, Daryl produced another two baskets full of almond cranberry biscuits, and everybody took one. Daryl winked at Cid.

"They know what side their bread's buttered on," he said. "Got to be sure to sample what the Village Elder's cooked up."

Lyle scoffed. "I think they just like your biscuits, Grandpa."

"That too," Daryl admitted.

With the repair work underway, Cid found himself with a surplus of free time. He took the chance to wash a few things with water from the well and clean up some of the dishes he'd borrowed from the Thankful Feast. Daryl took them gratefully.

"Thanks, lad. I was missing these, to be honest. I don't own that many bowls," Daryl responded. "And these were my nice ones."

Eventually, Cid ran out of other things to do besides farming. He went out to the field he'd planted the previous day to see what had sprouted. Just as Daryl had said, small offshoots of green were already peeking through the dirt. Zucchini grew quick in these parts.

Well, they were watered with water that passed beneath a Mana Tree. And there's a Mana Cavern that runs under the entire farm.

He suspected that might have something to do with it. Still, 'unnaturally fertile earth fed by a Mana Spring' wasn't exactly a problem. If he could get the hang of the farming thing, he might have accidentally made the best choice of his life in buying Oak Tree Farm.

With thoughts of enormous mana-fed vegetables

dancing through his head, he returned to the house to fetch his tomato seeds. It was time to plant the rest of the field.

Daryl nodded at him when he came into sight. "You saw?"

"Growing quick."

The old man gave him a sharp look, and Cid looked down at his feet. He trusted Daryl, but he didn't want to tell him about the Mana Cavern just yet— not until he had more of a sense of what it did and what it meant.

"You use a spell to till that field, lad?"

"How'd you know?"

"No man could get a field that size ready in a day. Even a strong one like you."

"Well, you know my secret."

Sort of.

"Aye. Those tomato seeds you're holding?"

Cid held up the bag so Daryl could see them better. "Yep."

"Tell you what. Bring me some large, ripe tomatoes when they're ready. That'll be in exchange for the help on the house."

It didn't feel like enough, but Cid nodded. "It's settled."

Then, he set off for the field, whistling all the way. The sun was shining, but the day was still cool. Perfect growing weather. He didn't have to worry about his new plants being scorched by the heat.

He smiled as he started sowing the rest of the field.

Forgot to ask Daryl about his planting methods. Well, it didn't seem to matter that much. If his zucchini had sprouted already, he must be doing something right.

He worked at a leisurely pace, and his bag was still half

full of tomato seeds by mid-afternoon. After all, he had until sundown to plant them all— and with the work done on the house and the townspeople doing some of his repairs for him, he was ahead of the schedule he'd set for himself on the farm. He could afford to take his time.

Suddenly, he heard screaming from near the farmhouse, and he froze, the tune dying on his lips. He dropped the bag of tomato seeds and sprinted back to the house, wishing he'd taken the time to learn healing magic when he was still in the Guard.

He could see a cloud of dust rising from the farmyard, and the panicked villagers were scrambling to get away from it. They looked like ants from this far away.

Someone could be hurt, really hurt.

His legs were burning, and he was breathing hard, but he pushed himself to run faster. He had to help. If someone had been injured working on his farm, he'd never forgive himself— especially since they were doing all of this for free.

When he got back from the field, though, he saw a group of Havenites staring blankly at a collapsed cow barn. Edd was shaking his head at them, looking irritated.

"Is anyone hurt?" Cid asked, trying to catch his breath. "Is everyone ok?"

"They're all right," the carpenter said. "Your barn, on the other hand..."

"It just collapsed!" said a large man to Cid's right. His face was flushed, and he looked embarrassed. "I knocked on one of the beams to see if it was sound, and the whole thing went down. The support beams broke clean in half. I've never seen rot damage that bad."

> You've failed Personal Quest: Home Sweet Home I!

> As the barn has been destroyed, you've failed to complete the mission of restoring basic functioning.

Cid sighed and ignored the blue screen before returning a response. "It was in pretty rough shape. Shame about failing the Quest though," Cid said. "It's not your fault. Seriously, though— everyone's alright?"

"Right as rain. Sorry about the Quest, but don't be too hard on yourself. You know, sometimes we get Quests that are too big for us to manage or something else interferes. There was a lot of rot damage. Looked like it was partially hollowed out from something like termites too, " the large man said. "Anyways, I'm Roger, the town baker. You've made quite a stir around here, Cid Dawnshield."

"Oh," Cid replied with a grimace as he watched the chicken coop— at least, what was going to be the Chicken Coop — fall to the ground. "Really?" he exclaimed.

"Nothing bad," replied Roger, not understanding that Cid wasn't talking to him. "We just don't see many newcomers here, and we're glad this land is being put to use. It's been a shame to see the old Oak Tree Farm so empty for so long."

"Mary," a tall woman said, stepping up to shake his hand. She had long dark hair tied back in a long braid. "I've got a little farm up the hill. Nothing this big. And I help Maggie with her brewing when she needs it."

Maggie.

"Is she here?" Cid asked, striking a casual pose.

Edd laughed. "Maggie? Not a chance. She doesn't go in for this kind of thing."

"Fixing barns?" Cid asked.

"Volunteering," Mary said with a laugh.

"But I—" Cid stopped, thinking about what he'd seen the previous day, Maggie getting up early to clean up all the trash from the Thankful Feast alone. Well, it wasn't his place to tell on her. If she wanted to keep it a secret, that was her business.

"Anyways," Edd said, shaking his head, "sorry about your barn, but there wasn't much we could have done for it. It was rotted all the way through, top to tail. Would have taken an expert to fix it, and they would have had to come in years ago when there was still a chance of saving it. As it was, we're just lucky it didn't do any real damage when it came down. Like I said, for this to be a Quest, that's just tough luck. Not all of 'em can realistically be done."

The villagers dispersed to clean out the tool shed, leaving Cid, Daryl, and Edd staring at the collapsed barn alone.

"Sorry about that," Daryl said, looking sheepish as he took a bite of a biscuit. "We did our best, but we should never have tried to take this one on. We just don't have people with the skill around here."

"I do my best," Edd said, looking guiltily at the barn. "But I'm a village carpenter, not an engineer."

"We don't really have the resources to rebuild a barn as rotted as that. We'll make sure to haul the old wood away, at least, so you don't have to deal with it."

Cid waved it off. "It's no big deal. I can use it for firewood. It might even be a good thing not to have that old barn there, anyways."

Daryl frowned. "Really? I thought you said you wanted animals."

Cid grinned. "I said I wanted animals. I didn't necessarily say they had to be cows."

He thought of old Nightshade, his loyal horse, stuck with the green and callow Billy Bagwell as a rider. He wondered if there was a way he could get him back. He was getting a bit old to be a Guard's mount, anyways. Maybe it was time for him to get a new job. Plow horse might suit him well.

"Edd," he said. "Have you ever built a horse stable?"

"I have. Built one for my mare last year. Can't claim I'm an expert, but she seems to like it all right."

"Do you think you could make me one just like it? Maybe a little bit bigger for more than one horse just in case I decide to get a few more."

"I think so. Give me a few days to draw up a plan. I'll come back, and we can look it over together."

"You buying a horse, lad?" Daryl asked, eyes dancing.

"Maybe. I'm going to try. There's one I have in mind."

He was already composing the letter to Lord Vanstone in his head. He'd emphasize the fertile land, the rolling hills, the green fields of Oak Tree Farm. It was the perfect place for a horse to retire to. Cid wasn't much of a writer, but he'd try his best for Nightshade. He'd have a better life here than he would with Billy Bagwell bouncing around on his back.

"You'll get your horse," Daryl said. "You're determined, lad. I can see it in your eyes. You won't stop until you get him."

Cid grinned. "I hope so.

CHAPTER 28:
GLACIAL FREEZE

After the incident with the barn, Cid spent the afternoon planting the rest of the tomato seeds while the villagers dragged what remained of the barn into a pile in the corner of the farmyard. He took frequent breaks to watch them work from his vantage point on the hill. The Havenites clearly weren't professional carpenters, but they were diligent and worked well together.

Must be nice living in a place where everyone knows you so well.

That was him now— or it would be someday. He didn't yet feel like he was fully a part of the community. After all, he'd just moved here. But this was his home now. Maybe next year, he'd be the one helping a new arrival get his farm set up.

It was a nice thought, and it gave him a boost as he finished his work for the day. When he was done, he cleaned his hands at the well and took the empty seed bag back to show Daryl.

The old man was sitting on the porch enjoying the last of the summer sunlight, and he nodded when he saw Cid returning.

"All wrapped up, eh?" He grinned.

"Yep. I've got zucchini and tomato in the ground now."

"You'll want to wait on the pumpkins, lad. I'll tell you

when to plant them. And I can give you advice on what to do with the empty bag."

"I should do something with the empty bag?" Cid asked, looking blankly at the scrap of canvas.

"Waste nothing," Daryl said. "We use up everything we can around here. Good quality canvas is hard to come by."

"Feed bag," Edd said tersely, coming over the porch. He was chewing on a stick of hay. "It'll be good for your horse when you get him."

The old man nodded. "Aye. Good idea, Edd."

Cid folded the bag up and left it in the basement then sat down on the porch steps next to the others.

"Where's Lyle?"

"Ah, that boy," Daryl said, shaking his head. "He's probably off running around somewhere in the woods. Got too much energy for his own good."

Mary and Roger, the baker, approached, looking tired. Mary was carrying a clay jug, and Cid looked at it hopefully.

I wonder if that's what I think it is.

"I think we're wrapping up for today," Roger said. "Mind if we sit down for a bit before heading back to the village? The others are going straight back, but we've got something we want to share."

"There's not enough for everyone," Mary muttered, carefully watching the other villagers as they packed up and headed out. When they were safely around the corner, she lifted her jug high.

"Is that ale?" Cid asked.

"You guessed it. Straight from Maggie's tavern. She couldn't come up today, but she sent it along for us to share."

He grinned. "That was kind of her, but I don't have any cups."

In the end, they drank straight out of the jug, passing it around between them on the porch. Roger had brought some good bread, cheese, and sausages, and they followed it up with the rest of Daryl's cranberry almond biscuits.

"Next time you're coming, let me know in advance," Cid said, taking a big swig of ale. "I'll catch some trout for all of us."

They sat in silence for a few moments, watching the sunset. Then—

"Do you hear that?" Cid asked.

The sound of jingling bells was coming toward them on the road, and he stood up to see what was approaching. A ragtag cart drawn by a fat grey pony was trotting their way. An old man with a long beard held the reins, eyes fixed on the farmhouse. When he arrived in the farmyard, he pulled the pony up quickly and stepped down from the cart.

"I'm Old Levi," he said, bowing so low his beard touched the ground. He was wearing a brightly colored patchwork coat. "Anything you need from my cart?"

"Uh," Cid said. "Can you be more specific?"

"He's a merchant," Daryl said. "Plumber. Jack of all trades. Comes around here a few times a year. If there's anything you need, he'd be a good person to do it. Great carpenter. I've used him a few times myself."

"Better than me," Edd admitted, stuffing the last biscuit in his mouth.

"I could use a stove," Cid said. "I've just been cooking everything over an open flame. And a toilet. Oh, and a bathtub. That stream's refreshing now while it's hot out, but it'll be a lot less pleasant in January."

Old Levi nodded and turned back to his cart, unstrapping a large piece of fabric to reveal a pile of used appliances in the back.

"A wood stove, eh?" he muttered. "I think I've got something you might like. It's used, but still good. Has a few years left in it."

"So do we all." Daryl grinned. "Let's see it then."

Grunting with the effort, Old Levi slowly dragged an old iron stove off the wagon. Cid moved to help him, but Daryl held him back.

"Don't bother," he said. "He won't let anyone else touch his gear. He's the only one who's allowed to."

"Not even to get it into the house?"

"Nope!"

Cid shrugged and stepped out of the way as Old Levi struggled to get the stove into the kitchen.

"I'll get you a toilet, too," the merchant said before he disappeared inside. "And a bathtub. Not to worry."

"Let's let him work," Daryl said, rolling his eyes. "He'll do what he wants no matter what we say. Are you happy with all we've done today, lad?"

"I think so." Cid grinned. "We got the farmhouse all fixed up, yeah? The repairs are all done there?"

"Yep. And the hole in your roof's fixed. Good thing, too. There's a lot more work to be done here, but your house is in good shape."

Cid took a deep breath. He'd had to swallow his pride a bit to accept the help, but he was glad he had. They'd all done much more in one day than he could have on his own.

"Alright," Old Levi said, huffing and puffing a bit as he

came back outside. "Stove's in. Want to pick out a bathtub and toilet?"

"I don't care much about the toilet," Cid admitted. "As long as it works. But as for the bathtub—" He paused. What he was about to say felt unbelievably decadent. "Do you have a big clawfoot tub, one big enough for me to lie down in?"

He'd always wanted one, but it hadn't been possible while he was in the Guard. He'd always had to use the cramped dormitory baths.

Levi stroked his beard for a moment then nodded. "Yep. I think I've got one of those. One second."

He rummaged around on the back of his cart then moved a pile of tin cans to reveal the most beautiful clawfoot tub Cid had ever seen. It was everything he could have imagined and more.

"It's perfect." He grinned. "I'll take it, whatever the price."

"Fifty gold pieces? For all three— the stove, the tub, and the toilet."

Cid winced. That was more than he'd hoped to pay, but it was worth it to have the tub. He just hoped Oak Tree Farm drew a profit this summer.

"Alright. Sold."

He handed over a sack of gold to Old Levi, and the merchant set to work hauling his purchases upstairs to the farmhouse bathroom. Cid felt a little guilty watching the old man push the tub up the staircase, but once again, Daryl shook his head.

"He won't accept any help. Reminds me of someone else I know, actually."

He gave Cid a significant look.

Once the tub was installed, Old Levi summoned them

upstairs to look at it.

"You've bought a lot," he said. "I'll give you something special for free."

And to his surprise, the old man took up a spellcasting stance, and his new appliances started to glow a vivid green.

"I'm casting [Flow Casage] on them. And the broken sink in here too. I can make it work. And [Portal]. This'll give you running water so you don't have to haul well water in and heat it on the stove."

"Really?" Cid asked. He couldn't hold back a grin. The thought of a warm bath tonight after a long day of work was exhilarating.

"Really. Hot and cold water too. My treat." Next, Levi took them downstairs to show off the new stove and ice box. "I've got a trick for this too," he said. "People love it."

This time the ice box glowed an icy blue.

"[Glacial Freeze +5]," Levi said. "It'll keep your food fresh."

"My trout." Cid grinned.

"Sure. Or, uh, whatever else you want. It doesn't have to be trout."

He didn't feel like explaining.

"You're right lucky Levi happened to be coming through," Daryl said. "This is just what the house needed."

"You want anything?" Cid asked. "Biscuits? Cheese?"

The merchant wiped his brow. "Well, if you've got any ale left, I wouldn't say no."

He nodded. "Coming right up."

CHAPTER 29: PINTS AND BITTERS

Old Levi drained the rest of the ale in Mary's jug and looked at them expectantly.

"Uh," Cid said. "Good work, Levi."

"Thanks. You're happy with it?"

"Thrilled." He was already thinking about that tub and how good it would feel to soak in it later. And the ice box was a huge improvement, as was the stove. He wouldn't have to cook everything over an open flame anymore. Life was good.

"Well," the merchant said. "If you don't want to buy anything else—"

"I think I'm tapped out," Cid said, turning his pockets inside out. They were empty. He had more gold in his pack, but not all that much.

"I'll be off then," Levi said, moving toward his cart. "Hope you like everything you bought."

He drew the fabric back over the pile of appliances and strapped it down. Then, he tossed his long beard over one shoulder and hopped into the driver's seat. The pony pricked up its ears expectantly when Old Levi took the reins as if it knew it was about to head home for a bucket of oats.

"Thanks, Levi," Cid said. "Truly. It's been a big help."

"No problem."

And with that, the old man was off, bells jingling merrily as the pony trotted down the road away from the farmhouse. They all watched him go from the porch. Then—

"I'm out too," Mary said. "Got a big day tomorrow at the brewery. Maggie's making a fresh batch of her amber ale."

"You'll have to save me some," Edd said, mounting his horse. "I'm out all day on a project. Replacing all the doors in Old Miss Jade's house. Boring but lucrative."

One by one, they all dispersed, leaving Daryl and Cid alone on the porch. The old man peered into the woods, shading his eyes from the setting sun.

"Where's that damn boy?" he asked. "He's been gone for hours. And he missed dinner. I'll have to find him something to eat now."

They saw a flash of red in the distance coming their way at high speed, and Daryl relaxed. "There he is."

Lyle was galloping toward them like a horse, and they tried not to laugh as they watched him approach.

"You think he's been running like that all day?" Cid asked.

Daryl shrugged. "Who knows?"

"Did you get everything fixed?" the lad asked when he got to the porch. "In the house, I mean?"

Cid nodded.

"Great. Can we go home now?"

"Sure can." Daryl laughed. "Cid Dawnshield, you want to come with us?"

"Uh." That hot bath was calling his name.

"Come back to town. It's been a hard day, and your barn

just collapsed. Let's go have a drink."

Hm. The hot bath did sound good, but a cold pint of ale in a warm tavern also sounded good. Maybe he'd still have time for the tub afterward.

"Alright," Cid said. "Maybe just one."

"Cid's coming to our house?!" Lyle asked.

Daryl laughed. "No, lad. Cid's coming with me to the pub. You'll go stay with Karl."

"But I hate Karl."

"You don't hate Karl. Remember when you two spent the whole day chasing sheep?"

"Yeah."

"Well, you can do it again."

That was enough for Lyle, and the three of them set off down the road toward Haven in the warm summer twilight. Cid whistled an old marching cadence as they walked, and Daryl hummed along.

"I remember that song," he said when they finished. "From my time back in the Magic Knight Corps. We used to sing it when we'd get sent out on long journeys. You remember how it was, I'm sure."

"Right," Cid said, looking down at the ground. He was starting to feel a bit guilty about lying to Daryl— about not telling him he'd been a Guard all along and that he was never in the Corps at all. He needed to fix that when he could. He just didn't know how.

When they got back to town, Lyle ran off down Water Street toward a tiny clapboard house next to the mill.

"He's going to go stay with Karl, the miller's son," Daryl explained. "He's a little— well, odd. But then again, Lyle's odd too. The two of them get along, I think. Or they hate each other. It's a little hard to tell sometimes."

"Hm." Hopefully things would be all right. Cid might not have been here long, but he'd seen enough to know the lad could be a handful.

"What do you say? Maggie's Tavern? Or would you rather split a jug of ale on my back porch? I've got some fresh-picked blackberries sitting in a pail in the kitchen."

"Let's go to the tavern. I can meet some more people who live here in Haven."

The fact that Maggie would be there had nothing to do with his choice, of course. Nothing at all.

They took a corner table in the back room of the bar, and Cid went to the front to grab two pints.

"Light or dark?" Maggie asked.

"Uh. What do you recommend?"

She looked him up and down, sizing him up. "Dark. I think you can handle it."

"And for Daryl?"

"Daryl Nightgreen? Definitely dark. He's been around the block, that one."

Cid looked back at the Village Elder who was carrying on a vibrant conversation with a white-haired old woman. Both of them were laughing. "Really?"

"Yeah. I know he always seems to be in a good mood, but he's had some hard times. Anyways, here's your beer. Two darks. I'll add them to your tab."

She moved off to talk to the next customer, leaving Cid alone with two steins of ale, wondering what exactly Daryl's life had been like. Cid felt a moment of disappointment that she didn't stay longer, but it wasn't the right time. *I'll have to find a better time than when she's working to talk to her and update my Quest.*

"Ah," the old man said, taking a large sip when Cid set the pint down in front of him. "That hits the spot, lad. Thanks."

"Not at all. It's only fair. You got the last round here."

"Maggie tell you all my secrets?"

"Well," Cid said, wondering what he should say next. "Not exactly. She just steered me toward the dark ale for you."

Daryl laughed. "Did she, now? That's Maggie for you. She's got an eye for— well, an eye for something, all right."

"What did she mean?"

Daryl sighed. "Well, lad, it's complicated. You know by now that I was a Mage Knight when I was younger, that I wasn't really cut out for it, and that I was better off staying in Haven."

"Yes," Cid said, taking a sip of ale. "I remember all that."

"I went into battle quite a bit in the Southern Lands back when the war was on. My portion of the Corps was very active. We saw a lot of action. It was— well, I don't want to spoil a good day, but it wasn't easy. I can tell you that much. When I left the Corps, I just needed to get away. I wanted to get as far from the Southern Lands as possible. Haven was that place for me. You know, when I was growing up here, I always thought it was boring. But after my time in the Corps, it was just the place I needed to be. Peaceful. You know how it is, lad, I'm sure."

It was time to bring it up. "You know, Daryl, I'm not sure I've been completely truthful with you."

"Go on."

The old man was looking at him expectantly, and Cid swallowed hard.

"Well," he said. "I know you think I was a Mage Knight. And I've definitely let you think that. I was flattered you believed it, honestly. But the truth is—"

"Oh, out with it, lad. I knew you weren't a Mage Knight. What were you— common soldier?"

"City Guard," Cid said a little sheepishly.

"Well, there you go. And I bet you were a good one, too. You've got that air about you."

"How long have you known I wasn't in the Corps?"

"A while, lad. Honestly, I was waiting to see how long it would take you to tell me yourself."

"I guess it did take a while," Cid said, rubbing his neck. "I just wasn't sure how to bring it up. How did you know?"

"I actually was a Mage Knight, remember? I can sense magic, and I can tell how much someone's got. And I hate to say it, Dawnshield, but while your spellwork was impressive today, you don't have enough to have been in the Corps. Nowhere close."

"Oh," Cid said, a little deflated.

"But I have to tell you, my time in the Corps was hard, but there are things I miss about it sometimes. The comradery. It's nice to feel that again. I didn't realize how much I'd missed it. You were a guard at least, right?"

"Aye. City Guard at Hardhearth," Cid responded.

"Then you know what I mean," Daryl replied, being good natured.

Cid thought back to his time in the Guard— of the hard beds and the hard times, of all the nights spent staring into the darkness, waiting to see if something would happen.

"Yeah," he said finally. "I know what you mean."

The old man smiled. "See? I knew I liked you, lad. Do me a favor, then, will you? Tell me a story— a good story, a real story — and all will be forgiven."

CHAPTER 30: THE PRICE OF A STORY

Cid frowned and took a deep drag of his ale. "A story? That's what you want from me?"

"Aye." Daryl nodded his head. "A tale of your time in the Guard. Something to get these old bones excited. Remind me of my younger days when I was a hot blooded youth."

"Oh, um, ok," Cid responded. "But I'm not really the bard. My mate Bran from the Magic Knight Corps was the real storyteller. Being a Battlemage, he could really blend his magic into his storytelling. Never seen anything quite like it. 'For effect', he would say before launching off a fireball."

"Don't worry about any of that. Focus on you and your stories. Do your best, lad," Daryl said. "I know you can think of something. You were in the Guard for how long?"

"Twenty years, maybe a few more if you count unpaid training years," Cid admitted.

"See?" remarked Daryl. "That's a whole career, one to be proud of. I'm sure you've got plenty of stories to tell. Make it something exciting. Full of adventure. Battles. Derring-do. A tale an old man would want to hear to make him feel young again."

Cid wracked his brain. His time in the Guard had been eventful, true. Hardheath wasn't a quiet town, even at the best of times, but he didn't have any stories to match Bran's wild tales of far-flung adventures and monster slaying. Fighting the undead outside of the city didn't have the same kind of glamour to it as slaying a Dragon or Frost Giant. And if Daryl was telling the truth about his own experience in the Corps, it had been much more exciting than Cid's life had been.

"The story needs to be long too, a real epic," the old man said. "I want to drink a few more pints here tonight. Give me something to fill the time."

"Alright," Cid said as he frantically searched through memories for something to fit the request. "I've got it. Have you ever heard of a village called Boarshead?"

"No, never," Daryl admitted, and Cid could see the excitement in the old man's eyes.

Hopefully this tale lives up to his expectations.

"There's no reason you would have," he said. "It's a tiny place in the middle of nowhere about fifty miles north of here even smaller than Haven— and much poorer. I've only been there the one time, and I hope never to go there again. They didn't have a proper amount of anything. I was used to rough accommodations, and that was beyond rough."

"What brought you there, then, lad? A mission from the Guard?" Daryl asked, pressing for details, his face pensive and thoughtful.

"Aye. I was sent there with three others from my post to clear out a reported necromancer's den in the forest just outside the village. It ordinarily would have been a job for the Magic Knight Corps, but they couldn't spare anyone due to the Battle Royale Testing. But mission requirements being what they were, something had to be done. So it fell on us to make it happen. Me and my mate Gavin were in charge, me as senior and him as my second. We had two others under our command, an old greybeard who went by the alias

Hatcher and a green recruit by the name of Patrick Shanley. No alias. Gotta earn that first. They wouldn't have been the men I would have chosen— aside from Gavin, Gavin was a good man— but the others? Eh. They were the ones I was assigned to lead. It was a violent year in Hardhearth, and the Guard couldn't spare anyone else either. We were lucky to at least get Hatcher. He wanted one more mission before he retired, and Commander Vanstone thought young Patrick needed to get more experience in the real world. I knew enough by then to know that there was no point in objecting to the Commander's wishes, so off we went."

"I had a few missions like that when I was in the Corps," Daryl said. "I know how it is. A blind hand leads."

Cid nodded and continued. "It was the dead of winter and brutally cold. We shivered all through the two day journey to Boarshead. No matter how many furs we wore, we couldn't seem to get warm. All the trees were grey and skeletal. They looked like grasping claws. Just right for a face-off with a necromancer."

Cid took another sip of beer and grinned. He was settling into a rhythm now, and Daryl seemed engaged by what he was saying. It was surprisingly easy to tell a story. Maybe he'd do it more often.

"We were expecting to see a lot of terrified villagers when we got into town, but no one was there when we showed up. No one at all. The village was totally deserted. Not a soul in sight. And the weirdest thing was that it was as if everyone had just up and vanished one day, leaving everything just as it was. Apples were rotting in a cart as if the owner had just walked away and left them there. A full shelf of pies stood in the window of the bakery— now spoiled with flies buzzing around them. I sent old Hatcher inside some of the houses to see what he could find, and it was the same story in pretty much every place checked. Books left open on tables, food spoiling on kitchen counters, toys strewn all over living room floors, meals left uneaten on dining room tables. The villagers had put out the fires at least— lucky for us, or the whole town would likely have been ablaze— but that was all they'd done. No one seemed to have packed to leave at all. It was eerie. No reason for it."

"Except for that necromancer," Daryl interjected, and Cid nodded. "Yeah, except for the necromancer."

"Oooh." Daryl shivered. "This is a spooky tale, lad. Can't tell where it's going, but with a necromancer involved, it can't be good."

"No," Cid said. "It wasn't."

He saw movement out of the corners of his eyes and glanced over to see what it was. Some of the other Havenites had gathered closer to his table. They all turned away when he looked at them, trying to seem casual, but it was clear that they were listening in, eager to hear where the story went next. Cid took a drink.

"We wanted to see if there was someone, anyone, who could tell us any more about what had happened, so all four of us searched the town. Door to door, every house. Nothing. No sign of any fighting either, at least, not until we reached the Town Constable's post at the jail."

"What did you see there, lad?"

"The Boarshead jail was tiny, just one cell and a little holding pen with a Constable's office in the front, and there had clearly been a struggle there. The door was splintered as if someone— or something— had to beat it down to get in. And when I looked inside, there were streaks of blood on the floor. They led to the lone cell. When I went back outside and told the others what I'd seen, I could see the fear in their eyes. All but Gavin. Some dark force had clearly done what it wished with the town, and it was left to us to pick up the pieces."

He paused for effect, holding the silence a beat too long. More Havenites had come over toward his table, and he could feel the impatience in the room.

"Well, get on with it, lad," Daryl said finally. "What was inside the jail?"

"I'm coming to that," Cid said. "Just trying to set the scene first."

"Aye, you've done that, now tell us what's next!"

"Right. Well, it was clear from the jump that I was the only one who'd be going inside the jail that night. Young Patrick and Hatcher weren't up to the task, and Gavin needed to stand guard outside. So, I unsheathed my sword, took a breath, and went inside. Followed the trail of blood. It was clear that was where I needed to go. And the cell, when I got to it, wasn't empty. The Constable was locked inside, and he was in rough shape."

"Was he able to tell you what had happened?" Daryl asked.

Cid laughed darkly. "That, he was not. The man was alive— sort of— but he'd never tell anyone anything again. He'd become one of the Undead. The necromancer's doing, no doubt. And he'd clearly put up a good fight before being turned, too. His armor was torn and ragged, and one arm was covered with blood. The cell door was locked... from the inside."

"From the inside?" Daryl asked. "Didn't know the Undead knew how to work a lock."

"They don't. But a living man— one who knows he's about to turn and doesn't want to hurt anyone— can. The Constable had been bitten in the fight at the jail and locked himself in the cell so he couldn't turn anyone else. I could still see the keys in his hand."

"That's courage."

"There's not much else he could have done," Cid admitted. "He was going to become a zombie no matter what. As far as I know, there's no way to stop that process once it's started. But it *was* quick thinking that he locked himself in before he was too far along."

"And you said the man was still alive?" Daryl breathed.

"I said 'sort of'. He was sitting on the floor, twitching and groaning, and he hissed at me when he saw me come in. Tried to attack. Battered himself against the bars. Luckily, they held him in. He could move, but whatever intelligence— whatever soul— he might have had was gone. He was just a blind destructive force, like an animal in a trap."

"Poor man."

"Aye," Cid said. The image of the Constable beating himself bloody against the bars of the cell still haunted him. It wasn't the kind of thing a man forgot. "But that's not all. He did something else before he turned."

He took a long drink, enjoying the look on Daryl's face as he got more and more impatient.

"Well?" the old man asked. "What did he do? You're a good storyteller, lad, but this is driving me nuts."

"He wrote a word on the wall in his own blood. One single word. I could see the writing get sloppier and sloppier with each letter— as he started to turn, I guess. And it trailed off, in the end. He never finished it."

"And? What did he write?"

Cid drained his beer. "It's getting late. We had a long day today, and I've got an early morning tomorrow at the farm. Perhaps we can come back tomorrow night, and I'll finish the tale then?"

Daryl slammed his stein down on the table, and Cid grinned. It was entertaining seeing the old man get impatient.

"Cid Dawnshield, you have every man, woman, and child in this tavern waiting to hear where this story's going to go. You really think we all want to break it off here and come back tomorrow?"

Cid looked around. It was true. Every Havenite in the bar was now crowded around his table, and none of them were even pretending not to be listening to his story anymore. All eyes in the tavern were on him, and they all looked annoyed.

"Well?" asked a large man with ruddy cheeks. "Get on with it. What did he write on the wall?"

"Aye!" said a red-haired woman across the tavern. She looked too young to drink, but she had a stein in her hand just the same. "What did you do with the zombie Constable? Did you kill him, or let him stay Undead forever?"

"What about the necromancer?" asked a scrawny girl sipping on a glass of juice. "This was all his fault, yeah? Did you get him? You did, right?"

A dark-eyed man leaning against the far wall spoke up, smirking. "What about the others? Gavin? Patrick? Hatcher? Did they make it out alive?"

Cid wasn't quite sure how to respond. He had genuinely planned on leaving and returning the next night to finish the tale, but it was starting to seem like that wasn't an option.

"See?" Daryl asked. "We all want to hear the end of the tale. Stay one more round, lad. I'm buying."

"Yeah?" Cid asked, raising an eyebrow.

"Yeah." Daryl motioned over towards the bartender. "Maggie?"

"Another pint of dark ale," the bartender said, raising her eyebrows. "One for each of you."

There was a massive hubbub in the bar as everyone else

tried to order more ale all at once. No one wanted to be dry for the second half of the story. Cid took a moment to collect himself as Maggie passed out glasses.

"I didn't think my tale would be so popular," he admitted. "Like I said, I'm no bard."

"You've got what it takes, lad," Daryl said. "Now, finish the tale. We all want to find out how it ends."

He nodded and glanced over at Maggie, trying to see how long it would take her to get him a beer.

Definitely just waiting for the beer. That's the only reason I'm looking her way..

She caught his gaze and grinned. "Coming right up, Dawnshield. I wouldn't keep you waiting. In the meantime, nobody likes a cliffhanger. Keep going!"

The little girl who'd been drinking juice earlier carried two fresh glasses over to their table.

"Alright," Cid said, taking his new pint from her. "Just this once. I'll stay late and finish the story."

CHAPTER 31: OUT OF THE BAR

"One moment!" Maggie shouted out. "I know everyone just topped off, but here's a round on me. Don't get used to it." The barkeeper poured out the ales, and once everyone had another drink and was gathered back around his table, Cid took a deep drag of his ale, polished it off, and started on the other Maggie had just given out before he started telling his story again.

"The Constable had tried to write one word on the jail cell wall. Ominous. Dark. Just 'below'," Cid explained.

"Below?" Daryl asked. "What does that mean? In the basement or something?"

Cid paused for effect and glanced around the room. Maggie got impatient with him and threw a wash rag. "Get on with it!"

He shrugged. "Same question I asked myself at the moment. But before I could investigate further, Gavin burst through the door telling me reinforcements had arrived. Commander Vanstone had learned how bad the situation in Boarshead was. Apparently, a man from the village, young enough to be almost a lad still, had managed to make it out. Screaming about horrors and terrors and the like, he ran the whole way to Hardhearth alone. I never knew how he'd managed to do it."

Cid looked over at the youngest of those listening in on

the story to really accent his next point. "It's remarkable what someone can do when the need is great. Gavin and I went out to greet the new arrivals. Both of us were thankful and relieved by the arrival of back up. There were about fifty men outside on lathered horses. They'd clearly ridden hard and traveled the same distance in one day as we had in two, and they looked exhausted. But they were willing and ready to fight. One thing, though: none of them was a mage. We didn't have any magic, and fighting Necromancers needs a magic edge."

"For a mission like that?" Daryl asked, looking incredulous. "Not having a Battlemage? I can't imagine it."

"Well, of course you can't," Cid said. "You were in the Magic Knight Corps. Spellwork is a big part of what you did. But in the Guard, things are trickier when you don't have magic. I didn't until a few weeks ago. So, we always needed to figure out another way."

The old man nodded. "Difficult work, that is. It's not the same, I know, but I had this bad case of the Doules that practically dried up my mana channels…"

Cid cast a side eyed glance at the elder but didn't say anything. Instead, he just continued the story. "I knew there was no time to lose. I left Gavin with Moses, Patrick, and a few of the other men and took the rest inside the jail to show them what we'd found. The Boarshead man— went by the name of Elric— came with me up front. He was horrified by what he'd seen in the village and eager to take out the necromancer who'd done it. I watched him carefully. I was younger than I am today, but I already knew well what could happen when a man gets too set on revenge. When the blood is hot, the brain stops working. You know how it is. Mostly, I was afraid he'd be a liability."

Daryl nodded his head. *He knows exactly what I'm talking about.*

Cid continued. "Anyways, we put the Constable out of his misery before moving forward. He didn't deserve to spend the rest of his days like that. No one did. And then we went below. You're right, Daryl. The jail had a basement— a large one— and we could hear eerie sounds drifting up from it— the most unearthly shrieking you can imagine. I hope never to hear anything like it ever again."

Daryl shook his head. "I can imagine."

"We went down the stairwell towards the basement, and the shrieks grew louder. We were getting closer to their source. Elric pushed ahead, and he quickly figured out where they were coming from. There was a jagged fissure in the basement wall just large enough for a man to squeeze through. Someone — or something— was living under the jail."

Cid paused, letting his words lingering as he took a sip of his beer. The Havenites were hanging on his every word.

"We pushed our way through, one by one, and we were attacked by zombies almost immediately. They clearly once had been villagers— but not anymore. Now, they were like that poor Constable in the jail cell upstairs. There were more of us than there were of them, and Guardsmen have always been good fighters, especially in close quarters. We were attacked almost immediately by ghouls. We made quick work of the Undead and pushed forward into the narrow passage. We were in a massive cave system under the jail, and we spent hours making our way through it, fighting zombies at every turn as we went. I won't bore you all with the details. It was a real dungeon grind. But suffice it to say that by the time we got to the heart of the cave, we were all exhausted. And the real battle was just about to begin.

"The passage opened up into a large recess deep beneath the earth, and it was full of dead villagers neatly stacked. I could see the anger on Elric's face when he saw what we were looking at. 'Those were my friends', he had said. 'My family.

And he just—'"

He paused, the memory as vivid as the day it happened. To continue, he had to take a deep drink of his stein.

"He trailed off, rage sucking away his breath and bringing him to tears. I tried to get him to calm down, to focus on the task ahead, but without much luck. And truth be told, I understood. The necromancer had clearly killed the whole village. Everyone Elric knew was dead. I don't know what I'd do in that situation.

"And then," Cid went on, "the necromancer came out. A portly man whose skin had gone the color of powder. I had to hold the lad back from attacking him right away and revealing our position. Turns out the necromancer came from Boarshead. He was the local miller. His wife had died in a tragic accident a few years before. Horrific. Got a foot caught in the waterwheel, and was dragged below and drowned. And it had been partly the miller's fault, too. He'd gotten distracted by a pretty girl selling apples on the road and neglected to watch the wheel. He blamed himself, and was never the same. In the end, he'd turned to the dark arts to try to bring her back."

Daryl shook his head sadly. "I don't endorse it. But I understand it, at least partly. When my own dear wife died, I wasn't sure how to go on."

The Havenites in the tavern murmured in agreement.

"I hear that," Cid said. "But the man had killed everyone in the entire village. Nothing could justify that. When the Necromancer saw Elric, he greeted him with a smile.

"'Good to see you again, Elric. How's your mom and dad?' the necromancer asked. When Elric didn't respond, he shrugged and said, 'Don't worry, lad. I'll be with you in a minute.' He seemed to have no idea that what he'd done was wrong. It chilled my bones to see it, because I know it meant the man was insane. And a mad necromancer was likely to be even more dangerous than a sane one.

"Elric wailed and tried to launch himself at the man, but I stopped him from doing anything. The lad was in pain and likely to get himself killed if he tried to fight now. Meanwhile, the necromancer turned to me with a sly smile. 'I can do it now,' he said, eyes wild. 'I finally have enough sacrifices. I can bring her back. She'll come back to me.'

"At that moment, I finally understood. He'd killed all of Boarshead to harvest the power of their departing souls. He was performing a mass casting ritual to bring his wife back.

"'Just... now,' he said, marking an X on the ground with chalk."

Cid drained his glass and held it up. Maggie took it immediately and refilled it.

"He'd hoped to bring his wife back," he started again, his face solemn as he recaptured the events so long ago. "But he brought something else instead. A heinous monster from the lower depths, the likes of which I'd never seen before. It burst out of the earth with a roar as if it was rising from the grave. Everything about the beast felt wrong. Wherever it had come from, it wasn't meant to be here on earth. The men behind me fell back, vomiting, as it dragged itself out of the ground.

"When it saw us, it summoned a massive wall of bone that cut off the only exit. We had no way to retreat. The only way out was forward. We knew we had to defeat the beast and kill the necromancer before he could sacrifice more people and summon more.

"The men around me roared and readied their swords to attack, but they were cut down by the monster's bone spears before they could move an inch. The mad necromancer seemed unfazed by the creature he'd summoned by accident. He was laughing, eyes rolling back in his head— and he was laughing still when the monster crushed him between its jaws and swallowed him down. It was just us standing against it now— standing between it and what remained of the village.

"And you had no magic to speak of," Daryl said, eyes wide. "Not a drop, lad. It's a miracle you're still alive today to tell the tale."

"I got lucky," Cid said. "That's all it was. There I was, in that cavern, with half the men I'd brought lying wounded on the floor. I kept my wits about me and tried to drag as many of them out of the way as I could. There were small outcroppings of rock around the edges of the cavern, and I left the injured men there where they'd have some shelter from the monster's attacks. Young Elric had been hit, and the lad was in a great deal of trouble. I almost felt bad to move him for fear of making his injuries worse. But he was a brave lad, he was. Foolish, yes, but brave."

"I take it by your words that the lad is no longer with us," Daryl said.

"All in good time," Cid replied. "All in good time. Once I got the wounded out of the way, I turned my attention to the beast. You spoke the truth, Daryl, when you said I didn't have a drop of magic to work with. But I did have this."

He made a show of reaching into his front jacket pocket to pull out the scroll he always kept there. Even now that he'd started his new life as a farmer, he had no intention of giving it up. *Just in case.*

Daryl squinted down at the piece of paper on the table. "What's that, lad? Is that what I think it is?"

Cid nodded. "A scroll I got one year from Commander Vanstone. He gave them to all of the team leaders. He knew I might need it one day, and by the gods was he right. [Blessed Scroll – Reinforcements]."

The Havenites looked back at him blankly.

"Tore up the scroll and tossed it on the ground," Cid said. "And the walls of the cave immediately began to rumble and shake. The beast snarled and readied its next attack."

He paused for a long moment.

"And...?" Daryl prodded.

"Are you sure you don't want me to wrap it up here and finish the tale tomorrow?" Cid smirked. "It's getting late, and I've been talking a long while."

The old man glared at him. "I'm not even going to dignify that with a response, lad."

"Alright, alright. Where was I? Oh right. Just threw down my magic scroll. The cave was shaking, and the beast was about to attack. I'd never used [Reinforcements] before, and I wasn't quite sure what to expect. So imagine my surprise when a flash of blinding purple light filled the cave and a portal opened in the ceiling. And guess what was inside?"

"Another monster?" asked the little girl who'd brought him his beer, eyes wide.

"Elric!" Maggie grinned.

"Good guesses, but no. Out poured a unit of Magic Knights. The strongest military might of the kingdom at my fingers. They were from the Corps, at least that's what I assumed. I never got the chance to talk to them to see where they'd come from. Their horses ran on the air like they were on the ground, and they were carrying glowing lances. Myself and the lads watched them in wonder. We'd never seen Magic Knights up close before. And they didn't even take a moment to acknowledge us. Except for the healer on their squad. Just went straight for the monster."

"All business," Daryl said, looking a little guilty. "That sounds right for Magic Knights. Especially when— no offense meant, lad— dealing with the City Guard."

"It's alright," Cid said. Under normal circumstances, he might be annoyed by Daryl's comment, but he was riding high on the success of his story. It would take more than that to bring him down.

"The monster wasn't the only thing to come out of the hole in the floor, so I didn't have much time to look at the knights. An army of minor summons soon followed— and those were more my speed. I left the Corps to deal with the big beast and turned my attention to the smaller ones. Did my best to keep them away from the wounded men. They took out a few— I'm only human, after all— but they didn't get all of them. I feel good about that."

"You did good, lad," Daryl said. "I'm sure you did."

"Meanwhile, the Corps took on the great monster. I've seen some strange and wild things in my life as a Guard, but I can tell you what I saw that day was the greatest battle I've ever seen in my life. The monster sent volley after volley of bone shards at the Knights, but they drove its attacks back with waves of purple fire. One of their spellcasters threw glowing orbs at it from afar while the rest either attacked it with fire or charged it with their magic lances. The beast had hands like lobster claws, and it was able to block their attacks— at first. But as time went on, some of the Knights' hits landed and it started to get tired. Slowly, they drove it back toward the hole it had risen from."

"What was it like to see the Knights in battle?" the little girl asked. "I've only seen them riding through the village once or twice. They didn't look at me."

"You've got a former Knight here," Daryl said good-naturedly, puffing up his chest. "You could ask him."

But all eyes were on Cid tonight, and it was his answer they wanted.

"They were magnificent," he said. "Like avenging angels. It was truly the greatest thing I've ever seen. Almost made me wish I had some magic in me so I could have joined the Corps. Almost. Not fully. I'm a Guard, through and through, and proud of it."

The Havenites raised their glasses high to the Guard.

"Throughout, I did my best to fend off the minor summons that appeared so the Knights could focus on their own task. And I tended to the wounded as I could. It was the least I could do. In the end, we won. It was a hard battle, and there's much I wish could have gone differently, but the monster lay dying on the ground, the Knights departing without a word."

He fell silent for a moment, remembering. In truth, it had stung a bit that they hadn't even acknowledged him. But that was how Knights were.

"And?" Maggie asked finally, winking. "Did you ever leave that cave?"

"Aye." He laughed. "I did. We got the wounded out of the cave. I carried Elric on my back myself. Yes, the lad survived, although he never returned to Boarshead again. When the work was done, I rode back to Hardhearth to give my report. And those of us who survived agreed to meet for drinks after I'd spoken with Lord Vanstone."

The bar was silent.

"That's it," Cid said awkwardly. "That's the end of the story."

"And a damn good one," Maggie said from across the room. He looked up. She was smiling broader than he'd ever seen anyone smile before. "Now, it's after midnight. Everyone, get out of my bar."

CHAPTER 32: DEDICATED SERVICE TO THE MAGIC KNIGHT CORPS

"Now, then, Miss Maggie," Daryl said, rising to his feet and pretending to look offended. "Is that how you treat someone who's brought in a good story on a Monday night? Besides, I was hoping I could talk to you about something."

"Alright, alright," she said, rolling her eyes. "You can stay a bit longer, if you must, but I'm closing shop soon. Seriously. That goes for the rest of you too."

Cid grinned and looked down at the table. He was starting to get the measure of the gruff Miss Maggie. She wasn't as tough as she tried to seem.

Some of the Havenites had packed up and left when she'd first told them to go, but there were still enough listening that Cid thought it was worth giving his story an epilogue.

"I rode back to Hardhearth as fast as I could, leaving Gavin and the rest to clean up the village and wrap things up with the wounded. I told him to keep a special eye on Elric. I wanted the lad to survive."

"I'm glad he did, lad," Daryl said. "There's a happy ending

to that part of the story, at least."

"Part of the reason I went to Vanstone so quickly was because I knew how important it would be to give a full report of what happened," Cid said. "So we could get the official tale out before the rumors started going. But that was only part of it. I also wanted to get a drink with Gavin and anyone else who'd come along so we could talk about all we'd seen. I have to admit, the thought of a pint or three of ale around a roaring tavern fire got me through the long, cold ride home."

The old man nodded. "As it should. I know the feeling. A night of drinking after a hard fight is sometimes the only cure to what ails you."

One of the villagers laughed, and Daryl glared. It wasn't a pun.

Cid nodded in agreement. "The Lord Commander looked grave as he took down my story, and I could tell he was troubled by what he'd heard. None of us had any sense going in how bad the situation was in Boarshead. 'I'm sorry I sent you into that with so few men,' he said once I was done. 'You did well. But it could have gone a lot worse than it did.' I was just glad he'd acknowledged it.

"With my duty done, I moved on to the Dead Horse Tavern down the street. It wasn't the nicest bar in town, but it had cheap drinks, live music, and a two-for-one Guard discount if you came in a group. That was enough to get my business. Gavin was still finishing up in Boarshead, so I settled in for a pint alone. Or alone enough. I was lonely though, and I took my comfort where I could. I didn't mind. Besides, there was a fiddle player going in the corner, and the pub was warm. It wasn't a bad way to spend part of the evening.

"After a few minutes, a large group walked into the Dead Horse. I glanced over— and then I did a double take," Cid continued, noticing that Miss Maggie looked impatient for him to finish. "They were Magic Knights. And not just that. It was the same group I'd summoned with my scroll earlier that day."

"A bit of a lucky coincidence, lad," Daryl said. "You sure the story you're telling is fully true? You've already shown a certain... talent for stretching the truth."

"Every word, Daryl" Cid replied "I swear it. I was just as surprised as you are now, and I was fully expecting them to ignore me, just as they'd done earlier that day. After all, I was just a lowly Guard to them. And at first, they did. But as the group loosened up, took off their coats, and started drinking, some of them started looking my way. And one in particular— a guy around my age, a little less fancy-looking than the others, sent me a round, and we started up a conversation.

"So that's how I met my mate, Bran. The same one that sent you a letter of introduction," Cid continued. "He saved my butt down in the necromancer's dungeon, and he bought me a pint of ale afterwards. He's the one who taught me pretty much everything I know today. He was just a regular Magic Knight when we first met, not the Battlemage he eventually became and is now, but he was an ambitious lad, and was already on the rise, even then. Our first mission together, albeit accidental — since I just panicked in the dungeon and dropped the scroll — was enough of a success that we were teamed up more and more on harder assignments. Whenever the Guard needed the support of the Magic Knight Corps, Bran was there. Or the other way around— there were times when the Corps needed the Guard's knowledge of the City and enough bodies skilled at fighting in close quarters. You can't do a magical volley in a narrow alleyway. It was a good partnership, over the years. It truly was."

Cid trailed off, remembering some of the missions he'd done with Bran and the Corps in his youth. They'd taken out an organized crime ring and saved a group of mage children from kidnappers who wanted to traffic them south. They'd done a lot of good together. They'd tried their best.

"That's a good tale, lad," Daryl said gently, setting his empty glass down on the table and eyeing the door. "And you told it well. Kept an old man entertained on a hot summer night. But as you keep saying, it's getting late now. I think it's time for me to wrap up and head to my bed."

"Understood," Cid said, looking around. The crowd around him had almost completely dwindled, but the villagers who were left were looking at him with respect. "I guess I've been talking for a while, huh?"

"About two hours." Maggie grinned, wiping down the bar counter. "And we all appreciated it. But as I said earlier, we're closed. It's time for you lot to clear out. I don't care much for who your friends are or used to be. You're one of us now, remember?"

Grumbling a bit, the rest of the Havenites downed their beers and left. Daryl was the last to go, and he gave Cid and Maggie a cheery wave as he walked out the door.

"See you soon, lad," he said. "There's still a lot of work to be done on the old Oak Tree Farm!"

"Don't remind me." Cid groaned.

Cid realized he'd been rude and helped to clean up. He carried the empty glasses back to the counter for Maggie to wash.

"Come back to the storeroom," she said, pushing her way past him toward a small blue door at the end of the bar. "I'll deal with those in a second."

He froze. His heart was pounding. She wanted him to come back to the storeroom...? What could she possibly want from him there? She couldn't possibly be interested in him that way... could she?

"Come on!" she called back from the open door. "I don't have all night!"

Breathing hard, he moved toward the tiny room— and she dropped a heavy case of apple bitters into his arms and a recipe card.

"Oof," he said. "Is this what I think it is?"

"A gift from everyone, and a reward? Yes. I threw in an extra Apple Bitter as a thanks for the story," Maggie responded.

She was rifling through the drawers of a storage cabinet, clearly looking for something.

"What am I supposed to do with this many apple bitters? " Cid asked, looking at the label on the crate. It was fairly clean, as if it had just been opened.

"Figure it out, maybe regift them. That's what I'd do. Sell 'em if you need to or get low on coin," Maggie said, still looking through her cabinet. "Do something. Impress me."

"My story wasn't impressive enough?" Cid responded curiously.

She gave him a look. "It'll take more than a story, Dawnshield. You wouldn't be the first hero to weave a grand tale and think that was enough. Ah. Here we go."

She pulled a few notecards out of the drawer and handed them over. He squinted at them, trying to make out what was written on them. Maggie's handwriting— or at least, he assumed it was Maggie's— was spidery and hard to make out.

"What's this? Six cups of 'hoo'?" Cid asked, struggling to read the handwriting.

"Recipes," she said, looking at him like it should be obvious. "For some craft beers. I invented them myself. It's 'hops', not 'hoo'."

"And you want me to try to make them?" he responded.

She grinned. "Like I said, impress me. A little effort goes a long way."

"But," Cid said, frowning. He didn't really want to try to make beer. He had no idea how to do it. "Can't I just come here and buy them from you? You are the barkeeper after all."

"You could," She shrugged, closing the drawer and moving back into the bar. "I wouldn't hold it against you, but I'd certainly judge you for it. Everybody in town knows how to make these."

He sighed. This was clearly a test.

"Alright," he said. "I'll do my best."

You've received the rewards for Friend of Haven I!	
You have returned to Miss Maggie to collect your reward. This is a benefit bestowed upon all new arrivals to town once it is determined that they intend to make Haven their home. No one single villager is responsible for this gift, everyone helped. Enjoy responsibly.	
Rewards:	A Crate of Apple Bitters Recipe Card — Apple Bitter

He pocketed the recipes, hoisted the crate of apple bitters on his back, and headed for the door. It was a long walk home this time of night.

As he passed the bar, though, something glinted in the shadows behind Maggie and caught his eye. A letter, framed, covered in glass, and mounted to the wall next to her bottles of liquor. The seal of the Magic Knight Corps glimmered at the bottom. It was hard to make out what it said, but he got the gist: it was a letter of appreciation from the Corps for dedicated service made out to "Dame Madeline of the Thorn".

He was about to move closer when he saw Maggie's face. She'd caught him looking, and her expression had gone hard and withdrawn.

"Good night, Dawnshield," she said firmly. "See you next time you're in the tavern."

"But—" Cid protested.

"Good night," came the firm reply.

He frowned but obediently headed out into the night. *What was up with that?* There was clearly a story there, and it wasn't one that Maggie wanted to tell. Well, there was no point in pushing. He'd have to trust that all would reveal itself in time. And, keeping that in mind, he stepped off for home.

CHAPTER 33: THE DEPARTED

Cid woke up with a groan on the hard floor of his bedroom the next morning. He hadn't made it to his bedroll, and his back ached. Everything was stiff. The sun was pouring through the window.

Bright. Too bright.

He might have gotten a little carried away with the ale the night before. To be fair, he'd been buoyed up by the success of his tale. He hadn't thought he'd be any good at storytelling, but somehow, he'd managed to hold the villagers' attention. It made him think. He had lots of exciting stories from his life in the Guard. Maybe he could gather them together once things with the farm got underway, and write a little book. It would be a good way to pass the time on a long and snowy winter night— and he suspected that there were plenty of those in his future here in Haven.

He went ahead and updated his log. *I've been neglecting this.*

Personal Log Entry IV
Start of Day Nine.
The locals of Haven are accepting you. Maybe it's because of your relationship with Daryl, maybe for other reasons—

it's difficult to know— but there are friendships brewing. The townsfolk are beginning to respect you, and you them. Continue on this path and lean on others as needed.

Active Quests	
Mana Harvest I	Reach the Leyline within the mana cave. Time Remaining: 32 Days
No One Left Behind	Acquire Nightshade from the City Guard of Hardhearth.
I Speak For the Trees	???
Completed Quests	
What Plants Crave	Secure a water source for your farm and finish unlocking the farmer class.
Friend of Haven I	Rewards claimed! A Crate of Apple Bitters Recipe Card — Apple Bitter
Friend of Haven II	Prove yourself a friend of Haven. Enjoy the festival, break bread with the villagers, and embrace the custom of thankfulness.
Farming Class	3/3 Conditions Met!

	Class has been rewarded!
Failed Quests	
Home Sweet Home I	Due to unfortunate circumstances, you were unable to reclaim the Barn and Chicken Coop. You have managed to recover the Tool Shed.

Not doing so bad currently. I need to get back to that cave at some point, though. Just not today. For now, there was still a lot to do on the farm. He stood up and did his best to stretch out the kinks from lying on the floor all night. His body was killing him. He needed a bed— and soon. *Though... I need to not go quite so heavy next time. I could also use some more furniture. Definitely before winter comes.*

The tub, sink, and stove had been welcome additions to the house, but it was still uncomfortably empty. His footsteps echoed in the bare hallway as he went out to inspect the work they'd done the day before.

The house was looking a lot better. Daryl and Lyle had scrubbed the entire place clean of dust and grime, and Edd had patched the hole in the roof. Cid was pleased to see that the floors were actually pretty nice once the dirt was off them, and the walls were in pretty good shape. They could use a coat of paint, but the underlying structure was there.

Hm. Paint. That would be a good place to start. A painted house.

The idea was appealing. He could make his house— and every room in it— any color he wanted. He'd never had that power. The Guard dormitories were all the same sterile white.

Lord Vanstone felt it made them easier to clean.

But he had no idea what color they should be. He'd never decorated a house before. *I'll have to get someone's advice. Daryl, maybe. His place feels pretty homey.*

Or... Maggie.

Cid shook his head to get the thought out of it. Maggie had done a nice job with her tavern, but there was no way she'd want to help him decorate.

That reminded him. He fished her recipe cards out of his pocket and took them down to the kitchen along with his new crate of apple bitters. He'd have to figure out what to do with them.

Another thing on the list.

He didn't mind this one much, though. He'd been a bit annoyed when she'd first handed them off, but it might not be a bad thing for him to be able to brew his own beer. It would save him a long walk to the tavern on nights when he was too tired from work to move.

Well, he'd deal with that later. For now, his growing plants needed him. He headed out to the well and drank down half a bucket of cold water then headed out to the field.

His heart lifted as soon as he got there. His zucchini was growing quickly, and some of the shoots were already starting to sprout tiny leaves. The tomato plants he'd planted yesterday were already starting to emerge from the ground, too. Things grew fast here.

It's the Mana Cavern. Its energy makes things grow.

He knew he still needed to investigate that further on a day when he could give it his full attention. But that day was not today. For now, he had weeding to do— a lot of weeding. The Cavern made his plants grow quickly, but it also did the same thing for weeds. A nasty-looking vine was already snaking its way through the zucchini patch, threatening to kill his little plants before they had the chance to bear fruit.

He spent most of the morning tearing up weeds and tossing them into a heap next to his field. The pile was almost at waist height by the time he was done. Cid thought about using **[Earth 1]** but largely avoided it, except when he needed a little extra power to move some of the larger rocks he came across.

If I had a horse here, that bunch of weeds would be a nice treat for him.

He paused his work, feeling guilty. He'd meant to write Lord Vanstone about Nightshade last night, but he'd been distracted by Daryl's invitation. He'd have to write that letter today and figure out how to send it. His old horse deserved better than young Billy Bagwell.

Once he was done weeding, he set about watering his plants by pulling water from the well and carrying it over in a bucket. It wasn't an efficient process, and by noon, he was sweating.

I need to figure out how to make this easier.

The well was too far from the field for him to be able to get water to his crops quickly, and walking back and forth ate up a lot of time. Cid wondered if he could figure out a way to get a store of water closer in. A trough, maybe, that he could fill once a week. Or— even better— a little irrigation ditch that would ferry water from the stream into a pool next to the field.

He'd figure it out. For now, his work here was done, and he was pleased with the progress. He already had his eyes on the next field over. It was still fallow, untilled, and full of rocks, but it was on the south side of the hill and got a lot of sunlight. A perfect spot to plant— well, to plant something.

He'd have to ask Daryl what might grow well there the next time he saw him. Corn, maybe. Or wheat. He could try to talk to Roger, the baker, about supplying the bakery with fresh flour. That would be a good source of income for the farm.

But he was getting ahead of himself. In good spirits and whistling a jaunty tune, he left his crops to grow and headed back down toward the farmyard. The old barn was gone now — its remains were piled in a sad heap on the other side of the yard— but the dilapidated chicken coop was still standing next to the toolshed.

Maybe I can fix it up.

If he could source some chickens in town, they might do well in that little coop. He could build a run for them so they could get a little time outside to peck for bugs in the dirt. He'd heard that letting chickens eat bugs in addition to grain made their eggs taste better.

Eggs.

His stomach growled. It would be good to have eggs and an occasional roast chicken for dinner. That settled it, then. He'd work on the coop this afternoon.

It was in rough shape, though— even worse than the barn— and it was clear no hens had lived here for a very long time. Most of the wood was rotted almost all the way through, and two of the walls were so worm-eaten, it was a miracle they hadn't collapsed already.

"Well," Cid said aloud just to hear someone talk after a full day spent alone. "If I replace one wall at a time, maybe I can make it work."

No such luck. He stuck his head inside the coop to get a closer look, and as soon as he touched one of the walls, the whole structure collapsed around him just as the barn had.

"Damn," he said, looking sadly at the pile of rotten wood that had once been a hen house. He was unhurt— just a little surprised— but it was still a disappointment. It would be a while longer now before he could have fresh eggs for breakfast.

Well, there was one thing he could still do today, at least. Gritting his teeth, he dragged the remains of the chicken coop onto the pile the villagers had made of the wood from the collapsed barn. Then, he took his spellcasting stance. [**Fire 1**].

The wood was wet and soggy, and it took a while to catch, but finally a thin wisp of smoke emerged from the remnants of the barn roof. Cid focused all his attention onto it and poured his energy there.

Fire. Come on! Fire!

The wood caught, and in a few minutes, he was standing next to a large bonfire. It burned slowly and produced large quantities of foul-smelling smoke, but at least it was going. After a frustrating afternoon, it was nice watching the barn and coop go up in flames. Cid smiled as he felt the heat on his face. He'd hoped to fix up the existing buildings— but building something new, something that he could call his own, might be an even better plan.

And this is one way to get rid of old garbage.

It might not be the most efficient way of doing it, but it was very cathartic.

CHAPTER 34: RASPBERRY TART

It took a while for the fire to burn down, and Cid stood around until it did— partly because he enjoyed watching the flames and partly because he was worried a spark would jump and burn down his house if he wasn't monitoring it. It also helped that the heart of the fire was oddly soothing on his skin. It was a good moment to relax. Farming was hard work, but if he'd been afraid of hard work, he could have just taken his pension and tried something else. *I like working hard. Tilling the soil, moving things. Keeping my body strong. Limber.*

I always need to get my eye on that. That's why I'm here. I want to enjoy my life and be content. The thoughts trailed away, and Cid watched the fire. Once the blaze was out, he raked the ashes into a pile.

This might make good fertilizer.

He'd heard of ashes being used in barren fields, although it might be an old wives' tale. He didn't want to mess with his existing crops since they were already growing so well, but he could test them out on the next field he tilled and sowed. It would be a good experiment to see which did better: the plants that grew in ash-infused soil, or the normal one.

But enough for now. He'd done enough for the day, and the sun was hot. It was time for a swim— and time to see if any trout were sunning themselves in his fishing hole. He wanted to test out his new stove, and with no crops ready yet, there wasn't much else to eat but fish.

Cid's stomach growled. He was starving, and when he'd checked for the rest of the food Daryl had given him, Cid couldn't find it anywhere, but considering his state the previous night, Cid didn't count out the possibility that he might have eaten it already. Regardless, he didn't have any food, and it would be a while until he got any. He had to catch the trout and cook it before he could eat, and trout was what he was craving.

Now that I have that ice box, I should start getting some food stores ready.

It would be nice for times like this, when he'd done a full day of work and didn't have much energy left over to gather ingredients and cook. He didn't have much choice but to grit his teeth and do it for now, but if he could make his life easier in the future, he would.

Work done, he headed for the stream. As he pushed his way through the bushes, though, something caught on his shirt and scratched his forearm.

"Gaugh!" he shouted, holding his arm up to look at the damage. A thin line of blood ran from wrist to elbow. It didn't hurt much, but it was annoying. Something in this stand of bushes had thorns.

It was silly, but after the day he'd had, Cid wanted revenge. He tore through the undergrowth looking for the offending plant— and froze when he saw it. It was a tall bush with plump red berries hanging from every branch, and they looked delicious.

A raspberry bush.

"You weren't trying to attack me," Cid said. "You were trying to get my attention."

He knew it was ridiculous— it was a bush, not a person, and hadn't been 'trying' to do anything— but it made him feel better to think of it as having its own intentions. And who knew? Perhaps it did. After all, it had grown on top of a Mana Cavern. That might do something to plants— make them more intelligent or something. They might just be super delicious. Cid wasn't fully sure how it worked yet or how it affects everything around it.

"I'll come back to you," he said. He wasn't sure if he was imagining it, but it felt like the bush waggled its branches in acknowledgment.

I need a dog. I've been alone on this farm too long. I'm starting to see things that aren't there.

He was also seeing some things that *were* there, though: a large cluster of raspberry bushes exactly like the one he'd just encountered, every one of them covered in ripe fruit. His stomach growled again.

"You, too," he said. "All of you. I'll be back."

Swim first, eat, then... find a basket.

He checked his fishing hole and was pleased to see two fat trout swimming in circles inside it. They scattered when he kneeled down to take a closer look, and he took the moment to widen and deepen the pool, digging with his hands into the soft mud of the riverbank. Soon, he'd doubled the size of the hole. It was large enough now to fit five or six large fish inside of it.

Large enough, I think.

If it got any bigger, the sun wouldn't warm the water enough to attract the trout. They liked basking near the surface— which was good, because it made them easier to catch.

Job done, Cid moved down the stream away from the fishing hole so he wouldn't scare the fish away while he was swimming. Then, he stripped down and jumped into the cool water.

After a long, hot day in the sun, it was heaven. He spent a long time just splashing around, getting the grime off the fields off of his body. When he was done, he floated on his back for a few minutes, looking up at the fluffy clouds drifting across the sky above his head.

Perfect.

The day might not have gone exactly as planned, but he was still making progress. He liked having something to do, liked having a project to work on— even one as challenging as this one. There was still a long way to go, but he was starting to be more confident that Oak Tree Farm would be something to be proud of and provide for all of his needs. Every single day, he got one step closer.

His stomach growled again.

Okay, okay. Time to go.

He dried himself off and checked the fishing hole. The fish had come back, and he quickly pulled his fishing line from where he'd left it in the dirt and hooked one for dinner. Then, he slung the trout over his shoulder and made his way back toward the raspberry bushes.

"Dinner and dessert," he said.

Or I could try to whip up a raspberry sauce for the trout. Or mash it up as a glaze and rub it in.

He wasn't much of a chef, really, but he could do his best. After all, he was on his own now without the Guard's mess hall and the old cook around to make sure he was fed. He needed to be able to take care of himself, and part of self care wasn't just finding food, it was also making good food.

Well, for now, he was going to snack on the berries he'd found. They were delicious: perfectly ripe and sweet with just the barest tang to them, and he soon found himself shoveling them into his mouth by the handful.

Easy, easy. I don't want to choke. No need to rush.

He didn't want to eat them all at once, otherwise there wouldn't be any left for later. Plus, the bushes needed at least some berries left on them in order to seed more bushes. If he played his cards right, he could get a little raspberry operation going next to the stream.

He didn't have a bag, so he stripped off his shirt and dropped a small pile of berries into it, then he took both the fruit and the fish back to the house. Old Levi had been thoughtful and provided him with a small pile of firewood next to the stove, and he quickly got a fire going. He could have tried to use **[Fire 1]**, but it felt... unnatural to him. Then, he quickly gutted the fish and dropped it into a pan, covered it with a lid, and put it inside to cook.

It's a whole lot easier than trying to cook it in clay over an open fire.

That had been fun to do. He'd have to bring it back once in a while. But it was good to have an easier option now.

The top of the stove was warm from the fire, so Cid mashed up some of his berries into a makeshift sauce and put them into a little pot to simmer. It wasn't much of a recipe, but he'd see how it worked. There were still a few left over, and he snacked on them while he waited for the fish to cook. When he got to the bottom of the pile, he frowned. The fruit had stained his shirt with red juice.

I seriously need some new clothes.

He still had some time until the food was ready to eat, so he let his mind wander— and it kept returning to Roger, the baker. If Cid *was* able to grow wheat in his second field — and he'd have to ask Daryl if that even seemed possible— the bakery might be a good buyer for it. But he might have something for Roger to buy even sooner than that.

"These would be great on a tart," he said to himself as he popped the last raspberry into his mouth.

He'd have to have the baker over sometime soon to get his opinion on them— or maybe Cid could take him a bag next time he went into town if he could figure out a way to carry them without turning them into berry-flavored mush.

He could get Roger's advice, too. Cid knew he didn't have the faintest clue how to bake, and he knew that he'd need to learn how if he wanted to feed himself through the winter on Oak Tree Farm. Thoughts of cakes, cookies, and fresh-baked bread danced through his head. He could snack on his own baked goods while he wrote his book on long, cold nights when the fields didn't need to be tended to. *Or... I can make time to explore the mana cave.*

The delicious smell of baked fish and raspberry sauce rising from the stove jolted him back to reality. That was all for the future. For now, dinner was ready, and it was time to eat. Not a moment too soon, either. He was starving.

CHAPTER 35:
FARMERS MARKET

The fish was delicious— even the raspberry sauce, which he'd been a little skeptical about— and Cid ate it greedily before settling in for another night on the floor. After staying up late talking the night before and a full day of work, he slept like a rock even with the uncomfortable 'bed'.

He'd looked forward to sleeping in a little, but once again, he heard banging on the door before dawn. This time, he knew exactly who it was. He'd heard that particular knock before. It was almost a signature.

"What do you want, Lyle?" he asked, opening the window and looking out. The sun was still below the horizon, but he could see the lad standing on his porch in the gray pre-dawn light.

"Wake up, Cid!" Lyle shouted. "The farmers market is today!"

Cid yawned. "Huh?"

"Are you deaf or something?" The lad grinned. "It's the Haven farmers' market today. Are you coming?"

"I didn't realize the town had a farmers' market."

"We do. Every Saturday in Hopkins Square. Everyone— and I mean *everyone*— comes out for it. People sell all their stuff there. And sometimes, it's really good stuff!"

"Oh," Cid said. "Well, that sounds nice, Lyle. Thanks for letting me know. I'll come next week and check it out."

But the lad was already shaking his head. "My grandpa saved you a spot— and a good one, too. Right by the road. That's one of the places everyone always wants. He'll be upset if you don't show up, and so will everyone else who sees the space is empty."

Cid sighed. He'd been looking forward to a slow morning, but it didn't sound like he had much choice but to go. And it could be good for the future of Oak Tree Farm. If people liked his vegetables, they'd come back. Even if he could only provide a sample of what they'd get later, once the plants were finished growing, it would be worth it.

"Anyways," Lyle said. "If you want to sell anything, you need to have your stuff in town in an hour. The market doesn't last that long. Haven's not *that* big."

"Noted," Cid said. "And thanks, Lyle. It was really nice of you to let me know. And it was nice of your grandpa to save me a spot."

The lad beamed up at him. "We want you to like it here!"

He's a good kid.

"I owe you a favor," Cid said. "I'll pay you back. Promise."

"Cool!" Lyle said. "I'll remember that!"

And he was off running down the road toward town, his red hair flashing in the growing light. Cid watched him go, waiting until he was out of sight around the corner before closing the window.

He's a good kid, but I wonder what he's going to ask me to do as payback for the favor.

If there was one thing he'd learned about Lyle, it was that the lad often had some creative ideas— and 'creative' was a mild way of putting it.

He'd worry about that later. For now, he needed to get ready and figure out what he could sell at the market. It would take him about twenty minutes to walk into town. Ten more, maybe, to get his booth ready. That meant he had about half an hour to get dressed and gather whatever vegetables might be ready.

There's no way anything will be ripe yet. The zucchinis have only been in the ground for a couple of days.

Hopefully the Mana Cavern had done its work. If not, he'd have to improvise.

He got dressed in a rush, washed his face in the sink— he was pleased to see the water came out so hot it was steaming — pulled his boots on, and headed downstairs. The sun was peeking over the horizon by the time he reached the field, and he knew he didn't have much time.

Why did Daryl spring this on me?

Well, there was no knowing what the old man's motives were. For all he knew, he was doing it because he thought it was funny to see Cid scramble.

When he got close enough to see his crops, though, he was stunned. They weren't all fully ripe yet— not by a long shot— but to his surprise, several of the zucchini plants had produced vegetables. They were small still, but they'd be good for samples at his first outing to the farmers' market. He could take a few and leave the rest to grow.

Even more surprising was an unfamiliar shock of leaves sprouting in one corner of the field. They weren't tomatoes or zucchini, and they definitely weren't any of the weeds he'd seen yesterday. Cid bent down to take a look, trying not to get his pants dirty. He was going into town today, and he wanted to look presentable.

He dug up one of the strange plants and held it up in front of his face.

Turnips.

But he hadn't planted turnips. Where had they come from? They must have gotten mixed in with the other seeds Daryl had given him when he planted them. Well, however they'd gotten here, they were ready to harvest. He could take them along with the zucchinis and hopefully sell at least some of them.

Whistling and in good spirits, he headed back to the farmhouse and retrieved the empty seed bag Daryl had given him. The old man had told him he'd want to use it again someday, and he was right. He could carry his wares in it when he traveled to the market. It wasn't large— but then again, he didn't have that many crops. It would do for today.

Back in the field, he cut five small zucchinis from their plants, dropped them in the bag, then pulled up almost all the turnips, leaving just a few to keep growing in the corner of the field.

They grow quickly. They'll come back.

By the time he was done, his sack was almost full. He wouldn't be able to fill his stand at the market, but he'd have enough vegetables there that he wouldn't embarrass himself. That was progress, at least.

Enough dew had collected on his plants overnight that Cid probably wouldn't need to water them until the afternoon, so once he had his sack ready, he slung it over his back and headed toward town. Some mist was still rising off the damp road when he set out, but the rising sun was burning it away. It was going to be a hot day.

"Hey!" said a voice behind him. "Cid Dawnshield!"

It was Mary, one of the women who'd helped clean up the farm two days earlier. She was carrying a bag twice the size of Cid's with no apparent difficulty.

"You going to the farmers' market?" he asked, eyeing her bag. This was his competition.

"Yep! Got some fresh corn that just came in. People always love the corn from my farm— although I wish I had a little more space for it."

"Yeah?"

"Yeah. I'm working a tiny holding. It's my family's— passed down through the generations— but there are times I wish that my great-grandfather had thought to buy a little more land for us when he put it together. You know how it is."

Cid didn't, but he nodded as if he did.

"Oak Tree Farm, though," she said. "That's a gorgeous piece of land you have, Cid. Plenty of room for corn there. You planted any yet?"

"Not yet," he said, sighing. "I've got zucchini and turnips in this bag. There's a field I've got my eye on for corn, but it's in rough shape."

"I can imagine. That farm's been dead for years."

"So they tell me."

"We're all glad you came, Cid Dawnshield," she said, her expression softening. "Everyone in Haven. Your story last night was spectacular. And we're glad to see that farm being worked again. It was time."

"I really appreciated your help," Cid said earnestly. Then, he shifted his sack to the other shoulder. It was getting heavy, and he didn't have much time before he needed to be at the market.

She clocked him looking down the road toward Haven and grinned. "Aye. We both need to get going, don't we?"

"It's my first farmers' market. I don't want to be late."

"Nor do I. I'll race you there, Dawnshield."

"I think you'd win that race," he admitted.

"Maybe," she said. "Maybe not. But seriously, we're here for you. All of Haven wants this farm to succeed. And I think you'll find that we're a stubborn lot."

He grinned. "I've already figured that one out."

Before he could say anything else, Mary was walking down the road away from him at high speed with her sack of corn strapped to her back, bound for the market. Cid couldn't match her pace, but he walked a little faster just the same. It would be rude to show up late after Daryl had saved him a spot.

CHAPTER 35: BOOTS ON THE GROUND

Cid was breathing hard by the time he got to town. He'd tried to keep up with Mary, with no luck. She'd quickly pulled away from him and vanished into the distance.

How did she do that?

Maybe Haven's Mana-infused water gave its residents unnatural powers of strength and speed. It would be unusual but not unheard of.

He could hear the sound of hammering coming from around the corner. They must still be setting up the booths for the market. Cid looked down at his sack of vegetables, feeling a bit sheepish. He'd felt good about his wares when he'd set out that morning, but now, his bag felt small and a little pitiful. Hopefully he wouldn't embarrass himself in front of the townspeople today.

"Hey!"

He looked up. Daryl was striding toward him, beaming. The old man had clearly dressed up for the special day. He was wearing a long green coat with matching shoes and hat, and his hair was neatly combed, slicked back, and parted.

"Was I supposed to wear something nice?" Cid asked. His clothes were clean, at least, and free of dirt stains. But they weren't exactly fancy.

"No, no, lad, don't worry about it. We're just glad you're here. How was your journey in?"

"Not bad. Thanks for the invite. Hope this is enough."

Daryl glanced at Cid's bag, face neutral.

"Aye," he said finally. "I think that'll do. Truth be told, I wasn't expecting you to have even that. Things grow fast up where you are."

"They sure do," Cid said, looking down at his feet. He still didn't want to tell Daryl about the Mana Cavern.

I'll do it soon once I've had a little more time to explore it.

"Well, come with me, lad," the old man said, grinning again. "I'll show you around the market. You can see what everyone else is selling. Then, I'll help get you set up at your booth."

"About that," Cid said. "Lyle told me you got me a nice spot by the road. I don't— I don't have enough stuff to make much use of a really nice booth—"

But Daryl was already shaking his head. "Did he tell you that? Well, I suppose he was doing his best to get you to come. We can excuse the lad a little white lie. I got you *a* spot, lad. Can't promise it's a nice one. There are a lot of rules about these market booths, I'm sure you can imagine. Everyone's always fighting over the best ones. And people here have long memories."

"Oh," Cid said, relieved. Daryl had his back. At least he wasn't accidentally taking someone's spot and stepping into a minefield.

"Here," the old man said, leading him toward Main Street. The road had been blocked off with wooden sawhorses at either end, and it was a flurry of activity as everyone tried to get their booths set up in time for the market to start. "Now,

Maggie's got a spot at the end. You can see she got in early and made sure she was all ready. She's selling a pumpkin ale this week, I think. Not my taste, but some people like it."

"Sounds good," Cid said. Pumpkin ale wasn't really his taste either, but a new brew from Miss Maggie was surely worth a try.

"We've got a baking section on the other side," Daryl went on. "Roger's got the main stall, of course. But a lot of people in town do a little baking as a side business and bring things to sell here for extra money. And he's a good sport about it. Always tries everyone else's recipes, and sometimes even suggests some improvements."

"That's nice of him."

"He's a kind man, Roger. A bit lonely but kind."

"Aye?"

"Aye. His wife left him for a rival baker one town over a few years ago. She's still there, but he was never really the same after that."

"Oh," Cid said, taking a closer look at Roger. He was smiling as always, but there was something sad behind his eyes. "Poor guy."

"Ah well. We all have our hardships to bear. Anyways, over there's the butcher's. Not much there right now— mostly cured meats, chicken, and what's left of the spring lamb. Fall's the best season at his booth. Cheeses here. We don't really have a good cheese seller in town. Everyone just brings in what they were able to make from their own milk. And then finally, fruits and vegetables. It being summer, as you can see, there's a lot of fresh fruit set out."

Daryl looked at him as if he expected a response.

"It's very nice," Cid said. "The fruit looks good."

Hopefully people wanted zucchini.

He saw Mary setting up her booth next to an apple seller. She unloaded her bag onto the table, and a heaping pile of corn came out of it. It was impressive— and a little intimidating.

Hm.

He looked at his own sack and shrugged. He was never going to be able to compete with that. He'd just have to do his best and sell what he could with a smile.

"Let's go to your booth, lad," Daryl said. "I can help you get set up. Lyle and I built it this morning, so you won't have to worry about construction, at least. I'll take a look at what you've got to sell and see if I can arrange it so it looks appealing."

"It's mostly zucchini," Cid said. "And some turnips. They were a surprise."

The old man smiled. "Then you're doing well! The zucchini will be a hit this time of year. Turnips— well, we're a little early for them. But I'm sure they'll sell too. There's a lot you can do with a turnip."

"I'll take your word for it."

He followed Daryl to his booth, clocking his competition as he went. Everything looked delicious. It was clear Haven had a lively farming culture already.

"It's not much, lad," Daryl admitted. "But it'll do for a start."

The stall wasn't exactly in a plum spot for attracting customers. It was situated toward the back of the market where it wouldn't get much foot traffic, and it was small and dark. It didn't match Lyle's description at all.

"He said it would be near the road," Cid said. "I mean! I'm

not complaining! I just—"

"I'll have to have a talk with young Lyle," Daryl said. "I know he meant well. Just wanted to make sure you came out. But it's not right to mislead people like that."

"Oh. Well. It's really not that big a deal."

He didn't want the lad to get in trouble on his account.

"But look," the old man said. "I know it's plain and doesn't have much to draw the eye, but if you keep coming back to the market, we can fix it up. Decorate it."

Daryl looked so hopeful that Cid had to grin. "It's perfect. Honestly, my crops aren't that great yet either. The booth and I can improve together."

"That's the spirit, lad. Now, put your wares on the table, and we'll sort it out."

Cid did as he was asked, and to his relief Daryl nodded approvingly.

"Zucchinis are small but good quality," he said. "In a few weeks, they'll be looking nice. And the turnips are turnips. You can't mess up a turnip, lad. You'll do well today!"

"Thanks," Cid said. "Let's hope so."

"Now, where's that boy?"

Right on cue, Lyle appeared, pushing his way through the crowd. His hair showed up first. It was so red, it almost glowed in the bright morning light.

"There you are," Daryl said when he got to the booth. "Now, can you help arrange these vegetables on the table while I go get something for Cid? And don't tell him what it is. I want it to be a surprise."

Without waiting for a response, he vanished into the

market. Lyle looked up at the table.

"Nice wares," he said.

Cid crossed his arms. The lad crossed his arms right back.

"Nicest booth in the market?" Cid asked.

Lyle looked a little abashed. "I wanted you to come."

"You shouldn't have lied. That might get you into trouble someday."

"It wasn't a lie. Not *really*. It could be the nicest booth in the market if we all fixed it up a little bit. And I think it will be. Grandpa's got something nice for you, and I'm sure he'll have more stuff next week."

"Okay," Cid said. "I'll give you that. But— close to the road? We're way in the back. There are three rows of stalls ahead of us."

"That's still close to the road," Lyle said stubbornly. "It's closer to the road than my house. Or Oak Tree Farm. It's technically true."

He had to laugh. "Alright. You'll be a lawyer someday, mark my words."

The lad made a face. "A lawyer? Boring. All they do is sit around all day. I told you, I want to be an adventurer. Or a Magic Knight."

"Stick to being an adventurer. The Corps isn't an easy life."

Lyle looked like he was about to protest, but Daryl showed up again before he could say anything. Cid quickly rearranged the turnips on the table to make it look like they'd been doing something while the old man was gone.

"Looks good, lad," he said when he got to the booth, fixing his piercing gaze on the pile of vegetables. "The arrangement makes it seem like you have more wares than you actually do."

"That was definitely intentional," Cid said.

"Here. look at this."

Daryl was carrying an old wooden sign under one arm, and he set it gently on the table. The paint was peeling a little, but it looked nice. A little bit vintage.

"Oak Tree Farm," Cid read. "What's this? You've clearly had it for a while."

"Years. Since the last owner. Well— not Old Talley. He was never really that into farming. I hope he likes his beach, though. The man before that."

"You knew him, then."

"Lad, this town's not that big. Of course I knew him. Stole the sign when Talley took the place over. Not my finest moment, but I was worried he'd throw it away. I've held on to this thing for— oh, years it must be. Almost threw it away a few times, but something made me hold on to it. Now, I'm glad I did."

"It's a nice sign," Cid said.

"It's yours if you want it, lad. We can hang it out in front of your booth. Hopefully, it'll attract a few customers. People still remember how it was at Oak Tree back in the day. Not young folks like Lyle, here. Us old timers."

"What was it like?"

"Oh, fun and merriment. In between bouts of hard work, of course. The man who owned the place was called Bevin. We grew up together. Everyone in Haven knew him. And— well

— Bevin liked a party. Couldn't find anyone more generous, either. He'd give you the shirt off his back if he knew you had a need for it."

"Where did he go?" Cid asked.

Daryl's face fell. "He died, lad. A long time ago. But I kept his sign."

"Oh."

He felt like a total jerk for asking the question. *Should have seen that one coming.*

"I love the sign," Cid said. "It's perfect for the booth. Maybe it'll make people think of the old days."

"Let's hope so," Daryl said, climbing on top of the table full of turnips. "Here, hand it to me, will you? I'll tie it up here. There we go."

They both stood back to admire the sign. It did give his booth a little extra draw.

"It's perfect, Daryl. Thank you."

"Oh, it was nothing, lad. Just glad you could use it. Now, we need to talk about what you're going to charge for these vegetables."

"Uh," Cid said. He had no idea what a fair price was. "Advise me?"

"Well, how much are you looking to make from the market today?"

"Uh," Cid said.

"Alright, let's start at the very beginning. Baby steps. How much money do you have, lad?"

"Uh," Cid said again, looking down at his feet. "Well, to be honest, Daryl. I don't have much."

"How much, exactly?"

"Um. None. I don't have any money at all. I got a little gold when I retired, but I spent it all on the farm."

Daryl laughed. "That so? Well, you're dedicated, that's for sure. I can respect it."

"I really need to sell something today," Cid said, trying to push his zucchinis together so it looked like he had more of them. "Otherwise, I won't be able to keep fixing things up."

"You'll be alright, Dawnshield. Never you worry. Just do your best. You might not come home with a treasure chest full of gold, but you're sure to make something."

"You think so?"

"Aye. Remember, Haven wants you to succeed. We all miss old Oak Tree, and we're glad to see it being worked again. I wouldn't be surprised if people make a point of stopping here just to pick up a turnip or two and drop a coin in your bag."

"Let's hope so."

Daryl picked up a turnip and weighed it expertly in one hand.

"I think a bronze coin each would be enough," he said. "For these, and for the zucchinis too. It's a fair price. A little on the cheap end, even. I think with that rate, you'll get some good business."

"Got it."

Cid had no idea what a fair price was for a turnip, so he'd just have to trust the old man's judgement. Daryl pulled a small chalkboard out of his cloak and wrote "Turnips and Zucchinis — One Bronze Each" on it in a careful hand. Then, he leaned it up against the side of the booth where people could see it.

"Alright," he said. "People are showing up to the market

now. We'll see how many come over this way."

Cid quickly took a count of his wares. Six little zucchinis and thirty-four turnips. If he was able to sell them all, he'd earn forty bronze coins.

Whether he could drum up that much business, though, remained to be seen. He set his face in a big smile as the market started to fill up. Whatever happened today, it wouldn't hurt to look friendly.

CHAPTER 36: THREE BRONZE RESERVED

Cid watched nervously and subtly rearranged the turnips on his table as the market started to fill up with people. With so many stands full of lush vegetables, would anyone want to buy what he was selling? He could only hope.

"Don't worry, lad," Daryl said, laughing. "It'll be fine."

But he didn't relax until he sold his first turnip to an old man with a long gray mustache.

"This is Perkins," Daryl said. "A sign painter. Perkins, Cid Dawnshield."

The old man looked up at him with rheumy eyes. "Dawnshield. Where have I heard that name before?"

"He just bought Oak Tree Farm."

"Oh!" Perkins said, smiling broadly. He was missing a few teeth— but only a few. "I painted that sign you've got there, my boy. Was— oh, about a million years ago."

"Feels like it," Daryl said. "Speaking of, might be due for a touch-up."

"Huh?"

"On the sign. Paint's peeling."

"Oh," Perkins said. "Sorry, Daryl. My hearing's not as

good as it once was. I think I can manage the sign, though. Dawnshield, will you be back here next week?"

"I think so," Cid said. "If my crops keep growing."

"Make sure of it. I'll bring some paint for the sign. And here."

Perkins dropped another turnip in his bag and set a second bronze coin on the counter. "I'll take another to help bring Oak Tree back."

He was gone before either of them had time to thank him, blending seamlessly into the crowd as if he'd never come to the booth at all.

"He moves fast," Cid said. "For an old man like that."

"Hm?" Daryl said, looking back at him blankly. "Oh. Well, maybe. Perkins was always ahead of the game."

It was a weird response, but he didn't have time to let it trouble him. His booth was already attracting a lot of attention, and he was soon overwhelmed with customers. He greeted each one with a smile and a little speech about how much he liked it here in Haven, and most of them bought something— even if it was just a single turnip. His pile of wares was diminished by half in about fifteen minutes, and the crowd showed no sign of slowing down.

"See?" Daryl said, looking pleased. "I told you. People want to buy what you've got. Not to overpraise myself, but I think the sign made a difference."

Cid grinned. Three people had already commented on it that morning, even without his doing anything to draw their attention to it.

"It sure has," he said. "And it'll look even better once Perkins has had the chance to paint it."

He was even starting to get into the patter that came with being a merchant.

"I've got raspberries, too," he said to the next customer that came in, trying it out. "Bushes full of them."

"Fresh trout," he said to the one after that. "Fat and juicy. I'll bring some next time."

"You'll have to, at that," Daryl said. "I love trout, lad."

The promise of raspberries and trout seemed to meet with a good response, so he turned to the next person in line ready to advertise both— and froze.

It was Miss Maggie.

"Hey!" he said, sounding just a little too enthusiastic. "Here for some turnips?"

She was clearly trying not to laugh. "Was actually hoping to look at your zucchini. How's it growing?"

"Right. Right. It's right there."

He gestured to the small pile of young zucchini on the table, and she took a look.

"They weren't ready to be harvested yet, Dawnshield," she said. "They're still a little small. But good effort just the same. I'll take one."

She dropped a coin on the table and tucked a zucchini into her pocket.

"Thanks," he said, pocketing the bronze. "How's business?"

"Things are going well over at my ale stall," she said. "Left Mary in charge for a few minutes while I checked out the rest of the market. Think we'll be sold out soon."

"That's great," Cid said.

"I can set a growler aside for you if you like. Three bronze."

He felt how many coins were in his pocket already— a good number. "I think I can afford that."

"Great. I'll pick one out for you. You know, your zucchinis are pretty big already considering you just started planting. They can't have been in the ground more than a few days. What's the secret?"

Probably the Mana Cavern.

"Um," Cid said. "I'm not sure. I'll try to figure it out after I learn more about farming."

"Keep growing."

And with that, she was gone, vanishing just as quickly as Perkins had. *How did she do that?*

Cid frowned. Something felt strange today. Mary's super-speed on the road, townspeople appearing and disappearing out of nowhere... What was going on? He'd spent enough time in the Guard to know when something strange was happening.

Relax. You're being paranoid.

Lack of sleep was making him see things that weren't there. That was it. He was in sleepy Haven now, not Hardhearth. There was nothing going on here at all— and that was a good thing.

He spent the next hour focused on selling his turnips and what was left of the zucchini, making a decent profit. Daryl had been right. It felt like almost everyone in town came through the booth at some point to buy something. Speaking of:

"You seen Lyle, lad?" the old man asked, popping up in

front of the counter with a turnip in his hand. "Also, I'll buy this."

"You can have it for free, Daryl—"

"Absolutely not. I'm the Village Elder. Not only am I on salary, I also set an example for everyone in town. I'll be paying my share."

Defiantly, as if daring anyone to argue with him, he dropped a bronze coin on the table.

"Thanks," Cid said. "And no, I haven't seen Lyle. He ran off a few minutes ago while I was dealing with a customer— thought he was looking for you—"

He was interrupted by shouting coming from Main Street, and he and Daryl left the booth at once, pushing through the crowd toward the source of the noise.

"It's Lyle," the old man said, teeth gritted. "I know it."

He was right. The lad was standing at the center of a cluster of shrieking children, fists raised high to cover his face. He was facing off against a much larger lad with a mean-looking face and a close-cropped haircut. Before Cid could reach him, Lyle rushed at his opponent, swinging his arms wildly, and the spectators cheered.

"Kids!" Cid shouted, wading into the crowd. "What are you doing? Knock it off!"

The crowd watching scattered, but Lyle kept trying to fight until Cid physically pulled him off the other boy. He was bleeding from a scrape on his forehead.

"No fighting!" Cid said, setting the lad down on his feet but holding him back.

"You're never gonna see your mom again, because she's dead!" the other lad said, sticking out his tongue before running away into the crowd. Cid waited until he was fully gone before letting go of Lyle's arm.

"What were you doing?" he asked. "Is that the kind of thing your grandpa would want you doing?"

"Definitely not," Daryl said, looking exhausted. "You'll be the death of me, boy. I swear it."

"That's Tommy Crawford," Lyle said, wiping some of the blood and dirt off his face. "He's a bully and a terrible person."

Daryl shook his head. "That's not something we should be saying about other villagers—"

"You heard what he said, Cid! You heard! About my mom being dead and all. He's been saying stuff like that all day for no other reason than to be mean. I couldn't take it anymore!"

Cid sighed. "Yeah. That was pretty bad. But take it from me, Lyle. Fighting with him isn't going to solve anything. At least not on the street like this. Maybe we can talk to his parents and get them to intervene."

Lyle looked at his grandfather imploringly.

"Aye," Daryl said, looking grave. "I'll see what I can do. Now, boy, let's get you cleaned up."

Daryl and Lyle moved off toward the river to wash his face, and Cid headed back to his booth. The situation seemed as settled as it could be for now, but it was troubling just the same. The lad didn't seem to have many friends in town, plus something about the way the other villagers had been acting all day felt off to him— as if there were something going on that he wasn't aware of. As if they were keeping a secret.

Stop it, Dawnshield. You're being paranoid. And it's not like you don't have enough secrets of your own.

His thoughts turned, once again, to the Mana Cavern.

Maybe it was time to come clean about it at last.

Soon.

He sold the rest of his wares, counted his money, packed his booth up, and headed home. He'd made forty bronze coins, and they jingled in his pocket all the way back to Oak Tree. Three were reserved for Maggie's ale, but that left plenty for seeds. He'd have to return the following week and see if he could turn even more of a profit.

CHAPTER 37: TURNIPS, OR TURNIPS

Cid slept late the next day, and to his relief, no one came banging on his door this time. The sun was high in the sky by the time he rolled off his bedroll, stretched, and headed downstairs to make breakfast.

Let's see... turnips? Or turnips?

He'd held back some of the less attractive vegetables, the ones that he didn't think would sell, for his own use. Now, he retrieved them from the cellar, lit the stove with **[Fire 1]**, and popped them in to cook.

Should have gotten some wares at the market. Some other things to eat. Or at least some seasoning.

Well, lesson learned. He'd have to be smarter about that next week. For now, turnips it was. At least this would be better than the road rations he'd been stuck with his first week on the farm.

While he was waiting, he pulled out his bag and counted his money again. Forty bronze coins exactly. He'd sold everything. He knew it was a small victory, but it was still worth celebrating. Three were Maggie's— he'd have to pick up his growler of ale next time he was in town; another thing he'd forgotten— but the other thirty-seven were his to invest as he liked.

What does this place need?

Well, furniture, for starters. But thirty-seven bronze wouldn't be enough to buy much of that. He'd have to set his sights smaller and simpler.

Something outside the window caught his eye. Sunlight glowed on one of his untilled fields, currently full of weeds and crabgrass. The one he'd looked at the earlier, thinking it would be perfect for corn.

Could probably get some seeds with this money.

Corn seeds went cheap in these parts, or so he'd heard. He could get enough to plant at least half the field. And as for the other half— well, hadn't he heard old Mary complaining about the small size of her farm just yesterday morning? He could invite her to plant the other half, charge her rent— an affordable price, of course— and bring in a little extra income for both of them.

It was a win-win plan, and he grinned. Now, he was starting to think like a farmer and a businessman instead of a Guard. He'd run the idea by Mary next time he saw her and see what she said. Hopefully, she'd agree.

With his next steps settled, he pulled his roasted turnips out of the stove and dug in. They were a little bland but not as bad as he'd expected.

Must be the Mana Cavern.

He knew that he couldn't give the Mana Cavern credit for *every* good thing that happened on the farm. Some of it was probably just luck or his own hard work, but it did seem like it was contributing to his success in some way.

As he ate, he drafted a letter to Lord Vanstone.

Dear Commander Vanstone...

He frowned. No. That's not right.

Too informal.

To Commander Vanstone...

Too impersonal. The man had been his commander for twenty years.

Commander Vanstone—

Good. Short and to the point. The Lord would like that.

Hope all is well in Hardhearth. I'm settling in well on Oak Tree Farm, and I have a boon to ask. I'm sure you remember my old horse Nightshade— the sour one who hated being saddled. Best horse in the Guard. I know he's getting old, and I'm sure you're thinking of retiring him in the next few years. I've got a job for him here— and I'm willing to pay you....

He trailed off. What did a horse cost?

...double what a horse of that age might be worth if you'll let me take him off your hands. He can't be much use to the Guard now anyways. Remember when he bit Pierre in the shoulder?

I hope you'll consider my request,

Cid Dawnshield.

He signed the letter with a flourish and set down his quill.

There. Done.

He'd send it off the next time he had the opportunity. Hopefully Lord Vanstone would give it some thought.

With that done, he wolfed down the rest of his turnips and headed out to the fields. He spent the first part of the morning watering and weeding his existing plants and checking to see how things were growing. The zucchinis had grown a lot since yesterday morning, and the turnips had spread to an entire corner of the field. The tomatoes were growing a little more slowly, but they were already close to knee height. He'd have a good harvest for next week's farmer's market— and hopefully make more money next time.

Next, he moved on to the field he hoped to plant next and worked **[Earth 1]** to till the soil, cleared out any large rocks, and broke up the dirt clods that might keep his corn from thriving. It was a large plot of land, and he knew he would likely need another day or two to get it ready. His basic level Earth spell didn't cover the entire field. But it was worth starting now. Hopefully by the next time he went into town, he'd be ready to buy seeds and sow.

"Well done, lad!"

Cid spun around and almost shouted aloud.

Daryl Nightgreen was standing behind him, leaning up against the dilapidated fence that surrounded the field. He looked impressed.

"Sorry to startle you," he said. "I brought Lyle, and we weren't exactly quiet coming in. Figured you would have heard us, but I guess you were lost in thought."

"I'm still new to the magic thing," Cid admitted. "If I'm trying to work a spell, I don't have a ton of attention to spare. And with **[Earth 1]**, I have to focus on the objects I'm clearing out."

He felt a little foolish talking of magic to a mage as skilled as Daryl, but to his relief, the old man nodded.

"Aye. I know what you mean. And believe me when I say, lad, that the basic spells take the longest to master. It's because the entire concept is new to you— and working magic is strange indeed if you're not used to doing it. Have faith. It only gets easier from here."

"Thanks, Daryl."

Cid looked over his field. His work here wasn't finished, but he'd done well. About a third of the plot was fully tilled and ready for planting. Not a bad place to break off, at least for a little while. He sat down next to Daryl in the grass and stretched his legs out long in front of him.

"I brought you something from Maggie," the old man said, pulling a growler full of ale out of his sack. "And let me tell you, lad, she's none too pleased that you forgot to pick it up from her yourself."

Cid groaned. "I was hoping she wouldn't remember."

"Then you'd be hoping for a long time. Our Maggie doesn't miss a trick."

"Well, don't leave before I give you some money to pay her."

"Lad," Daryl said. "I think you might do well to pay her yourself."

Cid looked up at him, but the old man's expression was inscrutable. "Alright," he said finally. "I will."

"I brought you a few things, too, since I know your crops aren't ready yet. You can pay me when we get back to the farmhouse. Don't worry, lad, I've noticed you don't like taking things for free, and I respect it. So you'll pay the Haven rate, and we'll call that fair."

"Good," Cid said. "I don't want to take advantage of anyone."

"They're gifts, lad, but I understand. And speaking of gifts, why don't you use your magic more often? I've been watching you work for a bit now, and until you tilled that field, you did everything by hand. Why? You could make your life a whole lot easier if you did it by spellcraft."

Cid shrugged. "I don't know. I like the honest work. I'm used to it after a life in the Guard. The sweat on my skin, feeling my muscles ache. I'm not in a hurry. I'm retired now. This is the rest of my life, and I'm enjoying it."

The old man nodded. "Aye. I can respect that too, and I understand it. Well, as long as you know that your magic is there in a pinch if you really need it, I think you'll do fine. This farm is big, but you're keeping it well."

Cid grinned. The compliment meant a lot coming from the Village Elder.

"Now, I didn't just come here to give you things and chit chat," Daryl said, face grave. "There's something we need to discuss. Now, I'm sure you might have noticed that things were a little odd yesterday."

"I did. But I thought it was all in my head."

"No, lad, it was real. We've all talked, and I'm here to tell you what's going on. But let's go inside the house first. Lyle's about, and I wouldn't want him to hear some of what I have to say."

CHAPTER 38:
THE OTHER SIDE
OF A CLIFF

Cid was apprehensive as they walked back toward the house together. What secret could possibly be so terrible that the old man wanted to keep it from his own grandson? Had he made a horrible mistake in moving to Haven?

Daryl laughed when he saw his face. "Easy, lad. It's nothing terrible. I just don't want the lad to hear anything that might hurt his feelings, is all."

"Ah," Cid replied, still feeling uneasy

He followed Cid into the house and into the living room — although without any furniture, there wasn't anything to differentiate it from any of the other rooms.

"Do you want to sit down?" Cid asked.

"On the floor, lad?" Daryl asked, making an exaggerated motion with his knees.

"Aye. There aren't any chairs," Cid apologized. "Haven't been able to get any yet. Seems like every time I try to work on my farm to make a little extra, something always comes up."

Daryl shrugged but didn't say anything to that. Instead, the old man just had a sly smile on his face. Slowly, knees cracking, Daryl lowered himself onto the hard wooden floor. Cid watched him descend, feeling guilty.

I might have to help him get back up, Cid realized.

"Um, do you want some turnips?" Cid offered. "I could roast a few—"

"No, no," Daryl said, unlatching his bag and starting to pull things out of it. He'd brought good cheese and a loaf of bread, some corn from Mary's stand, and a few other vegetables of various types. It was enough to feed Cid for a few days until the rest of his crops ripened. "I've got better. If you have a knife, lad, we can cut into this bread now and have a little snack. You can pay me back when I'm on my way out or by listening to what I have to say."

A knife was one of the few things Cid *did* have, and he passed it over to the old man to cut into the bread. Soon, they were feasting on thick slabs of brown bread topped with creamy cheese. It was delicious, and Cid took a mental note to ask Roger for the recipe if he was ever able to grow his own wheat on Oak Tree. *Or... I can buy flour, I'm sure.*

"Your house is a bit empty, lad," Daryl said, chewing on a mouthful of bread. "It's a bit of a distraction. You should try doing something about that. I'll ask my missus if we have anything we can spare."

"Thank you" Cid responded, not wanting to get into it with Daryl about his wife not being around anymore. "You think? You should see the bedroom. I just sleep on my bedroll directly on the floor."

"Were you thinking of getting some furniture at some point?" Daryl asked pointedly. "Men shouldn't live like this forever."

"It's on my list," Cid said. "But I don't honestly know where to get it. And I've been so focused on getting the farm up and running, even that hasn't been a priority. I keep getting interrupted."

"So, you've just been living like this? We have our ways here in Haven," Daryl looked almost offended.

"Well, I wouldn't exactly call it 'misery'—" Cid started to respond.

"I would! Can you imagine? Sleeping on a hardwood floor?" Daryl laughed "That has to be hard on your back. I know I'd hate it."

"I mean, I—" Cid struggled to find an answer.

Daryl shook his head. "My missus would not appreciate this at all."

Cid paused for a moment to take that in. *It must be getting worse. That's the second time he's slipped up.*

"Are you ok?" Cid asked pointedly.

"Sorry. I mean, when she was alive," the old man said, recovering quickly. "She wouldn't have liked it. Wouldn't have allowed it, in fact. And neither will I. We'll get you some furniture, lad. Don't you worry about it."

Cid protested. "Daryl, I really can't accept any more gifts —"

"Not to worry. I know you have your pride, Cid Dawnshield, so it's not a gift this time. But I won't accept coin in exchange for the goods. I'll ask your help with a favor, instead— how's that?" Daryl offered.

Cid blinked. This was a strange way of doing business. But he guessed that that was how things were done in a small town like Haven. *Pushy, this lot.*

"I think that should be all right," he said, a little hesitantly. It would be just like Daryl to ask a tiny favor in exchange for the furniture— something that wouldn't even come close to covering the cost of the goods. The old man was really too generous.

"Done," Daryl said, smiling. "Then we have a deal. I'll help you here, Cid, and in exchange you'll help me solve a problem I've been having. I can't tell you what it is until we shake on it."

This time, Cid didn't hesitate. He held out his hand, and Daryl clasped it firmly. His handshake was surprisingly strong coming from such an old man, but more than that, a sort of magic power seemed to emanate out of the man as if sealing the deal between them. "But I also want to know what's going on. The thing you brought me in here to talk about. I didn't forget!"

"Aye, lad," Daryl said. "I didn't forget it either, lad. It's all part and parcel of the same issue."

"Then we're set," Cid replied, "You've done nothing but help me, Daryl, ever since I first came to town. I'd help you with your problem even without the furniture. Even if you didn't give me anything in exchange, you've more than earned it. Just tell me what you need, and consider it done. I consider you a friend Daryl. It's fine, really."

Daryl raised his free hand into the air and made a series of complicated gestures, and glowing silver ropes appeared out of nowhere to bind their hands together.

"Don't panic, lad, they'll be gone in a moment. I just cast **[Covenant]** to make our agreement binding. I trust you, don't worry, but this goes beyond trust. This is just an extra safety precaution. You learn to be very careful when you're a Village Elder, especially in a town so far from anything else." Daryl explained

"What happens if I break the agreement?" Cid asked.

"Oh, nothing bad. You'll just have trouble sleeping, be stressed out and anxious, that sort of thing. Until you fulfill the terms," Daryl responded, not quite looking Cid in the eye.

"Alright." He didn't love having magic worked on him without warning, but he supposed it was for a good cause. Or at least, he hoped it was. "What do you want me to do?"

Daryl clasped his hand tightly. "My boy's in trouble, and I need you to help sort it out."

"Lyle?" Cid replied. "What's wrong?"

He was a bit headstrong, true, and the fistfight at the fair had been a rough moment, but Cid had a hard time imagining the lad in serious trouble. He seemed pretty self-sufficient. But surely Daryl knew more about the topic than he did.

"Consider it done, then," Cid said. "If you can give me more details about what the problem is, I'll do whatever I can to help. It'll be a matter of honor to me."

Daryl nodded, and the glowing ropes vanished into thin air. He let go of Cid's hand and cut a thick slice of bread. "Want some? I've got a tale to tell you."

"Sure," Cid replied, feeling like they were wasting time.

The old man gave him a slice and rearranged his bag so he could lean against it, making himself comfortable. "Now, lad, I'm sure you've noticed some strange things around these parts. Not sure how much you've seen, and I know you've been busy getting the farm ready, but maybe you've encountered one or two things that have been a bit unusual?"

Cid chewed his bread and thought back to what he'd seen. Old Mary walking under what appeared to be [Haste], carrying a bag heavier than she should have been able and leaving him in the dust. Townspeople using advanced magic and occasionally appearing and disappearing at will. The whole issue with the Leyline, and they'd all seemed like they'd been hiding something yesterday.

"Yes," he said slowly. "There have been a few things. But I thought it was because—"

He paused. He'd been about to say that he'd thought it was because of the Mana Cavern. But he wasn't sure he wanted to give that away yet.

Daryl gave him a look then went on. "Aye. You're a sharp lad, so I'm not surprised you clocked it. The truth is, Haven's a bit of a special place. We're not a typical town. And there's a reason we're so far out here in the middle of nowhere, far from civilization. See, the village is made up of the families of Magic Knights and retired Magic Knights. More retired than current these days, though as I'm sure you can guess, a few of us are still considered to be in a reserve status. None of us are as young as we once were. Been that way for years. We traditionally don't let anyone else in. Haven has been exclusive for a long time."

"I'm not a Magic Knight," Cid said, feeling like he was stating the obvious. "I just bought the land."

"Aye." Daryl laughed and interupted. "We don't know to talk more about that one. There was quite a bit of controversy about letting you into the village among the decision makers, I can tell you that. You might have bought it, but we weren't forced to sell it to you. Prestique wasn't quite enough."

"Oh, sorry," Cid said, not sure how to take the news.

"No need to apologize, lad. You did nothing wrong. In the end, there were a few points in your favor. First, we really needed someone here to take over Oak Tree Farm. It's a shame it's sat empty for so long. Second, I've been thinking, privately, that it's a shame we've isolated ourselves so much. I've wanted to try to bring a non-Knight for a while, just to shake things up a bit. Somebody that didn't have magic all of their life. Third, your character. You're clearly a hardworking lad, and I like drinking with you."

"Thanks," Cid said.

"Of course. And fourth, you came with a letter of recommendation," Daryl threw out.

"A— what? From Lord Vanstone?"

"No, lad. He's an important man to some circles, but we don't take much notice of nobles like him in these parts. Your friend Bran wrote you a reference and sent the letter on ahead of you. He's got a lot of pull in the Magic Knights," Daryl explained.

"He did?" He'd have to buy Bran a drink— or six— the next time he saw him.

"Aye. That was what made the real difference, truth be told," Daryl admitted, "The people here like and trust Magic Knights, and Bran's one of the most powerful Battlemages in the country. A Knight Errant too as you know. That's a powerful person to have on your side."

"I had no idea he did that," Cid said. "That's—"

"He said he wanted you to have a good adventure and a peaceful retirement. His words were enough for me. And I have to say, lad, I'm glad you came." Daryl continued, "I think letting you in was one of the better decisions I've made in my time as Village Elder. I truly do."

Daryl paused, and Cid took a moment to process what he'd just heard. He was living in a town full of current and former Magic Knights who'd chosen to isolate themselves from the rest of the world. It wasn't the weirdest thing he'd encountered, but it was close. Still, it was nice to know the truth. The explanations he'd made up for yesterday's strangeness had been far more sinister than the real thing.

"Which brings me to Lyle," Daryl went on. "I know I told you a story about how his parents disappeared, lad, but I wasn't telling you the whole truth. Sorry for that. Wasn't sure if I could trust you yet. Lyle's parents were killed, but not by highwaymen. They were Magic Knights, and it takes more than a common scoundrel to take down a Magic Knight. They were on a mission to a kingdom far to the west— the Kingdom of White Lions on the other side of the long mist. But on their way there, they were beset by Dark Magi. They fought bravely, I'm sure. They were powerful Knights, Lyle's parents, but in the end, they were killed. That's how I ended up raising the boy."

"So Lyle's…?" Cid asked.

"Latest in a long line of Magic Knights, but he doesn't have the talent like they did," Daryl said. "It's a lot of pressure on a lad. And those were hard times, too, when the king fell."

"I remember. A lot of deaths around those times," Cid responded.

"Aye. Bad bit of business, that was," Daryl continued.

When the king had fallen, a great plague of feral undeath had spread throughout the land— particularly in the western kingdoms. Hardhearth had been mostly spared, but he'd heard stories and seen the terrified villagers on the road fleeing the Undead.

"And all the adventurers, remember?" Daryl asked, looking misty-eyed. "In the Guild. I was retired from the Corps by then, but we still got the reports. They lost a lot of their number when there was all that business with the Dark Lord up in the Dreadmoore. But they didn't let it stop them. They fought back, mourned all the S Rankers they'd lost, and cheered on their new Guildmaster."

"Yeah?" Cid said. He dimly remembered all of this

happening, but he'd been in the thick of his service in the Guard back then and had had more pressing things to worry about than the problems of another Kingdom.

"Well, anyways," Daryl started again with a shrug. "It was a strange and chaotic time. And we only got garbled reports of it out here. The western kingdoms didn't concern us much at the time. All I— all we— cared about was the effect all that fighting had on us, on Lyle's parents, and most of all, on my grandson."

Cid spread a thick layer of cheese onto another slice of bread and took a bite. "And?"

Daryl sighed. "Well, I've told you the lad's parents were Magic Knights."

"Yes, and?" Cid prompted him, feeling like the other shoe was close to dropping.

"And that I was a Magic Knight as well," Daryl said.

"Yep, I remember," Cid replied. *He's repeating himself a bit. I wonder if his memory is acting up.*

"So he's the heir to a proud legacy. A family tradition, even. The Nightgreen family is famous— both in town and in the Corps," Daryl explained, "People here have been watching him since he was born, waiting to see where his talent was and how he'd use it."

"Wow," Cid said, feeling suddenly sorry for the boy. "That's a lot of pressure."

This explained a lot about Lyle, actually: the chip on his shoulder, his slightly tempestuous personality, and all the time he seemed to spend by himself. If everyone was constantly watching his every move to see what he'd do next, it made sense that he'd be wary of others.

"It *is* a lot of pressure," Daryl said. "I know I said he

doesn't have the talent of his parents, but that's not really correct. Everything is made worse by the fact that Lyle doesn't have any magic."

Cid blinked. "What?"

"Not a drop. Whatever powers the Nightgreen family may have, they seem to have skipped a generation. We've tried everything. You can imagine how hard it's been for him. Everyone else in Haven is a mage— literally every other person in town— except him."

"Wow," Cid said. "That must be devastating."

"I can't say how Lyle feels about it. He never discusses it at all. You know how he is. But I do worry about the lad. It keeps me up at night, it really does. Know that I've tried everything I could think of to awaken any magical abilities he might have. I had hoped that maybe they were just dormant, buried."

"And?" Cid asked, already knowing the answer.

"Nothing. We even used the Magic Knight Seal. Well, I used it. Held it over his head while he was sleeping. Tried it on his arm too. Not a hiss, not a burn. Nothing. Nothing happened. If he'd had any magic— any magic at all— that would have done the trick. When even that didn't work, I knew it was done." Daryl sounded defeated.

Cid looked down at the floor. The lad must have had a rough time of it here.

"I know he's a bit of a handful," Daryl said. "But I feel for the lad, I really do. His parents die, leaving him an orphan, and to make matters worse, he can't even avenge their deaths. Without magic, there's no way he'd be able to hold his own against a Dark Mage. And, while he never says it, I know it weighs on him that he can't carry on the family legacy."

"Poor lad," Cid said.

"Aye. It's been getting worse here for him lately, too. I've kept his lack of abilities a secret— or at least, as secret as anything can be in a town this small— but some of the other kids have started to catch on. He's at an age where children want to use whatever magic they have, even if they're untrained, and the others have noticed that he never joins in. Some of them have even started to try to hurt him just to see if he'll fight back with magic, they claim. But they know he doesn't have any. I swear they know."

"The Crawford boy from yesterday," Cid responded, taking a guess.

"Aye, and he's not the only one, either. It's a rough situation, Cid, and you can see why I'm coming to you to ask a boon. You're the only one here who can help him."

Cid blinked. "The *only* one?"

"Aye. The rest of us have had magic all our lives. We have no idea what it's like to live without it. But you do. Until recently, you didn't have any magic abilities to use at all."

"That's true," Cid said proudly. "Spent twenty odd years as a Guard without it. In some of the most dangerous neighborhoods in Hardhearth, too."

"So you know how to fight without casting any spells?" Daryl asked hopefully. "I'm sure you have a few techniques up your sleeve, tricks that could even things out a bit between Lyle and the others. Talking only does so much, I need the lad to be able to defend himself."

"I do," Cid said, trying to think of what might be useful here. The lad didn't have any real weaponry— and at any rate, he didn't want to teach him anything deadly. It wouldn't be good if any of the local kids got seriously hurt because of him. He just wanted to help Lyle defend himself.

Well, there is one thing I could teach him.

His secret technique. The one that had saved him many times in the winding dirt alleys of Hardhearth where the walls were too close for him to swing a sword, where scoundrels and mercenaries were waiting to jump you at any moment, where a man had to be on his guard at all times and bring his best self to every fight he landed in— or wind up dead in a gutter somewhere.

Daryl was looking back at him, expecting an answer.

"I've got just the thing," Cid said, smiling.

A pocket full of sand had saved his guts more times than he could count. It was a simple thing, but throw it in an enemy's eyes and you'd have him blinded and bellowing. Even more effective— and worse for whoever was picking the fight— when it was salt sand. Easy pickings, even if he was twice your size. And best of all, it didn't cause any permanent damage. Perfect for a lad trying to take down a bully.

The old man beamed back at him. "I don't need to know what it is. That's between you and the boy— as long as it's something a Village Elder would approve of. I'm just glad you're able to help."

"I'll come by later today," Cid promised. "Once I'm done with work for the day. I really do need to get some work done."

"Aye, sorry about that," Daryl said, slowly getting to his feet and heaving his heavy pack onto his back. "That'll work out well. I'll tell the lad to look out for you. He'll be glad you're doing this, lad. I really think he will be."

CHAPTER 39: INTO THE THICK OF IT

After one more slice of bread and cheese, Daryl took his leave.

"Got to get back to work. I've got a few meetings with the villagers today about a new mill. Haven's growing, lad, and our mill's growing with it. Keep an eye out for Lyle, will you?"

"I thought he came with you," Cid said.

"He did, but he ran off into the woods as soon as we got here. Haven't seen hide nor hair of him since then."

"I'll look out for him."

After the story he'd heard about the boy, it was the least he could do.

Cid spent the next hour sorting through what the old man had brought and taking it down to the cellar. There was still half a loaf of bread left for dinner, half a wheel of cheese, and an assortment of fresh vegetables— a bundle of spinach, tomatoes, peppers, and a few potatoes. And all of Mary's corn. It would feed him for a few days if he could figure out how to stretch it.

Maybe I can get some flour from Roger and make a pot pie or something.

Well, that was a matter for another day. He'd have more

bread and cheese for dinner— the cheese was good enough for a real meal, and he didn't want to put it in the ice box. That would be enough for him.

With that settled, he went back out to the fields to do a little more tilling. Daryl had interrupted his flow when he showed up. **[Earth 1]** came easily this time, and he grinned as he watched the soil turn over. He was getting good at this. Maybe he'd be a real mage someday.

The thought took the smile off his face. *Lyle.* He had to help the boy. And so, once his spell had done his work, he shouldered his pack and headed into town to look for him.

Surely he's back from whatever he's been doing in the woods by now.

It was a bright summer day, and the sun was still high in the sky as he made the walk toward Haven. Even with a late start, he'd still gotten in a good day's work with plenty of time left to enjoy himself before sundown. He was getting faster and stronger, and it made him feel optimistic about his future. Farm life wasn't easy, but it wasn't all hard work and drudgery. He'd still have time in his retirement to do other things.

When he got to the bridge Lyle liked best, he found Daryl Nightgreen sitting on the railing looking irritated.

"Boy's run off," he said when Cid got close enough to hear him. "I'd hoped he'd be home by now, but there's no sign of him."

"Oh," Cid said. "I hope he's all right."

"He'll be fine, lad. He does this sometimes. Usually when there's something I need him to do around the house," Daryl responded.

"I was hoping I could start teaching him to fight today," Cid explained.

"Then that's reason enough for us to try to find him. Come on, lad, let's look. We can search the village first. There's a good chance someone's taken him in and given him a hot meal. Lad eats like a horse, but he's still skinny as a beanpole."

They checked the neighboring houses, but no one had seen Lyle. From the way the neighbors talked when Daryl asked them, it seemed like this sort of thing happened a lot.

"Check the mill?" asked a roly-poly man who'd stopped by Cid's stall at the farmers' market. "All the kids are up there right now learning about the new water wheel."

Privately, Cid was skeptical that Lyle would want to be anywhere near a large group of other kids after they'd been bullying him for months, but water wheels did seem like something that might interest the boy. Daryl thanked the neighbor for his advice, and they headed toward the river.

"Frank was right," he said. "I bet the boy's there."

But Lyle wasn't at the mill, and he wasn't anywhere else in town, either. Haven wasn't that big, and after about an hour of searching, they'd looked everywhere he could possibly be—with no result.

"Let's head back to the farm," Cid said. "That's the last place you saw him, right?"

"Right. And he does like wandering in the woods. But this is a long time for him to be gone, lad. He usually gets bored after a couple of hours and comes back."

"I'm sure he's still at Oak Tree. Where else would he be?"

Trying not to worry, Cid led the way back to the farm. Once again, they checked everywhere, splitting up so they could cover more ground. But when they met back at the farmhouse an hour later, neither of them had found Lyle.

"The woods around here are dense, lad," Daryl said. "If

he's wandering in the forest, there's no chance we'll find him unless he wants to be found. We'll just have to wait for him to come back on his own and hope he's all right."

"There's not somewhere else we should che...." Cid trailed off. He had a nagging feeling that Lyle wasn't in the woods. That he was still on the farm somewhere. *But where could he be?*

Then, it hit him. The Mana Tree. It was just the kind of thing that would attract a curious boy.

"Daryl," he said. "Before we give up, I think we should check one more place."

"Aye? What's that?" Daryl asked.

"Well...."

It was time to come clean.

"Just as you've been keeping a few things from me," Cid said, "there's something I've been keeping from you. There's something special about this farm."

"More than my fond memories of young Bevin?" Daryl's eyes were dancing.

"There's a Mana Cave beneath this land. I found it when I first moved in. I think that's why my crops are growing so fast. And— well— there's also a Mana Tree at the top of that hill over there. I wonder if Lyle found it."

Daryl frowned. "You saw the Mana Tree?"

"Clear as the day is long. I swear it," Cid responded.

Cid led the way toward the creek and up the hill with the Mana Cave under it. When Daryl saw the tree, his eyes trailed down toward a now grand gate that stood where the cavern opening used to be. He whistled appreciatively.

"Well now," he said. "That's new. That can't be good."

"You think it's a bad sign?" Cid asked.

He'd assumed the tree was a good thing, that it had been the reason for the little bit of his farm's success. It hadn't occurred to him that it might not be.

"It might be a bad thing, maybe not. Depends," Daryl said. "It's a little early for testing, but it looks like your instincts were correct."

He pointed. A line of Lyle-sized footprints wound their way through the dirt toward the tree and under its roots, heading in the direction of the Mana Cave.

"We're on the right track," Cid said. "I know where he's going. Wait? What do you mean, testing?"

Was the Mana Cave safe for a kid?

Daryl waved the question away, and Cid followed behind. He didn't press, he was sure he was about to find out. With Daryl in the lead, they made their way toward the gap in the rocks under the tree's roots. Daryl shook his head gravely when he saw it.

"You think he went down there?" Cid asked. "This is the Mana Cave I was talking about earlier, right?"

"Yep. And yep. If these are Lyle's footprints, he's gone in," Daryl responded.

Cid stared. "Is it safe down there?"

Daryl sighed. "I don't know. It's been a long time since I was tested, and I never went in alone before. I was part of a team, either as a protector or prospect."

Cid heard all he needed to. He needed to get to the boy. He looked at the cave entrance with some trepidation and pushed the door open. It was beautiful on the other side, but he could feel the magic power flowing through the air. Anything that powerful always made him nervous.

"Alright," he said. "Going in."

Cid squeezed his way through the narrow entrance and stepped into the darkness. After a moment, he realized that Daryl wasn't following him.

He turned. The old man was still standing outside the cave.

"I can't go inside!" he explained. "See?"

Daryl raised a hand out in front of him. It hit what appeared to be an invisible barrier when he reached the cave entrance, as if there were an ultra transparent pane of glass blocking his way.

"Interesting," Cid said, heart dropping. That didn't feel like a good sign.

"I'll stay up here and guard the entrance, lad. And I'll try to work out some way to get through. You'll need to hurry before Lyle triggers the testing!" Daryl exclaimed "Please, hurry."

"Great. I'll keep pushing forward and try to find Lyle," Cid muttered to himself.

Trying not to assume the worst— and wishing he'd thought to bring his sword— Cid moved deeper into the cave.

CHAPTER 40:
STARTING TRIAL

Cid moved forward into the darkness, taking the time to let his eyes adjust to the dim light. Once again, the cave got brighter as he got closer to the large cavern full of mana crystals.

"Lyle?" he called. No response. But soon, it was bright enough to see the floor— and he could see the boy's footprints in the dirt ahead of him, leading deeper into the cave. He was on the right track.

"Lyle!" he yelled again.

Still nothing. *Well, Lyle had been gone for hours.* He might have traveled a long way in that time.

Cid turned a corner and found himself once again in the main room of the cave. The crystals cast an eerie flickering light on the path as he picked his way through the cavern, careful not to step on or touch anything. He still didn't know what the crystals did, if anything, or if they were dangerous. All he knew was that they were incredibly powerful. He could feel it.

Finally, he found himself back at the wall full of doors, but something had changed.

Are there more doors here now?

It was hard to tell. He'd been so stunned by the cavern itself the last time he was here that he hadn't taken a good look at them. And the past few weeks had been so full of farm work that his memory wasn't as clear as it could have been.

Still, it felt like the wall was different. Four doors stood ahead of him, each one made in a different style. One was gold, one silver, and one bronze. The fourth was the most intricate. It was covered with gold and silver lettering in an intricate script that he didn't recognize. If he ever got out of here, he'd have to ask Daryl if he knew what language it was, and what it might say.

Which one do I go through?

It seemed like the most ornate one was probably the right choice— and the one most likely to attract a kid's attention— but he couldn't be sure.

"Lyle?" he shouted, taking a total shot in the dark. "Are you in there?"

This time he got a response. The lad sounded very far away, but it was clearly his voice. It was coming from the biggest door, as Cid had guessed, and it seemed like he was calling Cid's name.

"Got it. Coming!" he shouted. *Stay safe, kid.*

How do I open this thing?

The door had no handle, only a large bronze knocker. Taking a guess, Cid walked up to it and knocked three times. The sound echoed through the cave, and with a groan, the door swung open.

"Cid!" Lyle shouted, more clearly now that there wasn't a giant door in the way.

Hopefully this isn't some kind of trap.

If it was, he'd have to deal with it when it came. His time in the Guard had prepared him for that much, at least. Once again wishing he had his sword on him, he stepped through the door.

It immediately swung shut behind him with a bang. He was in a small, circular room lined with doors. Once again, each one was in a different style, and each one had a glowing character etched into its surface, bathing the room in eerie light. It seemed to be the same mysterious script as had been on the door he'd just come through.

Is this the test Daryl was talking about?

"Lyle?"

No response this time, and Cid sighed. How was he supposed to know which door was the right one?

"Lyle?"

This time, one of the doors— its character glowing a fiery red— opened, and he heard a shriek from down in the darkness. It was the boy, and he was clearly in some kind of trouble.

Heart pounding, Cid raced forward into the cave. "Coming, Lyle! Hold on!"

He was in a narrow and winding passageway, and the walls were encrusted with mana crystals. They all glowed the same red as the character on the doorway, and the tunnel was getting brighter the farther he went.

"Cid! Help!"

Lyle's voice was very close now, and Cid picked up the pace. This took him back to his time in the Guards, rescuing the children of Hardhearth from deadly danger. It was a good feeling. He didn't want to do it full time— not anymore— but it was nice to be reminded of the old days.

"Coming, Lyle! Hang on!"

He rounded the corner and found himself standing in a large room. The walls and ceiling were covered in red mana crystals, all flickering as if they were on fire. And the floor—

The floor was lava.

He could feel the scorching heat from where he was. There was a door on the other side of the room on a low platform. Clearly, he needed to get to it, but how?

"Cid! You're here!"

Lyle was crouched on a small rock in the middle of the lava pit, cringing back from the heat of the fire. A line of rocks led toward him, barely rising above the lava. They were set far apart— not a hard crossing for a man Cid's size, but a very difficult one for a young boy.

It's a miracle that he got that far at all.

Whatever Lyle was trying to do here, he must be determined to succeed at it.

Cid backed up until he was almost at the wall of the cave, then sprinted toward the pit at high speed. He leaped onto the first rock, wincing as he felt the heat rising off the lava below him.

Two more rocks and I'm there.

He jumped once, twice, and then Lyle grabbed on to him and clung to him for safety.

"Cid!" the lad shouted. "I thought you wouldn't come!"

"Easy," Cid said. "Well, if you wanted me to come help you out, you could have told me where you were going instead of.... whatever this was."

Lyle grimaced and let go, moving toward the side of the

rock that was closest to the far door. Cid could see tear tracks on his face. "We need to get to the next one."

The distance to the next rock in the chain was much longer than any of the others, and Cid joined him to take a closer look. There was no way the lad would have been able to jump the gap. Cid didn't think he could do it himself, and his legs were twice as long as Lyle's.

"I don't think we can make it," he said. "We'll have to turn around and—"

"No!" Lyle shouted, looking close to panic. "We have to make it to the other side!"

Cid frowned. "Why?"

But there wasn't time for the lad to respond. The lava was starting to rise, and the pit was getting hotter. If they didn't get out soon, they'd both be burned alive. Cid scouted around the rock, hoping there might be something they could use.

To his surprise, he saw a few long boards piled at the rock's high point.

That's a little too convenient.

But Daryl had called this cave a test, which meant there had to be some way of passing it. Maybe the boards had been left there for that purpose.

"Okay," he said. "Lyle. Lyle! Calm down! We're going to get out of here."

The lad was clearly panicking, but he forced himself to breathe slowly and get himself under control. Cid was impressed. Not everyone had that skill.

"We're going to use those boards to span the distance to the next rock. I think they'll make it. I'll throw them across, and you go first. The next few rocks look easy to get to, and then you'll be at the door out."

"Okay," Lyle said. "Okay. Will you come, too?"

"I'll be right behind you," Cid promised.

Cid gathered the boards in his arms and carried them to the edge of the rock. He'd need to tie them together somehow.

Well, there's nothing else I can do except what's been tried and true.

He tore off his belt and, hoping his pants wouldn't fall down in transit, and quickly lashed two boards together. Then, he dangled his makeshift bridge over the lava pit to test it out. The belt held, and he gently lowered it down, closing the gap to the next rock.

"Go!" he shouted, and Lyle dashed across. Cid followed, praying the boards wouldn't break under his weight. The heat from the lava was searing.

The bridge held— barely. As soon as Cid made it across, it collapsed into the pit and burst into flames. They didn't have time to watch it sink, though. With Lyle leading the way, they jumped from rock to rock and onto the platform at the far end of the room.

It was still hot up here, but the heat was bearable enough that they could take a moment to catch their breath. Once he'd had a moment to recover, Lyle gave Cid a big hug.

"Thanks for coming for me," he said. "I knew you'd show up!"

"You just said otherwise! What the hell are you doing here?" Cid snapped. "It's not safe. You wandered into a room full of lava on your own?! What were you thinking? What was so important that you had to come down here?"

The lad sighed. "You have to know by now, I'm sure Grandpa told you. I don't have any magic. And if you don't have magic, you can't live in the village. We were able to keep it a secret for a while, but now, everyone is talking about it. I'll have to go soon, and— and this is all I've ever known!"

Lyle was clearly close to tears.

"Wait, what?" Cid asked. He hadn't realized the lad would be kicked out of town for not having magic. That seemed unnecessarily cruel.

"It's true," Lyle admitted. "But I have a plan. As soon as I saw this place, I knew that if I came down here, I'd be able to find a way to stay."

"Why here? Is this about the test Daryl was talking about?" Cid asked.

"That was the first part. I passed— *we* passed— thanks to your help," Lyle explained "This cave is where the prospects go to become Magic Knights. If they can make it through, they're worthy. Even if I don't have any magic, I know I can do it. And if I can get through the Mana Trials, they have to accept me in the Corps. And then I won't be kicked out of Haven!"

"Oh," Cid said. He wasn't really sure what to say.

"So," Lyle said, squaring his shoulders and looking at the door ahead of them. "I'm going to keep going. Are you coming or not?"

Cid shrugged his shoulders and looked back. *No use going that way.* "Alright, but you need to listen to me, and no going off on your own."

CHAPTER 41: YOUR OWN REASONS

The lad clearly wouldn't be dissuaded, and Cid sighed, looking back at the door they'd come in through on the other side of the room. With the board bridge gone, there was no turning back now. The only way out was through.

"Alright," he said wearily. "I'm coming. Can't let you get yourself killed down here on your own. But be careful, okay?"

Lyle shook his head. "You can't be careful in the Mana Trials. That's the whole point. It's a test of courage. The Magic Knights are the bravest warriors in the entire kingdom."

Some of them are.

Some of them, on the other hand, were arrogant jerks. But it didn't seem like a good idea to tell the lad that now.

"Look," he said. "Lyle. You don't have to do this. All this business about you being kicked out of Haven for not having magic… It's total bull. I don't agree with it, and you don't have to buy into it. We can find another way out. There has to be a way for those who don't pass the Trials to exit the cave. You'll be fine. And having magic isn't so bad. I lived that way for years, honed my wits and my strength. If the village won't accept you as you are, there are other places you can live."

"No," Lyle said. "I'm going to pass."

"Alright."

Well, I tried.

He moved toward the door, but the lad quickly moved ahead of him. "I have to knock. It's part of the trial."

Cid stepped back. "Go ahead. Knock then."

Lyle stepped up and banged on the door, and it creaked open. It was hot in the room beyond it— boiling hot— and they both took a step back.

"You sure?" Cid said.

"Dead sure."

Together, they walked through, and the door slammed shut behind them. They were in the first trial room.

"What are we in for?" Cid asked. "What are these Trials?"

"We're not supposed to know about them. They're supposed to be a surprise to everyone who goes in. But of course everyone talks about it."

"Sounds about right." Get a Corpsman drunk on some fine ale, and he'd often spill things he shouldn't. Even Magic Knights loved a good story, and they particularly loved being the center of attention while they were telling it.

"There are four," Lyle went on. "One for each of the four elements: fire, earth, air, and water. You have to fight something bad for each one of them. A monster, I think. If you can beat all of them, you're a Magic Knight."

"Great. Let me guess: this one is fire."

"Yeah. And the lava pit was just a warmup to get rid of anyone who wasn't serious. This is the real trial."

"I guess we're serious," Cid said.

"I am."

The lad was a little obnoxious— and maybe half-mad — but Cid had to admire his commitment. Peering into the darkness, Cid cast around for a weapon. There wasn't much, and he settled on a sharp-looking stalagmite that jutted up from the ground like a crooked tooth. Lyle watched him skeptically while he tried to break it free.

"Do you think you're going to beat the monster with that?" he asked.

"I think I'm going to try."

Looking unconvinced, the lad led the way farther into the cavern. The same eerie flickering red light from before lit their way, and the air got hotter the farther they went. The back of Cid's neck prickled.

"Something's down here," he said. "Something bad—"

An awful noise, halfway between a roar and a shriek, pierced the silence, and Cid raised his stalagmite high in front of his face as the creature crashed to the ground ahead of them.

"It was on the ceiling," Lyle said, eyes wide. "Waiting for us to—"

The monster shrieked again, cutting him off. It was a massive beast, ten times the size of a man, made of dark rock covered in molten lava and raging flame. Its eyes were glowing red, as were the large horns that erupted from the sides of its head. It roared a third time, and Cid flinched back from the scent of its breath. It was baking hot and smelled of sulfur and burning flesh.

"What is that?" he asked. "A fire golem?"

"I think so!" Lyle said, close to panic. "Don't you know?!"

"How would I know?! I was never a Magic Knight! I was a City Guard at Hardhearth! We didn't have to deal with this kind of thing!"

"We're going to have to fight it!"

"Yes, Lyle, we are obviously going to have to fight it!"

Cid forced himself to take a deep breath as the golem slowly got to its feet. There was no point in arguing with a child—even if he was the one who'd gotten them both into this mess. The only thing he could do was try his best to take the monster out.

But it was hot down here, and getting even hotter as the fire golem approached. Its footsteps echoed in the empty room. Cid brandished his stalagmite— which felt like a feeble weapon now. Why had he thought it would do any good?

Gathering his courage, he raced toward the beast— and was pushed back against the far wall by a blazing wall of heat. It was summoning its fire magic into its palms, and whatever it was about to do wasn't going to be good.

"Cid!" Lyle shrieked. "Watch out!"

He ducked and rolled as the golem launched its attack. A massive fireball slammed into the wall behind him, right where his head had been, and he winced. The beast roared and squinted into the darkness with its piggy eyes, looking for him.

It's slow on its feet. Maybe I can use that to my advantage.

But how? He couldn't even get near the thing. The air around it was too hot— it would burn his face off if he got within three feet of it. And if he died, the lad died too. He couldn't let that happen.

Maybe he could launch the stalagmite like a javelin. He'd always been good at ranged attacks.

Cid backed up against the far wall and tried to stay out of the golem's line of sight. It was still looking for him, and he took a moment to aim the stalagmite carefully. If he could just hit the back of the creature's head in the weak point where its skull met its neck, he might have a chance. Once the golem was on the ground, he could keep hurling weapons at it until it was dead.

It turned its head away from him, and he saw his chance. With a roar, he threw the stalagmite as hard as he could. It arced through the air toward the golem, and he could see the look of triumph building on Lyle's face—

Bellowing, the golem slapped the weapon down, and it shattered harmlessly on the ground. It knew where he was now, and it advanced on him, eyes glowing, as it once again built a fire attack between his hands.

Well, blast.

It was all over. The tricks he'd learned in the Guard hadn't worked, and now he was going to die before he even got to enjoy the rest of his life. *Some retirement this turned out to be.*

But he wasn't resigned to death yet. Wracking his brain for something— anything— a thought came unbidden, and he wracked his brain that much faster for an answer to it: *What would Bran do?*

He tried to put himself in his friend's place. Bran was a professional Battlemage. He'd probably obliterate the golem with an overpowering jet of water— the kind of spell Cid didn't have the skills to pull off. A **[Water 1]** spell wasn't exactly going to cut it here.

Or would it?

His Guard training wasn't enough to take down the golem on its own, and neither were his weak spells, but maybe there was a way to combine them. A way to use both the wits that he'd earned in Hardhearth and the power he'd gotten from Bran. A way—

"Cid!" Lyle shouted. "Do something!"

He snapped back to reality. The golem was only a few feet away from him. He didn't have enough water to destroy the creature completely, but maybe he could do something to weaken it. What were its vulnerable points? The back of its head— but it was facing him. Or its joints.

There's an idea.

He took his spellcasting stance, praying this would work, and cast **[Water 1]** at the creature's right elbow. A weak jet of water spouted from his hands. Feeling a little foolish, as if he was watering his crops instead of fighting a massive fire golem, he poured as much energy as he could into the spell. The creature roared with fury as the fire went out around the joint, leaving nothing but dead black rock. It reached out for him again, snarling with frustration. Its elbow no longer bent.

"You did it!" Lyle shouted from the other side of the room. "Cid! Keep going!"

Easier said than done.

But he had to try. Quickly, before the beast could move again, he shot another spout of water at its other elbow. Now, it couldn't move its arms, and it roared its anger. But it was still dangerous, could still walk, and was still on fire. It advanced on him menacingly, brandishing its horns, as Cid tried not to pass out from the blistering heat coming off its body.

"Magic!" Lyle said triumphantly. "We need to use magic to beat it!"

In retrospect, it should have been obvious. The Mana Trials were meant to test the villagers' ability to become Magic Knights. Of course the solution was magic, but Cid had fallen back on his twenty years of Guard training automatically— he'd never had magic in the Guard. He wouldn't make that mistake again.

Focus, Dawnshield. Don't let it get close to Lyle.

He used **[Water 1]** on the golem's knee, and it sank to the ground, roaring. It was still on fire, still a threat, but largely unable to move. He could feel his power draining, though. He'd never used this much magic before— and never in such a dire situation. And if the lad was right, he had three more enemies to fight. What if he couldn't keep it up?

It wasn't an option. He had to finish the job. Summoning what remained of his strength, he doused the creature's other knee with water, and it lay immobilized on the ground in front of him.

Now, what do I do?

"Finish the job!" Lyle shrieked. "Kill the monster!"

"Right. How?"

"Put the fire out! Put the fire out!"

The lad was jumping up and down with excitement, and Cid gave him a skeptical look. Did he even have enough magic in **[Water 1]** to cover the whole golem with water, or would he have to douse the creature a little bit at a time? If the latter, they'd be here all day.

Better get started then.

He shot a jet of water at the beast. It definitely wasn't enough to cover it. But if he worked his way along its body, he could cool it off. It roared its fury as he slowly got the fires out, turning it to solid rock a little bit at a time. Finally, its eyes dimmed as its head lowered to the floor. The golem was dead— nothing but a lifeless pile of black rock remaining.

Lyle waited a moment, just to be safe, then sprinted over to Cid and gave him a big hug.

"You did it! We did it!"

"What do you mean, 'we'?" Cid asked, but he was

grinning. This was the first real battle he'd fought since leaving the Guard, and to his surprise, it hadn't gone badly. He wasn't as old and out of shape as he thought. And he was better at magic than he'd expected to be.

That said, they weren't done yet— nowhere near.

"I'm going to need you to help in the next room," Cid warned. "I can't do everything myself."

"Done. I was already going to say that. I want the next kill. I know I can do it!"

"Easy." He didn't like a lad so young talking about killing.

Before he could say anything else, a glowing blue portal appeared in the center of the floor a few feet away from what remained of the fire golem. It pulsed gently as if it was summoning them.

"Guess it's time to go," Cid said. But Lyle was already on it.

"Whee!" the lad cried, leaping right into the center of the portal. Instantly, he sank through the floor and vanished.

Might as well follow him.

Cid took one last look back at the immobilized golem and stepped onto the portal.

Instantly, the fire room vanished around him, and he found himself back in the main room with the four doors leading into what Cid assumed were smaller chambers, and the sealed exit behind him. Lyle was already there, and he was beaming.

"We did it!" the lad said. "We passed. Look!"

He pointed at the door Cid had gone through to get to the lava pit. When he'd first seen it, a mysterious character was glowing red on the door's surface. Now, it was dark. They'd completed their task in that room.

With a creak, a second door— this one with a green character etched into its face— swung open. Green light poured out of the passageway beyond.

"What do you think?" Lyle asked. "Which element, Earth?"

"Seems like it," Cid said. "Green. Plants. Right?"

"Then let's go see what an earth monster looks like!"

Before the lad could move, Cid grabbed him by the arm.

"Lyle," he said, sounding as stern as he could manage. "Stay here. Seriously. I was just giving you a hard time in the room before. It's not safe."

Lyle crossed his arms. "No way. I'm coming."

"You're just a kid. I'm an old man. If something goes wrong—"

I've already lived a full life. He didn't want to say that to Lyle, though. It felt a little dark. And he definitely didn't want to point out that only one of them had any magic to speak of.

"Cid," the lad said. "You don't understand. This is the trial. The only trial. I have to do this—have to at least try to help out. If I can do this, I can stay here in my home. It won't even matter that I don't have any magic."

Cid sighed. "You really want to stay here? Even though they're trying to kick you out for what's— I'm sorry— a ridiculous reason? Lyle, there are other places."

But Lyle was already shaking his head. "No. I'm doing it."

He nodded. He might think the lad was fighting a losing battle, but he could respect his determination.

"Alright, lad," he said, cringing as he realized he sounded

a bit like Daryl. Was he already that old? "Let's go on. Earth room it is. We'll see what the Mana Trials have in store for us."

And they moved on together into the next passageway.

CHAPTER 42:
NEXT STOP

"Okay," Lyle said as they moved further into the cave. The walls were glowing an ugly, eerie green that turned Cid's stomach. "What's the plan?"

"What plan? There is no plan."

"We need a plan. Cid, I have to pass these trials."

Cid clapped a hand on the boy's shoulder and smiled. "We'll figure it out as we go along. Adapt to the situation we find in the room. It's the way of the Guard, Lyle."

"Alright." Lyle looked skeptical, and Cid grinned.

"You think I knew how to beat that fire golem before I actually did it?"

"Well… no. Clearly."

"See? I figured it out."

The lad fell silent, clearly pondering what he had said, and Cid took a moment to look around. The passage was getting wider and brighter as they moved along. They were clearly close to the first part of the trial— whatever it might be.

"Lyle," he said. "When I first came here, you said you wanted to be an adventurer, to travel the world and get out of the village. Now, you want to stay in Haven so badly that you're willing to risk your life in order to do it. Why? What changed?"

Lyle looked down at his feet. "You're right. I did want to be an adventurer. And I still do! Someday."

He fell silent, and Cid waited for him to speak again.

"It's— well— I used to think Haven was boring!" he said. "And it still can be sometimes. And I don't like the bullies. And you're right, the magic thing is dumb. It's not fair. But when you came to town, things got exciting. You have so many stories, and this whole big job in the Guard, and it just sounds like you had a really cool life with a lot of adventures even though you mostly just stayed in one place."

Cid grinned, touched. He'd never thought of the Guard as 'cool' before. "You know, a lot of lads would think the Magic Knights were the ones who had adventures. They're the ones who actually get to see the world."

"Magic Knights are boring," Lyle said. "I used to want to be one, but not anymore. It's easy to just solve your problems with magic. Being a Guard is a lot harder and better. You have to actually use your wits and learn to fight."

"Yeah?" The lad had a point. He'd always taken pride in that aspect of Guard work.

"Yeah. Plus, I mean, it's not like I'll ever be a Magic Knight. I might get to stay in Haven, but they'd never let me into the Corps without any magic. But I could be a Guard someday if I wanted and I worked hard."

"You'd be a great Guard, lad," Cid said. "You're hard-working and determined. Those are the qualities any good Guard needs the most."

The lad beamed up at him, red hair practically glowing in the green light of the cavern.

"And one more thing. Even if we don't pass, even if they try to kick you out, you'll always have a place with me.

Whether that place be on Oak Tree Farm or elsewhere."

"You'd leave Oak Tree Farm?" Lyle asked, looking stunned.

"I wouldn't want to, but if it came to it, yes. I wouldn't want to live in a town that treated its youngest so badly. But let's hope it doesn't come to that."

Lyle was grinning from ear to ear now, and Cid led the way into the cavern. "Now, let's go kill some monsters."

The passageway soon opened up into a large cave lit by green Mana Crystals, and they took a moment to take stock of the situation. They were on a high platform suspended above a giant pit full of sand. Another platform with a door on it stood on the far side, some distance away.

"Not as bad as the lava pit," Lyle said. "At least it's not hot."

"Aye, it's more comfortable here. But watch the sand. I bet there's something unpleasant beneath it."

The lad shuddered. "Like, what do you think?"

"I don't know. Let's watch and wait."

They didn't have to wait long. After a few moments, the sand started to ripple as if something large were making its way to the surface. Cid could see the shape of the monster, whatever it was, moving under the sand like a snake.

Then its head broke the surface, and they both recoiled in disgust.

"It's a worm!" Lyle said. "Ugh!"

It was the biggest worm Cid had ever seen with a large and predatory-looking mouth full of razor-sharp teeth. It didn't seem to be able to see them— the worm had no eyes— but it clearly knew they were there. Its head moved back and forth rhythmically as it tried to figure out where they were.

"We have to get to the other side," Lyle said.

"Right."

But how?

The sand didn't look stable, and Cid suspected that it would just suck them down if they tried to cross it on foot. And the worm looked hungry. He didn't relish the thought of being its next meal.

Wonder if it chews its food or just swallows it whole?

He shook his head hard to dislodge the thought from his brain. No need to be thinking that way right now.

"We need to make a bridge or something," Lyle said. "Like we used in the lava pit."

"Yeah, but—"

There were no convenient boards lying around this time. They'd have to figure something out for themselves. He looked down at the pit, baffled. The worm had given up trying to track them and was now swimming in vaguely menacing circles, half-submerged in sand.

Ugh.

Suddenly, he remembered a story Bran had told him. He himself had never seen a sand pit like this, never traveled to the deserts of the Southern Lands, but Bran and the Corps had. They'd seen dunes far bigger than this. His friend had told him a tale about being trapped out in the open in the middle of a thunderstorm— and about what happened when lightning struck the sand.

It had turned to glass.

Hm.

Maybe he could use that. He didn't have any power over lightning, but he *did* have [Fire 1]. Any heat would do the trick. He'd seen glassblowers do it all the time in Hardhearth.

"Lyle," he whispered. "Watch this."

And, taking his casting position, he shot a jet of flame at the nearest patch of sand, the one just below the platform they were on. They almost whooped with joy when it turned to hard glass— not a big piece but large enough for them both to stand on it. They had their strategy.

Lyle moved to jump down onto it, but Cid held him back.

"Wait," he said. "Let's wait for the worm to dive. And I don't think we want to jump. It can probably sense vibrations on the sand around it. We'll need to climb down as quietly as we can."

The lad was clearly impatient, but he waited for the worm to be fully covered in sand before slowly climbing down from the platform and into the pit. The creature was still swimming, but it had clearly gone farther away from the surface. If it stayed there, they might be able to pull this off.

Cid climbed down after him, and to his relief, the glass held firm at the surface of the sand.

Would have been a bummer if it sank under my weight.

He cast [Fire 1] again, and they had their next step in the pathway. Lyle lightly jumped across, and Cid followed. They were now out in the open, well away from the safety of the platform, and there was nowhere for them to go but forward. If the worm surfaced now, they'd really be in trouble.

Quickly, he cast again, and the lad scurried forward onto the glass bridge.

"Watch the worm while I make the bridge," Cid hissed. "Let me know if it's getting close."

Lyle nodded, face pale, and they kept moving across the glass bridge as fast as they could. Cid could feel the sand rumble beneath his feet whenever the worm passed directly beneath them. They froze every time it happened, hoping it couldn't sense them above it, but it was still unsettling.

Finally, after what felt like hours, they were almost at the far platform. Cid was just about to cast **[Fire 1]** again when Lyle tugged at his sleeve.

"Cid," he whispered. "Cid. Cid. It's coming."

He turned. The lad was right. The worm was clearly moving closer to the surface, and he could see its bulk moving beneath a thin layer of sand.

"Watch it. I'll cast as fast as I can."

They jumped onto the next piece of glass. *Only two more.*

But the beast was gaining on them fast, and moving upward as it did. It knew where they were.

"Cid!" Lyle screamed, no longer bothering to whisper. "Go faster, Cid!"

"Trying!"

He cast the spell, and they jumped. *One more.*

With a hiss, the worm broke the surface of the pit. He could hear its belly scraping against the sand as it raced toward them.

"Cid! It's almost here! Cid!"

He cast one more time, and they jumped— and then they were scrambling up the side of the platform mere feet ahead of the worm. Its gaping jaw was open wide, and it struck— and missed. Its head slammed against the wall, and it shrieked.

"Hold on, lad!" Cid shouted. "Don't let it shake you loose!"

Hanging on for dear life, they climbed up onto level ground, breathing hard. The worm couldn't reach them up here— but it was trying. It kept ramming the rock below them with its head, and Cid could feel the entire platform shaking as it did.

"Let's go," Lyle said. "It's not going to stop. We need to move on."

The lad was right. If they stayed, the platform was likely to collapse into the sand pit with them on it. Cid let Lyle lead the way through the door and closed it firmly behind them.

They were in another cavern, smaller than the first, lit by the same eerie green light as the others. Cid tried to move quietly to avoid attracting attention as his eyes adjusted to the darkness. No point in letting whatever was in here get the drop on them.

A screech pierced the silence, and Cid and Lyle exchanged a look. It was a strange noise, like rusted metal being bent into shape.

The lad frowned. "What do you think it—"

A massive suit of armor with glowing green eyes clanked into their line of sight. It didn't look friendly.

"—is?"

"An iron golem," Cid said. "I've seen one of these before back in the Guard. One of them got loose in Hardhearth and destroyed half a neighborhood before we were able to stop it."

"So it's pretty dangerous? More than the fire golem?"

"Very. But different. And I think I— we— can take it. I've done it before."

The golem was getting too close for comfort, its armor clanking loudly with every step, and they both backed up against the wall of the cave as far from the monster as they could get.

"Okay," Cid said. "So it's weak at the joints just like the fire golem. We need to target it there and try and get it to freeze up."

"Target it with what?"

Cid looked at the ground and grinned. "Sand."

It was almost too perfect. He'd originally gone into Haven today in order to teach Lyle his sand technique, and now he was getting the opportunity to do it. The stakes were a little higher than he'd originally intended, but you couldn't have everything.

"This thing is slow," Cid went on. "As long as we keep moving, we're fine. I'll start— use my magic to disable one of its knees so it can't move— then you join me. Throw as much sand as you can handle."

Lyle nodded, looking a little bit like a green Guard recruit in his first year.

A little young, maybe, but he'll shape up alright.

They each broke in a different direction— Lyle went left, Cid right. The golem wasn't sure which to follow, and in its moment of confusion, Cid struck. He took his casting stance and used [Air 1] to blow a massive cloud of sand toward it. It wasn't the most efficient technique, but it worked. He heard the ugly sound of metal scraping against sand as the golem came to a halt. One of its knees was seizing up.

"Go, Lyle, go!" Cid shouted, and the lad did as he was told. He threw handful after handful of sand at the golem from his side of the room while Cid kept casting [Air 1]. After a few rounds, it got hard to see through the clouds of sand and dust, but he could still hear its joints breaking down at the center of the cavern. They were winning.

And the lad didn't even need magic in order to be of use.

Well, Cid's spellcraft had made things a lot more efficient. But he wasn't about to say that.

When the dust cleared, the iron golem was lying dead at the center of the room, and the glowing portal had once again appeared on the floor.

"You did it!" Lyle said. "Beat the Earth room!"

"We did it," Cid said. "I couldn't have done it without your help."

To his surprise, he was in high spirits. The Mana Trials were almost fun. Fighting monsters was easier than fighting people— less complicated— and it was nice to know they'd likely reincarnate as soon as they left the cave. It made him feel a little bit better about killing them.

"You'd make a good Guardsman someday," he said. "Quick wits, and you follow orders. It's a good start."

The lad grinned, stepped onto the portal, and disappeared. Cid followed, and in a blink, they were both back in the room with the four doors. The earth door had gone dark as well now, leaving only two glowing characters: one a deep aquatic blue, one a bright white.

Water and Air. We're halfway through the Mana Trials.

Before he had time to wonder which was next, the water door creaked open, revealing a blue-lit corridor beyond it.

"You ready?" Cid asked.

The lad nodded his response, and they moved on toward the water trial together.

CHAPTER 43:
TINKER, TAILER

In the brief time since Cid had magic unlocked for him by Bran, he'd never used so much of his mana. He was already exhausted, and the end was still a while away. *Assuming I've at least crossed the halfway mark.*

"Can we take a minute?" he asked, taking a seat on a well-placed rock. "Just want to see if I can recharge a bit."

He wasn't even sure if magic worked that way. Mages recovered their drained power after a rest period— he knew that much thanks to Bran— but he had no idea how long that rest period needed to be. Maybe he'd need to sleep before he could fully recover.

We're only halfway through the Trials. This isn't good.

He wished Bran were here, or Daryl, or someone who knew anything about magecraft. But all he had was Lyle— and the lad wasn't likely to know anything.

Or— wait.

He was the son of two celebrated Magic Knights. Even if he'd been young when they died, he might have some sense of how they'd worked.

"Lyle," he said. "I need your help with something."

The lad looked pleased to be asked. Cid frowned, unsure

of how to bring up the topic of Lyle's parents.

"So," he said. "I talked to your grandpa about where you came from. About—"

"My parents," Lyle said. "They had magic. I'm the only freak who doesn't."

"Uh," Cid said. "Right. He didn't put it that way, but he did say they were pretty powerful."

"Yeah. They were, I guess. I don't remember them that well."

But they didn't have time to talk about the boy's sad childhood right now. Gently, Cid steered the conversation back to the point.

"Did they ever show you any skills? Teach you anything about magecraft? How long did it take them to fully recover from a mission?"

"Oh," Lyle said. "Yeah. They tried to teach me some— although there was only so much they could do, you know. And after a mission— I'm trying to remember. I think it could take a while. Depends on what they were doing. And I didn't always know what they were doing. Sometimes, it was top secret, and they couldn't say."

"Ah. Got it. A while, like 'overnight' a while?"

The lad frowned. "I think so. Are you— are you low on magic?"

"I'm no mage, Lyle. I'm a farmer with a few basic level spells. I could never be a Magic Knight with this little power. It's a miracle we've made it this far through the Trials."

"We have to succeed!"

Cid sighed. "And we will. But I might run out of power at some point. And if I do, we'll have to solve our problems without magic by using our wits like the Hardhearth Guard."

Lyle still looked worried, but he nodded. "Like the Guard. I'll follow your lead, Cid."

"Very well then."

Cid stood up and took a moment to take stock of how he felt. His rest had helped— a little. But he still wasn't at full strength. He wasn't sure exactly how long his magic would last, but it was likely he'd run out at some point in the Trials.

Well, nothing for it.

They'd just have to figure it out when the moment came.

They moved through the narrow, blue-lit hallway until it opened up into a large room. Once again, they were at the top of a high platform. Once again, there was a matching platform with a door on it at the other end.

I'm starting to notice a pattern.

Every Trial seemed to have a warm up room of sorts before the main event. And if the pattern held, there was a water golem of some kind behind the far door. He wondered how they'd beat that with his energy running low.

"Do you think there's a way to harvest the energy from the Mana Crystals?" he asked.

The lad blinked.

"That's the source of the Cavern's power, right? There's magic embedded in them? Maybe I can use them to recharge in some way."

"I don't know," Lyle admitted. "I don't know if anyone's ever tried it. Mana magic is different from the magic we— they — use. My parents always said that. But I don't know how."

Cid looked more closely at the crystals lining the wall of

the cavern. He could feel their power buzzing in the air around them.

"It's worth a shot, I think," he said. "If it comes to that."

But first, they had to focus on the matter at hand. He wasn't sure, but he thought he had enough magic left to get them through at least the first of the two remaining trial rooms.

He walked to the edge of the platform and looked down into the pit. It was a large pool of water— and it looked very deep, very cold. Small chunks of ice floated on its surface.

"Can you swim?" he asked Lyle.

"Yeah. My grandpa taught me, but I don't know if I want to go in there. It's too cold to swim in the river in the winter. It's dangerous. When I was really young, almost a baby, a kid fell through the ice and froze to death."

Cid grimaced. He'd hoped there would be an easy answer to this Trial, but the lad was probably right. Even Cid didn't think he could cover a distance that large in icy water before getting hypothermia. They'd have to find another way.

"Maybe there's a way to warm it up?" he suggested. "Magically?"

"My parents always said that kind of thing took a lot of power, and a lot of energy. They'd use warming spells when they went on winter missions, but they always came in potion form and were made by other Knights. Experts."

Cid didn't have a lot of power, and he didn't have a lot of energy. That ruled out that solution.

"Maybe I can make a bridge," he said. "Get us across."

He didn't have the skill to make a real bridge, but he could use [Earth 1] to fill in part of the pit so they could walk to the other side. It wouldn't be elegant, but then again, Cid wasn't exactly an elegant man. He was a Guard and a farmer. What was important was that the strategy worked, not that it looked good.

Lyle didn't seem to have any objections, so Cid got to it. He cast the spell and was pleased to see a wall of earth taking form in the pit, bisecting the pool of water like a dam. In seconds, a rough dirt pathway had appeared that led straight to the platform on the other side.

But something was wrong. He was feeling woozy, and black spots were floating in front of his eyes. Feeling light-headed, he took a knee, breathing hard.

"I think I'm tapped out," he croaked. "Don't think I have any more magic in me."

The lad went pale. "Do you think we can rest, or—?"

"I think I'd need to sleep in order to get my power back. We'll have to rely on our skills."

Lyle squared his shoulders. "Should we turn back?"

"Sorry?"

"If you're out of power, and— and there's no way we're going to win, maybe we should give up and turn back. You've helped me out so much already. I don't want you to get hurt because of me."

"And if you get kicked out of Haven?"

"Then I get kicked out of Haven," Lyle said. "You're right, Cid. There are other places to live. If that happens, I can figure out some other way."

Cid sat down and looked at the bridge he'd made. "No. Let's keep going."

The lad stared back at him, surprised. "Really?"

"Yeah. This is kind of fun. Crazy but fun. Reminds me of my past. And I want to see if we can beat the Trials even without magic."

"Without magic? Do you think that's even possible?"

"I think we're going to find out," Cid said. "Plus, if this is a test, it's unlikely these monsters will actually kill us if we fail, right?"

Lyle looked uncomfortable. "Um. Well. People have died in the Trials before. It doesn't happen a lot, but it happens."

"Oh."

Well, that was sobering. "Can we get out if we get into trouble?"

"Yeah. I think so. If you pound on the main door really hard it eventually gets the message and opens. I've only heard of it happening once or twice when someone got really stuck."

"Alright. We'll do that as a last resort if we have to. Until then, we'll try to do the Trials Guard-style."

"Guard-style!" Lyle said. "I like the sound of that."

Cid wasn't sure how long his earth bridge would hold with his magic as weak as it was, so he left the conversation there and scrambled down the platform and into the pit. Together, they moved as quickly as they could across the large pool of water. He could see creatures moving in the deep, but nothing came for them.

"This one wasn't so bad," Lyle said when they reached the far platform. It was just in time, too. Parts of Cid's earth bridge— the ones back by the entry platform— were already starting to crumble as the water leached into the soil. "Maybe the Magic Knights put it here to give people a break."

"Might be harder if you don't have Earth magic," Cid

mused. "If someone's really specialized, they might need to be really creative to figure out how to get through."

And maybe they made it easy because the water golem fight is going to be really hard.

He didn't want to say that part aloud, though.

They scrambled up the far platform and faced the door together. It was glowing the same blue as the rest of the cavern and pulsing faintly.

Here goes nothing.

"Lyle, you want to do the honors?"

But the lad stepped back. "You should open the door this time. Since it was your idea to keep going."

Cid reached out— and the door swung open before he could touch it. He blinked at it for a moment, trying not to be disappointed.

Fine. Moving on.

They moved on into the water cavern, keeping their eyes out for the water golem. Like the other golem chambers, this one was about half the size of the larger cavern before it. A pool of dark water stood at the center of the room.

"I think the golem sleeps there," Lyle whispered. "I bet—"

Right on cue, the water started to bubble as if something very large was moving under the surface. Both Cid and Lyle backed away as a large figure, made entirely of water, rose from the pool and snarled at them.

"How do we attack it?" Lyle asked. "It doesn't really have a body."

Cid was wondering the same thing. The technique they'd used on the first two golems— attacking the joints—

wouldn't work here. The water golem didn't have any joints.

"I'm going to see if my magic works," Cid said, and Lyle nodded.

He took his spell casting stance and tried to cast [**Earth 1**], hoping it would still have a weak effect, at least. Nothing happened. He was out.

At least I didn't get sick this time.

Small blessings.

"Okay," Cid said. "Next plan. We both need weapons. Look around the cave and find what you can."

He pulled up another stalagmite from the side of the cavern, and Lyle grabbed a rock off the ground. Together, they waited for the golem to come into range. When it was close enough, Lyle hurled his rock at the creature's chest.

"Take that!" the lad shouted. "Guard-style!"

The rock splashed harmlessly onto the golem's belly, sank through its liquid body, and dropped harmlessly to the ground. Cid groaned.

"Of course it doesn't have a real body," he said. "Water golem."

This one isn't going to be easy. But what's holding it together?

When the golem got within a few feet of them, he saw the answer. A glowing stone sat in the middle of its torso, right where its heart would be. It was a magical core. If Cid could knock the core out of the golem, the whole thing might fall apart.

But how?

Throwing a rock at it hadn't seemed to work. He needed

to get more creative. Ducking as the golem swiped at his head with a watery fist, he sprinted to the other side of the cavern to buy time to think.

"Lyle!" he shouted, but the lad was already following him. The water golem was slow and clumsy just like the others, and they had a while before it would reach them. In the meantime, Cid took stock of what he'd brought with him.

He had his pack and whatever was in it. The clothes on his back. His stalagmite. And not much else.

"Lyle, can you go through my pack and take a quick inventory? I'll watch the golem."

It was getting closer. They'd need to either strike at it or move soon.

"Snacks," the lad said. "A mini frying pan. A helmet. Spare boot laces. Um, there's not much else."

"Got it."

The frying pan would be useful, as would the helmet. If there was one thing he'd learned in his month on the farm, it was that sometimes you had to improvise with whatever materials you had available.

Quickly, he unbuttoned his shirt and stripped it off. He set it on the ground and put the frying pan at the center of it, then heaped the rest of the contents of his pack on top of that. Finally, he tied the sleeves of his shirt around the pile of random items until he had a neat— and heavy— bundle. The sleeves were still long enough that he could use the shirt and its contents as a makeshift weapon.

As the golem approached, Cid swung the shirt in circles over his head, waiting for his moment to strike. Lyle was crouched on the ground behind him next to his now-empty pack.

When the beast got within range, Cid struck out with his weighted shirt. To his relief, he struck the golem's glowing core. It fell to the ground with a clatter, and he held his breath waiting to see what would happen next.

The golem's face contorted with fury as it tried to hold its body together, but it was no use. It splashed to the ground in a puddle of water, soaking Cid's shoes.

"Yeah!" Lyle said. "Three down, one to go."

The lad leaped into the glowing portal that had just appeared on the floor and vanished. Cid took a moment to retrieve his shirt and gear and winced as he untied the bundle. The shirt was soaking wet.

No point putting that back on.

Sighing, he put the shirt into the pack with the rest of his things. Apparently, he was going to do the last Trial shirtless.

CHAPTER 44:
BETWEEN US

Cid stepped on the glowing portal and teleported back to the main room.

Just one more.

He didn't like to admit it, but he was feeling his age. Hopefully, he could make it through the last Trial. He felt like he could sleep for a week.

Lyle was waiting for him in the main room, as usual, beaming.

"How'd you do that?"

"Do what?"

"Make that whole weapon up on the spot!" the lad said. "I've never seen anything like that before."

Cid blinked. "...Never?"

"Everyone I know just uses magic for that kind of thing. They wouldn't have been able to figure it out."

That made sense. If Lyle had spent all his life in a society made up entirely of very powerful magic users, he probably wouldn't have encountered many people who'd learned how to improvise like Cid had just done.

Funny.

He'd always envied the Magic Knights a little. He was proud of his career as a Guard, of course. The Guard had the best men in the kingdom. But the Knights had always had the glamorous job. There weren't that many kids in Hardhearth who dreamed of being a Guard one day. But every lad in the city — and many grown men as well— had a Magic Knight name picked out just in case the Corps came calling.

But using magic for everything might not actually be a good thing. He'd seen it when the Guard and the Corps worked together on missions. The Guard were always better at finding new solutions to unusual problems. The Knights usually just used spellcraft to blast through everything in their way.

Well, it's something to think about.

"Let's get on our way," he said. "We've been down here a long time. Your grandfather will be worried."

"Yeah! Let's finish the job!"

Three of the doors were dark now, and the white-glowing door that led to the air trial was the only one left. Cid took a breath, stretched his back out, and led the way into the narrow passageway.

"Do you think you're going to try to use the crystals to recharge your magic?" Lyle said, trotting along behind him.

"I don't know. I might try to finish the job without magic now just to prove it can be done."

"Wow!"

Cid grinned. It was good to know the lad was so impressed.

Once again, the corridor turned a corner and opened up into a large cavern. Once again, they were on a platform overlooking a large pit. This one had nothing at the bottom of it— as far as he could tell. It was just a deep hole that trailed off into darkness.

"Do you think it goes on forever?" Lyle asked.

"I don't know," Cid said. "I think we'd be wise not to fall into it. We'd be falling for a while."

He looked down into the pit in dismay. Maybe it was a trick of the eye, but it seemed larger and wider than the others. How were they going to make it across without magic?

Something whizzed past his face, and he jumped back away from the edge.

"What was that?"

Lyle pointed at the air above their heads— high up. A large rock was flying across the pit at high speed. When it reached the other side, it bounced off the wall and came back in their direction. And it wasn't the only one. While Cid was watching the first rock, a second one dislodged itself from the wall of the cavern and started whizzing back and forth. Soon, the air above their heads was full of flying rocks.

"Okay," Cid said. "I guess that's our ticket across the pit."

"But how? They're going way too fast for us to catch."

"I know."

Cid flinched as another rock zoomed past them. They were dangerous missiles, and he didn't relish the thought of what might happen if one of them hit him or Lyle. They'd split his head open like a summer squash.

How would I solve this if I did have magic?

He could use **[Earth 1]** to trap one of the flying stones in a wall of rock, maybe. Or even better, use **[Air 1]** to create a wind strong enough to hold it in place. Magic made everything so damn easy.

There's no point in thinking that way, though.

He had to figure out a way to do it with the assets he had, not the ones he wished he had. That was a lesson he'd had drilled into his head from his first day in the Guard, and it had saved his life many times in the rough streets of Hardhearth. Standing back close to the wall, out of the path of the flying rocks, Cid assessed the situation.

They were going fast, but they were also following a regular pattern. Each stone took the same path to and from the far platform. That was good. This wasn't a chaotic situation where anything could happen. The rocks were consistent and predictable.

And how fast are they actually going?

Once they got away from the platform, they were actually moving at a fairly moderate speed, slow enough that someone could ride them across without being blown off. They just felt unmanageably fast when they were six inches from his face.

"Okay," he said to Lyle. "I have a plan."

The lad looked at him and said nothing.

"I'm going to try to grab one of the flying rocks as it goes by," Cid said. "I'll hold it in place. You hop on, and we'll ride it across. We'll need to jump off before it hits the far wall, obviously, but I think we can do it!"

He tried to put a positive spin on it, but the lad looked skeptical.

Well, he always looks skeptical. He'll see.

Cid ripped the sleeves off his wet shirt and wrapped them around his hands so he could grip the rocks better. He felt a moment's irritation that the boy's wild quest had caused him to lose one of the only two shirts he owned then tamped it down. He could always buy more shirts.

Once he was ready, he stood at the edge of the pit and watched the rocks fly by. He needed to pick the right one: large enough that it would hold him and Lyle but small enough that he stood a chance of catching it. He let three go past before he spotted the one he wanted. It was a good shape— broad and flat, made of nondescript gray granite— and he thought he could manage to hang onto it long enough for the lad to hop on.

He crouched low, gathering his strength, as the rock flew toward him. Once it was within range, he grabbed it— and held on for dear life as it fought against his grip. It was much more powerful than he'd expected it to be, and his feet skidded on the platform's surface as it dragged him toward the pit. When he was only inches away from falling off, he gave up and let go.

"Wow," he said, breathing hard. "That was—"

That was something.

He'd have to try again. And he'd have to choose a smaller rock. "Lyle, can you help this time?"

The lad nodded and stepped forward to join him at the edge of the pit, and together, they watched the rocks fly across the cavern.

"That one was too big," Cid said. "I couldn't hold it. We'll need to pick a smaller one next time."

"But that means—"

Lyle trailed off, but Cid knew what he'd been going to say. The rock he'd just chosen was as small as they could get while still fitting the two of them on top of it. Any smaller and they'd have to make two trips.

Well, it is what it is.

With that settled, he scouted another rock— a brown one this time— and waited for it to come close. This time, and with Lyle's help, he was able to hold it. Barely.

"Get on!" he shouted, feeling the sweat drip down his face as he tried to keep the rock from flying out of his hands and across the pit. "Quickly. Now!"

The lad scrambled onto it— but as soon as he was settled, the rock jumped forward suddenly, catching Cid by surprise. In seconds, he was suspended over the pit, still hanging onto the rock, flying through the air at high speed.

"Cid!" Lyle screamed. "Don't let go!"

"Not a chance."

He wasn't about to end his days falling forever into a bottomless pit. There wasn't even any honor in that. He'd been smart to wrap his hands, at least. He could feel his palms sweating under the fabric, and his arms were aching from the effort of hanging onto the rock above his head.

This is terrible.

Soon enough— although not soon enough for Cid— they were approaching the far platform.

"Lyle!" he shouted. "Jump off as soon as we're over solid ground!"

The lad gave him a thumbs up, keeping his eyes locked on the wall ahead of them. Cid's arms were killing him, and as soon as he was no longer over the pit, he let go of the rock and dropped. Lyle leaped off just before the rock crashed into the opposite wall and bounced back toward the other side of the cavern.

That was surprisingly graceful.

Cid took a moment to shake his arms out then turned

toward the final door. The final challenge in the Mana Trials. It felt like they'd been in this cavern forever.

"You ready?" he asked.

The lad nodded, and together, they pushed open the last door.

The room on the other side was large, glowing white from the crystals that lined the walls— and empty. It was brighter than the others with no shadows for a golem to hide in. Moving slowly, Cid took stock of the cave, wary that something might drop from the ceiling. Nothing did.

"Where is it?" he asked just as something slapped him in the face.

He fell back, reflexively striking out at whatever had hit him. But his fist encountered only empty air, and he spun around, baffled. Nothing was there. Before he could think any more about it, something struck him on the back, lightly, as if it were trying to mess with his head. He turned. Nothing.

"Did you see what hit me?" he asked. The lad shook his head.

It must be invisible.

It made a certain sort of sense. A golem made of air wouldn't have a body for him to see, anyways. But it made his life difficult. How could he fight it if he had no idea where it was? For now, it seemed like it was just trying to confuse him, and its attacks weren't serious yet. But he knew it was likely to get down to business for real soon— and if he couldn't think of a way to fight back, he was a sitting duck.

It whacked him hard on the arm, and he moved away to another part of the cavern to think. *Hopefully, this one will be as slow as the others.*

An image popped into his mind unbidden: the swirling

dust storms that his mother had once called "dirt demons" when he was a boy.

There's a solution.

If he could figure out where the thing was and throw dirt on it, he might be able to make the unseen golem visible.

"Lyle!" he called to the lad on the other side of the room. "Sand again. Lots of sand."

"You got it."

Cid also gathered sand, making a large pile in what remained of his shirt, and waited for the air golem to strike again. When it did— slapping him in the back of the head even harder than it had before— he threw a handful in the direction he thought the creature might be. To his relief, it worked. Some of the sand filtered into the air currents making up the golem's body. He could see a dim outline of the creature now, silhouetted against the bright mana crystals behind it.

Quickly, he dumped more sand onto it. Lyle sprinted over and did the same, and soon, the golem was fully visible as a vaguely man-shaped dust cloud standing at the center of the cavern. It was hard to tell, but it looked annoyed.

What's holding it together this time?

The water golem they'd already defeated had a glowing mana crystal in its chest, and he wondered if this one might have one too. It would be invisible, probably, but it might be there. He'd have to get close enough to reach in and grab it.

Getting close would be a problem, though. Before he could take a step forward, the air golem raised its arms, and a powerful wind blew him back toward the other side of the cave. He hit the far wall hard and dropped to the ground.

"Cid!" Lyle shouted.

"Alright. Alright."

He stood slowly and took stock. His back hurt where it had made contact with the wall, but nothing seemed broken. Yet. He might not be so lucky the next time. They needed to take the golem out before it could do any more damage.

He glanced over at the crystals lining the wall of the cave as the golem readied its next attack. If he was able to recharge his magic, he'd have an easier time of it…

No. Call him a fool, but he was a stubborn fool. He'd only try the crystal idea if he really got into trouble.

He advanced on the air golem, holding his stalagmite in one hand, just as it launched its next strike. The wind hit him hard, but this time, he dug in his heels and held his ground. Then, wincing against the force of the golem's attack, he took a step forward. Then another. The air golem poured more power into its spell. Cid pushed back harder. He took another step.

He could hear the lad cheering him on behind him. "Go Cid! You can do it!"

He was about halfway to the golem now and still making slow and painful progress. If he could just reach it, he could knock the crystal out of its chest with his weapon.

"That's the worst you can do?" he taunted, and to his surprise, the wind didn't pick up. Maybe this was the worst the golem could do.

He covered the last few steps to the creature, trying to keep from sliding backwards. Then, he forced his arm up toward it, stalagmite in his hand. Eyes closed against the wind, he struck— and hit home. The crystal clattered on the floor, and he almost fell over as the golem's air attack suddenly stopped. The creature was gone.

He turned to Lyle— and to his surprise, the lad looked

back at him gravely, arms crossed.

"Congratulations Cid," he said. "You passed."

CHAPTER 45: LEYLINE

For a moment, Cid thought that he must have misheard what Lyle said. "What? You want to repeat that?"

"You heard me correct. You passed the Mana Trials, Cid, well done," Lyle responded, his voice a little firmer than it had been before. "You should be proud— and without magic for the second half, too. I don't think anyone in Haven has seen anything like that in a long time."

"No, no, no," Cid said, shaking his hand. "No. You passed the Mana Trials. You're the one who dragged me down here. I spent all day looking for you so I could teach you how to defend yourself from bullies without magic."

Lyle sighed, and Cid could tell the lad had regrets. "Yeah, sorry about that one. It was a ruse. I told my grandfather not to do that, told him you should know the truth, but he insisted. Said there might be trouble otherwise if you were let in on the secret in advance and didn't pass."

"What?" Cid asked. He was still having trouble processing this turn of events. He was mad. *What's going on with this town?* It seemed like there were secrets stacked on secrets here.

"Let's go back to the main room," Lyle said and pointed toward the exit. "I'll explain everything once we get there. It's creepy here in the golem cave, and I don't want to wait around for the respawn and have to fight it again."

Cid followed the lad through the glowing portal and into the room with the four doors. The exit remained sealed. All four of the doors had grown dark, and the crystals on the ceiling glowed with multicolored light. Just in case, he tried the door— the main one that led back to the larger cave and the exit— but it was still sealed fast.

Lyle shook his head. "Not that way. Ours is down. The harvest isn't over."

"Down? What do you mean by down, Lyle?" Cid asked, his voice edged with some of the anger he was feeling. *Don't do anything hasty. Just see this through.*

With a grinding noise, as if it was moving on rusty gears, the room started to descend.

"Down," the lad said as if that alone explained anything. "That'll take us down to the Leyline that supports this Mana Cave. The crystals wouldn't be able to grow here without it. But it'll take a while. This thing moves slowly. While we're waiting, I can try to fill in some gaps and tell you the whole story."

"Ah, yes. How kind. Thank you," Cid said tersely before responding. "I expect the whole story this time."

"Right," the lad winced. "Sorry. We're not used to outsiders here. I know there were a lot of secrets. Grandpa and the others probably didn't handle it as well as they could have. I know some of them weren't exactly thrilled with you being here, and others weren't happy about this whole charade, but it was insisted by the Corps that we include you in the village. And what the Corps says, we do."

"Right," Cid said. He'd heard Bran make that complaint often enough to know the lad was speaking the truth.

"Everyone always knew there'd be someone coming in without magic," Lyle said. "My grandfather told me what he told you, and that most of it was the truth. Most. Not all. The others were pretty suspicious. Nothing personal, but a lot of people here are legacies and didn't want a non-magic user in the village. But your friend Bran, he's a Knight Errant, and that means something in Haven. Even without the title, Bran is a legendary Battlemage. It's been floated that he'll take over for my grandfather as Village Head when he's ready to become a reservist."

"He's a good tavern buddy too," Cid said. "I doubt he wants to end up here. I think his future involves the beach somewhere."

"I have no idea if any of that is supposed to be good or not," Lyle admitted. "Anyways, the one thing no one expected was that you'd show up with magic. Even most who get marked with the Corps Seal only manifest one or two abilities max. The town agreed to take you anyways, but when the observers said they spotted you using spells on Oak Tree Farm, people were pretty surprised— and impressed! They're basic level, but you made good use of them. That got folks to thinking. And once the Corps heard about them, they asked my Grandfather to watch you so he could see how much potential you had. That's one reason we were around so much on the farm. Well— we were mostly around to help you. We aren't spies here or anything, but we had to do what the Corps was asking."

"Interesting," Cid said. He was curious in spite of himself. How much potential did he actually have? "And?"

"And according to what the others told me, you've got a lot of power! Not enough to be in the Corps, at least I don't think so since you didn't grow up on top of a Leyline like we all did, but enough to learn some basic and midtier battle magic. Bran didn't randomly give you those spells. He gave them to you because he thought you might have some ability and he wanted to see what you'd do with them if the seed took hold in the little bit of magic you had in you."

"Oh," Cid said. *Have I always had magic ability?* How long had he spent not knowing it? He could have had a much easier life if he'd known. On the other hand, it was good that he'd learned to survive in the Guard through wits and skill. If he'd been aware of his magic, he might never have done that.

"You were really impressive," the lad went on. "Or so my grandfather says. Anyway, when the Corps heard about it, they came knocking again, wanting to see if there was an untapped line of recruits, but more so, if you could be brought up in power. They wanted us to put you through the Trials with this Mana Harvest and get you initiated as a Magic Knight. But... they didn't want you to know about it."

"And why not?" Cid asked, irritated. Who were the Magic Knights that they got to play games with people's lives like this?

"Because it was sort of unconventional, and they weren't sure if it would work. Something about the call of retirement softening a man. It wasn't our idea! I'm just telling you what they said. You're obviously older than the other Knights, and they weren't fully sure of how your magic would come out in a battle situation. And you haven't gone through Knight training, either. The Guard is different. But they thought it was worth a shot. They wanted to see if your training crossed over. And it did. You passed. And you passed in a cooler way than I did," Lyle responded

The lad looked so impressed that Cid almost forgot to be annoyed about what had happened. Almost.

"And you were— what?" he asked through gritted teeth. "A proctor?"

"Yeah. Well, proctor and examiner. I was supposed to keep tabs on you," Lyle admitted. "Sorry I wasn't very helpful. I'm not really allowed to fight with you. This was kind of a weird one, though, since you weren't supposed to know what was going on. So I cheated a little bit so you wouldn't get suspicious. Throwing the sand was fun!"

"How does a kid with no magic get to proctor a Mana Trial for the Magic Knights?" Cid asked.

"Yeah," Lyle said, looking down at his feet. "About that. I wasn't exactly truthful with you before."

"You had magic the whole time, didn't you?" Cid responded.

"Yeah, I did. I'm sorry I lied. I didn't like it— swear I didn't— but it was what they wanted me to do. The Corps thought you'd never go into the Trials unless you were protecting someone else, someone you thought was weaker. I'm actually a Magic Knight— well, a Magic Squire. Just commissioned last year after my own Trial during the Harvest."

"How wonderful.," Cid said dryly. "At your age and everything."

"Yeah!" Lyle said. "I'm not the youngest ever, but I'm definitely in the top twenty! It's because my parents always knew I'd be a Magic Knight when I was younger with our family legacy being what it is. They trained me up well."

"And your parents...?" Cid asked, already feeling anger rising up in him again.

"They're actually dead," the lad said, eyes downcast. "That much was true. Killed by Dark Mages all the same. But I will get to carry on their legacy."

He said this with pride, and his face was grave.

"What about that bully, though?" Cid asked. "Wasn't he beating you up because you don't have magic and everyone else in town does?"

Lyle shook his head. "That guy? No. He's just an asshole."

Before Cid could respond to that, the moving room shuddered to a halt, and the main door swung open. Light poured into the room through the open door, shimmering in every color of the rainbow. It was easily ten times brighter than the light from the crystals in the cavern above.

"The Leyline," Lyle whispered. "We're here! Come and see!"

Cid warily followed the lad out of the room and into the cave beyond. There were no crystals here. Instead, the light seemed to be coming from the air itself.

"Tiny particles of mana. Living magic," the lad explained. "Like dust, in a way. They eventually settle into crystals like you see in the rest of the cave. But they're more powerful this way."

"Wow," Cid said.

It was all he could think of to say. The Leyline was absolutely beautiful— possibly the most beautiful thing he'd ever seen— and for a moment, it drove everything else out of his head. He'd certainly have a lot to say to Daryl Nightgreen and the Magic Knight Corps when he got back to the surface. They'd jerked him around, and he wanted to make it absolutely clear that that wasn't acceptable. But for now, he had to admire the beauty of this place.

"This isn't even the best part," Lyle said, grinning. "Wait until we get to the big room."

The lad led the way down winding corridors and into the largest cavern Cid had ever seen— so large, he couldn't see the wall on the other side. The entire room was ablaze with shifting light.

"Is that...?" he muttered. It was hard to see against the

glowing mana dust, but it seemed like someone was standing in the middle of the room. He was wearing a long black cloak with the hood up, but Cid would recognize that familiar slouch anywhere.

"We need a senior Magic Knight here to confirm you passed the Trials and certify you as a member of the Corps in this year's Harvest," Lyle said. "He came down early to wait"

The cloaked figure turned to look at them. Just as Cid had thought, it was Bran.

CHAPTER 46:
EXTRA DUTY

Bran looked exhausted, as if he hadn't slept for days, but he still had the energy to grin at the look on Cid's face.

"Surprised to see me?" he asked. "You should see yourself. You look good. Tanned enough, little skinnier though. The farm life must be really working you out."

"Jackass," Cid said irritably before responding with a good-natured smile for his old friend. "How much of this was your idea?"

"Practically zero," Bran responded, and Cid took note of the *practically.* "I've been on a campaign in the Southern Lands until two days ago. More undead out of the Kingdom of the White Lion. Anyway, when I heard what the Corps had planned, I commandeered the swiftest horse I could and rode up here as fast as I felt was needed. I even gave the Corps officers who set the whole thing up a real piece of my mind, too."

"Thanks." Cid raised his hands in frustration. "This was — something."

"Will you see it through?" Bran asked. "Certify and join the Corps? Nothing serious, this is only for the reserves. Short of an all out invasion, you'd never even be called into action. I should know, I'm one of the people that makes the decision when to make the call, and they still needed someone to sign off on the whole thing and to certify you as a Knight if you passed. And I figured I was the only one you wouldn't kill when you found out what had been going on, so I told them I'd do it."

"You're pretty confident I'm not going to kill you," Cid said. "You sure about that?"

"Tell me the truth," Bran said. "On a scale of one to ten, how pissed off are you right now and compare that against the time I bought us the bad soup in that port city."

Cid shuddered, "Alright. Compared to that, I'm at like an eight and a half, and mostly because I'm not hunched over a latrine after asking 'are you sure this is safe to eat' a million times."

"See, progress already." Bran raised his hands as if that solved everything. "That score could be worse. Could be a ten."

"Could still become a ten," Cid said. "Depends on how the rest of this conversation goes."

Cid walked over toward the other man, curled his fist, and punched him right in the face. Bran landed hard on his back. "Alright, we can continue talking now. That takes care of that *practically zero,* you mentioned."

Bran nodded and got back up. He understood. Cid was pretty annoyed, but this didn't seem to be Bran's fault. Even a champion Battlemage had limited control over what the Corps did.

"Alright Bran, we'll have to get a drink after this," Cid said. "I'll show you the farm. It's still kind of a mess, but I've got a nice setup going. It'll be even nicer once I've got some more fields tilled and ready. Things grow pretty quickly here."

"I figured that's what I remember most about living here. Everything grows so quickly," Bran said. "You're right on top of that Leyline. That tends to have an effect. And I'd like to see what you've done with the rest of old Oak Tree Farm, or what you're looking to do. I spent a lot of time here in Haven, you know— as do most Magic Knights. I spent even a little time on that farm checking it out. It was abandoned even then, except for the occasional bivouac. Bet it was in pretty rough shape when you came in."

"You have no idea. Those spells you unlocked for me really helped out, and I was able to shape a few into permanents," Cid admitted.

Bran looked pleased. "Aye? I hoped they would. And in truth, I was curious to see what you'd do with them. I always thought you might have some power, but I could never tell how much. It was good to see I was right."

"Yeah," Cid said, feeling a flash of irritation as he remembered that this wasn't just a casual conversation with his old friend. "Speaking of— that can't happen again. Ever. Jerking me around and putting me through secret trials? Total bullshit. Tell your friends in the Corps that from me."

"Trust me," Bran said. "I already have. But I'll tell them again."

"And if they ever do this kind of thing again," Cid warned, "I'll go to the Corps offices and break their door down myself."

"Aye. I'll pass that one along. Speaking of which— technically, you're officially a Magic Knight now. If you say yes, that is. No commitment besides a yes. So, congratulations. You did it. We can do the ceremony now."

Cid smiled in spite of himself. "Fine. I'll humor you. Yes. But do we have to?"

"Kind of," Bran responded. "But we can do the short one."

"Yeah. Let's do that, the short one. I'm ready to go home, to MY home. The one that I bought and paid for with my time and pension," Cid said.

Bran nodded. "Message heard loud and clear. Okay. Kneel."

Cid knelt, and Bran called forth a glowing orb of light into his palms. It cycled through the four colors from the trial doors over and over: red, green, blue, and white. Elemental magic.

"By the power invested in me by the Kingdom of the White Tower, inherent in my rank as an Errant within the Corps of Magic Knights, bestowed upon me by the Cardinal of Region Three, and upon my own judgement as witness of the first Mana Harvest of the season for reverse outpost one, I dub thee Sir Dawnshield of Oak Tree Farm," Bran said in a deep voice that sounded totally unlike his normal speaking voice. "Protector of the weak, defender of the kingdom, pledged to fight evil throughout the land. Do you accept?"

"I pledge to protect the weak and defend the kingdom. Here. Around my land," Cid responded, emphasizing the point. "And maybe elsewhere if things get really bad, but I'm not signing up for any other commitments."

"Okay, I think I can scribble that in," Bran said in his normal voice. "Fantastic. That's it. Now you're a Magic Knight."

He snapped his fingers, and the orb vanished.

"I don't want to be a Magic Knight," Cid said. "I want to be a farmer. That's the whole reason I moved here and bought the farm. Get my hands dirty and everything. We literally had this conversation with you complaining about Gold Bay and girls and tiny glasses for drinks."

"Yeah," Bran said. "I heard you loud and clear. I'm already ahead of you. I already talked to the leadership about that, and they wanted some feedback about you and your fit here in town. They're really looking for a Town Constable kind of position. Haven doesn't have one right now, and with the number of Knights that come through this place or retire here, it really should. You should still be able to work the farm full time. Don't even have to serve, really. Just gotta help out if something happens."

"Great," Cid said dryly. "My favorite gift Bran. You bring me extra duties."

"It's not that bad. Besides, you're kind of old to train as a full-on Magic Knight, anyways." Bran grinned. "But, wait, I've got more to tell you about the positives. It comes with a small salary and is entitled to a warhorse."

Cid was feeling worked up and practically shouted, "I know I'm too old. That's why I'm *retired.*"

But he felt a little better, at least— he wouldn't have to give up the farm because of all this nonsense.

"You know," Bran said. "I'll never understand why you wanted to retire to a farm in the middle of nowhere when you could have had pretty girls in Golden Bay. This is almost a good thing, yeah? Get some excitement?"

"There you go again about Golden Bay. Don't push it, buddy," Cid growled.

Bran laughed and turned towards Lyle. The lad hadn't said anything yet. "Hey, how's your Squireship?"

"It's been kind of bland," Lyle admitted, "Not much has happened yet. This thing with Cid is kind of my only mission so far."

"You guys know each other?" Cid asked.

"Yeah," Bran said. "All Magic Knights know each other. Kind of. The Corps isn't that big. I was here when this guy got initiated."

"I remember, it was at last year's Mana Harvest." Lyle said excitedly.

Cid frowned. "I keep hearing that, what do you mean Mana Harvest?"

"It's when all this mana dust from the Leyline comes together into crystals. Well, some of it does. It fuels the little trial dungeon, and that's when we rotate out our prospects. It happens once a year, and it's our biggest festival here in Haven. Even bigger than the Thankful Feast! The Magic Knights who get initiated at the Mana Harvest are the luckiest knights of all!"

"Oh. Am I getting started at the Mana Harvest? You're going to rope me into another task? Another holiday I'll have to attend when I've work to be doing on my farm? Is that what's happening now?" Cid was getting testy.

"Uh," Bran said.

"No," Lyle said. "It's not for another month. But when it happens, there'll be a big party, and everyone's invited!"

"Interesting," Cid said. "Well, Lyle, let's go upstairs. I have a few things I want to say to Daryl Nightgreen. Bran, I'll catch you later."

"I'll bring beer!" Bran shouted out as Cid and Lyle took off. The Magic Knight didn't bother to follow them out. He knew when to leave a little distance.

Cid and Lyle left Bran down in the Leyline cavern and went back into the elevator. The lad was silent for the entire ride up, and when the moving room finally shuddered to a halt, he hesitated before getting out.

"What are you going to say to Grandfather?" he asked, looking paler than Cid had ever seen him.

"Nothing terrible," Cid replied tersely. "But there are a few things that will need to be understood if I'm going to keep living here."

He led the way back across the Mana Cavern with Lyle trotting along anxiously at his heels. When he reached the entrance, Daryl was standing just outside the door. The old man smiled when he saw them coming— but his smile dropped when he saw the look on Cid's face.

"What's wrong, lad?" he asked. "You look displeased."

"I *am* displeased," Cid said, dropping down onto the grass just outside the cave. It felt good to get off his feet. After his long day in the Mana Trials, he was even more tired than he'd thought. "Everything that's happened in this town since I showed up has been ridiculous. Not the gifts, or the help with the barn— thanks for that, by the way— but all this, whatever you want to call it.. What the hell were you thinking? Why did you think I'd be ok with that?"

Daryl at least had the good grace to look ashamed. "Aye, lad. You're right to be angry—"

"Yes! I *am* right to be angry! I came here for a peaceful retirement. I don't know if you know this Daryl, but life out there isn't exactly easy, but it's easy enough here. But you manipulated me at every turn. I don't want to be a Magic Knight— but if the Corps insisted on doing this trial thing, you could have at least told me what was going on. I'd have run the Trials if I had to, but at least then I'd have known what I was in for. And what was the point of sneaking around at the farmers' market? Did you really think a professional Guard— a man from Hardhearth, no less, where thieves and scoundrels lurk around every corner— wouldn't guess something was up? I thought this would be a nice, quiet town. But all I got was a bunch of trickery!"

"You're in the right of it, lad," Daryl said. "We've treated you poorly. And I'm sorry for it. We let our distrust of outsiders get in our own way. If there's anything we in Haven can do to earn your trust—"

"Yeah!" Cid said. "I can tell you exactly what you're going to do. Deal with me straight from now on. No more sneaking around. No more spying on me to see how much magic I have. No more waking me up early in the morning when I'm trying to sleep. Let me tend my farm in peace, live like a normal member of the town, and maybe I'll trust you all again."

Daryl's gaze was firmly fixed on the ground. "Aye. We can do that much, at least. I'll tell the others and make sure they do what I say."

"And one more thing," Cid said. "According to Bran and the Corps, I'm now the Town Constable. Didn't really ask for the position, but here we are. You're the Village Elder. If I'm going to be doing this job, I want the full respect that's owed to my position. I need to sit in on town meetings, I need the keys to community buildings, and I'll need an assistant."

"An assistant?" Daryl asked, brow furrowing. "But who —"

"Lyle," Cid said. "He was involved in this whole mess. I'll need an aide as Constable, and I could also use a helping hand around Oak Tree Farm if we're going to have a full harvest by the end of the summer after all of your shenanigans. Lyle can assist me. It'll help make up for the Mana Trial thing. And maybe he'll learn something."

"Aye," Daryl said. "It'll be good for the lad to have honest work instead of running around the woods all day. If he agrees, I'll consent to that."

"Can I teach you more magic?" Lyle asked.

"Alright," Cid said. "But we'll be doing a lot of farm work the old-fashioned way. It'll be a lot of hard work. No spells. At least for you."

"So, Guard-style?" Lyle asked.

"Yeah. Guard-style."

"Then we're settled," Daryl said. "And truly, lad. We really are happy to have you here in Haven."

"Sure," Cid said tersely as he stood up. "Glad to hear it."

He turned his back on Daryl and Lyle and headed back down the hill toward the farm. It would take a while for him to trust the villagers again after they'd taken him for such a ride, but he'd worry about that later. For now, he was off to town to pick up some food. Bran was coming over later with a cask of ale, and after the month he'd had, they had a lot of catching up to do. Cid woke early the next morning, thinking of his old horse.

Hopefully, Lord Vanstone writes back soon.

To his relief, no one was banging on his door today. The farm was empty, and he had time to relax for a bit before heading off to work. Wishing he had some tea, he sat out on the porch to watch the sun rise above the trees. It was peaceful out here, still cool before the heat of the day had set in, and the air smelled like growing things. After spending so many years in the city, this was exactly where he wanted to be.

He'd asked Edd to build a stable for him, but the scrawny carpenter hadn't come back to the farm since the day the old cow barn had collapsed. He'd have to follow up with him soon before the weather got cold. And until then, he'd need to find or build somewhere for Nightshade to stay. Luckily, there was no shortage of empty pasture land around here.

Once he was tired of sitting, he got up, stretched his back out, and headed toward the fields. After a quick look at his growing crops— all seemed well there— he moved farther out toward the land that had once been used for cow pastures back when the farm had been solvent. There were a few fields he could use, and he inspected them carefully, trying to decide which one Nightshade would like best.

There was one that provided easy access to the stream, but it was low on the hill, muddy, and small. He wanted his horse to be able to stretch his legs. A few others were clearly out as well. One was too rocky, and he worried Nightshade would hurt himself as he galloped around the field. Another was dark and gloomy in the shadow of a stand of tall oak trees.

That left the main pasture— the largest and lushest one by far. In retrospect, it had been the clear choice from the start. It might seem silly, but he wanted Nightshade to have a nice time in retirement. The old horse had served him well over the years, and he deserved better than the tiny stall he'd had in the city.

The Guard had had a small pen for their horses to get outside, at least, and they'd all gotten plenty of exercise at work— but it wasn't the same. And it had been hard sometimes seeing the luxurious stables and acres of rolling fields the Magic Knights got to use. In their years of partnership, he'd sometimes been able to take Nightshade to one of the Corps' pastures when it wasn't in use just to give the old horse a chance to roll around in the grass. But those times had been few and far between, and it was time to make it up to him.

Maybe I can get him a friend. A pony or something.

But he was getting ahead of himself, as usual. First, he needed to inspect the pasture and get it ready for Nightshade to arrive— if, as he hoped, he did.

The grass was a bright green and looked to be of good quality. The horse would eat well here if he got enough time outside. Cid wouldn't have to supplement his feed much until after the first frost, at least.

That's a good thing, because right now, I can't afford hay.

Hopefully, his first big harvest this fall would bring in good money. If not, he might have to ask Daryl Nightgreen for a loan to get him through the winter.

While the field itself was in good shape, the fence was another story. It was made of rough wood harvested from the forest, and while it was well-made —that it was even partly standing after years of neglect was a testament to its quality— it was in need of extensive repairs if he wanted to keep a horse here.

He took a closer look at the nearest stretch of fencing. It was made in a style he recognized from his time in Hardhearth. The villagers just outside the city made their sheep pens the same way: two lines of foraged wood with the bark still on, woven together. He'd never tried to make one before, but he thought he could do it. Or at least, he could repair what was already there.

Anything for Nightshade.

He relaced his boots a bit tighter and strode into the woods to gather materials. He'd need young wood— not too hard but still green and springy. He'd need to weave the branches together stick by stick until they formed a dense barricade too thick for an animal to get through. It was painstaking work, but it didn't require nails or a lot of other supplies. That was why so many poor villagers used the technique.

He kept a wary eye out as he ventured deeper into the forest, and he grabbed a large stick as soon as he found one. There were fewer wolves and wildcats in this part of the kingdom than there once had been, but they were still out there. The last thing he needed was to get mauled on his own farm.

He was in good spirits, though, overall, and his mood improved further when he found a stand of young ash trees not too far from the big pasture. There was plenty of green wood here. They'd serve his purpose well. He took out his pocket knife and cut some branches off, making sure to leave enough on each tree that it would continue to grow. When he had a large bushel, he slung it over one shoulder and headed back toward the field.

Let's see if I can figure out how to do this.

He was a Guard, not a weaver, and it took him a few tries before he was able to make a successful braid. Once he had a section ready, he wove in line with the existing fence. It wasn't as nice as his predecessor's work, but it would do.

This is going to take forever, though.

Well, it wasn't like his horse was going to show up any time soon. He'd just have to keep at it a little each day until the fence was done. It was a nice, contemplative project that he could do in the evenings after he'd finished his other work. And it was pleasant to be out here in the sunlit field.

Hope Nightshade is grateful for all of this.

He would be. He was a good horse.

Cid made a few more trips back and forth to the ash tree stand then stood back to take stock of what he'd accomplished. He'd fixed one whole side of the fence— just the short side of the rectangle, but still. It was a good amount for one day, and his hands ached from weaving. *Time to go do something else.*

He walked around the pasture, looking for anything else that needed to be improved.

"Hm," he said when he reached the south side of the field. Three concrete watering troughs were attached to the fence, big enough for many animals to drink from at once. A large herd of cows must once have lived here. Well, at least Nightshade would stay well-hydrated.

The troughs were disgusting, though. They were full of black and brackish water that seemed like a haven for mosquito larvae, and mold coated the sides of each basin. No animal of Cid's could be allowed to drink from these troughs. It wasn't humane.

But he didn't want to touch the nasty water. Even Cid had limits. He headed back toward the farmyard to see if there was anything in the tool shed that could help him out. Daryl had given him a small spade, but maybe there was a larger shovel somewhere that he could use.

When he got to the shed, he dug around in the back — and sighed. He'd already looked back here when he was thinking of digging the fishing hole, but he'd hoped there would be something that he'd missed the first time. No dice. He'd have to use the spade after all.

This is going to take forever.

That seemed to be the theme on Oak Tree Farm today. But, as with the fence, there was nothing to do but get started. He carried the spade back toward the moldy troughs, took a breath, and got to work.

The job was even worse than he'd thought it would be. The spade was plenty good for digging in the dirt, but it barely held any water at all. Worse, the handle wasn't long enough to keep Cid from getting splashed as he tried to empty the first trough. He'd obviously faced much worse in his life, but it was still disgusting. After only half an hour of work, his arms were black with grime, and the basin seemed just as full as ever.

Has anything changed at all?

If he squinted, it looked like the water level might have gone down an inch or two. But it wasn't much of a change.

As it was, even emptying a single trough was likely to take all afternoon and leave Cid filthy. His arms and shirt were already covered in mold and algae.

There has got to be a better way to do this.

And now he'd have to wash his shirt, too. He dropped his spade, irritated, and laid back in the grass to relax for a moment. Fluffy clouds drifted across the blue sky above his head, and he smiled. Life wasn't so bad. This task was annoying, but at the end of the day, he still owned his own farm. That alone was something to celebrate. And things could be way worse. It could be raining.

Rain. There's an idea.

An memory popped into his head: a massive sea storm that had once blown through Hardhearth back when he was barely more than a fresh recruit. The Guard had seen it coming before it arrived: a tall funnel spinning toward them across the harbor. There'd been nothing anyone could do— most of the Corps' Battlemages were out of town on a mission, and they were the only ones who could stop a storm of that size. It had hit the city like a hammer and blown down half the marketplace before someone could be summoned to dispel it. The baker's stand had been sucked up into the funnel and carried high into the sky. It had never come back.

Maybe I could make something similar.

He wasn't sure if he was powerful enough— but then again, this didn't need to be a massive spell. Just large enough to clear the water out of a few troughs. He took his casting stance and cast [**Air 1**], keeping the sea storm in mind as he did. Hopefully, that would be enough to make the funnel take shape.

The wind picked up as the spell started to take shape.

Funnel, he thought. *Funnel.*

To his surprise— he still wasn't confident in his magical abilities— the air bent to his will, forming a miniature waterspout. He gestured at the troughs, feeling a bit awkward, and the funnel siphoned the water out of them and dumped it on the ground outside the fence.

"Um," Cid said. "Go away now."

The funnel twirled one last time and vanished.

Congratulations, you've unlocked a new ability!

After testing your magic, you've managed to learn how to cast a new ability through a higher level of Spellweaving.

[Wind Funnel] has been unlocked!

Cid grinned. He'd learned a new skill and made his life easier while doing it. He took a moment to savor the victory then got back to work. The troughs might be empty of water now, but they were still caked with dirt, rotting leaves, and green-black mold. Grimacing, he picked up his spade again and started scraping the debris out.

Wish there was a spell that could help with this. It's disgusting.

But he'd used up all his casting energy on clearing out the water, so the rest of the work would have to be done by hand. The shovel made an unpleasant noise on the concrete as he cleaned, and at this point, his shirt was so dirty that it was basically unsalvageable. Still, if it got him his horse back, it would all have been worth it.

The sun was low on the horizon by the time he finally cleared the last of the dirt out and stood back to look at what he'd accomplished. The troughs weren't pristine, but they were serviceable. He wouldn't be ashamed if someone saw them.

That's how we operate around here. Just good enough to work.

Well, as long as it worked. He headed back toward the farmhouse to change his shirt and relax for a bit before heading to sleep. After a long and frustrating day in the field, he'd earned it.

EPILOGUE PART 1: A FEW MONTHS LATER

"Gee-up, Nightshade," Cid said with a warm pat, and the old horse sprang into motion, straining against the harness traces. They were clearing out a downed tree in one of the lower fields, getting it ready for next year's growing season. It was late summer now, too late for more planting, but he wanted to have things set before the first frost put an end to his fieldwork. They'd done well this year— especially for the farm's first season— but he wanted to double his output next season. Maybe then he could hire a few more hands to help out.

Nightshade dragged the old tree through the farmyard next to the house and stopped, looking at Cid as if he wanted feedback on his work.

"Good lad," Cid said. "You did well. This'll be good firewood for the coldest of days."

He didn't want to think about it yet, but winter was coming— and according to the villagers, winters here were harsh and full of snow. He'd need to use the timber he had sparingly if he wanted to stay warm.

Whistling an old Guard's tune to help guide the tempo of his working, Cid unhooked the horse from the tree and led him back to his pasture. He'd been pleased— and happily surprised — to see that the 'swift horse' Bran had ridden to the Mana Trials was his former mount. As Bran had said as he handed over the horse's bridles with a huge smile, "For your troubles."

Cid grinned at the memory. It wasn't just his troubles. After all, old Nightshade still had a lot of spirit in him. The letter of complaint from Lord Varnstone had arrived only a few days after Bran. As it turned out, young Billy Bagwell hadn't been able to handle the horse— and none of the other Guardsmen could either. The commander had been happy to give him to Cid and get him off his hands.

"You're a one-man pony, aren't you?" Cid asked.

Nightshade ignored him, the horse's eyes fixed on the fresh grass in his field. He'd been living outside most of the summer in a large pasture next to the stream, but Edd had quickly gotten to work and had been working hard on a stable to house the horse. He did it for free too, without any cost to Cid. Edd, like most of the villagers, had been trying hard to make up for their behavior toward Cid earlier in the summer when he'd been a fresh outsider to the village. They hadn't quite made it up to him yet, but he figured he'd get there eventually.

"Cid!" Lyle shouted as he ran over. "Cid." The lad was running toward him as fast as he could. Cid let Nightshade into his pasture and waited for Lyle by the fenced gate.

"Edd says the stable is about ready," Lyle explained, "You want to come take a look?"

"Sure. Let's go," Cid responded. *Hopefully, everything is a go.*

They walked back to the farmyard together. Lyle had proven himself to be a hard worker and eager to learn— and to Cid's surprise, he'd been happy to do things without magic. They worked, at times tearing their hands and tearing the soil. They'd done a few magic workshops, too, after their work in the fields was done. Cid had picked up a few things. Namely, the **[Jailer]** ability and had upgraded **[Water 1]** to **[Water 2]**.

The stable was a cozy building in the same place the old cow barn had been with a little pen next to it so Nightshade could still get outside if ever Cid didn't have the time to lead him out to the field. *It looks good, but I need to check it out.* Cid walked in.

"Hey there, Cid," Edd called out as he worked to attach a hinge to one of the last stall doors. "It's nothing fancy, but I think it'll do. I should be done in a day or so."

Cid nodded his approval. The building had four big stalls, each with a window to the outside, a hayloft above, and a small room where he could store tack and other gear. Nightshade would be happy here.

"Good," he said appreciatively. "Keep up the good work. Thank you. This means a lot."

"Cid, we did a lot," Lyle commented, proud of his work. "Edd was teaching me how to put shingles on a roof today!" Lyle said. "And he's going to let me do the last bit of it myself tomorrow."

"You should be proud," Cid commented. "That's not a bad set of skills to learn. That will serve you well long term, but we need to be off to the fields now."

The lad followed him out of the stable and stayed close behind him as they proceeded across the property, chattering about farm tasks the whole time. Even Daryl had been surprised at how quickly Lyle had taken to working on Oak Tree Farm. He seemed to like the work even better than Cid did.

It was almost time for the fall harvest season, and the fields were lush and full with every manner of growable from green to orange. Cid had planted several more types of crops since early summer: giant turnips, tall okra, and several rows of corn. They said hello to Mary as they passed her field. She'd taken Cid up on his offer of opening up some growing space on his second field for her to use, and her corn was doing well.

It was a good way to live and a good way to pass the time. They spent most of the morning weeding, watering, and checking the plants for bugs. Basic upkeep to ensure the plants grew and thrived.

"So, Cid, when are you going to teach me some more fighting tips?" Lyle asked, sprinkling water on a big tomato plant. "Something the Guard would use for up close fighting, like in a tavern brawl? Please?"

"Alright, fine, but you'll have to prove you know the basics first," Cid responded. "Quiz time. What do you do if you're in a fight in a narrow street? Close corridor but still outside. Think of the city, think of Hardhearth, or the biggest city you've ever seen before. Tall buildings, barely room for an elbow."

The lad looked back at him blankly, not quite sure how to respond, or how to imagine what Cid was telling him.

"Remember what I told you," Cid pressed in the teaching point. "Never allow yourself to get cornered. But if you do, you need to move and find your back to the wall, and that's where you shine. Otherwise, you're screwed."

"Right," Lyle said. "And I should take every cheap shot I can, right? A man's honor means a lot less than his life. It's not just about winning a fight, it's about not getting hurt or killed."

"Absolutely," Cid responded, "You can flat-out brawl if you want to end up old and crippled before your time, or you can be smart and rely on technique and ability instead."

"And what do you suggest I do?" Lyle asked, and though Cid knew the lad had training and magic, but didn't want to use them. The one answer that mattered most kept coming to his mind.

"I suggest you use your magic and be done with it. It's not worth taking a chance if a better way is possible," Cid admitted. "If something is one way nine times out of ten, it's that tenth time you want to be careful about."

Lyle considered his words as they kept working. Cid pulled up a big weed, stood up, and looked around the field. They'd done plenty of work here for the day and had reached a good place to stop.

"That's a good place to stop for the day," Cid said as he got up and brushed sweat off of his face. "Go wash up real quick and put on your uniform," he said. "It's almost time for our rounds."

"I almost forgot about rounds!" Lyle said as he scrambled up to go get changed.

EPILOGUE PART 2: CONSTABLE

Lyle ran down the hill toward the farmhouse. Cid followed behind at an easier, slower pace. *No point in rushing and wearing myself out for no reason. Patrolling can wait a few minutes on us.* He smiled as he enjoyed the feeling of the wind on his face and took in the scene of the leaves starting to change colors on the edge of the farmstead.

When he got back to the house, Cid went straight upstairs and washed up before changing into his Constable's uniform. The Corps had sent it to him a few weeks after he'd passed the Mana Trials and taken up Bran's offer for the post. It was a dark blue three-piece uniform with a dark bronze button. It was quite a bit more dapper and polished than the simple grey uniform he'd had as a Guard. *It makes sense though, the Magic Knights Corps has a lot more resources and financial backing than the Guard ever did.* Cid couldn't help but admire himself when it was done. He wasn't a vain man, but he thought he cut a sharp figure in the uniform.

One of a few good things to come out of this whole ordeal. Cid thought as his mind turned towards Nightshade and how grateful he was to be reunited with his old horse.

"Lyle!" he called out as he walked down the stairs. "It's time to get going." He headed towards the door and called out again with no answer. *The lad must have already headed out.*

Well, I'll just have to meet up with him in Haven. It would be nice to have a short walk alone with his thoughts for a bit.

Cid set off and grabbed his Constables Blade before leaving. He left Nightshade behind to rest in the field. For what he was doing, the horse could take the day off and enjoy the sun. They both needed it. Cid had been trying to absorb as much sun as he could on the trip into town, knowing that it wouldn't be long before the weather turned and it started to get colder. Part of him— for now, a small part— was looking forward to the winter. It would be nice to have some quiet time by himself, and the snow would keep the villagers from interrupting him all the time. It would give him plenty of time for reading and writing in front of the fireplace.

Lyle was waiting for him outside the Nightgreen house in his squire's uniform. Cid could see Daryl watching from the front window, but he didn't acknowledge him. He wasn't quite ready to be on more than polite terms with the Village Elder yet after his experience with the Trials. Maybe eventually. But not yet.

"Come on Lyle," Cid called out, and the lad got up, waved goodbye to Daryl, and set off with him. Soon, he and Lyle were out on a foot patrol, walking together in silence as they made their rounds of the town. Lyle kept his head on a swivel and kept an unlit torch on his person for when it got dark. Cid was pleased to see the lad taking his duties seriously.

He'll grow up to be a good man one day, just needs a bit of guidance.

"Look!" Lyle said, pointing at something on the ground next to the water mill. "What's that?"

They hustled over to look at it. There were tracks in the mud by the water wheel, and they seemed to have been made by a three-toed reptilian creature. Cid bent down for a closer inspection.

"Monster tracks," he said finally. "Something's prowling around here. Might be a recent spawn or something that's gone unnoticed for a while that just upgraded. We'll have to keep an eye on it."

They searched but found no other sign of monsters or any clue as to where the spawn was. Eventually, as it got dark, Cid sent Lyle home to Daryl's house and headed to the tavern for an after-work drink. Maggie grinned when she saw him walk through the door.

"Hey, it's my favorite wandering guard," she said, pouring him a pint of his favorite ale. "Come have a seat. Are you going to have any pumpkins this year I can use for a few recipes?"

Grumbling a bit at being called 'the wandering guard,' Cid sat down at the bar and took a drink. "I think so. Though, the baker has signed a healthy commitment for an order if I can meet it."

"Ah, well, hopefully you'll have plenty. Anyways, I've been watching you with that lad," Maggie said. "You've done well with him. Lyle was a real hellion before, but he's shaping up. It's good for him to have found himself working for you, it seems to have built some character."

"Thank you," Cid replied with a nod but didn't say much more.

Things had been a little tense with Maggie after the events of that summer, and the conversations didn't come easy between them.

"You know, Daryl's getting older," she went on. "And he's — well, you know. I don't know how much longer he's going to be the Village Elder. At some point, the lad's not going to be able to stay with his grandfather anymore, and he'll have to move on."

Cid sighed. "I thought of that. When that time comes, Lyle can stay with me on Oak Tree Farm. I've got more than enough room. He's been a big help around the farm already, and I can always use the extra hand. When he's old enough, he can decide for himself what he wants to do with his life. The Magic Knights will hold a spot for him if he wants to go active. If he doesn't want to do that, and if he proves himself here as Assistant Constable, I can write him a reference if he wants to be a Guard in the city. My name holds enough pull for him to get hired. Or he can stay here and keep helping me."

"You think the Corps would let him do that?" Maggie asked, and Cid knew she had more experience than he did with the matter— he just wondered if her question was just that, a question or a warning.

Privately, Cid had his doubts. But the lad was young yet, and who knew how much things might change with the Magic Knights by the time he was old enough to be looking for work?

"I think we'll have to see what happens," he said, finishing his ale. "Now, I'm off."

"Do you have to work late tonight?" Maggie asked with a lingering smile.

"Not too late, at least, I hope not. We saw monster tracks earlier today. I want to see if I can track the thing down and either kill it or drive it off. Dangerous in the dark, so I sent Lyle home. Hopefully, we've been away long enough for it to be less cautious now. Should be a quick clear," Cid explained

She smiled. "Alright. I'll stay open late tonight, just in case. Come in for a drink when you're done. On the house. I've got a new ale I want your thoughts on."

Cid shouldered his pack. Did he want to come back to the tavern?

"Well," he said finally. "Maybe just one."

He never could resist a good ale.

WANT MORE LITRPG?

To interact with other readers, try LitRPG Books on Facebook. Or the GameLit Society Facebook group.

Lastly, and my personal favorite, try the LitRPG Forum which has the best discord server.

For updates and to sign up for my spam check out https://fantasyunlimited.org

Join Me And A Few Other Authors in Our Discord

-The Hunter's Den-

https://discord.gg/htzB3CW62S

"To learn more about LitRPG, talk to authors including myself, and just have an awesome time, please join the LitRPG Group."

WOLFE LOCKE

* AUTHOR'S NOTES *

Thanks for taking the time to read Cid's story. I'm
not sure if their will be a book two, I'm not sure it needs
it. Sure. There's more story to tell, but not every book
needs a series. The town of Haven is roughly based
on the town of Dahlonega in the mountains of North
Georgia. You can google the why if you want to.

That said, if I get pestered enough on social media, I can do
another book, but mostly I just ask you take the time to review
and rate this story and like the reviews you agree with.

This is my author page
https://www.amazon.com/Wolfe-Locke/e/B0892M84JB/
Hit that follow button as well so amazon
will send you updates.

This is my book club. I send out new releases this way too. Sign
up. Its also on Amazon.
http://tiny.cc/BookClubonAmazon

For updates visit https://fantasyunlimited.org.

Free Download from the Publisher
Audiobook "Essence Weaver"

Free Download from the Publisher
Audiobook "Netherland: The Owl Eater's Legacy"

BOOKS BY THIS AUTHOR

The Retired S Ranked Adventurer Volume I: A Light Novel

★ Adventurers never die, they just fade away ★

They called him Sven, the Shatterfist.
One of a group of heroes who fought the Demon Lord Mannon.
He's finally returned home.
But for Sven, after returning from abroad, life isn't what it used to be.
Adventuring isn't what it used to be.
Things have changed. Something is different.

The obvious next step?
Retire.

Settle down. Start his own tavern. Drink with magic girls.
Maybe not in that order.

Get your copy of "The Retired S Ranked Adventurer" and set off for an adventure.

Casual Farming, Slow Living Litrpg

Embrace an adventure in the magical world of "Casual Farming", a wholesome and captivating young adult fantasy romance book set in a slice-of-life LitRPG world of farming.

Join Jason Hunter on his journey of self-discovery as he inherits an old farmstead outside of Summer Shandy. He'll face the challenges of taming the overgrown fields and fending off field monsters, all while finding a way to balance his duties, his chore-list, build his strength, and navigate the complexities of relationships if he wants to live the quiet life for himself in the country.

Experience the nostalgia and coziness of farm life while being swept away by a fantasy romance that will leave you breathless. This book is perfect for anyone who loves a good love story, adventure, and a touch of magic.

Don't wait any longer, hit that download button or order your copy today and start a happy adventure!

Dungeon Mercantile, The Ballad Of Shady Greg

I got dragged to a new world, and I can't even do dungeons?!

My name is Greg, and as a non-native of Jadera, the system won't let me into dungeons.
That's fine, though, I've got other skills besides fighting.
I'm an excellent Merchant, buying and selling the awesome loot that adventurers bring out of their delves.
Potions, weapons, armor, monster bits... you name it. Simple right? I'll buy it from you and sell it to the next one!
That goes triple for legendaries! And when my bitterest rival-- and former best friend--tries to run me out of business?
Well, let's just say that merchants have our ways.
Come, join me for a mug and I'll tell you all about it. Most of it will even be the truth.

Pick up a copy of "Dungeon Mercantile " today!

For Fans of - Dungeon Shops, Young Adult Friendly Fantasy,

Third Apocalypse

Decades ago, the world was changed by the arrival of the system.
One day, monsters spawned across the world, gateways to dungeons appeared everywhere, and the blue screens heralded the end of days. The apocalypse. The ruin of the world.

Amongst the ruins of the world, they survive.
The players.
Those granted power by the system and led by the 2nd regressor, the King of the Crows.
He who mastered the system, learned the truth of the apocalypse, and seized the keys of absolute authority.

But even a King cannot stop the fall of mankind.
No power is absolute. An end is eventual.
The final calamity and coming of disaster.

To fight against the overwhelming power of a mad god, the mark of the regressor will be passed on.
Jax Nolan is picked as the successor, the man destined to go back to the beginning.

Back to the start of the apocalypse and the advent of the system.
And become the hero of the story.

Get a copy today!
For Fans of: Second Chance Stories, Tower Climbs, Blue Screen Apocalypses, LitRPG

Rosie Hexwell: Witches Brew

Live, Laugh, Latte: Unwind with Rosie in a world of brewing delight. Embark on a magical adventure with Rosie to not disappoint her grandmother—get your copy now on Kindle & Kindle Unlimited!

In the captivating town of Mystwood, where magic and mundanity intertwine, lies the Witch's Brew—a quaint, slow-living café nestled in the heart of a magical wonder and normality.

Enter Rosie Hexwell, a charming yet reluctant witch, who expertly crafts tantalizing concoctions and wondrous brews with the help of her loyal pumpkin golems. Together, they create a haven for their cherished, sometimes more than human customers who've been enchanted by the café's charm for years.

But tranquility teeters on the edge as a formidable rival threatens to shatter their idyllic world. A powerful, arcane enterprise seeks to claim the Witch's Brew business as its own, and Rosie must summon all her wiles and elbow grease to protect her magical coffee sanctuary.

As the battle brews, can Rosie unlock the full potential of her untapped powers to save her family's legacy and preserve the cozy comforts of her enchanted abode?

From Wolfe & Falcon, the imaginative minds behind the best-selling Mana Harvest and The Retired S Ranked Adventurer, comes a heartwarming, cozy fantasy that weaves a slice-of-life tale of friendship, magic, and the unrelenting spirit of a witch determined to safeguard her heritage.

Prepare to be spellbound by Rosie Hexwell and the Witch's Brew, where every sip is an enchanting experience, and every visit is a whimsical adventure!

Now with more pumpkin spice! Seriously, snag it on Kindle & Kindle Unlimited today!

Isekai Park

Welcome to the enchanting world of Parnival Wonderland, where magic and adventure await at every turn.

Grey had always known that something was missing from his life, but he never could have guessed that it would come in the form of a mysterious girl named Billie. When she offered him a job, Grey was hesitant at first, but the chance was too good to pass up.

He was transported to a world beyond his wildest dreams. Filled with familiar sights and rich delights, the park was a place where the impossible became possible, and the unexpected was always just around the corner.

Billie, the spirit of the park, entrusted Grey with the critical task of managing the park's magical energies, which kept the park alive and fended off dark spirits seeking to destroy it. But as Grey delved deeper into the secrets of Isekai Park, he discovered that not everything was as it seemed, and the park was in greater danger than anyone had realized.

With a steady stream of mana to manage, Grey must quickly learn the ropes of Parnival Wonderland to keep the park alive and protect it from the dangers that lurk within. As darker spirits threaten to destroy everything he's worked so hard to build, Grey must use all of his wit, charm, and magical abilities to fend off the incursions and keep Parnival Wonderland safe.

Join Grey on his whimsical and thrilling tale of adventure,

where the impossible is made possible, and the unexpected is always just around the corner. Don't miss this captivating novel that will transport you to another world filled with magic, wonder, and danger. Download or buy today on Kindle and Kindle Unlimited to experience the journey of a lifetime in Parnival Wonderland!

Tower Reborn

Inside the Tower, there is only one choice—climb or die.

John Mavren and his comrades eventually reached the 100th floor, five years after the desolation of the outside world and twenty years after the Tower first appeared. In a violent battle to ascend, John was struck down even as he dealt the final blow to the last boss.

Those who survived were granted passage off ruined Earth and into worlds unknown, but they refused. Instead, they asked the Final Guardian for only a single grace—that John be returned to life.

Time moved backwards.

Bestowed with a fragment of his original power and with almost no memory of what had happened before, John wakes up in the past only one year after the arrival of the Tower.

With a sense of impending doom and a single, desperate hope for survival, John knows he must conquer the Tower and defeat those who dwell within.

He must become powerful enough to overcome a forgotten future and stop the apocalypse.

From Bestseller Wolfe Locke comes Tower Reborn in the

Realm Grinder Series, a new Tower Climbing LitRPG about an apocalypse, a Tower of Realms, and a Hero going from strong to stronger.

Made in the USA
Las Vegas, NV
29 December 2023

83621685R10201